THE
MARRIED
MAN

BOOKS BY K.L. SLATER

THE MARRIED MAN

K.L. SLATER

bookouture

Published by Bookouture in 2024

An imprint of Storyfire Ltd.
Carmelite House
50 Victoria Embankment
London EC4Y 0DZ

www.bookouture.com

Storyfire Ltd's authorised representative in the EEA is Hachette Ireland
8 Castlecourt Centre
Castleknock Road
Castleknock
Dublin 15 D15 YF6A
Ireland

ISBN: 978-1-83618-270-2
eBook ISBN: 978-1-83618-269-6

For my mum, with love always x

ONE

LIV

When Liv wakes from her nap, she glances at the wall clock. It's 11 a.m. and they've been gone an hour, so not too long before they are due home.

The Find My Friends app on her iPhone is confused. Whirring around, it's still placing Rich in the house nearly two hours ago. She calls his phone to check their ETA, but is immediately diverted to voicemail, which would usually mean he has a poor signal as he rarely turns his phone off.

When Liv thinks about her husband, and their young son, Maddox – who turned three just a week ago – an uncomfortable feeling starts to unfurl in the pit of her stomach. Should she have stopped them going today?

Her son is very young, but he's also very determined. From the moment he unwrapped the shiny blue wrapping paper from his birthday gift just a few days earlier – an enormous colourful kite with his favourite character, Sonic the Hedgehog, on it – his big blue eyes have shone with excitement.

Despite Rich's efforts during the past week to contain his

enthusiasm to the garden, due to the rainy weather, little Maddox had only grown more determined. 'Fog hill,' he'd repeated, over and over, pointing a chubby hand towards the front door. 'Me go big hill!'

Frog Hill is a popular local beauty spot where they often go walking as a family in finer weather. Maddox has seen older kids flying their colourful kites up there, standing transfixed each time, his wild curls blowing as he stares with wonder at the twisting shapes and trailing ribbons. Liv or Rich often have to tear him away as he reaches towards the sky with a grasping starfish hand. That's what had given Rich the idea to get him a starter kite.

Liv looks out of the window, watches the tall conifers at the bottom of the garden bending and swaying in the wind. She can't deny it's great kite weather, but a severe storm warning has been issued for later.

'We'll be home long before the storm kicks in,' Rich had said before they'd left. 'You get some rest and we'll be back before you know it.'

They'd had the best time last night. Maddox had been bouncing around all day waiting for the big event. Liv had planned a little party for him at home to celebrate, just the three of them. His nursery friends had attended a bouncy castle bash on his actual birthday, but yesterday was a chance for the three of them as a family to mark the day. At least, it had just been the three of them to start with. Shannon, Rich's mum, had dropped Maddox back in the morning, having babysat him Friday night, but then she'd turned up again yesterday afternoon, just as Liv was setting the table with party poppers, glitter sprinkles and celebration napkins. Liv had noticed before that she often did this on important occasions: turned up unexpectedly and affected a mortified expression when she 'discovered' they had other plans that didn't include her.

'I must've got the time wrong... I thought your little celebration was tomorrow!' Shannon had pressed her fingers to her cheeks and turned to Liv. 'I just thought I'd pop those new towels round I bought you from the sales.'

'Stay and have a glass with us, Mum,' Rich had said, earning himself a glare from Liv.

'Oh no, I don't want to intrude. I really should be getting back,' Shannon had said mildly, eyeing the bottle of champagne Rich had started to open. Despite her protest, she hadn't moved an inch.

'Nonsense,' Rich insisted. 'One glass won't hurt. It'll be nice to celebrate with us, right, Liv?'

'Of course.' Liv had forced a smile.

Liv is very fond of Shannon, but it irks her that Rich doesn't seem to notice his mother pulls this trick on a regular basis: anniversaries, birthdays and any kind of celebration where she and Rich make the effort to grab a few hours together. Just the two of them, or as was the case today, the three of them. Thankfully, last night, as it stood, Shannon had downed just the one glass and gone home.

Rich had opened a bottle of wine with dinner and another one after that, so no surprise that Liv had felt a bit worse for wear this morning and Rich, who never seems to get hangovers, had offered to take Maddox up to Frog Hill.

'He can fly his new kite there and burn off some energy,' Rich had suggested when Liv had admitted to feeling a bit rough. 'You can rest and recharge your batteries and then we'll have nice, chilled family time when we get back.'

She'd hauled herself off the sofa and followed them to the front door. After their customary goodbye hugs and kisses, Maddox had skipped down the short driveway, chatting excitedly to his daddy. Liv had watched as Rich's powerful arms swept him up so easily and into the car seat. Her heart had felt so full as she'd waved them off.

Now, she heads to the kitchen. She'd needed that nap, but

there are things she needs to do: laundry, cleaning up after leaving the dishes last night. But there are *always* things to do in any busy household. Instead, she pushes a pod into the Nespresso machine, flicking the radio on low for a bit of background music. Then she takes her coffee and a house interiors magazine over to the squashy sofa in front of the glass doors.

When people come to the cottage for the first time, they often say it could easily grace the pages of a glossy design magazine. She and Rich had bought it from an elderly couple when it was still dark and worn. It had been neglected for years, but they'd spent a lot of money and time and now, it couldn't look more different.

Liv casts her eye approvingly over the exposed wooden beams adding their rustic charm to the kitchen. They'd preserved original fireplaces in some of the other rooms that provide a warmth and authenticity that perfectly complement the new soft neutral tones and elegant fixtures. The overall effect is a seamless blend of old and new, giving the space a timeless appeal.

She adores this house and feels so lucky and content here with her little family and Betsy the pup, who they'd got from a local rescue centre just six months ago.

Liv picks up the interiors magazine and puts it down again. She can't settle. Her coffee begins to cool, the magazine remaining untouched while she stares up at the grey clouds that race across the sky. The troubled churning in the pit of her stomach is back, but she doesn't want to think about what is bothering her. Now is not the time and, besides, it is too late. Far too late to make it right again.

She considers the chores again, but the thought of a long soak and time to read a few pages of her new book is too tempting to ignore.

Upstairs, she runs a hot bath and drizzles in some Jo Malone London bath oil that Shannon generously gifted her last Christmas. She undresses, dropping her clothes in a heap, and climbs into the pomegranate-scented warm water that bathes her aching limbs like a healing cocoon. Liv closes her eyes and takes a few deep breaths. She opens her new book and reads the first chapter twice before giving up and setting it down on the floor.

She washes her hair and endures another fifteen minutes in the bath before getting out, drying herself on a fluffy towel and wrapping up in a warm fleecy dressing gown. She lies on the bed for ten minutes, staring at the ceiling and trying to ignore the unpleasant swirling sensation in her stomach. She can't rest.

When she gets up to dry her hair, she glances at her phone. Ninety minutes have now passed since Rich and Maddox left the house.

Back downstairs, Liv puts a load of washing on and makes a half-hearted start at tidying up the kitchen; last night, Rich had been adamant they shouldn't bother with the mess before they went up to bed.

'Tonight's special,' he'd said, touching her cheek tenderly. 'Too special to spend it doing chores.' They'd looked at each other for a few poignant moments before she'd nodded in agreement. Of course, he was right.

Another thirty minutes pass and they're still not back. She tries his phone but it goes to voicemail again. There could be a thousand plausible reasons to explain their delayed return, and yet, when Liv opens the iPhone app again, the location still won't settle. She takes a screenshot.

Frog Hill and the surrounding area is notoriously bad for signal. There are parts where it disappears completely, and so she isn't altogether surprised when her call goes through to voicemail again, and she tells herself not to worry.

However, when another hour passes and her efforts to contact Rich by phone, messages that don't get two delivery ticks, and even email, come to nothing, she pulls on some warm clothing and jumps in the car. It's a ten-minute drive to Frog Hill from the house, a journey she knows like the back of her hand.

As she approaches a gravelled stretch of pot-holed ground the locals use as a free car park, her heart lifts when she spots Rich's car. Not hard, as it's the only vehicle parked up there.

Liv gets out of the car and turns to the hill, looming behind her. There is nobody up there. No tell-tale giant rainbow-coloured Delta kite swirling high above the ground. Liv pulls her puffer jacket tighter around her neck. The wind is picking up and the temperature has dropped a few degrees from earlier in the day.

She walks slowly around the base of the hill, all the time looking up towards the top. From down here, she can see the big frog-shaped rock at the summit that gives the hill its name. Maddox loves that rock; he even made a papier-mâché model of it in his nursery class that's now proudly displayed on a shelf in his bedroom.

Liv has brought Maddox up here herself a few times. She has taken pictures and filmed video clips of him fearlessly climbing on to, and then jumping off, the rock. They both lay down on top of it last summer and counted the fluffy white clouds in a picture-perfect blue sky.

But now her boy is not up there, and the clouds above her are steel grey and billowing wildly.

Again, Liv walks slowly around the circumference of the hill until she's scoured all sides. Dejected, she heads back to the waste ground.

Rich's car is a black Mercedes GLE bought on lease last year. It has plenty of room for the three of them and Rich's fishing gear when he camps out. Through the tinted back window, she can see the outline of Maddox's car seat. She tries the door and of course the vehicle is locked. Although there's a spare key at home, she hasn't thought to bring it with her.

If not for the fact that Rich's car is still parked here, Liv might have assumed their journeys had perhaps crossed and they had missed each other.

But worryingly, the car *is* here, and so that can't be the case.

Her heart is thumping now, and she feels sick. She calls her mother-in-law.

'If his car's there then they must still be around,' Shannon says calmly, but Liv can hear concern weighing down her words. 'If you can't see them up on the hill, look around the surrounding areas. See if they've gone for a walk or something.'

Liv ends the call and slowly scans across flat stretches of fields and the rough land that borders them strewn with bracken and long grass. There are small clusters of trees and bushes dotted here and there, but no one else is around.

They haven't gone for a walk, she's certain of that. The storm is approaching; she can feel its bite in the heavy, humid air. There's no way Rich would hang around this long, putting Maddox at risk.

At around two, she calls Rich's phone and gets his voicemail again.

'Rich!' Liv yells into the worsening weather at the top of her voice. There's no one around to hear, but she's compelled to do it. She must go through all the motions. Get everything in the right order for her own sanity.

The gathering wind whips the strength from her voice and so Liv tries again and again, turning full circle to catch any movement or sound. But there is nothing. There is no one.

She's done everything she can think of. She stands there, her insides turning to liquid. Her mind refusing to function. *Think.*

Liv looks again at the Mercedes, and it suddenly occurs to her that there might be something wrong with the car. Of course! If the car wouldn't start, Rich would just leave it there and call a cab to pick them up, not wanting to bother her when she was resting.

But his phone has no signal. Or he's out of charge and that's the reason her calls won't connect. The hill, the wind, the car... it all feels like a film set to her. None of it feels real.

Liv gets back into her Mini and sits there for a couple of minutes, confused and staring hopefully up at the hill as if her son might suddenly spring from nowhere, running and waving with his wild dark curls and ruddy cheeks.

As if this is a bad dream and she doesn't have to worry after all.

When that doesn't happen, Liv starts the Mini and drives home.

Back at the house, she calls Rich's phone yet again and leaves a message.

She calls her mother-in-law. She lost her own mum to heart disease years ago, long before she met Rich. His father – a bitter man who didn't approve of any of Rich's choices in life – had already died. Shannon has seemed to consciously install herself as a substitute mother figure in Liv's life. It can be quite irritating. But at times like this, Shannon does have the ability to think coolly and logically.

When Shannon answers her call, Liv says, 'I've looked everywhere and there's no sign of them. They should've been back home ages ago now. I'm really worried, especially with the storm brewing.'

'Try not to fret, Liv.' Shannon makes a sympathetic noise. 'There must be an explanation. Do you want me to drive out there and look around?'

'No. There's no point and the wind is really getting up now. I'll call you if there's any change. I've no choice but to wait a bit longer and pray they come back.'

'I'm sure it'll be fine, love,' Shannon says.

She's irked by Shannon's seemingly unconcerned tone. But

Rich's mum is a practical woman and there have been occasions where her level head has saved Liv from having a meltdown. Like last year when she'd forgotten where she'd parked her car in a multi-storey and thought it had been stolen. Shannon had happened to call her on another matter just as she was on the edge of a full-on meltdown and about to call the police. She'd calmly suggested Liv might be on the wrong floor. Which of course turned out to be the case.

But this is different. Liv needs Shannon to take her seriously. It is important.

'Try not to worry. I'm sure there's no need to get alarmed just yet.'

'Maybe I should give it a little longer before I start panicking,' Liv says grudgingly.

Shannon sighs. 'There'll be a perfectly good explanation. You'll see.'

Liv ends the conversation and then, despite what she's just said, she immediately calls the police. The sooner they get involved, the better.

TWO

'I know it's hard but try not to panic.' The kind young police officer, Susan, hands Liv a clean tissue. Susan has been at the house about fifteen minutes, now. Long enough to make Liv a cup of tea and to explain that she's a specialist-trained family liaison officer, here to offer her support, 'at this very worrying time'.

'Frog Hill and the surrounding area is crawling with police officers as we speak and there are more on the way,' Susan continues in a calm voice. 'Nine times out of ten there's a perfectly normal explanation in circumstances such as this one. Rest assured, if your husband and son are out there then we will find them.'

If. Liv nods and snuffles into the tissue, dabbing at her eyes. 'Thank you,' she says in a wobbly voice. 'It's just... well, they've been gone for over three hours now. They're never out that long, and with the weather worsening... can't you trace his phone at least?'

'That's in hand too, although if a mobile phone is turned off, it can be significantly more challenging to locate it. Not impossible but takes a little more time.'

'How long?'

Susan opens her mouth to reply just as another officer cranes his neck around the kitchen door. The handmade cupboards and the cream Aga usually distract visitors, but his eyes gravitate to the dirty crockery and empty wine glasses from last night's celebrations and Liv feels her shoulder muscles tighten. It feels like she's being judged; as if somehow, the police think she and Rich having a good time last night might be a factor in what's happened. The officer beckons to Susan. 'Quick word?'

'Back in a mo,' she says to Liv, moving quickly out of the room.

Liv stares out of the window. The swaying row of conifers at the bottom of the garden have started to bend quite steeply with the stronger gusts of wind. People will no doubt be quick to criticise. Say they were foolish parents, even neglectful, to allow Maddox out in this weather, but as Rich said, it was perfectly fine when they set off late morning.

She takes another sip of the lukewarm tea and then sets it aside, wondering what the officer wanted to say to his colleague without her hearing. She turns at a shuffling noise in the doorway. The two officers are back.

'I have some very good news, Liv,' Susan says with a smile. 'Our officers have just located Maddox. Your son is fine. He's tired and a little cold, but safe and unhurt.'

'Oh, thank God!' Liv's eyes squeeze closed and she murmurs a prayer of thanks. 'Where was he?'

'He was right up at the top of the hill, in a kind of ground den covered in bracken. It looks like something older kids have constructed at some point and it seems Maddox had crawled in, probably afraid of being alone up there. With the weather worsening, it was a smart thing to do.'

'He mustn't have heard me shouting because of the wind,'

Liv says softly, her heart squeezing. Then she looks at Susan again and says, 'What about Rich?'

Susan glances at her colleague. Hesitates.

'What is it?' Liv whispers, looking from one officer to the other. 'What is it you're not telling me?'

'I'm afraid there's no sign of your husband yet.' Susan takes a step forward and extends a calming hand as Liv starts to shake. 'Try not to worry. We'll keep looking until we find him.'

The police officers eventually leave two hours later when Shannon arrives amid torrential rain from the storm, promising the search will continue the second the weather improves.

While Maddox's gran makes him some warm milk, Liv sits with her arm around him, stroking his hair. The temptation is to gently question him, but the police did all that with her before they left the house.

'Where did Daddy go, Maddox?' Liv had asked him after guidance from a specialist officer.

'Me not know,' Maddox had whispered, his eyes wide and fearful.

'What did Daddy say before he went away?' the officer had gently asked.

'Kite.' Maddox had turned from the officer and buried his face in Liv's side. A tangle of unnamed emotions had clenched from inside her.

'Let's leave it there for today,' one of the officers had said. 'We can try again tomorrow when he's had some rest.'

'I think it's time for me to take this exhausted little boy up to bed,' Shannon says now as Maddox sips the hot milk.

Liv shakes her head. 'Actually, Shannon, I really think we need to protect Maddox from the police presence and all the attention. Could you take him to your house, just for tonight?'

Shannon frowns. 'But you've only just got him back. Surely you want to keep him with you?'

Liv looks down at her hands. 'I'm scared. Worried about Rich still being out there. I don't want Maddox picking up on that.'

Shannon considers this for a moment. 'Why don't you come back with us too, love? I can run you back in the morning. I don't want you dealing with this on your own.'

Shannon's face looks pale and strained. Although she is greatly relieved that Maddox is now safe, Liv knows she'll be hiding her own concerns that her only son is still missing.

Liv shakes her head. 'Rich might come back here and I have to try and get my head together,' she says, fighting back tears. 'I need space to make sense of it all.'

Grudgingly, Shannon agrees. She gathers a few things for Maddox, wraps him up warm, and together they walk him out to the car, battling the elements. Liv kisses her son and waves them off, watching the car until it turns at the bottom of the street, rain lashing her face and drenching her clothes.

Alone in the house at last, Liv pulls off her damp fleece and splashes some cool water on to her red, puffy face before going upstairs to her bedroom.

It's dark outside now. All the streetlights are lit, the sky above looks ominous as the storm continues to brew. Liv knows that behind their half-open curtains and blinds, the neighbours will be buzzing with curiosity. Desperate to find out details now the police cars have all left.

Everyone wanting answers. Everyone except her.

Liv picks up the framed photograph on the windowsill and studies it. A happy snapshot of their day trip to the coast that summer. Maddox's face is lightly tanned, a blob of chocolate ice-cream caught in the corner of his mouth from a cone Rich has just bought him. Liv herself looks happily tired, following a day walking back and forth to collect sea water for the turrets and moats the boys had built together on the beach. Rich has an arm around each of them, hugging them close. His handsome face radiates happiness and contentment.

Liv pulls the bedroom curtains closed before opening the wardrobe door to look calmly at the rail of her husband's work shirts, T-shirts and a couple of pairs of trousers. Three pairs of shoes sit neatly at the bottom. There are no suits, jackets or coats in there. Not now. The motorcycle leathers he told her he'd worn in his twenties that he could never bear to part with are also missing.

Anyone coming in here and looking around the house would see Rich's presence everywhere. In the bathroom, his toothbrush and razor sit on the glass shelf above the sink. A tangle of his worn clothes wait to be laundered in the wicker basket. In the garage, they would find his electric bike, still plugged in and charging and, right by his favourite leather armchair in the living room, a half-watched episode from his favourite series of *Game of Thrones* paused yesterday on his iPad.

It's all an illusion and no detail has been overlooked.

Just as Rich said in their hasty planning conversation, 'It's simple, really. You showcase certain key things people expect to see, and they will arrive at the desired conclusion and not question a thing.'

Those motorcycle leathers and the other missing things were hastily packed up with the rest of his belongings and taken a hundred-and-fifty miles away, to the storage facility which they'd pre-paid in cash for, for the next twelve months.

It's surreal, looking around the house now that he's gone. Knowing that everything is falling into place. Just as they intended it. Just as they planned.

So far, everything has gone perfectly and there is every chance it will continue to do so.

Provided they both stick to the rules.

THREE

KAIT

I watch Daniel carry our cups of tea over on a small tray. He's recently embarked on some kind of new running regime and after six weeks he looks fitter than ever with his broad shoulders and defined biceps.

More importantly, he's kind, loyal and hardworking and most of the time I feel like the luckiest girl on earth, being with him. When I reached my mid-thirties, with a whole bunch of bad relationship choices behind me, I'd already done a great job of convincing myself that the whole marriage-kids-settling-down kind of life wasn't going to be for me, after all.

I'd told myself that particular life path wasn't everything it was made out to be, anyway. Sure, there were times I felt lonely, but at that point in time, just before Daniel and I met, I had a promising career, I owned my own apartment in a vibrant area of the city and I had a decent social life. My older sister, Kirsten, has settled down, but happily for me, her partner, Ellie, has a phobia of flying, which left Kirsten and me able to go abroad together a couple of times a year. Life wasn't perfect, but it was good. I had no real complaints.

Then three years ago, just as I'd come to terms with the fact I probably wouldn't find 'the one' after all, Daniel Hatton walked into my life.

Daniel bends forward now and offers me the tray. 'Tea is served, madam.'

'You're spoiling me again.' I take a mug, noticing the ginger thins he's piled on a little bone china saucer. 'If I eat many more of your sweet treats, I'll have to be rolled off this sofa.'

He laughs. 'You deserve to be looked after and I take my job as chief spoiler very seriously indeed.' Daniel sets down the tray and sits next to me. 'Besides, the tea is decaf and the bickies are low sugar. How are you feeling?'

'Much better than I did, thanks.'

He nods, and I watch as he drifts off momentarily, the familiar frown lines crinkling on his brow. Lately, he seems to have the weight of the world on his shoulders, but every time I ask if he's OK, he waves away my concern as if it's nothing.

I know he's worried about me and the baby, but recently, something happened that suggested to me that it might be more than that and nothing at all to do with the baby. It occurs to me that maybe, just maybe, he's found other interests while I've been recuperating.

'Good you're feeling better.' Daniel's worried expression dissolves as he snaps to attention again. 'Really good.'

I can't fault the attention he gives me, even though recently, he seems to spend more time out of the house than he's ever done. He's been properly doling out the kid-glove treatment since the hospital diagnosed me with pre-eclampsia three weeks ago. I'm thirty-six and it's the first time I've been pregnant, so when I started experiencing severe headaches and my lower legs and feet swelled up, I didn't really think of it as a serious warning sign. Until I collapsed when I was out shopping for baby equipment in town.

Daniel was at work when they rushed me to the City Hospital where a consultant ran a series of tests including liver and kidney function and an ultrasound scan. I'd called Kirsten and she had frantically tried to contact Daniel, even ringing around the local gyms. But nobody had a clue where he was.

'It's not an uncommon condition around the mid to late second trimester, but it can be dangerous if left untreated,' the consultant told me, reeling off a lengthy list of lifestyle changes including a regular exercise routine, getting enough sleep, together with eating healthy foods that are low in salt and avoiding caffeine. Sounded like I had a fun time ahead of me.

I was in the waiting room when Kirsten got to the hospital and Daniel rang her back just as we reached the entrance.

I looked at him. 'Kirsten tried to call, but you didn't pick up your phone. Where were you?'

'Can somebody just tell me what happened?' Daniel glared at Kirsten. I knew he instantly resented the fact she'd been the one with me even though he had been nowhere to be found. It struck me he ought to be grateful.

'I'll explain everything when we get back,' Kirsten said, shrinking back a bit from his glare. 'For now, we need to get Kait out to the cab.'

'Don't be ridiculous, I've got the car,' Daniel said, offhandedly. 'I'm taking Kait home. We can drop you off on the way if you need us to.'

I hadn't seen him like this before: so openly rude. He just seemed to have a short fuse lately. He was fine with me, but... others, not so much. I threw Kirsten an apologetic look, but I didn't say anything to Daniel about his attitude towards her there, in the hospital, with the medical staff and other patients nearby. At the time, I didn't have the energy to start refereeing between them.

'I'll make my own way home.' Kirsten gave me a strange look I couldn't identify, her voice softening. Usually quick to temper, she didn't seem her usual incendiary self, which I felt relieved about. 'I'll text you later, Kait. Get plenty of rest.'

Since then, Daniel has embarked on a mission to ensure all the consultant's instructions are carried out to the letter. I soon forgot about his manner towards Kirsten and, instead, feel constantly grateful he's so caring and takes such an interest in my pregnancy and wellbeing. But one question still prevails from that day: where was my husband when Kirsten couldn't reach him? What was he doing that was so absorbing he continued to ignore his phone? I'd promised myself I wouldn't get like this again, but... I had good reason to be suspicious.

'I thought we might have a little walk around the field when you've finished your tea,' Daniel says.

I look out of the window and wrinkle my nose at the drizzle and the low grey clouds skimming above the fields beyond the house. One of the reasons I'd instantly loved this place was its semi-rural location. Fresh air and open space while still within striking distance of the city. 'I'd prefer to just rest most of today, I think,' I say. 'I feel really tired.'

'No problem. We'll go for a walk in the morning then.' Daniel downs his tea before standing up. 'If you're going to rest, I'll pop out now and deliver those protein powder orders while you're resting.'

My chest tightens. In his work as a personal trainer, he's always gone the extra mile for his clients. Sourcing and delivering equipment for them – at a good mark-up, of course – and lots of his male clients are keen on bulking up and buy their nutritional supplements from him. But these days, he always seems to be 'popping out briefly', which is a total under-estimation of the time he's gone. Sometimes he's out for a few hours and he's often late home from work several days a week these days. 'Are they just local deliveries?'

His phone vibrates with a notification. Distracted, he glances at the screen, his frown lines returning. 'Mostly local, yes.' He pats his pocket for his keys. 'Anything else you need before I go?'

'No, I'm fine. I'm quite capable of getting up and moving around the house if I need anything.' I hesitate. 'Just try not to be out too long. I miss you.'

He bends down to kiss me on the forehead. 'Miss you too. I'll be back before you know it, but you've only got to call if you need me.'

Like Kirsten did that day at the hospital.

I say, 'I'll try not to disturb you.'

He rests his hand gently on my bump. 'I'm always here for my queen and her precious cargo. I'll lock the door when I go, OK?'

I give him a little nod but I don't say anything. I learned a long time ago I wasn't going to win a battle about home security. I'd go so far as to say my husband is bordering on paranoid when it comes to it. The door must be locked when we're home and he fitted window locks and brackets so they can only open so far, which is a pain in warmer weather.

'We got robbed when I was younger,' he told me. 'You never forget something like that and it doesn't hurt to take a few sensible precautions.' So now, to keep him happy, I make sure I lock the doors and windows, too.

As Daniel walks away, his phone begins to ring. He digs it out of his back jeans pocket and heads towards the door. As he does so, a folded piece of paper falls out and flutters to the floor.

I open my mouth to tell him, but Daniel is already in what sounds like a gruff conversation with someone, so I don't disturb him.

It'll wait until he gets back.

FOUR

MADDOX

Maddox leaves football training, walking slower than he needs to because he doesn't want to go back home. Doesn't want to face his mum. Once he has turned the corner on to Main Road, he slows his pace to a saunter, searching out larger stones to kick along the pavement as he goes.

On the outside, everything in his life seems the same as always. Same school, same footie, same online gaming performance. Inside though, Maddox has somehow found himself in a place that is unfamiliar and stops him feeling relaxed and content. He knows exactly when it happened, and he doesn't like the fact he can't get it out of his head.

There's something up with his mum and it's making him nervous. For as long as Maddox can remember, it's just been the two of them. Him and his mum against the world since the day his dad went missing. But for the last couple of months, she's started acting strangely. Out of character. She spends ages online at the kitchen table in the evening instead of watching TV and chilling out like she used to do. There's a load of empty wine bottles in the glass bottle bin outside, too, and she hardly ever used to drink in the house.

Maddox kicks a large, smooth stone hard enough that it bolts way ahead of him.

It's the reason he looked at her laptop when she was at work a couple of weeks ago. There was a passcode which used his birth day and month – 9 October – along with his birth year, that she used for everything. He'd spent an hour going through her search history and ended up wishing he hadn't.

His mum has always been the one to give him confidence, tell him he could do anything he wants to.

She's always told him, ever since he was a little kid: 'The world is your oyster, Maddox. You can reach the stars if you put your mind to it.' But recently, she's added, 'I can't talk specifics, but I want you to think – I mean really think – what it is you'd love to do in life, because soon, money won't be a barrier. You'll be able to go for exactly what you choose.'

The first time she'd said it, Maddox had looked at her like she'd gone bananas. At home, money had always been a barrier to *everything*. His mum worked hard, but there was only ever just enough.

Maddox manages to get most of what he needs online for his football training and gaming. There are loads of good quality used equipment and clothing marketplaces out there if you know where to look and, rather than asking his mum, who he knows is hard-pressed, he tries to pay for it himself using the crappy wages he gets from his part-time job.

But if something goes badly wrong at home, like when the hot water tank flooded the bathroom just before Christmas and ruined the kitchen ceiling, then they have to do without something so they can pay the unexpected bill.

That's just the way life is, and Maddox has never known it to be any different. But that's also why it's so weird to hear his mum speaking in riddles about money. As though a better life is just around the corner when Maddox is old enough now to know that the next few years will just be more of the same. Scrimping and scraping and making do with less.

That one comment she made keeps playing on loop in his head – 'soon, money won't be a barrier' – is the reason he had a look around his mum's laptop when she had a late shift at the care home. Found some stuff that made him want to throw up. Stuff he doesn't want to think about too much, at least until he figures out what it properly means.

Maddox spots another stone, even bigger than the last one, and boots it, hard as he can directly in front of him.

'Oi!' His heart jolts when he sees a chunky, familiar guy striding towards him, his face set into a snarl.

'Shit,' Maddox curses under his breath. Looks like the flying stone found a target. At sixteen, Brandon McFadden is a couple of years older than Maddox and used to attend the same school as him. He got excluded multiple times for dealing drugs in the playground before the local authority sent him to a special Pupil Referral Unit for kids who can no longer attend mainstream schools. Since he left the PRU, Brandon always seems to be hanging around here for some reason.

'Alright, Brandon?' Maddox mumbles. He's seen him hanging around school for the last few days and, unless he's mistaken, Brandon has been trying to catch his eye and occa-sionally, trying to strike up a conversation. Maddox feels slightly uncomfortable bumping into him again. Trouble seems to follow Brandon McFadden. Everybody knows that.

'No. I'm not alright! That rock you aimed at me hit me on the shin, you stupid little—'

Maddox backs away, holding up a hand. 'Sorry, sorry. I wasn't looking. I should've checked there was nobody around.' He tries to think on his feet to avoid a black eye. 'How're you doing, Brandon? Everybody's still buzzing about you at school.'

Brandon's scowl relaxes a little. 'Yeah? What they been saying then?'

Maddox shrugs. 'Everybody's been going on about how cool it was. That you basically did what you liked and stuck two fingers up to the teachers.'

'Too right!' Brandon stands a little straighter. 'Never looked back since I left the place, have I? Never earned as much cash.' He rubs his thumb and index finger together.

Maddox raises an eyebrow. 'Yeah? Lucky you.'

Brandon regards Maddox for a moment or two before leaning closer and murmuring. 'Not something I can shout about, if you know what I mean. Only a select few can be involved. That's what I've been trying to talk to you about.'

'Right.' Maddox manages not to roll his eyes. Everybody knows Brandon lives in La-La-Land courtesy of the weed he constantly smokes. 'Sounds like you're doing well, mate. Hope you—'

A boy on his football team and his dad walk past. Parents know about Brandon – his record of bad behaviour and the fact he has been permanently excluded from the school. The dad does a double-take, glancing at Brandon and then Maddox before unlocking a parked car and getting in it with his son.

'I might be able to let you in on it. You're the sort we need.' Brandon smirks. 'I can't go into all the details now, I have to get clearance from my boss. But there's an opening available that's an amazing opportunity to make a lot of cash. How's that sound?'

'Sounds good,' Maddox murmurs, still not quite understanding exactly what might be expected of him. 'But... is it illegal?'

Brandan laughs. 'Hey, can you imagine me doing anything illegal?' He holds out his arms as if he's an open book. 'Not illegal. But my boss says you have to register interest before there are any more details given. D'ya get me?'

Even though Brandon is claiming this job is above board, it feels distinctly dodgy to Maddox, and exactly the sort of thing he ought to stay clear of.

Brandon leans in and lowers his voice. 'Tell you what. 'Cos I like you, I'll speak to my boss, see what I can do.'

'Sounds great. Thanks!' Maddox adjusts the rucksack on his back, hoping Brandon will soon stop spouting rubbish. 'Better go then. See you around, Brandon.'

'Later, yeah?'

They touch fists and Maddox resumes his walk to school, resisting the urge to kick any more boulders on the way.

FIVE

KAIT

I open my eyes with a start. The full mug of tea Daniel made me before he left is still on the small table, now stone cold. I must have fallen asleep as soon as he left, more tired than I realised. I check my watch and see he's been gone about an hour and a half.

I sit up straighter and yawn, lacing my fingers together and stretching my arms above my head, the tangle of fleecy blankets and a furry cushion falling away. I'd rather not move away from this cosy nest here on the sofa, but I need the bathroom. Desperately so. I shuffle to the edge of the seat cushion and, being careful not to jump up too quickly, I slowly unfold my body until I'm standing.

Walking across the room, I notice the bit of folded notepaper that fell out of Daniel's back pocket. I bend to pick it up, tucking it into my cardigan pocket before heading across the hallway into the downstairs cloakroom.

In the kitchen, I flick on the kettle to make a fresh hot drink and, while I'm waiting for it to boil, I pull out the piece of paper. Unfolding it, I frown at the handwritten note in Daniel's distinctive scrawl.

F Forest upn X17 314 907 2600

F Forest? I've never heard of the place, but it sounds like an abbreviation for a stretch of countryside or something. Knowing Daniel, it will be something to do with his business. He's mentioned before he wants to get into the latest health trend of outdoor training.

The kettle clicks and I make myself a cup of tea. I flatten out the note and place it on the worktop so Daniel will see it on his return. Then I go back to the living room.

I glance at the big date on our calendar. Only four months until the baby comes and, until then, I'm supposed to be resting. Time is just rolling on relentlessly. So much has happened to me in my life since that early evening after work three years ago.

I was standing at a bar waiting for my sister to arrive. Kirsten called ahead to say she'd been delayed at work, so I decided to get myself a drink and grab a free table to wait for her.

As I took a seat, I heard a deep male voice behind me, 'That was lucky, they've only just gone.' I turned around to see a good-looking guy of about forty, grinning. 'Tables are like gold dust in here.'

I gave him a little smile and turned around again, checking my phone to see if Kirsten had messaged.

'I'm Daniel,' I heard him say. 'I've not been living in the area long and I spend far too much time in this place.'

I put down my phone and turned my chair around slightly so I could see him without straining.

'I've only been here a couple of times,' I said, taking a sip of my white wine spritzer. 'It's my sister's choice.'

'Your sister's got good taste.'

His easy manner, relaxed dress sense and five o'clock shadow seemed to suggest he didn't really know how fit he was.

His friendly banter seemed genuine rather than pure chat-up, which women in their thirties like me can usually spot a mile off. Turned out he was waiting for a delayed friend too.

The chat came easily. Daniel seemed impressed when I told him about my career in retail and so I asked what he did for a living.

'I managed to get out of my previous line of work and I'm helping a friend renovate a property he's just bought,' he said. 'It's only a temporary job until I can find something suitable.'

'I've always fancied doing a property up and selling it for a decent profit.' I grinned. 'There are one or two Facebook groups with great ideas for—'

'I don't do social media,' he said, pulling a face. 'Let's just say I got burned pretty bad once and I vowed never to go back to it.'

Before I could find out more, Kirsten arrived. I felt surprisingly disappointed when Daniel checked his watch and stood up. 'That's it for me. I'm giving up on my mate but—' he leaned forward and pressed a business card into my hand '—I'd love to continue our conversation soon. Have a nice evening, ladies.'

'Blimey, you're a fast worker.' Kirsten gave me a look. 'I'm only twenty minutes late and you've already hooked up with your next conquest. Thought you were done with men after your last one. You said you were having a break for a while.'

I shrugged. Trust Kirsten to try and rake up the details of my last long-term disastrous relationship that I tried hard not to think about anymore. After two years and planning to buy a house together, he'd announced he didn't feel ready to settle down after all. At the age of thirty-eight.

I felt a frisson of excitement in my belly as I watched Daniel saunter out of the bar, his wide shoulders and slim hips cutting an impressive form as he raised a friendly hand to the barman. It felt like something big just happened, like I'd met 'the one'.

When I turned back to Kirsten, she stared at me intently.

'I'll get the drinks in,' I said.

I texted him the next morning. Two minutes after I sent it, he called me. We went for a meal that night, talked and talked about our lives. He told me he'd finally broken free of a long-term job he felt had both saved him and begun to destroy him.

A few months into our relationship, Daniel said it had always been his dream to set up as a freelance personal trainer. Despite one or two niggles and Kirsten telling me I needed my head testing, I decided to back him. Loaned him three thousand pounds of my modest life savings so he could train to get the specialist diploma he needed to enable him to get the necessary insurance to become self-employed.

Kirsten went nuts. 'It's a textbook romance scam, Kait. I just read an article about a woman who got taken for twenty grand in an almost identical scenario. You'll get yourself in deep again.'

But within six months of starting his freelance business, Daniel had secured a few clients and had paid back every penny of the loan I gave him.

'You really need to get on Instagram and Facebook,' I told him. 'You're missing out on a lot of exposure online.'

I had Facebook and Twitter accounts, but I didn't use them very much. Seeing my tiny friends group on there only served to remind me how isolated I'd become from my life a few years earlier. I didn't see any of them in real life.

Daniel shook his head. 'Not for me. I like doing business face-to-face. I know where I stand then.'

He'd confided in me that he'd been scammed out of some money in a pyramid selling scheme about a year before we met. 'I lost a grand. A lot of money and could have been worse.'

'What happened?' I asked, genuinely interested. But Daniel shook his head.

'I try not to think about it. I dealt with it by putting it firmly behind me and promising myself never to engage on social media again.'

I got the message loud and clear, although I found it a bit odd. But a couple of colleagues at school had also ditched social media after parents had contacted them directly online regarding their child.

I told myself it was Daniel's choice, and I could totally understand being wary after such a horrible experience. But my concern was that social media would be a valuable boost in growing his business and in the event, Daniel proved me wrong.

Through word of mouth, his popularity and reputation grew to such an extent, he soon had a waiting list. I was impressed how clever he'd been. How he'd realised that regular gym instructors were ten-a-penny.

'See, I'm targeting wealthier clients who haven't got time to go to the gym, or don't want to train in a public gym environment,' Daniel told me. 'The secret is to make life as easy as possible for them.'

He implemented a policy to take on only those clients who were wealthy enough to have training facilities at their own home. And it worked. Some of the photos he sent me of the flash pads he worked in – always taken surreptitiously when the client was unaware, of course – made my jaw drop.

It wasn't a case of a couple of pieces of smart equipment and a few weights. Some clients had their own fully equipped gyms in slickly renovated basements or purpose-built outbuildings located in outsized, landscaped gardens. Full-sized heated outdoor swimming pools with elaborate coloured lights and electric covers were not uncommon.

That's when I started thinking about the people he might be training. The women who lived in these houses. Wealthy women with taut bodies and beautiful faces. It was a kind of joke, wasn't it? Bored, wealthy women screwing their hot personal trainers. Except it didn't feel remotely funny and I knew I had to fight my jealousy before it got out of hand.

Daniel didn't seem that impressed, but he did remark it was another world. 'Compared to the years I spent in my early career on the oil rigs,' he said.

'What was it like, working on the rigs?'

'The freezing North Sea, the constant smell of diesel and the lack of any home comforts. That was my life.' He shook his head in dread whenever he talked about the rigs. 'Sometimes I wonder why I stuck it for so long.'

It was obvious Daniel was uncomfortable talking about his unhappy past and I understood that completely. But he explained how he'd started on the rigs when he was eighteen, saying, 'It was a kind of escape, I guess.'

'An escape from what?' I didn't want to press him too hard, but it had taken him a while to open up and, besides, I was curious.

'My dad... he was a bully and he wasn't around that much for me.' He looked down at his hands. 'My mother put up with it even though he treated her like dirt over the years. She said that underneath it all he was a good man. But when I got older, I promised myself when the chance came, I'd do anything to escape his poisonous influence.'

'So you signed up to work on the oil rigs?'

Daniel nodded. 'Yeah. When my parents died within a year of each other, I felt pretty much untouchable out there in the middle of the sea where I didn't have to think too hard about the fact I was completely alone in the world. During my time off, I usually stayed in a B&B close to the sea, counting the days until I could go back out to the rig. It's only now I realise I was just running away from my grief rather than dealing with it.'

He only really confided in me that once. I tried many times

to encourage him to open up about more of his past although I was purposely sketchy about my own. I was lucky in a way as Daniel seemed to have an aversion to talking about his own past and hardly asked me about my own. I got the impression he didn't like to bring it up in case it opened the possibility of conversation about him again.

'Sounds to me like he's got some stuff he might want to hide. Don't we all!' Kirsten said on several occasions, and maybe she was right. But I've always felt Daniel and I are all about the future and so long as that future is filled with hope, trust and loyalty then I don't care about the past. It's all about a fresh start really, isn't it?

When Daniel finally gets back home about thirty minutes later, I insist on making him a coffee while he faffs around me. 'I've told you before, I'm not an invalid. Just let me be,' I chide him. 'Did you get all your deliveries done?'

'What? Oh yeah, all done.'

He's staring at his phone again and it's starting to drive me crazy. 'Put your phone down, Daniel. Let's have coffee and, you know, *chat*? Like we used to?'

Our life seems to speed along like a runaway train. We were married within eighteen months of meeting, and I fell pregnant early in the year. I'd been on the pill but one night, after a boozy meal out, I had a stomach upset in the middle of the night and... well, we never gave it another thought. I'd missed the odd tablet before and we'd been fine and I'd always suffered from irregular periods anyway.

We were both a little shocked but happy when I bought a pregnancy test and discovered I was already three months pregnant. I felt at the centre of Daniel's world: the way he treated me like a princess, wanting to spend every minute together. Until recently when that changed.

Daniel places his phone face down now on the low table. 'Sorry, I don't mean to act distracted all the time.'

'So why are you?' I glance at his phone, a burning sensation in my chest. 'Who are you texting so much?'

'Clients! It's a busy time, that's all. I want to keep on top of everything.'

'You can't work twenty-four-seven, though.' I can feel myself getting agitated, so I stand up. 'Everyone needs a break now and then.'

He follows me into the kitchen.

'Oh, a piece of paper dropped out of your pocket when you pulled out your phone earlier,' I say, spooning instant coffee into his cup. 'It's over there. On the worktop.'

I only look up because he doesn't answer and that's when I see him pick up the note. I watch as his face drains of colour.

'Is everything OK?' I say, concerned.

He tries to recover his composure but it's too late. And he knows it.

He blinks and a smile stretches unnaturally across his mouth. 'It's just an online training resource a client gave me. I'd left my phone in the car, so he wrote it on a bit of paper.'

'But it's your handwriting on the note.' I'm starting to feel sick; he's not being honest with me.

The smile disappears and he waits a few seconds before replying. He's taking some thinking time. 'Oh yes, that's right, the client told me about an interesting website, and then I wrote it down, OK? Please don't split hairs like this, Kait.'

'It doesn't look like a website.' I feel so tired and, even though my suspicion antennae are on high alert, I'm not sure I can deal with a full-blown argument. The last thing I want is a 'situation' where I say things I can't take back.

Daniel loosely picks up the note and then drops it again as his phone rings. He glances at the screen and curses. 'I have to get this.'

Very convenient. *Too convenient.*

'That's good news. I'll see him tonight.' He walks out of the kitchen, and I hear him speaking in low, urgent tones in the hallway. Acting on instinct, I snatch up my own phone and walk over to the worktop, taking a quick snap of the note. His quick brush-off doesn't quite wash, not least because he looked so worried when he initially saw the note. I jump a little when he strides back in, managing to surreptitiously slide the phone into the waistband of my leggings before facing him.

'Sorry about that. Awkward client.' Two hot little red spots have appeared on his cheeks.

I stare at him, unnerved by his obvious discomfort. I can't let this go without asking him more questions. 'What was it for, the reference you wrote down?'

'Jeez, how many more times? It was just from a client. It's an online training portal, OK?'

I frown. 'F Forest... what does that stand for? Is it a place?'

'Like I told you, it's just something a client mentioned,' he says irritably. 'He thought I might be interested in it.'

My eyes gravitate to the note again. 'You're acting weird. Is something wrong?'

He turns and looks me in the eye. 'No, Kait. I give you my word, nothing's wrong. Why are you always asking me that?'

I feel my shining future slip slightly. *I give you my word.*

'Can't we just talk about—'

'I don't want to talk about anything, Kait,' he says sharply. 'Can't we just drop it? I've got a hundred things on my mind.'

I'm shocked that he's spoken to me as abruptly and then just cut off the conversation like that. It's totally out of character for him.

I pick up the note. 'Shall I just throw this away then?'

He takes it from me, crumples it slightly and throws it into the swing bin. 'There, it's gone. Now let's get back to the important stuff. What do you fancy for tea tonight?'

I feel my eyes prickle and I fight hard to beat the tears back, dropping my questioning like a brick. A sudden cramping in my stomach takes my breath and I sit down heavily on a stool.

'What is it? What's wrong?' He's instantly alarmed, rushing over to me, rubbing my back. 'Let's get you in a more comfortable chair.'

I allow him to lead me into the living room where he helps me sit in the armchair and helps me lift my legs on to a footstool.

'Kait,' he sighs. 'I'm sorry, OK? I just wish you'd stop breathing down my neck.' He pinches the top of his nose and closes his eyes. 'That call... it was a client. I made a mistake with their nutrition order, so I'm going to have to pop out and swap their product. It's my fault, I'm trying to do a hundred things at once and I realise I need to slow down a bit. I shouldn't be too long and then we can talk.'

He goes back to the kitchen to make me a cup of tea. I'm emotional and a bit teary and that's normal seeing as my hormones are all over the place. Daniel is being as caring and attentive as ever now and I'm warmed by a sudden wave of affection for him. I want so much to believe we are stronger than how it feels right now.

Slowly, I get out of the chair and walk to the kitchen to tell him I'm sorry too. I stand in the doorway when I see the kitchen is empty. Daniel's not here. Then I catch movement behind the door.

I take a step inside and see my husband, his back to me, rifling through the bin. He stands up and straightens out a crumpled paper in his hand, wiping a smear of yogurt from it with the edge of his hand.

It's the note he claimed was nothing. The note he wasn't interested in.

I clench my jaw and silently take a few steps back. Daniel has made a mistake lying to me. Underneath my initial upset, I feel a new resolve forming. Something feels wrong and I know

now it's not my imagination after all. He's the father of my child and he's lying to me. I'm wondering exactly what it is about that note that's turning him inside out.

Daniel is up to something he doesn't want me to know about. I'm certain of that now.

The big question is, what is it?

SIX

LIV

The day after tomorrow is the day she's been waiting for, for so long. In two days the pretence finally ends, and her new life begins.

The last eleven, nearly twelve years have been building up to this point. The time when she can finally step out of the shadows and feel the sun on her skin again. No need to hide away. No need to keep her head down, trying not to draw any attention.

It is the reason she'd agreed to the plan. The reason she's waited all this time.

On Friday morning, seven-hundred-and-fifty thousand pounds will land in her personal bank account. Two-hundred-and-fifty thousand of it specifically for Maddox. Not life insurance. It will come from a source Liv doesn't want to think about.

The money will gift her son a good, strong future. It will give Maddox the power to fulfil his dreams. Whatever it may be that he wants to do.

That's what they'd agreed all that time ago.

Rich will get his own sum and Liv doesn't care whether it's more or less than hers. She's never been greedy when it comes to money, but this... this is different. This is an amount she deserves. She has earned every penny of it with her own blood, sweat and tears. And in keeping her mouth shut and agreeing to participate in Rich's crazy plan, she has secured her future.

She did it for herself and she did it for her boy. She did not do it for Rich. She could have happily strangled him when he told her what he'd done and the danger it had put them in.

She squeezes her eyes closed before opening them again. That was all a very long time ago. She got through it and in a couple of days' time, she and her son will finally reap the benefits of the sacrifices made.

Liv pours herself a glass of wine and walks to the bottom of the stairs. The sounds of warfare reach her ears.

'Maddox?' No answer. Liv bangs the heel of her hand against the banister. He'd come in from school earlier and gone straight up to his bedroom with only a grunt of acknowledgement to her calling hello. 'Maddox, you there?'

The sound of gunfire is paused, and she hears the bedroom door open a touch before he issues a reluctant, 'Yeah?'

'Fancy coming down and watching a film together?' Liv takes a sip of her wine. 'I can pop a pizza in the oven if you're hungry.'

'Nah, I'm not bothered, Mum.'

The bedroom door clicks shut again and Liv's heart sinks. She lingers for a moment or two, until the gunfire and explosions commence. These days, Maddox goes to school, football training, the café he works at part-time, and then heads straight up to his bedroom on his PlayStation until hunger inevitably brings him back down looking for food. She knows this is common behaviour for fourteen-year-olds, but it's not healthy.

Only a few weeks ago, they used to spend more time together, watch the odd movie, chat about their day at the very least. That has somehow stopped happening and, despite Liv asking him if he's OK every chance she gets, Maddox continues to shrug her off like she's just an irritation.

Why has he changed so suddenly?

Maddox had just turned three when Rich took him to fly his kite that day. Too young, she'd thought, for their plan to leave any lasting impression on him. Now, she isn't so sure. Maddox says he has no clear memory of what happened but he seems to be turning into a nervous and perhaps slightly depressed teenager for no apparent reason.

It's easy to write his behaviour off as normal teenage angst, but Liv has also heard of buried trauma and how it nearly always worms its way to the surface in the end. She feels increasingly worried this might be happening to Maddox.

She takes another swig of wine to numb the twist of guilt in her stomach and goes back to the sofa. Tomorrow, she tells herself, everything will change. She'll have enough money to sort out almost anything. She can take the two of them away for a break somewhere warm where they can order food to their sunbeds, swim in the ocean and have relaxed conversations on the beach.

Where there is no PlayStation and no distractions to get between them.

SEVEN

KAIT

Daniel has tiptoed around me all afternoon and evening. When he returned from his second trip out to supposedly sort out an unsatisfied client, he followed me around the house.

It's as if he can sense I've been pacing around while he's been gone, trying to sort out my thoughts. Trying to stop myself from slipping.

'Kait, I've said I'm sorry I had to go out again, OK? I have to keep my clients happy and make things easy for them, you know that. They pay me a lot of money.' He lets out a sigh of frustration. 'Why are you carrying it on like this?'

I keep seeing him – unaware I was watching – rifling through the kitchen bin, pulling out the note that he'd declared so confidently meant nothing. All lies. How come life can be so good for so long and then one little mis-step and it all starts to fall away?

I shake off his hand.

'Why do you keep walking away? I won't go away until you listen to me... you owe me that, at least!'

'You don't seem yourself lately, that's all.' I stop walking and turn to face him. I've already decided I'm not going to confront him specifically about retrieving the note. Not yet. I've felt something's up with him and I've repeatedly said so. Up until now, he's simply wafted me away like an annoying fly. Now I have something more solid to work with, I'm going to properly look into it. I've learned my lesson of where rushing in ends in relationships. My hand drifts to my stomach. Once the baby gets here, it will be far more difficult to do a bit of detective work.

Rich lets out a heavy sigh. 'I'm just tired, OK?'

'Join the club.' I turn away and he touches my arm and tells me the 'real reason' he's been so distracted.

'Kait, I... I'm worried about work.'

'Why haven't you talked to me before now, if you're so anxious?'

He hangs his head. 'I didn't want to worry you what with the pre-eclampsia and everything. To be honest, on reflection, things are probably not as bad as I think. I've just got to ride it out.'

Turns out he's lost a couple of clients, and so far he hasn't been able to replace them. 'I used to have a waiting list,' Daniel explains, placing his hand on mine. 'At one time, those slots would've been snapped up within a day but, as it stands, they're still free. That's why I'm worried and now you know.'

'It's just a couple of cancellations,' I say, moving my hand so his falls away again. 'You still have a good business.' The substantial monthly amount he pays into our joint account has remained stable.

I've been worried about money since I had to finish work early due to the pre-eclampsia. At my training level pay-grade, I don't get a lot more than statutory sick pay. Up until now, every time I've mentioned my worries, Daniel simply says, 'My money is enough. Stop worrying.' So I've agreed I'll just resign after my second scan in a couple of weeks' time.

'I know you're right about the business. I'm probably just

being a bit dramatic. It's just... I want everything to be perfect for when the baby gets here and, lately, my imagination seems to have run away with me. Asking myself what I'll do if it gets worse, if more clients leave.'

I'm dragging my body around like a lead weight. I wish I could just go up to bed early. Relax alone under the cool, crisp duvet and read my book in peace. Get away from what I know is another diversion from Daniel. It's upsetting and exhausting.

But Daniel hasn't finished yet. 'What will I do if I have to go back to an employed position at some poxy city gym for a quarter of the money I'm earning now?'

I give him a weak smile, unconvinced. 'It doesn't sound like the end of the world, Daniel. Certainly not at the stage where you should be losing sleep over it.'

His change of mood has crept up on me. When I think back to when we met, Daniel had been super-confident and so optimistic about the future. Now, increasingly, he gives off strong vibes of anxiety and tension as if he's under a lot of pressure.

Granted, losing a couple of clients is a concern when you're self-employed, but does that fully explain his snap change of mood earlier? The way the colour drained from his face when he saw the note? Saying it wasn't important and then fishing it out of the bin covered in slops? I'm not convinced.

Daniel's voice brightens. 'You get yourself comfy and I'll make my world-famous spaghetti bolognese for an early dinner. What do you say?' He looks relieved and leans forward to plant a kiss on my forehead. 'I want to make up for my grouchiness earlier and, from now on, I promise I'll talk to you when I'm worried about work.'

I catch hold of his wrist before he can escape to the kitchen. I have to give him one last chance. Myself, too.

'I've got one more question.'

'OK.' He grins, no doubt expecting me to continue his light-hearted banter. 'Fire away.'

'Does that note really have something to do with a client?'

His arm stiffens under my touch. 'What do you mean?'

'You seemed shocked to see it. Unnerved.'

Daniel gives what I've come to regard as his cover-up laugh. 'Shocked? Over a scribbled note? I don't think so.'

I think again about the colour draining from his face. His snappy answers. I say, 'I've noticed you don't come home straight after work anymore.'

Daniel stares at me, staying silent for just a beat too long. 'I like to go for a run as you know. Just an hour or two to wind down, process my day. And then I come home. Kait, why are you making such a big deal about this?'

'I'm just airing my thoughts while we're on the subject.'

A tiny muscle flexes in his jaw. 'Does it ever occur to you that sometimes you might just be plain wrong?'

I'm going to have to let it go. I don't know where I stand anymore when it comes to Daniel; whether I'm on to something or blowing everything up out of proportion.

On the one hand he still seems to be the man I fell in love with: kind, caring and authentic. But increasingly, I also catch a glimpse of someone else with faraway eyes and a brooding intensity that unnerves me. I've seen this side of him before, just briefly when it seems to slip through a chink in his armour.

I even asked him about it once. Before I fell pregnant and we'd both had a bit too much to drink. We put on a movie and I turned to make a comment to find him staring at the wall above the TV, clearly deep in thought about something. But it was more than that. He wore an expression I didn't recognise; his whole face had changed. The only way I can describe it is to say it was like he'd shed a mask and revealed a different personality underneath. He caught me watching him and, as if someone had flicked a switch, the 'real' Daniel returned in an instant. I said, 'I think you have another side to you that you try very hard to keep hidden.'

Daniel grinned. Slid his arm around my shoulders. 'Well done, you win. You've spotted the real me.' Then he laughed out loud. 'That's a joke by the way. I love you to bits, Kait. But when are you going to start trusting me?'

I told myself we all have different sides to us, like the moodiness I can be guilty of when I'm over-tired. That was the point I knew I needed to work harder to strengthen our relationship.

But this unsettling glimmer of Daniel I'm noticing more and more seems more worrying than that. Sometimes it honestly feels like there's a completely different person inside my husband. Someone I don't know at all.

EIGHT

RICH

They'd got married three months ago in a tiny church in the village. When the wedding march began to play and Rich turned around to see her, Livvy was a vision. She'd chosen an understated white satin sheath dress and Maddox, clutching her hand, had looked adorable in his little grey suit with its matching waistcoat.

Rich wore a black suit that fit him like a glove. Although his mother, Shannon, had remarked he looked more like he was going to a funeral than a wedding, there was no doubt they'd made a handsome couple. Everyone – apart from Shannon – said so, but that didn't dim his joy. He already knew that no woman, even though she liked Livvy, would ever be good enough for him in his mother's eyes.

If he was honest, it had been a bit of an impulsive decision to get wed. They'd already been together for a few years and they'd been blessed with having Maddox and, frankly, there had always been something more important to spend the money on. A family holiday, a new kitchen. But now business was really booming. The future was looking so bright and, as Livvy had reasoned, 'If not now, when?'

They'd had such a good time at the wedding. It was small and perfect in every way. They'd moved to this beautiful leafy village eighteen months ago and they'd fitted in perfectly with the established residents. So much so, Rich had been invited to attend the monthly Parish Council meetings and was occasionally, due to him being a property developer and investor, asked for his opinion on various land matters. It had pushed him way up in the unofficial village hierarchy and the locals rallied around when Rich and Livvy announced they were getting married in the January of the year everything fell apart.

The florist was the postmaster's son who owned a boutique flower shop in Nottingham. The food was catered by the village ladies' group who had a thriving cottage industry going for local weddings, celebrations and even funerals, and the tiered American-iced wedding cake with a spectacular sugar-flower bouquet was made by a retired baker who lived in the Old Forge, the cottage right next to the pub. Rich and Livvy knew every face there and the villagers talked about it for weeks afterwards.

The moment the vicar announced them as man and wife, Rich had felt like the luckiest man on earth. He had a healthy, strong son, a chocolate-box cottage they'd just finished renovating thanks to his thriving property business, and now he had his beautiful new wife, Livvy, who had every faith in him and the life Rich was building for them all.

Thinking back, remembering how happy he felt... it was just making him feel worse. He started to lose his grip a couple of months after the wedding. Felt himself sliding. He tried to anchor himself in his new life, focus on his wife and son, but it wasn't easy. He'd started to slide down an icy slope with absolutely nothing around to grab on to. It seemed there was no way of stopping himself falling.

The worst part was that just a short time ago, everything had seemed so perfect. Possibly *too* perfect.

He could see that now.

NINE

MADDOX

When Maddox gets to school, Brandon is waiting near the gates again.

'You up for it then, mate?' He takes out a vape as they begin to saunter down the street together. Brandon is standing right in front of him, so close he can see the bulging veins in his thick neck. 'Did you have a think about it? I told the head guy you were interested, and he wants an answer today. I've got to get this sorted before the end of term, so don't let me down.'

The last thing Maddox wants is to get on the wrong side of Brandon. There had been rumours at school that he lifted weights and took steroids to bulk up. Some people said the steroids made him aggressive and that's why he was always getting into trouble. Looking at the size of his biceps under his thin jacket, Maddox can easily believe it.

'Thing is, you haven't really told me what's involved.'

Brandon gives a wolfish grin. 'You know it's easy, you know you'll make a lot of money, right? It's up to the boss to tell you exactly what you'll be doing.'

'I'm still not sure.' Maddox dithers. 'I don't know this guy, don't know what's involved, so...'

'*I* know what's involved and you trust my judgement, right?'

'Yeah, but... my mum is a ball-breaker. If she found out, I'd—'

Brandon takes a drag of the vape and laughs. 'Mate, seriously. Your *mum*?'

Maddox feels heat flash into his cheeks and silently curses himself. He shouldn't have said that. He turns away from the sickly sweet odour and forces a laugh.

'I'm joking, man! Thing is though, I'm not free that much. I got commitments with my footie training and stuff.'

They both turn at the sound of a car engine purring alongside them. The passenger window rolls down smoothly and the driver ducks down to look at them. It's Mr Pinfold, head of PE and the head football team coach.

'Everything OK, Maddox?'

'Yes, sir.' He feels heat channel into his face as he studies his shoes and shifts from one foot to the other. When he glances up again, Mr Pinfold is staring at Brandon.

'What?' Brandon says belligerently.

'What're you doing around here?'

Brandon scowls, lifts his vape and takes a moment to inhale before answering.

'No law against walking on a public footpath, is there?'

Mr Pinfold smiles. 'Of course not. So long as you're not bothering our students.'

'As if!' Brandon makes a derogatory noise and turns to Maddox. 'Are you being bothered?'

'No,' Maddox says quickly. 'Not at all.'

'That's good. See you at Saturday morning's game, Maddox.' The car starts to move again. 'Look after yourself, Brandon.'

Brandon puffs out vapour and growls, 'Tosser.'

'Mr Pinfold's alright,' Maddox says mildly, earning himself a glare from Brandon. 'If you keep on the right side of him, that is.'

'Anyway. Before that prick interrupted us, I was saying: this job takes hardly any time at all, and you'll make sooo much cash. Trust me.' Brandon coughs violently before continuing to drag on the vape. 'You don't play footie after nine or ten at night, do you?'

Maddox shakes his head.

'So that's when you sneak out for an hour or two, yeah? Back for midnight or just after.' Brandon grins, revealing a missing tooth. 'Your ballbreaker mum's none the wiser.'

Maddox puts his head down as he walks and shoves his hands into his pockets. He could use some money, for sure. He's been working two days a week after school and before footie training as a pot-washer at a local bistro café that closes late. The pay is crap, and although it's only a few hours, the work feels long and hard, washing a never-ending stream of dirty dishes and caked-up pans while the pot-bellied chef constantly barks at him to go faster.

Brandon seems to sense his silent deliberations. 'No word of a lie, a few hours here and there can make you a hundred quid cash a night once you know what you're doing,' he says before stopping walking to cough up his guts again.

'You should ditch that poison.' Maddox nods towards the vape. 'It's rotting your lungs.' All the cool kids smoke one at school, but Maddox has resisted.

'I'm saving the good stuff for later.' Brandon winks. 'I've got a good supplier if you're interested. Quality weed. The best.'

Maddox frowns. Smoking weed and vaping would kill his fitness in no time at all. He's not interested in getting more money to buy drugs but... there's a girl he likes in his class. She's small and pretty and not loud and brash like some of the other girls. Maddox has caught her looking at him a couple of times in lessons. Last week, she'd looked away quickly, but yesterday, she'd given him a little smile.

If he had a bit of spare money, he could take her out to the cinema or ten-pin bowling. Maybe they'd go for pizza afterwards. A proper date. It would feel good to have the means to do that.

'Ha! You're warming to the idea.' Brandon nudges him. 'I can see it in your face.'

Maddox asks, 'Who's your boss?'

'Hey, ask no questions and I'll tell no lies.'

Maddox kicks a stone away as they walk. He doesn't like the way Brandon is controlling everything and talking in riddles. He's managed to describe a very well-paid job without telling him hardly anything.

'So... you in, or what?' Brandon stops walking and gives him a hard look. 'I've got people queuing up for a pop at this cherry, so it's cool if you're not interested.'

Maddox scuffs the toes of his trainers in the gravel and thinks about the stuff he found on his mum's laptop. The empty wine bottles she hides in the glass recycling box behind the wheelie bins and the way she is almost always wasted and in bed for 9 p.m. these days. Would she even notice he'd slipped out the odd couple of nights?

It doesn't sound like working with Brandon will interfere with his football training either, and he does have a few nights when he's free. All that money for just a few hours' work. His mum might keep talking about money being on its way, but the reality is, for now at least, he's stuck at the bistro in pot-washing hell.

If he doesn't like the work, Maddox figures he can easily make an excuse to Brandon and just drop out. That way he doesn't have to say no and risk losing what sounds like a great opportunity to make some easy cash, not at some vague point in the future, but right now. When he needs it the most. If the money his mum keeps banging on about comes through then he can drop this job. It seems like a win-win.

'OK then,' Maddox says. 'Count me in.'

Suddenly all business, Brandon gives him a curt nod and they swap numbers.

'Cool,' he tells Maddox. 'Keep an eye on your phone. You start tonight.'

TEN

NOTTINGHAMSHIRE POLICE

Detective Inspector Helena Price scans the list of live cases on the Computer-Aided Dispatch system and sighs.

'Sounds like you've got the weight of the world on your shoulders back there, boss.' Detective Sergeant Kane Brewster turns to face her from his seat at the desk in front. 'Problems?'

'On the contrary, Brewster. I'm just looking at our current cases and they're not exactly challenging me in the ways I imagined they might. I'm talking about when I joined the force. Back in the days I thought I could make a real difference to people's lives.'

Brewster pulls a face conceding agreement. 'This month's not turning out to be our finest hour in terms of stopping the wave of crime, for sure.'

Helena scrolls down the monitor, reading from the screen.

'Petty thefts from garden sheds again last week on the Ruffs Estate, vandalism to parked cars at several tram stations and an organised shoplifting gang operating in the Victoria Centre,' she continues. 'Add to that my agreement to mentor a couple of new PCs and getting an evaluation of the quarterly documentation to the super by the end of the week, and I've just about had it up to here.'

Helena lifts a hand above her neat brown bob.

'Wish I could help, but my CAD data's not looking much better.' Brewster scrolls up and down his computer screen and hesitates. Moves back up to something. 'Unless you fancy us looking into this latest entry, that is. A school at Clifton... the academy. Deputy head there has called in some worrying concerns this morning. Sounds a bit sinister.'

'Oh?' Helena perks up. 'Sinister in what way?'

Brewster reads out the data entry. 'Called into Control at 17:10 by Fairlawns Forest Academy's deputy headteacher, Mr Sanjit Patel. Concerns for pupil safety. Recent instances of possible county lines recruitment close to school's premises. Reported to headteacher by school staff and several parents.'

Helena frowns. 'Gangs recruiting school kids to deliver hard drugs in outlying areas of the county. It's only a couple more weeks until the end of term: the perfect time for them to find new runners for the summer. Not the first time we've come across this, but it's been a while.'

'Reports are rare,' Brewster agrees. 'These gangs are slick and careful. They intimidate and pressure vulnerable young people, hand them a few quid and, before they know it, they're in up to their neck.'

Helena walks across to Brewster's desk and peers at his screen over his shoulder.

'Wasn't there a tragic death in Mansfield last year?' she murmurs. 'A thirteen-year-old lad took his own life because of gang intimidation?'

'Yes, boss. Happened on the Oak Tree estate. Drug dealing's still rife there, according to a colleague I know at the Mansfield station, but the locals are too scared to talk to the police about it.'

'We'll need to move fast on this before the summer break.' Helena glances up at the wall clock. 'School will be finished now. Put us down to follow it up first thing in the morning.'

ELEVEN

MADDOX

Before he leaves the house, he waits until his mum has knocked herself out with the cheap wine she favours and has gone up to bed. He's dressed in dark clothing and a hoodie as Brandon had instructed in his WhatsApp message. He doesn't leave his mum a note of where he's gone.

It's eight-thirty. Maddox has left a little earlier than he needs to get to the meeting place – a piece of wasteland behind a disused car garage – for the stipulated time of 9 p.m. He wants to feel prepared and, bearing in mind the type of people who might be involved, it will give him time to stake the place out beforehand.

He walks down the road and turns into the first of a warren of streets that will take him to the meeting place via a series of shortcuts. Maddox feels oddly vulnerable. He gets a lift back home from a team mate and his dad after any late-night training or footie games. He isn't used to walking alone later in the evening. The back streets are deathly quiet and pitch dark, thanks to several streetlights needing to be repaired.

He usually finishes working at the bistro between five and five-thirty and Maddox always goes straight home from there or to his football activities. He has buddies there, and occasionally, they all arrange to go to important local matches together on the weekend, but the sport is the only thing that binds them.

He's popular enough amongst the footie lads, but he doesn't really have any close mates. He prefers it that way; it means you don't have to trust anyone. People only let you down, even the one person who's always had his back: his mum. At least he thought she had until a couple of weeks ago.

His feet scuff on the pavement, echoing around him. He's about halfway there now. The sun has set but most of the houses he's passing still have their curtains open. He can see families inside, watching television or eating. Wrapped up in their own safe little worlds.

If something happened out here, say if someone jumped him and knocked him to the ground, nobody would see anything.

Maddox picks up the pace, long legs easily increasing the length of his strides. He's not *scared* exactly. Just a bit jumpy. The sooner he meets Brandon and finds out what's expected of him, the better. If he doesn't like the sound of what's involved, he can bail at the last minute. Although Brandon's not going to like that.

Brandon is known as a bit of a troublemaker locally, not just at school. Petty vandalism and a charge of common assault at a football match last year had got him on the wrong side of the coppers. His older brother is currently in prison and his dad is a known drug dealer who has also done time... his mum would have a fit if she knew he was meeting him tonight.

Maddox takes a sharp right and jogs down a scruffy, narrow alleyway with a concrete bollard at either end to stop the trial bikes that used it as a rat run. He emerges on a better lit street before turning off again and jogging along, passing the odd boarded-up house until finally, he spots the peeling sign above the derelict garage forecourt.

He checks his phone. There's still a good ten minutes before the time he's arranged to meet Brandon. He pulls the hoodie down further over his eyes and takes a shortcut down the side of the abandoned garage to where the small back yard opens out on to a patch of rough land. It's very dark with no street lighting in place at all.

As Maddox's eyes adjusts, he catches movement to his right and then immediately to his left. He's suddenly dazzled by car headlights snapping on and blazing full-beam in his face.

He lets out a cry of alarm as an arm slips roughly around his neck, capturing him in a vice-like grip. 'Is that you, Brandon?'

'Shut your mouth and get into the car,' a voice growls that is definitely not Brandon's. 'Do it now.'

Maddox begins to walk but is half-dragged towards the vehicle in front of him. The door of the car opens, and somebody pushes him hard enough that he falls into the back seat. He only just pulls his legs in when the door slams shut and, for a moment, all is quiet.

It's only when he looks up, Maddox sees that he is not alone. There is barely any light inside the car, but he can see someone is sitting very still in the driver's seat, watching him silently through the rear-view mirror.

When his eyes adjust he can see it's an older man although he can't yet see his facial features.

'Alright?' Maddox mumbles awkwardly after sitting there for a few seconds in silence. Just him and this weird guy who does nothing but stare at him.

Maddox looks down at his twisting fingers to escape the man's penetrating look. He knows better than to start asking any questions. Just as he'd suspected when Brandon approached him, he's probably got himself involved in something dodgy.

And the worst part is, he can't walk away now even if he wants to.

TWELVE

'Maddox Leigh. That you?'

Maddox looks up, startled. The man's voice is not gruff or aggressive as he'd expected. In fact, he is quite softly spoken.

'Yes,' he says.

'Tell me a bit about yourself, Maddox.'

Those cool eyes again, still pinned to him in the mirror.

'I... I'm fourteen. Fifteen in three months. I go to Fairlawns Forest Academy in Clifton.'

Silence. He's getting nothing back from this guy. Nothing at all.

'I live with my mum on the Clifton estate,' Maddox adds.

'What road?'

'Pinewood Gardens.'

'I know it. Your mum working?'

Maddox nods. 'Two jobs. She's a part-time teaching assistant at Highview Primary and sometimes, she helps out at a local bar.'

The man gives a quick nod. 'You know, this job could make a big difference to both you and your mum's life. Nobody wants to be working two jobs, right?'

'My mum doesn't mind,' Maddox says carefully. He's not about to mention the money she keeps banging on about. 'She wouldn't want to be part of anything that's...' He racks his brain for the right word so the man doesn't take offence.

'Dodgy?' He throws his head back and laughs. 'Proper little angel, is she, your mum? Good job you've got more sense.'

Maddox remembers his football and how he's planned this will be his get-out clause.

'Thing is, I told Brandon I'd be interested in the job, but I have footie training a few nights a week and—'

'What about your dad?' the man says.

Maddox swallows. 'Sorry?'

'Tell me about your dad.'

'He... my dad died years ago.'

'Sorry to hear that. How did he die?'

Maddox feels sick. He never talks about his dad. Tries not to think about him, either. Sometimes he dreams about him, but he can't do anything about that. This man strikes Maddox as the sort of person who makes it his business to know everything. He probably knows everything about him already and is testing Maddox to see if he's being truthful.

'My dad went missing eleven years ago when I was three; twelve years in October. He was presumed dead four years ago,' Maddox says bluntly. It occurs to him it's his own fault he is in this horrible situation. Being forced to discuss his personal business with a menacing stranger who hasn't even introduced himself.

'*Presumed* dead. Interesting he's been missing for nearly twelve years but only presumed dead four years ago.'

'You can't be declared as presumed dead in this country until you've been gone for at least seven years,' Maddox says quietly. 'And if there's no body been found.'

If only he'd had the sense to tell Brandon he had no spare

time. He'd be in his bedroom now, playing Call of Duty. But he had been tempted by the money on offer and now he's explaining to a stranger stuff he usually refuses to think about.

Maddox sits up a little straighter as the man shuffles in his seat, but he doesn't turn around. He has broad shoulders and a powerful neck. He looks as if he might weight-train like Brandon, and Maddox wonders if he takes steroids that make him aggressive, too.

'Do you remember your dad?'

Maddox's fingernails drive into the soft flesh of his palms. He really needs to get out of here.

'Look, I'm sorry but there's been a mix-up. I came here tonight to tell Brandon that I can't do the job now because of my football training. I've just found out I have to fit in a few more sessions, so I don't have enough time to work for you.'

'And that's all happened since this afternoon, has it? After you agreed to come here?'

Something about how the man is talking softly in his offhand manner feels passive-aggressive to Maddox. But his heart is racing because he's not fooled. He's not stupid enough to speak out of turn.

'I forgot they told us last week we had to attend more sessions,' Maddox says. 'I thought I'd come and tell Brandon tonight as I'd agreed to meet him.'

'Very courteous,' the man says in his off-putting manner. 'You seem like a nice, polite lad, Maddox, and I like that. I really do.'

An army of invisible insects begin to march over every inch of Maddox's flesh. Burrowing into every tiny crevice on his body. At least that's how it feels. He glances longingly at the car door handle, itching to jump out and scarper. To run all the way back home and pretend it never happened.

But Maddox knows that people like this man... they don't

just shrug their shoulders and disappear into the night again. Not when they're going to lose face.

'Thing is,' the man says, 'I'm getting the feeling you might have changed your mind, Maddox. It feels a bit like you're trying to get out of the commitment you made and that puts me in a difficult position. Do you see that?'

'I'm not trying to get out of it!' Maddox can feel his heartbeat in his throat. 'It's just the footie training... I'll have to see if I can fit it in. Working for you and doing the extra training, too.'

'That's more like it. Now, where were we?' he says. 'Oh yes, I was asking if you remembered your dad?'

'No,' Maddox says, his voice flat now. 'I don't remember anything about him.'

'Do you remember the day your dad went missing?'

'Not really. Just... flying the kite. The wind.' Maddox shifts in the back seat. Scratches his forearms. Why is this guy so interested in his dad? A ball of heat builds in his chest. He has a right to put a stop to this.

'Thing is, I don't like talking about my dad,' Maddox blurts out. 'I was only three when he went missing, so I don't know anything.'

'Of course you don't,' says the man. 'But other people around you must know what happened. People like your mum. So what does she say about what happened to your dad?'

'She says nothing. She doesn't like talking about it either.' Maddox can't pretend he's not upset anymore. His face feels like it's made of stone. 'We don't talk about it, OK? There's nothing left of him. No photos or anything. He's just... he's just gone.' Maddox swallows as his voice breaks and he meets the man's eyes in the rear-view mirror. 'And anyway, I haven't come here to talk about my dad, I've come about the job Brandon told me about.'

The heat in his chest dims and Maddox braces himself for the man to suddenly whip round and grab him by the collar. Let him. Even that's better than the unbearable ache he has in his stomach right now.

But the man smiles. He smiles at Maddox in the mirror. 'Well, that's put me in my place,' he says softly.

'S–sorry,' Maddox stammers. 'I didn't mean to—'

'Never apologise for speaking your truth.' The man twists around fully in his seat and Maddox gets a full view of him for the first time since he got into the car. He expected a broken nose, bad teeth and an evil glare. But this guy is handsome and healthy-looking. He doesn't look as if he takes drugs. He has on a baseball cap and a thin scarf knotted around his neck.

'I'm Sammy.' The man stretches his arm and offers a hand through the gap in the two front seats. Maddox shakes it, keeping his own handshake firm and confident. 'You've got something about you, lad. You're growing into a fine young man with bags of potential.'

It's a strange thing to say, and it occurs to Maddox that Sammy might have plans for him in his dodgy organisation. Plans he doesn't want to be part of.

Sammy hands him something smooth and cold. Maddox can see, even in the dim light, that it's a dark metallic iPhone. The very latest model with the new camera configuration on the back.

'This is yours to keep,' Sammy says. 'It has an inbuilt SIM, so just charge it up and it's ready to go. Keep it safe and – more importantly – make sure it's always hidden. I'll contact you on this for business purposes. Don't use it for anything else, yeah?'

Maddox nods and slides the phone into his hoodie pocket.

'Oki doki, well, that's it for now. I'll be in touch.' Sammy touches something on the dashboard and there's an audible click as the central locking releases. Maddox reaches for the door handle as the internal light comes on. 'Wait. Couple of other things before you shoot off.'

Maddox hesitates and sits back in his seat again. Sammy stretches his hand through the seat gap. 'This is for you.'

He drops something light and firm into Maddox's hand. He looks down and gasps at the tight roll of notes in his palm.

'I– I can't take this,' Maddox stammers, his stomach fluttering.

'Why not?'

'I haven't done any work yet.'

'You're going to turn it down, are you? While your poor mum is working two crappy jobs to make ends meet?' Sammy frowns. 'Come on, Maddox, lad. You're better than that.'

Maddox rubs his thumb over the coarse paper money. His mum has always been worried about paying the bills. Until recently and the mention of the supposed windfall that's on its way when she's had a few glasses.

Only a few months ago, she was turning the heating down because of the higher energy bills. But she's always dreamed about a better life for as long as Maddox can remember, and it hasn't materialised yet.

'Think of it as an advance, yeah?' Sammy says warmly. 'A small taste of what you'll be getting once we get organised.'

'OK then. Thanks,' Maddox says awkwardly, pulling the door handle.

He looks back and Sammy grins and says, 'Welcome to the team, fella. No turning back now.'

Maddox unlocks the back door and slips inside the kitchen and waits a few moments, eyeing the empty bottle of wine and single glass on the worktop.

When he's satisfied the house is all quiet, he finally breathes out. His mum must still be dead to the world up there. He gets a glass of tap water and takes it upstairs after locking up and turning off the kitchen light.

Back in his bedroom, Maddox puts the new iPhone on charge. It's completely dead so there's nothing to see on there yet. He unrolls the wad of notes Sammy gave him and takes a sharp inbreath. They're all twenties, totalling two hundred pounds. *Two hundred!*

His mum has told him she earns roughly twelve pounds an hour averaged out over her two jobs. After tax, she'd probably have to work well over twenty hours to walk out with a similar sum to what he's holding in his hand. And yet this amount of money seemed to mean nothing to Sammy.

He should feel stoked to be given the money for doing nothing with plenty more of it promised soon. But he only feels confused.

Maddox came away from the meeting still without a good understanding of the work he's going to be doing, although he's not stupid. He can guess. But that guy, Sammy, he seemed more interested in asking questions about what happened to his dad than filling Maddox in on what the mystery job will entail.

And weirdly, he seemed to know loads about what happened back then without Maddox saying a thing. So why keep asking?

Maddox lies back on his bed fully clothed and stares at the ceiling, waiting for answers to come. When he's worried like this, he misses his gran. She was the best at giving advice and she didn't always agree with his mum, either. It was like she still understood what it felt like to be young, and she encouraged him to take chances. But his gran isn't herself anymore. She doesn't even know who he is.

What happened tonight must be a test, he decides. Sammy will need to know if Maddox can be trusted with his... well, you know, Maddox guesses, *his drugs*. He squeezes his eyes shut. His mum will literally skin him alive if she finds out what he's getting himself into. She sees things in black and white, good and bad. Until it comes to her own life, he thinks bitterly as he thinks about the fruits of his recent snooping. But she hasn't got a clue about what happens out there anymore, on the street. Won't realise how dangerous these people are once you get yourself entangled.

His mum won't accept that Maddox can't just walk away.

Not now he has two hundred quid of Sammy's money taped behind his headboard.

THIRTEEN

LIV

Her heart is pounding so hard, it's woken her up. Or maybe it's her mouth and throat: both as dry as if she's swallowed sawdust. It's all down to one thing though: the drinking. It has to stop. Liv knows this on an intelligent level, has known it for a while. But that doesn't stop the physical need. It's the only thing that eases the thoughts, takes the edge off her worries and gets her through the long nights.

Or maybe, just maybe, it was just the noise that woke her. It feels like she heard something downstairs and then the click of a door.

The glowing digits on her clock radio tell her it's just past midnight. She hasn't been asleep that long. Two or three hours maybe.

Liv lies there, listening, willing her heart to slow down. But the house is quiet, as she'd expect, so maybe she imagined it.

Today is the big day. Her mind starts racing. It's going to be impossible to sleep.

She gets up and wraps her dressing gown around her and steps out on to the landing. There's a thin bar of light emanating from the bottom of Maddox's bedroom door.

Liv frowns. He's not one to fall asleep with his light on; in fact, he usually turns it off when he's gaming at night. She opens the door softly. Maddox is sprawled out on his bed, lying on his back, shoes off but fully clothed. One arm is carelessly flung away from him, his dark curls unfurled like an ebony halo on his white pillow.

In a brief flash, the years peel away and for all the world he could still be that little boy who'd wake in the early hours asking when his daddy would be coming home.

She pads over to his bed and reaches to turn off the lamp, her hand faltering when she notices the iPhone plugged in and charging on the bedside table. She frowns, looking at his battered Samsung smartphone next to it. She knows the outrageous price of an iPhone – perhaps as much as a thousand pounds. Way beyond what Maddox could afford to pay from a handful of hours working at a local café.

She gingerly touches the screen, and it lights up, displaying the generic Apple graphics. The phone is not locked, so she presses the text messages icon and the app loads but all the folders are empty. There are no messages to view.

She flinches. Her eyes feel dry and tired as she averts her gaze. Is this phone stolen, or has someone bought it for her son?

Gently, Liv pulls the quilt across his body as best she can without waking him. His chest is broad and strong; his shoulders are thickening fast.

Her little boy is almost a man and now there's no doubt in her mind as to what woke her up.

Liv turns off the lamp and leaves the bedroom, shutting the door quietly behind her. Back out on the landing, she presses her back to the cool plaster of the wall and closes her eyes. She can feel a gulf opening between them. He's been evasive for a few weeks now, doesn't seem to want to spend any time with her. Tonight, he's been out until nearly midnight without telling her. She doesn't know where he went or who he was with, but there's one thing she's now certain of.

Maddox is keeping secrets from her.

FOURTEEN

KAIT

FRIDAY MORNING

It's 6.30 a.m. when I open my eyes. The bedroom is already light, the thin curtains no match for the invasion of even weak rays of sun. I move my hand gently across my bump. I felt my baby moving in the night as if she could sense I couldn't sleep.

Daniel and I decided we'd rather have the surprise at the end as to whether we'll be blessed with a son or daughter, but I know it's a girl. I just *know* in that way only a mother can and I've almost subconsciously started calling the baby 'her'.

I feel nauseous. Moving slowly and giving myself time so I don't faint, I get out of bed and peek through the curtains, down at the driveway. Both our cars are parked there now, illuminated by the streetlight outside the front gates. But when I checked in the early hours, Daniel's spot was empty. He was still out.

The hospital told me I must get quality rest at night, but how can I possibly do that when I'm so tense, second-guessing where my husband is? I prickle with fury at his thoughtlessness.

I reach for my phone. Daniel might be home now, but he didn't come to bed last night. He obviously didn't want to wake me, or more than likely, alert me to the fact he'd stayed out so long. This has never happened before, and I'm scared. I'm scared that me being ill, having to rest so much... maybe he's just been unable to cope with that. Or he's got fed up and has had his head turned by someone who isn't pregnant and boring. Someone who just wants to have fun. Because fun and having sex simply isn't on our agenda right now.

I've noticed things have been getting worse in terms of him being late home on a regular basis and then there was the note the day before yesterday. The note that apparently means nothing but drained the colour from his cheeks in a matter of seconds.

Everything seemed to be OK between us last night, after dinner. Until Daniel said, 'I forgot one of the orders earlier. The customer is expecting it today. I'll deal with it now and then we can watch a bit of TV together when I get back if you feel up to it.'

'OK.' I'd shrugged, clearing the plates from the table. He'd looked relieved when I didn't make a fuss, but our altercation the day before had knocked the stuffing out of me. I wasn't feeling great, my energy at rock bottom. The thought of having a bit of peace and quiet with the television off sounded very appealing. Naively, I believed him when he said he wouldn't be out long.

Daniel kissed my cheek. 'Leave the plates, I'll load the dishwasher when I get back. You shouldn't be bending like that.'

When I heard the front door close and the car start, I carried on loading the plates. It's no good just doing less and less, I'll find it even more difficult to keep active as I've been advised. Daniel would have me lying on the sofa barely moving each day if it was up to him and, if truth be told, I am already going a bit stir crazy, stuck in the house all the time and off work sick way before my maternity leave should kick in.

When the kitchen looked tidy, I went upstairs and rested on

the bed, playing a relaxation exercise on my phone for ten minutes. Afterwards, I'd have liked to just stay there in bed, but I knew Daniel would be back very soon so I went back downstairs and lay on the sofa, reading. After a few chapters, I glanced at the time. Daniel had been gone for an hour now and yet he'd given me the distinct impression he'd be back very soon.

In the end, I had a soak in the bath and went back to bed. Daniel still hadn't returned by the time I closed my book and turned off the lamp.

The next time I woke up for the bathroom was just after midnight and his car was still not on the drive. Thankfully, even though I was restless, I'd managed to drop to sleep at some point after that.

Now he's home and in the spare room, I check the Ring doorbell footage on my phone. It shows the front of the house and I have to scroll up until just before 2 a.m. when his car headlights swing on to the driveway. Where the hell can he have been until then when he said he'd be back soon to watch TV?

I'm just about to close the doorbell camera footage off when I notice there are two more clips that have loaded. He pulls on to the drive at 01:51 and then ninety seconds later he gets out of the car.

He walks slowly up the drive, shuffling his keys to find the correct one. His movements are awkward because his other hand is raised to his ear. He's on the phone.

'Yes, I just got back and—'

Infuriatingly, the twenty-second clip ends there. I curse under my breath that we left the settings on the shortest recording window when installing the camera. I close it and open the final clip. The crystal-clear footage shows Daniel putting his key in the lock and he is still on the phone.

'It's fine, stop worrying. The house lights are off so she's fast asleep.' A soft chuckle in response to something the person on the other end says. 'I know, I can't wait! I'll call you in the morning, sending—'

The footage ends and my face crumples. Sending what? Sending all his love? As fat tears start to tumble on to my cheeks, my hand gravitates to my stomach. To my unborn baby.

Daniel is taking me for a fool. He's having an affair while gaslighting me, telling me I'm imagining my worries. All this after swearing the baby and I mean everything to him. Well, two can play at that game.

Even though my heart is breaking, at least I know where I stand now. I know I'm not imagining it and that is a massive advantage.

Somehow, I'll find out exactly what he's playing at and who it is he's playing with before I confront him this time. I'll make sure he doesn't get away with this.

He won't just lose me, he'll lose this house and the rights to raise his unborn child, too. He'll lose everything.

FIFTEEN

LIV

Her eyes spring open even before the 06:45 alarm sounds.

She's had a restless night worrying about Maddox and silently debating whether to confront him this morning or say nothing and put her secret knowledge about his trip out and the new phone to use.

The danger in that approach though is that, very quickly, he'll slip further away from her and if he's stolen that phone, he might get himself into serious trouble she can't pull him back from.

Liv feels the clutch of guilt at her throat. She's partly to blame for this. Drinking every night and going to bed early, allowing herself to get distracted in the lead-up to today. But on the bright side, things are about to change. Both their lives will be transformed and she'll have more time to give to Maddox.

There are certain things she'll need to keep in place for a while and work is one of them. Too much change, too soon, will inevitably lead to unwanted attention and it was one of the things she and Rich discussed at length in the early stages of their planning.

Liv stretches out luxuriously, sensing sunlight trying to

push through the curtains on this, the first day of the rest of her life. Her head is fuzzy like every morning these days, but it still feels good to acknowledge that, soon, the struggle will be over. No more scraping to make ends meet. No more worrying.

At eight o'clock she checks the balance of the hidden account on the online banking app. There is nothing in there yet, but she doesn't feel alarmed. This is no ordinary bank account and Rich had explained that to her.

'I've had to pull some strings to get us both set up with what's essentially a secret, personal bank account,' he'd said. 'I had no choice but to do it via the dark web, so it leaves absolutely no trace back to us.'

It makes Liv shudder even now. *The dark web.* She's seen the phrase used many times online and in the press. This mysterious, dangerous place that inevitably brings trouble to the people who dabble in it.

'Only people who don't know what they're doing,' he'd laughed when she'd voiced her thoughts.

She could have asked Rich a lot more questions but chose not to at the time. Fear, doubt and denial were her overarching emotions back then and Liv can recall thinking that a little knowledge can be a dangerous thing.

She felt safer knowing next to nothing about the detail. That way, she'd reasoned, if she did get questioned by the police, she wouldn't need to put an act on when she said she didn't know what they were talking about.

Now, her stomach roils with an intoxicating mix of excitement and terror.

Today is the day. The whisper repeats in her head. Today is the day she has waited for, for so long.

Has it all been worth it? She doesn't want to think about that one. Not yet.

She just needs to see the money land. There will be five neat figures on her laptop screen when the first deposit hits her account. And there will finally be email contact from Rich. She needs that too so they can make a decision about what they will tell Maddox.

Not the truth about exactly what happened back then, but a story that will adequately explain his presumed-deceased father making contact and coming back into his life.

At 08:12 Liv rechecks the app, but the transaction isn't showing yet. Before that fateful day, Rich had spent hours researching everything thoroughly in terms of the payment details. He'd been in touch with a man he called his 'contact' and had told her the money would be paid via eighty-thousand-pound instalments and then a final balancing payment to total the seven-hundred-and-fifty thousand pounds they had agreed on.

'Banks have inbuilt checks to detect deposits of over a hundred thousand pounds, so we'll want to come in well under that. I'll also need to vary the payment dates so there isn't a pattern. It's important you don't panic when it comes to the day all our plans start to kick in.'

That was fine by Liv. However Rich chose to do it was fine... so long as she got her money. The important thing was that she and Maddox would one day get out of this place – the maze of concrete and streets strewn with litter and grimy houses. Away from the dodgy people he's possibly hanging around with. Somewhere they can finally escape the past.

Nine-thirty and there is still no deposit showing in her account. Maddox has left the house to go to school. Without stopping for breakfast, he'd stomped downstairs, grabbed his school bag and murmured a cursory 'see you later' to her as he slammed the front door shut.

The excitement that had been bubbling in her stomach has now disappeared and Liv is left only with a faintly increasing sense of panic that she must ignore before it takes over her logical thinking.

Rich would not double-cross her. She truly believes that. He would not betray Liv and he would not betray their son. Not after everything they'd been through. Liv had always been able to count on Rich, even when he made a mistake as big and devastating as the one that changed the course of all their lives.

She refreshes the screen. There will be a perfectly reasonable explanation for the lack of money, she knows it. But this is not a normal situation where she can do something to increase her feeling of control.

She stares at the monitor. There is no banking helpline she can call to query the status of the transaction. No friendly customer service manager she can contact to help her figure out what's happening. There is just this: an impersonal, unfamiliar screen. A shady place on the dark web she has no understanding of and no other point of contact whatsoever to assist her.

On top of this, Liv has no way of getting in touch with Rich. They had both agreed to a policy of zero contact. It was the safest way to ensure some IT expert or hacker wouldn't be able to find anything and blow open their ruse. It was the *only* way of steel-plating their plans from certain failure.

They agreed this measure would stay in place until the day the first transaction was made. Then, on the day and only that day, Rich would communicate with her via an encrypted email address that would be forwarded in the body of another email.

That encrypted address has not been sent yet.

But there is plenty of time, Liv tells herself. There is time for Rich to make contact and explain what the problem is. There is even time for the first deposit to land in her bank account today.

'The most important thing to remember,' Rich had repeatedly told her leading up to his disappearance, 'is not to panic. If you panic, you'll make mistakes. And one mistake could blow us out of the water.'

Liv leaves the laptop open on the worktop and pours herself a glass of water. Sitting looking out of the poky kitchen window, she stares at the scrap of garden and sips the cool liquid.

The garden had been so beautiful at their old cottage. She'd planted blooms that attracted bees and butterflies. Here, the grass is patchy and poor, the bare branches of a scraggy silver birch tree silhouetted against the pale grey swirl of clouds. Disappointment and dread swell in the tightness of her chest.

Liv recalls when she was a child, probably around eight or nine, waking up with excitement the day her father's sister was due to visit from her farmhouse in Bordeaux. There had been weeks of anticipation for Aunt Marie's visit. They hadn't much money as a family, but on the morning of her arrival, the cupboards were packed full of wonderful food they never usually ate. Freshly baked bread, fancy savoury crackers, and exotic cheeses in the fridge that Liv had never tasted before in her life.

Liv had spent the previous day painting a picture for her, had spent hours on a joyful scene of her and her parents standing outside the family home to welcome Aunt Marie, who was depicted as arriving with an enormous suitcase. Liv had gone to great trouble to make the picture colourful and had painstakingly studded the edges with tiny, screwed-up balls of coloured tissue paper in the colours of the French flag.

That morning, they had all waited in anticipation. Thirty minutes, then an hour passed. Her father checking his watch and sighing.

'She'll come soon,' her mother said.

'There'll be a perfectly good explanation,' her father agreed.

The neighbours peeked from behind their net curtains. Liv's dad had phoned the railway station to check on Marie's train and discovered it had arrived on time. In those days, with no mobile phones or email to contact his sister directly, he had been forced to drive to the station to see if Marie was stranded there.

He had returned frustrated and without answers a few hours later.

The next day they got word that Marie had not come, deciding it was too much bother. Instead, she'd embarked on a drinking bender, which had culminated in a hospital stay.

The disappointment, the anger, the disbelief of her parents. It had marred their orderly family life for weeks. She remembers deciding at the time that everything in life is a disappointment. Nothing ever turns out the way you plan or hope for.

Liv turns away from the glass doors. She hates this place, hates the area. She can tell it's even getting to Maddox now. He has problems, worries he won't discuss with her. She knows this as his mother but she can't get it out of him. They both need this fresh start like they need oxygen.

At nine-forty-five, she checks the bank and her inbox. No change. Liv begins to pace around the room, down the hallway, into the living room and back again.

She battles against herself. Tries in vain to quell the growing panic knotting in the centre of her chest. Panic that's making it more difficult to breathe. Liv tries so hard, but she can't block the question that has started to repeat on loop in her head.

Louder and louder. Faster and faster.

What if the money isn't coming?

SIXTEEN

NOTTINGHAMSHIRE POLICE

Brewster parks the unmarked pool car down the road from the academy, well away from the yellow-marked 'Strictly No Parking' zig-zagged zones outside the school that Helena knows will be rammed nose-to-tail with parents' cars in approximately thirty minutes.

She happens to know there are close to 2000 students on roll at this sprawling modern building and yet, as she and Brewster are buzzed through into reception, the outside areas are deserted and the communal areas around reception are quiet.

'We're here to see Mr Patel, deputy head,' Brewster tells the admin clerk standing behind a Perspex-shielded hatch. 'He's probably expecting us.'

They're asked to wait, and Helena takes a seat on a comfy orange chair in the pleasant waiting area that's flooded with light thanks to a feature ceiling atrium.

After a few minutes, an internal locked door whirrs open and a diminutive, suited man in his early thirties holds open the door.

'I'm Sanjit Patel, deputy head,' he says, holding out his hand with a friendly smile. 'Come through, we can talk in my office.'

'Nice and quiet in here and your facilities are impressive,' Brewster remarks as they walk down a corridor and past two modern glass-walled classrooms with rows of computers and students staring at the monitors. 'Bit different to how I remember school. It was all a bit spit and sawdust back then. All I remember are the draughty windows and peeling paintwork.'

Patel raises an eyebrow and grins. 'We make a point of applying for every penny of funding there is going, particularly in areas of capital spend like IT equipment and buildings. As an academy, we get much more control of how to spend our budget than a local authority-controlled school.'

They turn into another corridor, this one featuring an anthracite-coloured hardwearing carpet.

'This is us.' Patel stops outside a light-oak door bearing a 'Deputy Headteacher' plaque and ushers the detectives inside.

Helena looks around the mid-sized room. There's a round, low table set in the middle of a cluster of comfy chairs. The table bears a jug of water and four glasses. Aside from that is a desk, office chair and filing cabinet.

She can remember her own school deputy head sharing a corner of the jumbled school office, his desk covered in piles of messy paperwork and files. This room is sleek and organised, fitted out with pale wooden cupboards and units. The visible box files all match and Patel's desk is completely clear save for a notepad, pen, and an Ikea-style flexible reading lamp.

Brewster stands surveying the area from a small window that looks out on to the sports field at the rear of the building.

'Please, take a seat and help yourself to some water,' Patel says. 'Thanks for coming in, I'm impressed with your quick response.'

'We take this kind of report very seriously, Mr Patel,' Helena says, waving away the glass of water Brewster has just poured. 'Can you tell us in your own words exactly what happened?'

The deputy head nods and sits down in the chair opposite. 'Over the last week, we've become aware of rumours of a sixteen-year-old boy called Brandon McFadden hanging around the area. Brandon is known to many students as he was permanently excluded from the academy during the spring term.' Patel sighs. 'Without going into too much detail, as I'm sure you know, he has a lot of problems at home and a history of police cautions.'

Brewster gives a quick nod. 'We are aware of that, yes.'

'Anyway, he'd been spotted in the vicinity but not close enough to the school that we felt able to do anything about it.'

Brewster makes some notes. 'You had no reason to believe he was interacting with your students at this stage?'

'That's right. A teacher heard some of the kids talking in class about seeing him around but that was the extent of it. Our pastoral care worker casually asked around and the general consensus of opinion was that Brandon was on the lookout for someone but they didn't know who.'

'I see. But the situation has now developed?' Helena frowns.

'Yes. We had a couple of parents come in on separate occasions yesterday, reporting that they'd seen Brandon interacting with one of our current students in a worrying manner.'

Brewster looks up from his notebook. 'Worrying in what way?'

'Appearing to rough him up a bit then acting overly friendly, slapping him on the back. The parents both said the younger lad, still in his sports kit, had looked worried and nervous. Then after football training last night, our head of PE, Mr Pinfold, spotted the two boys and recognising both, he stopped his car to speak with them.'

'What's the younger lad's name?' Brewster asks.

'Maddox Leigh. He's fourteen, currently in Year Ten. Nice lad and a promising young footballer.' Patel frowns. 'I'm afraid

Brandon is the exact opposite to the kind of person Maddox should be associating with.'

'When Mr Pinfold stopped the car, what was said exactly?' Brewster presses him.

'He asked Maddox if he was OK and Maddox said he was. Then he said hello to Brandon and asked what he was doing around here, meaning the school particularly.'

'They weren't on school grounds?' Helena checks.

'That's right, and Geoff – Mr Pinfold – said that was basically Brandon's defence. A sort of brusque "back off, you can't do anything" kind of attitude.'

'Have you spoken to Maddox about your concerns?' Helena says.

Patel shakes his head. 'Not yet. The head thought it best we contact you for advice on what to do next. If there is drug dealing involved, we don't want to put our foot in it so Brandon and the people behind him simply move on to another school in the area.'

'Very sensible,' Brewster says. 'We can have a quick chat with him while we're here, if that's appropriate?'

'That would be ideal,' Patel says. 'But we're worried. Maddox – who has a hundred per cent attendance record – is absent from school today. Our school office chases all absence as we're required to get explanation from the student's parent, but so far they've been unable to contact Ms Leigh.'

Brewster says, 'What happens if he continues to remain absent?'

'The school attendance officer will pay a visit if we're unable to make contact. But we have more absence than we like at the academy, so as you can imagine, it might take a few days to get to that stage.'

Helena nods her understanding. 'If you provide us with an address, we're happy to call at the house when we leave here.

Due to the serious nature of your concerns, we'll need to confirm Maddox's safety as a matter of urgency, and we can let you know the outcome of that.'

'That's great, thank you.' Patel stands up, looking relieved. 'I'll get his contact information from the school office now.'

SEVENTEEN

RICH

SEVEN MONTHS BEFORE HIS DISAPPEARANCE

He'd unexpectedly met Caleb Mosley at a Spanish property trade fair at Birmingham's NEC. Caleb's name was well known in the circles Rich dreamed of moving in. Moreover, his company – Mosley Property Development – was not only a major player in the UK but was now garnering a strong reputation abroad for mid-range property developments on a more affordable scale for mainly British buyers.

After an uneventful first day at the fair, Rich attended a networking meeting and watched – over the shoulder of a boring little man intent on spouting on about the benefits of building sustainably – as Caleb Mosley expertly entertained the dense crowd of hangers-on that surrounded him.

It had been Rich's vain hope he might get to meet Caleb, but it soon became apparent there was little chance of that. It seemed everyone else had exactly the same idea.

Rich took in Caleb's made-to-measure suit, the burnished brown leather brogues and flattering tan he sported from, he assumed, working a good portion of the year abroad. Rich had always coveted that kind of attention, not from women, but from other men. Successful businessmen like the ones in this room. The way they seemed completely absorbed in Caleb's every word and laughing in all the right places for one reason, and one reason only. Caleb, a self-made man who'd grafted hard to get to his current status, was confident and successful, but more importantly, he was rich. Very rich and at the top of his game.

When Rich stood at the bathroom sink, he watched in amazement when Caleb Mosley walked up and began washing his hands at the very next sink. Something caught his eye as he turned and he bent down to scoop up a compact black leather wallet.

'Is this yours?' He held it out to Caleb, who shook droplets of water from his hands and took it.

'Jeez, I'd forget my head if it was loose.' He grinned, showing strong, even teeth and tucked the wallet into his trouser pocket leaving a tiny wet mark on what looked to Rich like Italian silk. 'Thanks, man.'

'No worries.' Rich moved to the hand-dryer, racking his brains for something impressive and dazzling to say to strike up a rapport with this property magnate who he hadn't got a hope of getting close to out in the networking suite. But his mind remained stubbornly blank.

Caleb wafted his hands briefly under the dryer next to Rich before making a final check of his appearance in the mirror, swiping a hand over his immaculate dark hair. 'Thanks again. See you around.'

Rich turned around to raise a hand and Caleb hesitated, his face growing serious.

'Survivor, or supporter?' he said.

'Sorry?' Rich frowned, his hands now bone dry.

Caleb tapped a small metal shape on his own lapel. 'The light-blue ribbon.'

After a pause, Rich looked down at his discreet pin badge, his expression telling Caleb it had completely slipped his mind he was wearing it. 'Oh, supporter. My dad died of prostate cancer ten years ago.'

Caleb turned away from the door and moved nearer. Close enough Rich could see previously invisible worry lines etched around his eyes and mouth. 'My old man died last year, same thing. Not sure I'll ever get over it.'

'I'm sorry to hear that, mate. It's a terrible disease.' Rich nodded to his badge. 'At least we're doing our bit, raising awareness.'

Caleb stared at the floor, his mouth set in a sad shape. 'Dad suffered so much, but he fought until his last breath. Never complained, you know?'

'I hear you.' Rich's face sagged in understanding. 'I did a charity run last year, raised a bit of money. Even then, it's hard to feel like you can really make a difference.'

Caleb looked at him then and Rich was shocked to see his eyes brimming with tears. Even more surprising, he made no effort to mask the emotion. 'You know, I'm surrounded by yes-men and leeches out there, desperate to associate with me for one reason and one reason only. To boost their business reputation. I've been here two days and I haven't met one genuine person until now – until speaking to you. What's your name?'

Rich felt his cheeks grow hot as he offered his hand. 'Richard Askew. Rich. That's nice of you to say, but I—'

'Do you know who I am?'

Rich hesitated a moment or two. Should he play dumb, or just admit he knew Caleb? I mean, who didn't? All Rich did was hand over his wallet, but he'd have done that for anyone. 'Yeah, I know who you are. Caleb Mosley.'

The other man nodded slowly. 'You got a stand here at the exhibition?'

If Rich tried to bluff that he'd had any kind of business

success, Caleb would smell the lie a mile away, so he shook his head, embarrassed. 'Nah. Bit out of my price range.' He gave a little laugh and tried not to look at his scarlet cheeks glowing back at him in the mirror. 'I've just got a small business, not much more than a start-up really. It doesn't really support—'

'Plenty of room on my stand.' Caleb headed for the door again and beckoned to him. 'We'll get you set up there tomorrow.'

'But...' Rich felt panic rise in his chest. He'd seen Caleb's exhibition space; it was hard to miss it. It consisted of a run of meeting booths, plenty of open space with display boards and comfy seats. All nicely bordered by an outward-facing wall of enormous 4K HD screens replaying MPD's most high-profile projects. There was no way Rich could offer Caleb even a fraction of the price he must have paid for this premium showcase corner.

Caleb did a double-take. 'Don't look so worried, the offer is gratis. No cost to you at all. You're not going to turn me down, I hope?'

'No! I'm really grateful. I can't thank you enough.'

Caleb slapped Rich on the back and they left the bathroom together. 'My staff will help set you up first thing in the morning so you're ready to go when the show opens. In the meantime, come and meet some of my associates. They're always looking to do business with good, honest people.'

Rich followed him blindly, the hundreds of chattering people that milled around them blurring into one faceless hum. It was crazy... a small miracle, even! He glanced down at the pin badge he'd picked up from a charity box on the way in as a nice touch in the unlikely event he got to speak to Caleb Mosley. If there's one thing he always did, it was his homework. With this in mind, a day before the exhibition, Rich had made a point of googling Caleb's most recent interviews and in one of them he'd opened up about his grief in losing his father last year.

Rich grinned as he followed Caleb's broad back, watching how people turned to watch him, nod admirably at him. Their eyes fell on Rich accompanying him and their admiration turned into envious glances.

Rich's old man hadn't died of prostate cancer. He'd been a cantankerous, lying old drunk who pickled his liver for sixty years and then whined constantly when the cirrhosis took hold until he finally popped his clogs.

Rich might not be a successful businessman yet, but he was an accomplished storyteller. And for now, that was seeing him through quite nicely.

EIGHTEEN

LIV

Liv closes the bank's webpage, dread coursing through her. She's checked numerous times now but the money still hasn't arrived. She can't put her visit to River Gate Care Home off for yet another day. Not if she wants to live with herself.

Liv's heart sinks when she spots Betsy, their eleven-year-old Staffordshire Bull Terrier, sitting patiently by the door. 'Come on then, old girl. Quick walk before I go.'

Betsy perks up, her tail wagging while Liv puts on her collar and lead. She crosses the road to walk Betsy around the small park.

While Betsy sniffs and pulls on her lead, Liv thinks about how she noticed the change in her mother-in-law about ten months after Rich went missing. At first, there was nothing overly concerning. Shannon would sometimes use the wrong word in conversation or forget what she was about to say or do and, crucially, would be unable to recall it.

Any mother would be devastated if, one day, her son just disappeared off the face of the earth, and Shannon was no exception to that. Liv told herself it was shock, grief. In time, she felt sure Shannon would be able to heal and settle a little.

Shannon had been the first person in her family to go to university and had been halfway through her third year of teaching when she met Richard Snr, Rich's dad. Twelve years older than her and set in his ways, Richard Snr had been very clear that he didn't approve of her working. 'I want a wife to come home to and a mother for my children,' he'd reportedly announced. Liv thought he'd sounded like a walking cliché but, as Shannon magnanimously said, Richard Snr was from a different generation and she gave up her beloved career.

When her husband died, Shannon immediately took on several voluntary positions in the education sector she had loved. Listening to children read at the local school, helping out during their swimming sessions and accompanying the younger classes on school trips. She became secretary of the PTA.

Shannon had always been very switched on, a formidable organiser and Liv's go-to person for advice, having lost her own mum to heart disease before she turned thirty.

Before he left, Rich placed his hands on her shoulders and stared into her eyes. 'I know you and Maddox will be OK. You're both going to get through this. But I have one thing to ask. A big favour.'

'Anything,' Liv whispered.

'Promise me you'll look after my mum. Just until this is all over. I know she's fine right now, but she's going to take it hard. It's any mother's nightmare, losing their son.'

'Of course I will!' Liv hugged him. 'You don't even need to ask.'

'I don't want her to suffer because of what we've decided we must do. She's been through a lot with my dad and...' Rich's eyes glistened with tears. 'It's just that eleven, twelve years... it's a long time, and Mum will be getting on when I come back.' He wiped his eyes with the back of his hand.

'Hey, I get it. I'll watch out for Shannon no matter what, OK?'

She'd said it easily, but she had meant it. Of course she would be there for Shannon, to give her support and nurture her relationship with Maddox.

But she hadn't anticipated *this*. Had never considered what it actually meant to be a twenty-four-hour carer. What that did to your work, your wellbeing, *your entire life*.

Another dog walks by and Betsy, despite her now stiff back legs and greying whiskers, strains on her lead forcing Liv to pull her back.

Liv had tried to keep her promise to Rich. She'd kept Shannon in her own home as long as she could. But in the end, when the meals Liv had prepared remained untouched in the fridge and the bathroom flooded when the taps had been left running, she had been forced to admit defeat.

Liv told herself she'd done the best she could, had done her mother-in-law proud. But it didn't feel like that and Liv had learned a painful lesson.

The concept of looking after someone was so different to the practical implementation. Liv's two jobs simply didn't allow her to spend the hours needed with Shannon, didn't even allow her to pop in several times a day. Not without becoming exhausted.

So Liv used Shannon's modest savings to engage carers who visited up to four times a day to ensure Shannon took her medication and provided her with meals. But when Shannon was found shivering on a neighbour's doorstep at midnight in her nightwear, Liv knew it wasn't enough.

She'd spent a few weeks checking out options and local facilities and had settled on River Gate, a modern residential home that boasted a recent accreditation of 'outstanding' by the Care Quality Commission.

Now, at seventy-two, Shannon lives in a residential dementia care home.

Liv takes Betsy back home and goes straight out to the car.

River Gate is only a ten-minute drive from Liv's house and she religiously visited Shannon three times a week. That is, until Shannon started her strange behaviour and Liv became more and more unnerved. These days, she has to force herself to go there once a week to visit.

On her way to River Gate, Liv picks up a small bunch of mixed freesias, Shannon's favourite flowers. Up until his disappearance, Rich always took some round when he visited with a box of Milk Tray chocolates. Only Milk Tray would do for Shannon. 'Pity the Milk Tray man can't bring them round,' she'd joke every single time, alluding to the old seventies advert. 'Handsome man with rippling muscles. What a tonic *that'd* be.'

'Cheers, Mum!' Rich would ham it up all glum-faced as Shannon howled with laughter, embracing him.

When Liv pulls up at River Gate, she bags a spot close to the door. She takes a deep breath to steel herself and gets out of the car, walking into the long, low building. She'd rung ahead and asked if the visit could take place in Shannon's private bedroom.

A smell of antiseptic and floor cleaner hits her as soon as she's buzzed into reception.

'Mrs Askew's assigned carer is off-duty now, but he left some notes,' the young woman behind reception says, picking up a printed sheet. 'The doctor has tweaked her medication to help with her insomnia. It says here, she's experiencing night terrors.'

Liv shudders. Shannon has never suffered with insomnia since she's known her, never mind night terrors, which sound awful. Her heart squeezes with sympathy for Shannon. Liv can't help but feel she's neglecting her. She's done her best for Shannon but when it comes down to it, she is Rich's mum. He's the one who should be back on the scene caring for her... and instead, where is he? Shacked up with some other woman? Living a new life, rolling in cash with a new identity in Spain?

The clerk is still speaking in a mechanical tone, reading out details from the sheet. Names of medications, Shannon's diet and her weakening ability to carry out simple tasks.

'Her motor skills are—'

'Is there any chance I could speak to someone about Shannon's sleep problems?' Liv interrupts. 'I'd really like to understand it better if I can.'

'I'll see if a senior carer is available,' she says, putting down the sheet. 'If you'd like to go through, I'll see what I can do.'

'Thank you.' Liv signs the visitors' book, thanks the clerk and heads out of reception and straight down the clinical-looking corridor to Shannon's room.

The door is slightly ajar. Liv taps lightly and pushes it open, stepping inside. Shannon is sitting in an armchair staring out of the window at the garden. Her head wheels around, but her expression of hopeful expectancy immediately falls away when she sees Liv. A shadow crosses her face when she sees the flowers and she looks away, her lips puckering.

'Hello, Shannon! It's me, Liv. How are you feeling?'

Shannon does not reply, but Liv is not deterred. She walks over to her and holds out the flowers. 'I bought your favourite blooms to brighten up your room and look at this treat.' Liv smiles and places the chocolates on the small table next to her. 'Remember the Milk Tray man, Shannon?'

The old lady turns to face her and Liv shrinks back slightly from the expression of pure disdain she's levelling her way. She jumps back as a pale, bony arm flies up and sweeps the chocolates and flowers from the table. She looks down at the floor, at the pastel-coloured petals scattered at the older woman's feet.

'Where's my boy?' she growls, her voice vitriolic. 'He's told me all about what you're up to.'

'What?' Liv whispers, shrinking back. Shannon has never mentioned Rich, has never asked for him since the dementia took hold.

'Who are you?' Shannon's features screw into a tight knot as she jabs a finger.

'Shannon! It's me, Liv! Calm down, you'll get yourself in a state.'

Shannon begins to wail and Liv sits there, her arms wrapped around herself. This is a new, troubling stage in Shannon's illness. The door opens and two women in pale-blue trousers and tunics rush in. 'What happened?' one says, sliding her arm around a whimpering Shannon.

'She just became upset when I came in,' Liv says, looking from one to the other. 'She knocked the flowers and chocolates off the table and...' She takes a breath. She's aware she's acting like she, herself, did something wrong, but she didn't. *Calm down*, she tells herself.

The carer squeezes Shannon's hand gently as her breathing begins to regulate, but Liv is very aware of her mother-in-law's distrustful stare.

'Can I have a quick word?' The lady in the darker blue uniform nods towards the door. 'Outside?'

Relieved to leave the building tension in the room, Liv follows her out, Shannon's eyes remaining pinned to her the whole time.

'Reception should have asked someone to brief you before you saw Shannon,' she says.

'She told me about the insomnia, the night terrors,' Liv says, unnerved.

She nods. 'I also wanted to forewarn you that Shannon has become increasingly confused over the last couple of weeks. There's a note on the file to say someone tried to contact you twice with an update but had no response.'

Liv locks her back teeth. There had been a missed call just over a week ago, and then an answerphone message a couple of days after that. She'd meant to call back, to get an update on Shannon's condition but... the guilt of Shannon's situation was so much easier to deal with when Liv imagined her comfortable and reasonably content in her pleasant en-suite bedroom at River Gate. It hadn't sounded urgent, and she'd been steeling herself to call back. Then, with the distraction of the count-down to today and the long-awaited money, and Maddox's distancing over the past couple of weeks, it had slipped her mind completely.

'Ms Leigh?'

Liv blinks. 'Sorry. I'd say she seems more volatile than confused.'

The carer shrugs. 'She's convinced her late son is in contact, that he comes to the window and visits her... whispering instructions to her in the night.'

'Oh God.' Liv's eyes widen. 'I mean, that's not possible, is it? That someone would be able to do that.'

The carer presses her lips together. 'I can't swear it's completely impossible, but you've seen the premises. The building itself is secure, but our grounds are open to the public road. Saying that, it's unlikely. *Highly* unlikely that such a thing could occur.'

Liv feels a weight pressing on the inside of her chest wall. 'Does Shannon's bedroom window open?'

'Only an inch or two like all the residents' bedrooms. Just enough to allow a little air to circulate in the warm weather. Rest assured nobody could feasibly enter the property through there.'

But that would be enough for what Shannon has claimed is happening. Liv feels slightly breathless. An inch or two would be plenty to hear someone whispering to her in the middle of the night.

Someone like her son. If Rich is back on the scene.

The money isn't coming today, that much is obvious. All day, Liv has been thinking of excuses. Reasons for what might be delaying the transaction, but underneath she thinks she knows why. Maybe she's always known the truth of it.

Rich has betrayed her. He has lied and double-crossed her. This man she's trusted with her life, her future. The man who is the father of her only child. She's forgotten her own conviction that everything in life turns out to be a disappointment. Even as she thinks it, she cannot quite believe it. She is desperately searching for a possible blip in their arrangements. A clue as to why it's all gone wrong.

Had she mis-remembered the agreement? It had been a long time ago. She's worked hard to blank the detail... but no. This detail is still crystal clear in her head. She's memorised every detail of the money. Of the final day of the plan.

Which leaves her with only one question.

Where the hell is Rich Askew now?

NINETEEN

KAIT

It's still before seven in the morning when I creep down the carpeted landing; I hover outside the spare room door. I've only been awake for about thirty minutes, but after discovering the doorbell footage and the stuff that's been constantly channelling through my head, it feels like I've been in purgatory for hours.

I can hear the steady deep snoring of my lying, cheating husband in the other bedroom. No surprise there, he'll be shattered after getting home in the early hours.

If there's one thing Daniel loves, it's his sleep. He's grouchy and lacklustre if he doesn't get enough of it. Annoying, but this morning, it suits me to keep him out of the way as long as possible, so I creep past the door and carry on downstairs.

I make a pot of decaf coffee, open the photos app on my phone and sit down at my laptop. I open an internet search page and, using the photograph of the scrap of paper for reference, type in the address bar: *F Forest upn X17 314 907 2600*

A second later, the results load. They look fairly meaningless and mostly numerical references found in various irrelevant lists. I clear the address bar and start again. This time I enter only *F Forest* in there.

The first page of results are all references of websites and pages with the word 'forest' in them. From Airbnb properties, football clubs and Instagram accounts, nothing looks relevant or right.

I try again with *upn* and then enter the run of numbers on its own. Nothing that comes up makes any sense at all. My heart sinks.

It looks as though my preoccupation with the note Daniel dropped is groundless. I thought he looked guilty and nervous, and I don't know what I expected to find here, but this is not it.

'It's just some training platform details I scribbled down for a client,' Daniel had said repeatedly. I don't know why I can't get rid of the niggle I feel inside, but somehow, his explanation isn't ringing true.

Maybe, just maybe, he *is* telling the truth and it's some kind of training platform. I've heard him mention them before and as I understand it, he's referring to a paid-up, subscription type of platform that offers personal training advice and exercise routines that people can access from home. It's possible that the long reference number could be a way into one such resource without a customer having to pay, or something like that.

Sounds almost reasonable, and I'd have almost been ready to believe him if I hadn't just watched that doorbell video clip. Over and over again. If I hadn't heard him talking to someone on the phone, telling them not to worry. That I'd be asleep and none the wiser.

I've grappled with this long enough on my own. Asking Daniel directly has proven to be a brick wall and there's only one person I trust enough to bare my soul to when it's something so personal.

I pick up my phone and text my sister. Ten minutes later, we've agreed to meet for coffee in town even though I'm supposed to be resting. I know all this stress isn't good for me, but what can I do? I have to find out the truth for me and my baby.

On my drive over there, I think about what life was like before I met Daniel. I had a social life, a handful of good friends and a few thousand pounds in my savings account. I was doing OK at the bank in my cashier training and, on the face of it, life was good again at last after troubled relationships where I'd seemed to have a knack of picking players and losers.

But every day, after leaving the office, I'd get back inside my smart flat and get changed. Then I'd make a cup of tea and sit in my padded, stressless recliner and take in my glimpse of the Trent between the frontline apartment blocks. Tell myself I was fine on my own. I didn't need a man. Try to ignore the fact it felt like I was kidding myself.

After a long hot bath, some reading, watching a bit of TV, a tidy round, it was usually bed before ten-thirty. Night after night. Until the weekend when, if I wasn't meeting friends, there were whole days and nights to kill, too. I had a good life but somehow, it always felt a dress rehearsal... like really, I was just waiting for the real thing.

Then I met Daniel and within days, everything changed. Almost immediately, we began to see each other every other night. Our first meets were largely set in town for a drink after work, or at the cinema and casual eateries during the week. Weekends, we'd sometimes spend a day at the coast or enjoy a long, lingering meal in fancy, low-lit restaurants with linen-covered tables set with polished cutlery and sparkling glassware.

Daniel stayed over at my flat for the first time two weeks after we met and I stayed at his slick, rented new-build the following week. His house was decorated entirely in bland neutrals and lacked any homely details or personal touches. Some might say that's just typical of a single guy. I thought so, anyway.

Our own mutual attraction however was instant and indisputable.

'It's really important to me we're honest with each other,' Daniel said, early on in our relationship. 'I want to be completely transparent with you and I hope you feel the same way.'

It was so refreshing, after playing so many games in my previous relationships. Men that told me stories to back up the image of the people they wanted me to think they were. When it became all too clear within a short time, who they really were. Someone I didn't want to be around.

I met my sister for a drink. Told her I'd met someone new.

'OK, so I guess what you said about having a good break from a relationship is shelved for now?' she'd said carefully, sipping her wine.

I'd pulled a face. I was allowed to change my mind! 'Daniel is different. He seems like a genuinely good man and I feel like a different person now.'

'You deserve to meet someone nice but... you have to be ready,' Kirsten had reasoned. 'He sounds like a nice guy.'

Ironically, Kirsten and Daniel have clashed for some time now and I don't feel in the mood for her lecturing when she hears the full extent of it all. Of what I've found out. There's not just me to worry about now: soon we'll be the proud parents of our brand-new baby. I can't be happy at what should be a joyous time while all this is rattling around in my head, leaving no space for happiness or optimism for the future.

But I have to know the truth. It's as simple as that. I need Kirsten's help as to the best way forward and I hope she can put her judgement to one side to give me some advice.

I park in the Victoria Centre and cross the road to 200 Degrees coffee shop on Milton Street. Kirsten is already sitting at a table for two near the back of the café.

'You look pale, aren't you supposed to be resting?' She frowns and stands up to embrace me, glancing down at my stomach.

'Don't worry, I'm taking it easy. Don't forget the doctors advised exercise, too.'

Kirsten presses her lips together, not altogether convinced. 'At least sit down and let me get the coffees in then.'

I watch Kirsten as she walks to the counter. Since I met Daniel, she's involved herself much more in my life. Me in hers... not so much because she's often working away. I like to think she's keeping a caring, sisterly eye on me but sometimes it feels like she's trying to be my keeper.

Periodically, her partner of five years, Ellie, gives me a call just to catch up. I've got far more in common personality-wise with Ellie. She runs a wellbeing practice at a peaceful studio in the city and holds regular retreats and workshop days that she's invited me to take part in several times. It occurs to me that now might be a good time to accept her offer. If I can only stop myself spiralling out of control with the stuff that's filling my head morning, noon and night.

Two weeks ago she rang and I could hear the tension in her voice. After the initial polite enquiries as to how the other was doing, Ellie said, 'I wondered if you've seen Kirsten much lately and if so, whether you've noticed she's a bit stressed out?'

Her question took me by surprise because Ellie had never asked me anything like that before. Our last couple of calls had consisted of her asking about the baby and trying to get me to attend her Yoga for Pregnancy classes.

'We've met up for coffee a few times and she seems fine,' I told her. 'She always seems more worried about my life than her own.'

'How do you mean?'

'Oh you know, she doesn't like Daniel, doesn't think I was ready for another relationship. Same old.'

There was a short silence before Ellie said, 'You have every right to be happy, Kait. Whether Kirsten agrees or not. Remember that.'

'Thanks, Ellie,' I said, genuinely appreciating her kind words.

'Oh, and Kait?'

'Yes?'

'Please don't mention to Kirsten I asked about her.' She hesitated. 'It's just... she'll be annoyed if she knows I've said anything about my concerns. She's very private person, as you know.'

I gave Ellie an assurance I wouldn't say anything to Kirsten and we ended the call. But I found myself thinking about it for a couple of days afterwards. Ellie had sounded strange and, although I hadn't got around to it yet, I reminded myself I should really call in and see her at the studio.

Kirsten told me that although Ellie seems zen, she's actually the sort of person who lives on the edge of her nerves waiting for catastrophe. 'She never recovered from the death of her beloved dad,' Kirsten told me. 'He was a man who worked hard and partied harder, a drinker who always battled with his weight and cholesterol levels, up to the day he suffered a massive heart attack at the wheel of a car and passed away. I think she's still grieving him and it's made her paranoid about her own health.'

I thought about my own beliefs, tinged by my childhood and I realised we bring so much heartbreak and misery with us from our early years. We tuck our heavy burden away where it can't be seen by others and the years roll by as we learn to live with the eternal aching.

Today, Kirsten is wearing olive-coloured yoga leggings and a short buttery-beige leather jacket that ends well before her neat, toned bum. In my current state, I feel bloated and slow, but who am I kidding? Even before I fell pregnant, I could never get away with an outfit like Kirsten is wearing in a million years.

Kirsten has inherited Mum's diminutive physique, whereas I take after our dad. We were both just teenagers back then but I was always Dad's favourite, and I felt something break inside of me when he died from lung cancer. When Mum developed the heart disease that finally took her, it felt like the worst kind of double whammy.

'Jeez, cheer up, Kait. It might never happen!' Kirsten says when she returns with our lattes and two flapjacks.

'Sorry.' I sit up straight, realising my features are pulled long and I'm slouching. 'Got a lot on my mind and I'm exhausted.'

'Sounds like low sugar. This should fix it, eat up.' She pushes a plate with a flapjack on it towards me. 'Are you feeling rough?'

'Yes, but not for the reason you might think. I'm feeling OK pregnancy-wise.' I pick up my latte and stare into the pale froth as if it might give me the answers I need. 'How are you feeling?'

She looks surprised. 'Me? I'm fine. Soldiering on as usual.' She takes a sip of her latte and narrows her eyes. 'Why do you ask?'

I roll my eyes. 'Does there have to be a reason? I'm just showing I care! How's Ellie doing? I haven't seen her for ages.'

She looks away and says shortly, 'She's OK, thanks. I'll tell her you're asking after her.' Kirsten sniffs. 'OK, spill then. What's up? You sounded pretty keen to meet when you texted.'

I sigh. No point in beating around the bush. 'It's Daniel. I think he's having an affair.'

'What?' Kirsten splutters and dabs her mouth. 'Seriously?'

'Yes. Seriously. I'm not imagining it.' I feel a spike of irritation because it's clear Kirsten is already exhibiting disbelief. 'If you give me a chance before judging me, I'll explain.'

Kirsten rolls her eyes. 'I don't want this to turn into a tit-for-tat trade of insults. I came today because you sound down about whatever's worrying you. Now I see why. So what's happened?'

I tell her about the note. 'I've since found out the note doesn't mean anything even though he looked so worried when he knew I'd seen it. But it was the backdrop to the next thing I'm going to tell you, which is the real problem that can't be explained away.'

Kirsten nibbles her flapjack and nods, watching me the whole time.

'Daniel said he had to pop out last night, something to do with a client. I knew something wasn't right as it was supposed to be his day off but that was the third time he'd been out and he'd been on his phone a lot. Anyway, I wasn't feeling great, so I went to bed. I didn't hear him come home, so when I woke up this morning, I checked the doorbell video footage to see what time he actually got back.'

'Ooh, clever!' I'm not sure she's taking me seriously.

'The footage showed he didn't get home until the early hours. It also caught some of the phone call he was on when he got out of the car and it sounded like he was talking to someone he'd been with. A woman.'

'You think that's where he'd been until the early hours... with a woman?'

'That's what it sounded like. He was reassuring her.'

'What did he say?' Kirsten puts down her coffee cup. At last, she is sitting up and listening.

I open the app and scroll down until just before 2 a.m. this morning.

I frown, peer closer and then scroll through again but there's nothing after Daniel left the house at eight o'clock last night.

The video clips of him arriving home in the early hours have been deleted.

'They were here. I'm sure...' I scroll furiously up and down the saved clips. I can feel my face heating up. Why the hell didn't I save the clips to my phone? 'I'm an idiot,' I mutter under my breath.

Kirsten stares. 'It's OK, Kait. You don't have to prove anything to me.'

'I know, but I wanted to show you the clip. So you can see him, hear what he's saying. It's here somewhere.' My search is fruitless. 'Daniel must have deleted the clips!'

'Hey.' Kirsten reaches across the table to still my busy fingers. 'Forget the clips. Talk to me. Just offload and tell me how you're feeling. There's no point getting stressed out and building everything up—'

'You think I'm imagining it!' I pull my hand away. 'It must be him who's deleted the evidence hoping I didn't see it yet.'

'No. I never said that, but things can seem bigger and more worrying when your emotions are in a heightened state.'

'Because I'm pregnant, you mean?'

'Being pregnant is a big deal, Kait, and you have pre-eclampsia, right? That's a lot to worry about and that's when anxiety can build up. Make you feel like the world – well, in this case, your husband – is against you.' I watch Kirsten stir some sugar lazily into her americano. I can't quite work out why, when she and Daniel always seem to be on spiky terms, she's seeming to jump to his defence on this issue.

There again, she's always been a pragmatic personality rather than emotional like me. I've never known my sister dither about anything much. A joint director in a global corporate leadership training company, she advises leaders in getting the most from their management team. Her no-nonsense, pragmatic approach to business has little space for emotional meltdowns. We're sisters, but we've always demonstrated very different responses to our own personal issues.

'I know you wouldn't be worrying like I am,' I say carefully. 'It's not in your nature.'

'Oh, I don't know. People change,' she says cryptically. 'But I do accept that's your approach. It's Ellie's mindset too, so I've been on the receiving end of it.' Kirsten pulls a face. 'It's not really helpful if you can avoid it. Look, for what it's worth, even though we have our differences, I reckon Daniel's one of the good guys,' Kirsten offers. 'It's obvious he adores you, Kait. I don't think he'd do anything to threaten that and it's important you're sure of what you're accusing him of. Once you accuse him and tell him how you're feeling, you can't take it back. Just my opinion.'

I'm beginning to wish I hadn't asked to meet up. Perhaps the time would have been better spent trying to access Daniel's personal devices while he slept. Why did I think this would help the situation? Since meeting Daniel, I've neglected my friendship circle to the extent that people have stopped trying and stopped inviting me out. I can't blame them. I'd fallen head over heels in love and I wanted to spend every single moment with Daniel. He liked it to be just the two of us and I felt the same way. Still do. But when I need someone to talk to, a sympathetic ear is scarce these days. There is only Kirsten left.

'You mentioned a note,' she says, shaking me from my thoughts.

'What?'

'What did the note say?'

I pick up my phone again and swipe at the screen before holding it up to face her. 'I took a picture of it.'

Kirsten's eyes scan over it a few times before shaking her head. 'Doesn't mean anything to me but ping it over to my phone so I've got a copy.'

'I'm not really worried about the note anymore, to be honest. Daniel swears it's just a training platform reference. I've googled it and can't find a thing to match it.'

'So why did you initially suspect something?'

'It was his face when he saw I'd found it. All the colour just drained from his cheeks.'

'Send it to me anyway,' Kirsten says. 'You never know.'

I sigh and AirDrop the photo over to her phone. The last thing I want to do is to impose on Kirsten's busy schedule, but despite my sister's thinly disguised belief I'm making something out of nothing, I can't rid myself of the nub of suspicion that sits in the middle of my chest like a hard, tangled knot of misery.

Kirsten narrows her eyes and squints at the photograph that's now displayed on her phone screen. I expect her to shrug and close it down, but she continues to study it.

'For the past six months I've been working with a representative from the government's education department. We're looking at possibly changing the way information is collected and retained in schools,' she says, still focusing on the screen. 'And I've become familiar with an acronym that's used a lot. UPN.'

I glance at the photo of the message still open on my own phone.

'See this?' Kirsten points to part of the message that reads: *upn X17 314 907 2600.* 'I think this might be a Unique Pupil Number.'

'Unique *what?*' I peer closer at the message.

'Unique Pupil Number. Every single pupil in the UK has their own numerical identity unique to them that's used throughout their education.' She looks up at me. 'That's what this could be.'

'I don't think so. Daniel said it was a training platform reference,' I say hesitantly, but occurs to me I haven't been able to confirm that's the case in my own searches, so maybe it's time to change tack.

'I'll ask my assistant to take a look at it. Claire's like a terrier when it comes to finding stuff out.' Kirsten gives me a strange look. 'I'm sure it means nothing, Kait, try not to worry.'

I turn my phone over so I can't see the note. I feel hot and sick.

Somehow, it feels like things are going from bad to worse.

TWENTY

LIV

Back home, the summer cold that started to hit this afternoon after she left River Gate feels like it's escalating.

I hope it's not flu, she thinks, as it seems to be so quickly getting worse.

Periodically, Betsy looks up from her bed hopefully as Liv shifts to get comfy on the sofa. 'Not just yet, girl. Another walk might just finish me off.' She'll ask Maddox to pop her out around the block later. She also hopes that, whatever it is, she didn't unknowingly pass it on to Shannon earlier.

She never used to get ill like this. Always a fan of plenty of fresh air and religiously taking her morning vitamin supplements, she'd enjoyed what seemed to be a steel-plated immune system up until now.

But this past year, the situation has been getting her down. Constantly lurching between believing everything will work out fine and worrying it will go horribly wrong, Liv has felt herself slipping. That's why she's taken solace in the odd glass of wine in the evening, just to get her through.

She hasn't the energy nor the inclination to get out for long walks with Betsy nor to sign up for one of the cardio exercise classes she used to enjoy. And she's got nobody to notice her increased drinking levels or her lack of getting out of the house.

As people head toward their mid-forties, some of them experience a sinking feeling that they are on the relentless march toward middle-age with no turning back. No time to achieve the goals they thought they had a chance of hitting. But not Liv. She's been looking forward to this time for so, so long.

A cool half a million pounds of her own, plus Maddox's amount, with the power to transform her and her son's life.

This is supposed to be the best time of her life, when everything comes together after the many years of sacrifice. It's supposed to be the better future she has visualised a thousand times. Now it's here, the reality is very different. Now, Liv finds herself unable to sleep and she can't shake the impending sense of doom that she may have been well and truly shafted by the one person she trusted. *Had* to trust because the alternative didn't bear thinking about.

All those years ago, she'd placed her trust in Rich and now it looks as if he has betrayed her. The question is, what does she do about it? Where does she even start? There has been no contact for over eleven years, just as they agreed.

Now she's got the building worry of Shannon and her repeated claim to carers that her son is visiting her during the night, whispering to her through the open window. The staff seemed to discount Shannon's claims but something about it makes the back of Liv's neck prickle. Has Rich secretly returned to see his mother, but with no intention of meeting with her, or his son, or keeping his promises to deliver the money?

But who can she turn to? Not Shannon herself, who seems to despise Liv a little more with every visit she makes. Certainly not her son, Maddox, now fourteen and brooding and holding his own secrets which she must address, and soon.

If he finds out what his parents did that day, how everything has been planned to the nth degree by his mother and his very-much-alive father, it will completely screw him up for life.

No stone was left unturned. They'd congratulated themselves that the plan was as close to perfect as they could get it. All loose ends had been dealt with. All eventualities satisfied. And their confidence had been proven right when Rich was legally presumed dead after seven years. Just as they'd hoped.

But now, the plan has seemingly fallen to pieces at the very last hurdle. Rich's promised contact has not been made. Other important agreements remain unfulfilled.

On top of all that, Maddox is behaving strangely. Liv knows him better than anyone in the world and something is bothering him. Yesterday, she'd tried tackling his morose mood and she'd felt completely unable to reach him. As if a yawning crevice had opened up between them without her noticing and now he's got a thousand-pound iPhone in his possession that he simply cannot have acquired by honest means.

It feels like the world around her is crumbling. Liv must have missed a detail in that perfect plan. A weakness she had failed to spot in looking after her own interests.

For so many years, she has blanked the past. Refused to relive what happened back then, refused to even discuss it with her son. She has trusted Rich and he is currently playing her like a fool. Could it be he's changed his mind at the eleventh hour and decided to keep all the money himself?

She has no way to contact him. Just a small business postal box she'd rented as they'd agreed, two years after he went missing. Every day without fail she checked on her online account if there was any mail to collect and every day, as per the last eleven years, the answer was always the same: *No new items.*

TWENTY-ONE

MADDOX

When Maddox gets home that night, his mum is lying on the sofa under a mound of fleecy blankets.

'Don't get too close, love. I still feel awful,' she says, sneezing into a tissue.

He strides across the room, uncomfortable he has to face her when he thought she'd be in bed. 'It's boiling in here. I'll open a window.'

'No, don't!' Liv puts a hand up. 'I can't seem to get warm. I'll be OK. It's kind of you to show concern though.'

Maddox feels a twinge of resentment as he considers her miserable expression.

The truth of it is that he doesn't feel concerned at all. She's only got a mild cold and that doesn't change the fact she's been lying to him basically his whole life. And what about the money that's supposedly soon going to be coming? The money his mum has been going on about non-stop? Sammy has explained things that have answered a lot of questions for Maddox. The hard part is that he must act normal. Sammy was very clear about that.

Maddox thinks about the money he'll soon be making from

his new job. Real money that helps out and makes a difference, and a warm glow ignites inside him. It feels good to have the means to be independent for when he leaves home. He just needs to think of a good story to cover up where the cash is really coming from. Like Sammy said, 'It's hard to hear this stuff, I know. But think about the future. Don't blow everything by losing it with your mum.'

He grudgingly makes Liv a slice of toast and takes her a couple of paracetamols in with a mug of strong tea, just as she likes it. Maybe then she'll fall asleep. He's trying not to think about the stuff on her laptop. The stuff she's done. Since meeting Sammy last night he feels more upbeat, like he's already grown up a lot. Like he's got someone who's on his side.

'You're a good lad,' she says now, cradling the hot mug in both hands. 'If I get plenty of rest, I'll still be able to help out at the school's weekend netball practice tomorrow morning.'

That's good, he thinks. *Good that she'll be out all day.*

In his pocket, Maddox's secret iPhone vibrates with a notification. He steps out of the room to see it's a WhatsApp message from Brandon. He opens it and scans the brief contents before pushing the phone back into his pocket.

'I'm going out again soon, Mum,' Maddox says lightly. 'I've been offered an evening job helping to coach primary school kids starting next week, and I have a meet-up later to find out more about it. Just a couple of days a week to start with.'

His mum's eyes light up. 'Oh that's wonderful news, Maddox! Are you going to accept?'

He hesitates for a moment before answering, as he feels guilt hit. 'Yeah. I'd be stupid not to.'

His mum looks up at him. 'Who is it you're meeting?'

'One of the teachers. He's taking me to meet his colleague who runs a proper club; it's all above board, don't worry.' Maddox is being a touch sarcastic but it's lost on her. He watches as her shoulders relax again. She's not interested in what he's doing, not really. It's all a show she puts on.

'I'm pleased for you, love. You get off when you like, I'll be fine once I get tucked up cosy in bed.' He turns away. She spends half her life in bed these days. 'Oh, and Maddox?'

He looks back. 'Yeah?'

'Keep your nose clean. If there's anything you want to talk about, you only have to say. Remember that one wrong decision can change your life, so think hard about who you want to hang around with.'

Maddox scowls. It's a strange thing to say, almost as if she knows he's up to something. Pretending she cares.

He slides his hand inside his pocket and rests it on the cool, smooth metal of the iPhone.

He does need to be careful. The last thing he wants is his mum ruining his plans.

SATURDAY

'Shame there was no answer yesterday from the contact number we have,' Helena says, when they get out of the car and walk down the street. 'I'd rather not just turn up out of the blue in a situation like this.'

'It's my understanding there's just Maddox and his mum living there,' Sanjit said as he handed Helena the student's contact details the previous afternoon. 'I'd say Ms Leigh is a supportive parent. She shows an interest in Maddox's education and his progress in the school football team, often attending key games. I understand she works as a teaching assistant herself, so has always been supportive of his education.'

Helena stared at the coloured picture of a good-looking lad with curly dark hair and piercing blue eyes.

'She's never contacted the school regarding any concerns of her own?' Helena asked and Patel shook his head.

'No concerns logged at all. But my guess is, she'll be very concerned indeed if it turns out Maddox has got himself involved with anything underhand. He's a good lad with a bright future. Hopefully we can stamp out any potential problems before it's too late.'

'This is it, boss. Number fifty-eight.' Brewster stops walking and points to a glossy black door in the middle of a linked row of new-build terraced houses.

There's no answer and so Helena rings the bell again. Brewster steps back and looks up to the top floor. 'We're out of luck this time, I think. Doesn't seem to be anyone home.'

There's rattling on the other side of the door, which suddenly opens, and a woman Helena estimates to be in her mid-forties appears, snuffling into a tissue. She's blinking against the light and patting down her dishevelled hair.

'Sorry, I was asleep. I know it's late morning, but I'm—' She falls quiet, her eyes pinned to the warrant card Brewster is holding up. 'Oh no... is it about—' She abruptly clamps her mouth shut, her face draining of colour.

Brewster waits for her to continue, but she remains silent, her eyes wide and filled with dread. As if she's fully expecting bad news.

'DS Kane Brewster and DI Helena Price from Nottinghamshire Police. We were hoping for a quick word with Maddox Leigh. Are you his mum?'

'Yes. I'm Olivia – call me Liv.' Helena watches as the woman's taut expression relaxes a little. 'I thought it was... never mind. Come in.'

They step into the neat hallway and Helena turns to Liv. 'You seemed to be expecting we might be here concerning something else,' she says, glancing up the stairs. 'Is everything OK?'

'Oh yes, everything is fine. Absolutely fine!' Liv's smile stretches unnaturally. 'I'll keep my distance, I'm full of cold.' She holds a tissue up to her face. 'Come through, we can talk in here.'

They follow her into the sparsely furnished living room.

The house is quiet. Too quiet, as though the very fabric of the walls is holding something in and out of sight from its visitors.

Liv sits down and looks at her hands as if she's gathering herself. When she looks back up, it strikes Helena that the woman's eyes look empty. Dark. There are two empty wine bottles and a glass on the floor at the side of the armchair.

A prickle starts at the back of Helena's neck. She has the feeling they're not going to get a lot from Olivia Leigh today. But she's got enough years as a police officer under her belt to know one thing. Something's not right here, in this house. With this woman.

Helena just can't discern exactly what it is yet.

TWENTY-THREE

LIV

Liv leads the detectives through to the living room and invites them to take a seat. She watches as the woman takes in the shabby room, the worn rug stretching in front of the clumsy electric fire.

Breathe, she tells herself. *Just. Calm. Down.*

The doorbell had woken her from a deep sleep. She'd barely rested at all last night, worrying about the money, about Maddox and what was going to happen. She'd fired off a quick text to her colleague to let her know she was going to have to give the kids' netball practice a miss.

Exhausted with her constantly whirring thoughts, she'd laid her cheek on the soft kitchen sofa cushion for a few moments and had dropped off into a dream full of anxieties and dread. Rich's face had loomed large in front of her, and he'd been laughing. Laughing, and taunting her that she'd been so easy to fool. That he had a new life now that didn't include Liv, nor Maddox.

She'd woken suddenly at the shrill ringing. Jumped up and rushed to the door immediately, the suffocating tentacles of the dream still clinging to her. Crazily – for a second or two – part of her had thought it might be him. Thought Rich might have actually come to see her to explain why the money had not arrived. To tell her that yes, there had been a hitch, but now everything was OK.

When she saw the two detectives, she'd fallen into a panic. Thought they'd found out what she'd done. What she and Rich had both done all those years ago.

'Liv? Are you feeling alright?' The female detective, DI Price, regards her curiously. 'Is there something you want to tell us?'

'What? No, nothing. Everything's fine.' Liv battles to calm herself and slow down her breathing. 'Sorry, I'm a bit disorientated, that's all. I didn't sleep well. I was fast on when you came to the door, and I think I jumped up too quickly.'

'I can get you a glass of water if—'

'No, no. I'm fine.' Liv remembers her laptop is open on the kitchen worktop. She gives Price a small smile. 'Thanks anyway. You said you'd come to talk to Maddox? He's not here.'

'That's a shame,' Brewster remarks. 'We were hoping to have a chat with him about some worrying reports the school has received.'

'About Maddox?' Liv frowns, her mind instantly flashing to the brand new phone he's in possession of. 'He's a good lad. Never brought me any trouble.'

'And we're not suggesting he's in trouble now,' Brewster says carefully, taking out a small notebook. 'We just need to check a few things out with him to satisfy ourselves he's not in any danger.'

'Like I said, he's gone out and I'm not sure what time he'll be back.'

'Did Maddox say where he was going?' Helena asks.

Liv hesitates, thinking. 'He usually has football practice on a Saturday morning.'

'You don't sound that sure,' Price remarks.

Liv frowns. 'It's just that yesterday he said he's been offered a job. Helping to coach kids at football. So I suppose he could be doing that.' Her frown increases as she remembers her concerns. 'He met up with one of his teachers last night who took him to see the person running the club.' The two detectives remain silent. 'It's all above board, he told me not to worry.'

She catches the detectives exchange a glance. She's starting to feel light-headed with the mother of all headaches beginning to stir. 'He's usually really good with things like that, but he was excited about this new opportunity.'

'Did Maddox perhaps mention the name of the teacher he was meeting?' Brewster says, his pen poised above the notebook.

Liv shakes her head and braces herself to be told Maddox is suspected of stealing an iPhone. 'What's going on? What reports have you heard from the school?'

'We're yet to confirm the details, but the academy Maddox attends has received several reports of possible county lines drug activity in the vicinity of the school,' Helena says.

'County lines?' *Drugs?* Oh please, God... no. Liv feels sick.

'Known drug dealers are recruiting young people in rural areas to deal their drugs, thereby extending their reach and boosting profits,' Brewster provides.

'Oh God!' Liv's hand flies to her mouth. 'And you think Maddox might be involved in this?'

'That's why we're here,' Brewster says. 'To make sure Maddox is safe. He was seen talking to a known drug dealer close to the school.'

Liv feels like she might faint. Her head is spinning even though she is sitting down. Everything seems to instantly fall into place. Maddox hasn't stolen the new phone at all.

He's bought it with money he's earned from dealing.

TWENTY-FOUR

KAIT

Daniel is attending a three-day training conference in Newcastle today and so left the house earlier than usual at 6 a.m. He'll be going straight to work on Tuesday from check-out, so won't be home till Tuesday evening. I heard him get up and shower, was aware of him leaning over me and kissing me on the cheek. I murmured a goodbye, turned over and went back to sleep.

Later, I wake naturally and know it's after seven by the light filtering through the bedroom curtains. I yawn and reach over for my phone. I always turn it to silent before I turn off the lamp, but I see the screen is lit up with an incoming call. It's 07:11 and only Daniel would call me this early. I yank it off the charging cable and immediately answer. 'Hello?'

'Kait? Sorry it's early, but—'

'Oh, Kirsten... it's you!'

There's a split-second hesitation from my sister. 'Is Daniel there with you?'

'What? No. Daniel left at six for a training conference up in—'

'Listen. I was right about the note and the UPN standing

for Unique Pupil Number,' Kirsten says a little breathlessly. 'My assistant, she checked it out and that is a valid number.'

'OK,' I say, a little baffled why I need to know this so early in the morning.

'Thing is, my assistant, Claire, she's... let's just say, very resourceful and she used one of her contacts to get a bit more information.'

'About the number?'

'Yes. About who it belongs to.' Kirsten pauses. 'It's just... I want to check that you're happy for me to give you this information, Kait. I don't want to force anything on you or give you even more to worry about.'

I let out a nervous laugh. 'This all sounds a bit dramatic. Just tell me.'

A moment's pause. 'OK, so that particular UPN belongs to a fourteen-year-old boy called Maddox Leigh. He attends Fairlawns Forest Academy in Clifton.'

F Forest – that had been the start of the note. According to Kirsten's assistant, it's an abbreviation for Fairlawns Forest Academy.

It still doesn't make much sense. I'm not sure it means anything at all. It could be the details of a client's son or something. But then... why wouldn't Daniel have just said that? Why would he act so strangely and lie, and insist it was a training platform reference?

'Kait, are you still there?'

'Yes, sorry. I'm just thinking.'

'I couldn't come over and tell you myself because I'm just about to board a train with a colleague to London for the weekend, as have client meetings there over the next few days and... well, I thought you should know right away.'

'It doesn't mean much to me at the moment. It's a strange one.'

'Kait, I hate to do this over the phone, but I want you to have all the information I've been given.' In the background, a loud-speaker announcement about train arrivals makes it harder to hear her. 'I'm sending you an email containing a bit more information. If you want to talk later today when I get to my hotel, just text me. OK?'

'OK,' I say, a bit non-plussed. 'What else did you—'

'Got to go, love. Train is just in. Speak soon.' And Kirsten ends the call.

I check my emails but there's nothing come through yet. I pop my phone back on the bedside table, slip out of bed and stand in front of the full-length mirror on the back of the bedroom door. I pull my nightie fabric tightly around my stomach, framing it, turning side to side to gauge its size. Like every morning, I say a silent prayer to keep my baby growing safe and sound.

I'm trying to take care of myself as I've been told to do by the hospital, but it's so much harder to do when my head is full of doubt and worry.

I pull on my fleecy dressing gown, slip the phone in my pocket and go downstairs to make a cup of tea. It's still early enough to feel cool in the kitchen with its wide glass doors, and I slip my feet into cosy slippers while I wait for the kettle to boil.

I take my drink into the living room, leaving the white, wooden slats of the blind closed, and flick on a lamp. I put the breakfast news on the TV and pick up my phone again.

As I refresh my emails, a new one pops up.

From: Kirsten Reeves
To: Kaitlyn Hatton
Re: Information

Just confirming those details:

I'm attaching all the info here. DO NOT SHARE.

If you want to talk, call me later. After six if poss.

Sending love, K

Do not share? With whom? I'm hardly going to share it with Daniel, that would be tantamount to admitting I don't trust him to the extent I've got Kirsten on the case. He already considers her overbearing and interfering; it would be like a red rag to a bull.

I double-click on the attachment and a scanned image of a one-page form loads.

PUPIL INFORMATION RECORD

CONFIDENTIAL

School Name: *Fairlawns Forest Academy*

STUDENT DETAILS:
UPN ref (12 digits): *X17 314 907 2600*

Name: *Maddox LEIGH*
Address: *58 Pinewood Gardens, Clifton Estate, Nottingham*
D.O.B: *09/10/2009*

Contact Details:
Parent/Guardian 1: *Ms Olivia Leigh*
Home phone: *0115 9784 6351*
Work phone: *0115 9223 7300*
Contact work: *Y/N*
Email: *OliviaL_79@gmail.co.uk*

Parent/Guardian 2: *N/A*

I scan down the form. All this means nothing to me. I know Kirsten just wants to help but her assistant has dug up confidential details of something that is nothing to do with Daniel.

I come to the end of the contact details and then the form is blank until the line:

Photo ID: *Maddox Leigh*

When the photograph loads, I can't tear my eyes away from the dark curls, the pale skin and those intense blue eyes.

My eyes swim, the details blurring in front of me. It feels as if fireworks are exploding in my head.

I don't know this good-looking boy. I've never met him and I've certainly never spoken to him.

But it's going to be impossible to ignore him any longer, because Maddox Leigh bears a striking resemblance to Daniel and that tells me I was right.

My husband is a liar and a cheat.

TWENTY-FIVE

RICH

Not in Rich's wildest dreams did he believe that only two months after his first meeting with Caleb, he and Livvy would be firm friends with Caleb Mosley and his wife, Alicia.

After meeting at the conference, Caleb took Rich under his wing, introduced him to invaluable contacts way beyond his reach and coached him in in the hidden tips and tricks of successful property development. The two men often sat for hours in Caleb's glass-walled office that overlooked Battersea Park in London, drinking twenty-one-year-old single malt Glenlivet whisky. Rich listened patiently to Caleb's seemingly endless tales of his late father and his struggles with his illness.

'You're the only person that really gets it,' Caleb repeatedly told him. 'The only one who's been through the same thing.'

Livvy and Alicia got on like a house on fire. They often met up for lunch or shopping when Livvy would come home with a designer silk scarf or once, an expensive cashmere sweater that Alicia had insisted on treating her to. Although Caleb and his wife hadn't got children of their own, they enjoyed lavishing attention and gifts on Maddox. He was now signed up to a private Saturday-morning football training academy exclusively for tots.

Happily, Rich's mum was a willing babysitter on the weekends the two couples would meet up for a drink or dine out at top-notch restaurants. Recently, they'd all enjoyed a short break in London together, taking in a few tourist sights and a West End show. Rich couldn't believe how quickly their lives had changed for the better, and yet, Livvy being Livvy, she managed to find something to worry about.

'I love going out with Caleb and Alicia,' she said one day when they sat on the neat patio of their newly landscaped cottage garden enjoying a glass of wine while Maddox played on his small slide. 'But we've used up our overdraft again this month. You must have noticed.'

Rich's stomach tightened. He had no choice but to brazen this out and appear as convincing as possible.

'It's only temporary.' He took a big gulp of wine. 'I'll get on to the bank in the morning, get them to increase our limit.'

Livvy put down her glass. 'That's not what I meant, Rich. We're clearly living beyond our means. It's impossible for us to sustain a lifestyle similar to the Mosleys'. We just can't do it.'

'Caleb paid for the hotel last weekend. They always shoulder the expensive bits without being asked.' They'd all gone for a night to London to see *The Lion King*. Caleb had very generously booked them two suites at the Mandarin Oriental. 'My treat,' he'd insisted when Rich had tried to protest.

'Yes, and it was amazing. But then you insisted on booking the show tickets which cost us a small fortune.'

'What could I do? I had to offer, and the tickets cost a lot less than the hotel.'

Livvy groaned. 'You're missing the point, Rich. We're socialising with high rollers here. Drinks, meals, even buying new outfits to go to the fancy places they take us... Caleb and

Alicia have been rich for so long, it doesn't even occur to them we can't afford to take turns buying bottles of champagne. It's going to bankrupt us if we're not careful!'

He'd put down his wine and held her hand. 'Try and think of it as an investment, a fast-track to the most influential people and deals so good there's barely any risk. In a few months, we won't have any money problems because thanks to Caleb, I've got something coming to fruition that's going to make us very well off.'

'What's that, exactly?' Livvy frowned and pulled her hand away. 'You've never mentioned anything recently. Only that dodgy Spanish villa devel... oh no! Don't tell me you've sunk a load of money into that after we talked about it!'

'Not a *load* of money exactly, just what we can afford.' He forced a smile, pushing thoughts of the secret maxed-up credit cards and bank loans she didn't know about out of his head. And the rest of it. If Livvy found out what he'd done, she'd take Maddox and leave him tomorrow. There was no two ways about it. 'My job is shouldering any business worries. Your job is to continue being the wonderful mum you are to Maddox.'

'My job matters too,' she said, her features knotting. 'I might not earn much, but I like to think I'm making a difference.'

Rich would never understand why Livvy insisted on keeping her part-time job at the local school. It fitted in well with Maddox, who was enrolled into a private nursery on the days she worked. But after his childcare fees were paid, Livvy's salary was almost wiped out anyway. Who'd choose to go out to work when there was no need to?

'Course I know you're making a difference. I'm just asking you to trust me in what I do for us, Livvy. I need you to believe in my ability to build a successful business.'

'I *do* believe in you,' she said softly, her finger tracing the face of his new Breitling watch that cost three times the amount he told her. 'I always have. I just worry you're getting carried away with the big dream.'

'I'm dealing with facts, not dreams. Soon, we'll be able to live this kind of life without even having to think about an overdraft and that's a fact. You'll see.' He stood up, drained his wine and held out his hand for a glass. 'Fancy another one?'

TWENTY-SIX

MADDOX

He takes his time walking back to the house. His mum probably won't be expecting him back yet. She'll assume he's gone to his usual Saturday morning football practice, so he's got plenty of time before she starts thinking about where he's got to. She doesn't need to know he's skipped footie practice for the first time ever. In fact, after his conversations with Sammy last night, the less she knows, the better.

He turns off the main road and enters the small park on his right where he'd walked Betsy before leaving the house this morning. There are a couple of young mums in there talking over takeaway coffees with little kids on the climbing frame but other than that the park is empty. Maddox sits down on a wooden bench at the far end of the grass and watches as a little kid zooms in on a yellow stunt scooter. Behind him is a man who is obviously his dad. They head for the kids' play area where the boy abandons his scooter and runs over to the swings.

The man picks up the scooter and leans it against a bench.

'Dad! Push me, Dad!' The kid laughs. 'Push me, high as the sky!'

A buzzing sound starts in Maddox's head. *Push me, high as*

the sky! A flash of blurred trees... throwing his head back... staring up at a blue sky while he whooshes: back and forth. A tall figure pushing and laughing, his face eclipsed by the light... his dad. His own dad.

Maddox squeezes his eyes shut to dispel the pictures in his head and hugs his arms around himself. He feels hot and a bit disorientated from walking too long in the sun. The squeals and laughter of the children fade as he thinks about last night and about what it means.

Yesterday, he ditched school and met Brandon mid-morning behind the shopping arcade as the text in the early hours of the morning had instructed.

Maddox raised his hand as he approached, but Brandon scowled back over the top of his vape.

'Alright?' Maddox said, as he drew closer.

'Do you know Sammy?' Brandon puffed out vapour.

'Yeah, course. I met him last—'

'No. I mean do you *properly* know him,' Brandon snapped. 'Like from before.'

Maddox frowned. 'No. How could I?'

Brandon said nothing and watched him through narrowed eyes, as if he was trying to make up his mind whether to believe Maddox. 'A car is coming for us in ten,' he said at last, checking his watch.

'Where are we going?'

Brandon shrugged. 'That's just it. I don't know. I'm supposed to show new recruits how it's done, right? I'm supposed to be their boss. But Sammy has different plans for you.'

Maddox looked at him, alarmed. 'Huh? Different like how?'

'How should I know?' Brandon scuffed his trainers on the pavement. Maddox could see he was put out about it.

Maddox scratched at the new patch of eczema on his hand. 'Where will the car take us?'

Brandon scowled. 'You're being dropped off at Sammy's place. Don't ask me any more questions.'

Maddox had felt his heart beat in his throat. This wasn't the expected plan, and obviously Brandon was puzzled, too. It felt like things were getting out of hand. Was it too late to make a run for it?

Maddox had looked up and down the street. There were no cars and no people around. He probably had three or four minutes tops to do one.

'Don't even think about doing anything stupid.' Brandon took a step towards him. 'I know where you live and more to the point, so does Sammy. You really don't want to hack Sammy off, trust me.'

Maddox had felt his breathing becoming shallower. The tight feeling in his chest was getting worse and his face felt like it was on fire.

'Don't worry about it.' Brandon eyed him cautiously. 'Everything's cool, man.'

But everything was far from cool because things had taken an unexpected turn. Even Brandon was surprised with Sammy's unusual interest in him.

The car had pulled up a few seconds later, its exhaust growling, engine roaring. Maddox recognised it as a souped-up Toyota with an outsized spoiler. He'd seen shots of them on TikTok reels filmed at illegal car meets.

Brandon opened the passenger door and pulled the front seat forward. 'Get in the back,' he said curtly.

Awkwardly, Maddox climbed into the half-size back and folded his long legs behind the driving seat. He was the tallest lad in his class and his mum reckoned he'd be over six foot within a couple more years. But he didn't want to think about his mum and what she might say if she could see him right now.

The driver didn't look at him or say a word. He wore a dark-grey hoodie pulled low on to his forehead. Maddox laid his head against the window and looked out miserably. He was officially an idiot for getting involved with these monkeys, but he had to face reality. He'd made the decision and all he could do now was to find a way out of his commitment before he was asked to do something illegal. He was happy to return the cash Sammy had given him. He just had to wait for an opportunity to explain he couldn't be involved now, after all.

After a ten-minute drive to the outskirts of town, the car turned into a big retail park.

Brandon pointed and mumbled something to the driver, and he slowed down, came to a stop outside a vast, brightly coloured bowling alley.

Maddox sat up straighter as Brandon opened the passenger door, got out of the car and pulled the seat forward.

'This is it,' he said grouchily. 'You'll find Sammy in the café.'

Maddox extricated himself from the cramped back seat and before he could say goodbye to Brandon, the door slammed shut and the car roared away again.

He felt hot and sick. Genuinely afraid.

But Maddox had got himself into this mess and he knew it was up to him to get back out.

Now, a football soars through the air and lands at his feet, bringing him back to the moment. The little boy runs over and stops a few yards away.

'Can I have my ball back, please?' he says without meeting Maddox's eyes.

'Sure you can.' He kicks the ball and the kid dribbles it impressively before turning back and kicking it towards his dad.

Maddox watches them for a few moments, a strange, hollow feeling in his chest.

He needn't have worried about seeing Sammy. He found him as soon as he arrived, sitting there in the bowling alley café, scrolling. The place was nearly empty of kids. Everyone would be at school where Maddox should be. He'd never ditched school before and he didn't feel great about doing so, but what choice did he have?

When he saw Maddox, Sammy put down his phone, stood up and patted him affectionately on the back. 'Glad you could make it, buddy.'

He didn't look nearly as scary as he had in the dim light of the car the night before. He had similar hair to Maddox but his looked cooler, partly slicked back.

'I've booked us a lane. I thought we'd have a couple of games then grab a burger and fries and have a chat. That OK with you, mate?'

Maddox swallowed down his surprise. 'I... yeah, that's good. Thanks, Sammy.' *He must be up to something*, Maddox thought, but he wasn't about to say so.

'Cool. Let's go then.'

They had a brilliant time. Sammy made him laugh and Maddox relaxed within a short time. They chatted about all sorts of things and thankfully, Sammy didn't question him about his home life as he had done in the car.

Over a burger, chips and a Pepsi, Maddox felt confident enough to speak up.

'It's been great today, thanks, Sammy. I thought... I wasn't sure what to think.'

'Go on. You thought what?'

'I felt nervous about coming here.'

Sammy grinned. 'Really? Nervous in what way?'

'I thought that—' Maddox hesitated again. Considered the right way to express himself. 'I thought you might ask me to do something illegal. Like... different to what Brandon said it would be.'

Sammy looked at him in this strange, intense way, pressing his face close and, for an awful moment, Maddox thought he was going to actually *kiss* him, which would have been beyond weird. School were always reminding them of gross stuff like the dangers of being groomed. The big sign was someone you just met taking care of you, buying you stuff, making you feel good, so you want to please them.

Now, the weight of his iPhone feels comforting in his pocket, but he shrugs off the thoughts. He's not an idiot and Sammy isn't a creepy perv. He's sure of that.

He thinks back to Sammy's response: 'No, lad. Nothing like that. You're meant for better things than the shit life the rest of the young ones aspire to. You're special. D'ya hear me?'

Momentarily mute, Maddox simply nodded. Now *that* was a slightly weird thing to say...

'Look. I know you've had it tough, losing your dad like you did. The memories you had of him all but erased. That's not right. It's not right at all.'

Maddox couldn't think of one thing to say. So he stayed quiet.

'There's something I need you to do for me, Maddox. Something that requires you to trust me.'

'OK,' he said quietly, drawing out the word. His mouth felt dry and the panic that had filled his chest earlier began to rise again.

Sammy inched his chair closer and began to speak in a low, urgent voice, telling him what he needed him to do.

'Do you think you can do that?'

Maddox swallowed, not knowing how to react. 'I... I didn't think this would be the job. Brandon didn't say—'

'Brandon knows nothing about this,' Sammy said quickly. 'Nobody knows but me and you, and that's the way it's going to stay. Do you understand?'

'Yes,' Maddox replied meekly.

'Are you going to do what I've asked?'

Maddox nodded slowly. 'Yes.'

'Don't worry. I'm not going to ask you to talk about that very painful part of your life again,' Sammy said. 'You don't know me well enough yet. But in time, you will. I promise you that.'

Sammy had taken him through the process with a small laptop balanced on his knees, showing Maddox how to right click on entire folders in order to save the contents to the pen drive.

'It's important you don't rush, so give yourself time to do the job properly,' Sammy told him. 'If you want me to help you find out the truth about your dad, you need to make sure I get everything that's on there. Every last document. Any questions?'

Maddox shook his head. He'd used pen drives loads of times in I.T. lessons but he let Sammy do his thing.

Sammy reached inside his front jacket pocket and pulled something out.

'I've got a gift for you here, Maddox. Ask no questions. Just take it. It's yours.'

Then he slid a small, white envelope across the table.

'Look at it when you get home.' Sammy paused and added pointedly, 'Make sure you're alone.'

'What is it?' Maddox ran his fingers across the envelope; there was something flimsy inside but he couldn't quite get a clue as to what.

Sammy said, 'One thing you'll learn about me, is I've got ways and means of getting things that are out of most other people's reach. And I got this precious thing for you. When you see what's in the envelope, you'll understand why I'm trying to get to the truth. We'll catch up soon, yeah?'

Now, Maddox looks across the park to the roundabout where the small boy is being spun faster and faster by his dad. He's squealing, his face red and alive with bubbling laughter.

'Faster, Dad!' he yells. 'Faster, faster!'

Maddox smiles and takes the envelope out of his pocket. He

looks at it, front and back. There is nothing written on the front of it.

While the boy's squealing and yelling fades into the background, Maddox inserts his fingertip at the top edge of the envelope and, very carefully and very slowly, he tears open the sealed flap.

TWENTY-SEVEN

NOTTINGHAMSHIRE POLICE

Helena is walking back from the kitchen with a glass of water for Liv when a key rattles in the front door. A tall boy with wild dark curls and pale skin stands in the open doorway, looking instantly alarmed.

'Are you Maddox?' Helena says, giving him a smile that is not returned.

'Who are you?' He closes the door behind him and throws his key on the stairs. Calls out. 'Mum?'

Helena nods towards the living room. 'Your mum's not feeling too good. She's in there.'

He shrugs off his jacket and stalks past Helena, without answering her.

He stops dead a few steps in, when he sees Brewster sitting there, causing Helena to pull up short behind him to avoid spilling the water. 'Mum? What's going on?'

'It's OK, love. Come on in, the detectives need to talk to you.' Liv takes the water and looks at Helena. 'This is my son, Maddox.'

'Detectives?' Maddox frowns.

'Hello, Maddox. I'm DS Kane Brewster, and this is DI Helena Price,' Brewster says pleasantly. 'We dropped by today to make sure you're OK.'

Maddox stuffs his hands into his pockets. 'Why wouldn't I be?'

'Well, we've had a couple of concerning incidents reported by your school.'

Helena watches as Maddox's naturally pale complexion drains further of colour. 'Hopefully there's nothing to worry about,' she says. 'Sit down and we'll have a chat.'

'I don't know anything,' Maddox says, remaining standing.

'You don't know anything about what?' Brewster says.

'Anything. Whatever the concerning incidents are.'

'Maddox, sit down.' Liv looks perplexed. 'What's got into you?'

Maddox sits down next to his mum but doesn't look at her.

'Your deputy headteacher contacted us concerning possible county lines activity in the vicinity of the school,' Helena says. 'Have you heard the phrase "county lines", Maddox?'

'No,' the boy mumbles.

'It concerns known drug dealers attempting to recruit young people in more rural areas to deal for them,' Brewster says, his expression grim. 'This recruitment often takes place close to secondary schools, and we've come by today to ask if anyone has tried to get you involved in anything like this.'

Maddox laughs. 'As if!'

'Maddox! Don't be so disrespectful!' Liv's cheeks redden as she regards Helena and Brewster. 'I'm so sorry. He's not usually like this.'

Helena hears the slight softening of her words. A slurring.

Helena looks sternly at the boy. 'This is no laughing matter, Maddox. These people can be highly dangerous, even if they appear friendly to begin with.'

Maddox stares straight ahead, a surly expression on his face. 'Like I said, I don't know anything about it.'

'Concerned parents and members of staff have reported suspicious activity to the school leadership team and your name was mentioned as someone they'd seen talking to a previous student of the school.' Brewster checks his notebook. 'Brandon McFadden. An older boy recently excluded from Fairlawns Forest. Does that name ring a bell, Maddox?'

'No,' Maddox says, still refusing to look at Brewster.

'Thing is, your deputy head, Mr Patel, he told us a member of staff, Mr Pinfold, was so concerned to see you with Brandon, he stopped his car to ask if you were OK a couple of days ago.'

'Is this true, Maddox?' Liv says faintly, her hand touching her throat.

'I might've spoken to Brandon, but it wasn't about drugs,' Maddox says easily. 'We were just having a chat.'

'A chat about what, exactly?' Brewster presses him.

Maddox shrugs. 'What he's been up to. Football. That kind of thing.'

Helena says, 'So Brandon didn't ask you to work for him, or for someone he knows?'

'Nope.'

Helena watches as he touches the pocket on the front of his thin denim jacket.

'Where is it you've been this morning?' Brewster says. 'Just now, before you came back home? Your mum said you're supposed to let her know if you go out, but you didn't.'

Brewster watches as the lad hesitates. 'I just went out. Football training.' He glances at the wall clock. 'I just hung around for a bit before coming home.'

'So, when we leave here and find Brandon McFadden, he's going to back up your story, is he? That you just chatted about what he's been up to and discussed football?'

Maddox's head spins round to face him. 'Don't drag Brandon into this, he's done nothing wrong.'

Brewster's voice hardens. 'When you say, "drag him into this", what's "this" exactly?'

'I don't know! Whatever it is you're going on about,' Maddox snaps.

'What's in your pocket, Maddox?' Helena says.

'What?' His fingers flutter over his top pocket and his belligerent attitude dissolves in an instant.

'You've been touching that pocket since you sat down. What do you have in there?'

'None of your business.'

'Maddox, apologise this instant! This isn't how you've been raised.' Liv stands up unsteadily. 'Have your got something in your pocket?'

'No.' Maddox folds his arms and looks at Brewster. 'Gonna strip and search me, are you?'

'Not at this stage, but don't push your luck,' Brewster instantly responds.

Maddox stands up. 'Can I go up to my room now?'

Liv looks at the detectives for approval.

Helena gets up from the armchair. 'Try and remember, Maddox, we're just trying to look out for you. We're on your side.'

Maddox stares at the wall and doesn't answer.

'Thank you both for your time.' Brewster hands Liv a business card. 'If you or Maddox need to get in touch about anything we've discussed today, there's a direct line here you can call.'

'I hope you've told them the truth,' Liv tells Maddox. 'I'd better not find out you've been lying.'

Maddox turns to face his mum, a sneer on his face. 'That's rich, coming from you.'

Colour rises in Liv's face like a crimson tide. Helena and Brewster exchange a glance.

'What are you talking about?' Her eyes dart to her son. 'Be quiet. You don't know what you're saying.'

'I do, though!' Helena looks from the boy's clenched fists to his sparking, tearful eyes. 'I know you've been lying to me for years about my dad.'

TWENTY-EIGHT

KAIT

My insides have turned to liquid. I've thrown up twice in between pacing around the house, racking my brains as to what's been happening behind my back.

I wanted to be wrong. I wanted Daniel to be true and loyal and honest, but he's turning out to be worse than even I could have imagined.

I can't seem to sit still, but I've forced myself back into the living room now to try and calm down. My tea has gone cold, and the lamps are still on in here despite the light flooding in through the slatted blinds.

Since I set eyes on the photograph of Maddox Leigh, the safe, loving life I've been building around me is now falling away bit by bit, like rotting leaves. When I fell in love with Daniel, I vowed to put the past behind me and start again. All the strange vibes I've had over the past couple of months that I've tried to shrug off, tried to convince myself I might be imagining, the constant niggling suspicion that he is up to something, maybe having an affair... it's all turned out to be completely valid.

I keep going hot and cold. I'm shivering.

Could it really be that Daniel has a secret son and that son has a mother, Olivia Leigh? Another family. People who were there way before he met me.

It feels real. It's really happening and my heart is breaking.

In the same way I've suspected things are wrong, I feel I know deep down now that Maddox Leigh is Daniel's son. A fourteen-year-old boy he's kept secret, kept silent and hidden away. His mother, a woman living nearby that he had a child with years before.

It's a forbidden area of his life he didn't want me to know anything about. The stuff he's done, the lives he's ruined... Daniel Hatton is rotten to the core.

I place my hand on my bump. She is my first child. But not his.

The day I told him I was pregnant, tears streamed down his face as he took me in his arms. 'I've wanted to be a father for so long. I'd almost given up hope it would happen,' he sobbed, holding me so tight I could hardly breathe. 'This is the best feeling in the whole world. I've never felt anything like it.'

I was three months pregnant before I even knew about it. I'd had what I considered to be a couple of light periods. I bought a pregnancy test while Daniel was at work. It confirmed I was having a baby.

I didn't know how I felt... confused, joyful but afraid that it wouldn't be what Daniel wanted. He'd been acting strangely for a few weeks by then and I just felt unsure.

In the end I told Daniel by showing him a picture of the three-month scan. That's when he cried and said all those wonderful things he didn't mean.

My body sags with a heavy dread as I reach for my phone. I'm so sad. And raging. A brief flutter of worry about my blood pressure and stress levels passes over me, but what can I do? I've got to deal with this. Got to face reality.

I should call Daniel. Tell him not to come home.

But then would it be best to tell him to come home and pack his things before leaving? To have it out with him and get some answers?

I unlock the screen and then put the phone down like it's burning my hands. I want to cry and scream. I want to forget the stupid note that fell out of his back pocket and pretend everything is OK.

I want him to beg for my forgiveness, tell me he can't live without me and our baby.

But before any of that, I need hard facts. Evidence. It's not enough that I know the truth in my heart. I owe it to my child that if I break up with her father before she's even born, I can say I made the effort to be one hundred per cent certain of the truth.

Even thinking about it makes me feel like I'm suffocating. I can't just sit here, doing nothing so I get up and walk out of the room.

I open the door at the end of the hallway and walk into Daniel's small, organised office. He spends a lot of time in here but there's not much paperwork lying around. His iMac sits front centre on his desk and there's a pot of pens and pencils and a yellow legal-type notebook on there with nothing written on it.

I sit down in his ergonomic Herman Miller office chair, which cost a small fortune when he kitted out his office last year.

'I work with too many people suffering from dodgy necks and creaking backs, thanks to sitting in chairs that promote bad posture for years,' he'd said when my mouth dropped open at the cost.

But I knew it wasn't the pain of his clients that spurred him on. Not really. As I'd got to know Daniel better, I realised that despite a frugal childhood and having parents who disagreed with any kind of material excess, he simply coveted expensive things. More than that, he genuinely believed he deserved the best of everything and had some catching up to do. Seeing his wealthy clients made him both aspire to that life for himself, for us, and also made him bitter that he might never quite reach those levels of financial security.

That's why I was surprised he'd chosen personal training as a career. It wasn't an obviously money-making venture. But Daniel didn't agree.

'You never know where things might lead,' he'd said.

There are three small drawers stacked down one side of his pedestal desk. They're all unlocked, so I open each one in turn and check out the contents. They house plenty of printer paper, sticky notes and paper clips and staples, but nothing out of the ordinary. Nothing to shed any light on my suspicions.

For a man who strives for a paperless office, most of this stuff seems redundant. I look at the large computer on his desk, wiggle the mouse to wake the screen and tap in Daniel's birthday: 080881. It lets me in right away, but I'm not surprised; Daniel has always been open with passwords for his personal devices.

He regularly attends training courses in different parts of the country and is sometimes away overnight. On those occasions, he takes his laptop with him but his desktop computer is always here, in his office. Freely available to me and for that reason, I've never thought to snoop. But it's just occurred to me that the two devices will be synced via the cloud. The contents should be identical.

I've never searched his office before today. Not once. Even during the last couple of months when I've managed to convince myself he's up to something, I haven't gone through his things. Until now. Perhaps the risk I might find something has always subconsciously outweighed the drive to do it. I don't know.

But now, I remember what he's capable of. I need to get to the truth.

My own computer desktop in the spare room is crowded with apps, including lots I haven't used for ages, but Daniel's desktop is pristine and organised like the rest of his office. There are a grand total of ten icons on there including an Office for Mac collection and various fitness monitoring apps.

I open up the documents and scan down the folders. *Clients. Workout sheets. Fitness reviews.* I open them all and scan down the list, double-clicking on random entries to check the contents.

Next, I do a blanket search of his documents for the name: Maddox Leigh.

Nothing comes up.

Next, I type in: Olivia Leigh. Nothing.

On Safari, I open up his search history and browse the list of websites visited. Training platforms, sports equipment wholesalers, nutrition information.

And then I find it.

A screenshot of a bank statement in Daniel's name alone with nearly three hundred thousand pounds showing on the balance.

Back in the kitchen, I force myself to stop endlessly turning over possibilities in my head and face the facts. I was under the impression our finances were joint and yet I've discovered Daniel has an account with a hell of a lot of money in it that he's kept secret from me. The fact that Daniel has lied to me about his personal finances has added fire to my determination to find out exactly who Olivia and Maddox Leigh are.

I push my still-raging thoughts away and try to focus. First, I open the attachment on Kirsten's email on my phone and read it through again. Then I take a screenshot of the form. I fetch my laptop from the sitting room, sit on the sofa and open up Facebook.

I search for Olivia Leigh and I get about twenty results. The women I sift through are mostly too young or live in the wrong country, but there are three possible matches, which I look at closer. I quickly rule out the shortlist. Two of the women look too old to be the mother of a fourteen-year-old and the final one lives in Cornwall.

I have her address right in front of me on Daniel's information form. I open Google Maps and enter the details. She and her son live just a twenty-two-minute drive from here, the house I've bought with Daniel and where my newborn daughter will live.

I clamp my hand to my mouth and squeeze my eyes shut. How could he do this to us?

Is this where he's been going when he finishes work or when he's supposedly out delivering protein supplements to his clients? The boy, Maddox, is fourteen years old... this is obviously an old liaison. Has he been in a continuous relationship with Olivia since meeting me and were they ever married? Maddox and his mother have a different surname to Daniel. He told me he'd been working on the oil rigs off the shores of Scotland until just before we met. If that's the truth then maybe they broke up years ago.

I try Instagram next and get similar results. There is no Olivia Leigh profile that fits the information I have about her.

I look at the screenshot of the pupil information form again. There are two workplaces for Olivia detailed there. I google the first one, a primary school in Clifton.

The home page of Highview Primary loads and I click on the 'About Us' tab. A mini-menu appears and I go for the 'Meet the Staff' option.

I hold my breath as I scroll down the management team and

the class teachers until my eyes settle on the fourth photograph down in the support staff section.

Ms Liv Leigh. Not Olivia! I read the short bio piece.

Ms Leigh is a member of our valued teaching-assistant team and has worked at Highview for six years. Liv says, 'Our pupils are all so lovely, it's a privilege to be trusted with their care and supporting their education. I can honestly say, I look forward to coming into work each day!'

I double-click on the thumbnail head and shoulders shot to enlarge the image.

Liv Leigh is in her mid-forties with light-brown wavy hair cut into a blunt bob. She's attractive with soft brown eyes, full lips and clear skin and she is smiling in the photograph. She seems friendly and approachable – the kind of person you could trust with the care of your child. The kind of person you could easily confide in or talk to as a parent.

My mind starts to whirl through awful possibilities. Does Daniel enjoy intimate chats – and possibly more than that – with her?

A seething jealous fury surges within me. It's a hard nut lodged fast in my throat.

I dip my head one side then the other to try and ease the tension in my neck and shoulders. I swallow but the nut won't budge.

Looking back at the student contact form, my eyes settle on her mobile phone number. Her email address.

Does Liv Leigh know Daniel is married to me and that we're having a baby together? I've noticed his increasing absences, but he's never gone long enough or often enough that he can be carrying on a full life with her and his teenage son, too. She *must* know about me, if he's visiting them.

Two other things have occurred to me. Why would Daniel write down the name of the academy and the Unique Pupil Number of his own son? Surely that is something he should already have. Backing up the possibility that something is wrong is the fact the form contains information for one parent only. 'N/A' has been handwritten next to the details requested for parent/guardian #2. The name 'Daniel Hatton' does not appear anywhere on the form.

On balance, it all seems to suggest that Daniel is not currently in contact with Maddox or his mum. Maybe he has his son's UPN so he can remotely track his academic progress. Kirsten said parents use apps for everything these days to keep in contact with school – from paying for students' lunches and trips to obtaining up-to-date feedback on their assessments and progress.

So far, of course, this is pure speculation. I will never know the full truth of the matter until someone in the know tells me. Daniel has consistently batted away all my efforts to speak to him about his changing behaviour. If I confront him with what I have about Maddox, he'll no doubt try and convince me that's all in my head, too.

There is really only one person who can give me the answers I need and that's when I make my mind up.

I need to speak to Olivia Leigh.

Later that day, Helena watches Brewster pacing around like a cat on hot bricks the whole time she's on the seven-minute call to HQ. When she finishes, he immediately strides over.

'Boss, remember you were convinced Olivia Leigh was hiding something from us?'

'Hmm...' Half-listening, Helena starts to make notes on the outcome of her conference call. If she doesn't get stuff down quickly, there's a danger she'll forget key milestones that were agreed, and the super is not going to be impressed with that.

She looks at Brewster, sees that terrier glint in his eye. He's clearly not going to go away until he's said his piece. 'You were saying?'

'I think I found out what it was you were sensing at the Leigh house.' He hesitates. 'I can see you're busy, but can you come over to my desk? It'll take five minutes, tops.'

Helena puts down her pen and smiles despite her growing irritation. Nothing Brewster has ever shown her has taken only five minutes but, there again, he doesn't often interrupt her if she's busy unless there's good reason.

She pushes her chair back. 'I've got a meeting with the

super in an hour's time.' They both know Superintendent Della Grey is not a woman who appreciates being kept waiting.

Brewster's expression brightens. 'Message received and understood, boss, but I can assure you it *is* good. It's also interesting and unusual and... well, it's best if I can just show you.'

When Helena sits down, Brewster taps his keyboard, and the monitor comes to life. A newspaper report fills the screen.

'This article is four years old,' he says and falls silent, allowing Helena to read it.

Missing local man presumed legally dead

The wife of a missing Nottinghamshire man has told the Post *of her sadness after receiving the news that her husband has now been legally presumed dead.*

Father-of-one Richard Askew – known to friends and family as Rich – had been missing from his home in Thunder Bridge, West Yorkshire since 13 October 2012. The self-employed property developer had taken his three-year-old son, Maddox, out kite flying to the local countryside for the afternoon, but he never returned home.

The alarm on that day was raised by Mr Askew's wife, Olivia. Police conducted a thorough local search and Maddox was found alone with no sign of his father.

The Post *reached out to Olivia Leigh, who now lives in Hucknall, Nottinghamshire, for comment.*

'Maddox is now ten years old and Rich has never been found. We're so very sad he has been declared as presumed dead. Now, it's time for my son and I to somehow find a way to move on from all the heartbreak. On that note, we ask that people respect our privacy and our right to finally put an end to any speculation following my husband's death.'

West Yorkshire Police had long suspected Mr Askew may have taken his own life on the day he disappeared or perhaps

*suffered a fatal accident after leaving the area for an unknown
reason.*

'Gosh, that's very sad,' Helena says when she finishes reading the report. 'And quite a turn-up for the books, too, bearing in mind Maddox accused Olivia of lying to him for years about his dad. How did you come across it, Brewster?'

'I did a basic search of Olivia and Maddox Leigh on the PNC. It threw up the police file on Richard Askew's disappearance and flagged the surname change from Askew to Leigh that Liv made a year after he'd gone missing. They moved from Thunder Bridge in West Yorkshire to Nottingham at that point in time, too. Natural she'd want to make a fresh start for the sake of her son, I suppose, but changing their identity seems to be a step too far.'

Helena nods. 'I'm not sure Richard Askew's disappearance is relevant to our county lines concerns, but it's very useful background information. We saw there was tension between Maddox and his mum yesterday and the boy mentioned his dad. The fact Richard Askew had been officially declared presumed dead four years ago will likely still be a major source of trauma for them both.'

Helena makes to stand up when Brewster says, 'I want to show you some interesting stuff in the investigation file, if you have a few more minutes?'

She hesitates. 'I could really do with getting back to my notes, Brewster. Can this wait?'

Brewster pulls a face. 'It can, but I think you'll kick yourself if you don't see what I've got to show you at the start of the investigation. It makes for interesting reading.'

'I'm sure it does—' Helena stands up '—but I'm not sure it's good use of our time to gen-up on a closed file for what seems like a fairly straightforward case.'

'But that's just it, boss. It wasn't straightforward at all.'

Helena stops and looks back at him. 'How so?'

'Olivia Askew, as she was still called back then, was initially suspected of involvement in her husband's disappearance. Detectives repeatedly interviewed her and basically took her life apart in the months following Richard Askew's disappearance.' Brewster pulls up an internal police report on the screen. 'Although she reported him missing, there were some facts that didn't add up. She was never charged, but the confidential case notes made by the senior investigating officer at the time make it clear they were never completely convinced of her innocence. They just couldn't gather enough evidence to prove it.'

'So, Maddox's comment about his mum lying to him about his dad... it's just possible there could be more to that than meets the eye,' Helena murmurs.

'My thoughts exactly.'

She turns around and walks back to her colleague's desk. 'OK, Brewster, you've just got yourself ten more minutes.'

THIRTY

LIV

After the detectives have left, Liv takes some paracetamol for her banging head and sits for a few minutes in the silence.

She feels so shaken. Despite feeling rotten, she's craving for a glass of wine to help steady her nerves, but that will only complicate matters. It's important she's clearheaded enough to think through all the information she's been given today. By the police and, inadvertently, by Maddox.

Turns out her gut feeling that her son is in trouble is correct. She can only pray that now the police are involved, any slide into him working for these county lines drug dealers will be firmly nipped in the bud.

Her boy – so bright and talented. Always managing to keep himself out of trouble and happy to focus entirely on his football and his dream of playing professionally. He's kept out of harm's way. Until now.

Things are changing. And there's something else that makes her want to throw up: Maddox's new off-hand attitude to the police, to her and – worst of all – his throwaway comment before he'd stormed upstairs.

I know you've been lying to me for years about my dad.

What did he mean? What could have possibly caused such an outburst? Certainly not the truth. He can't possibly know the truth of what happened. Nobody knows that but herself and Rich.

As much as it shames Liv to admit it, she's never sat down and addressed the issue of Rich's disappearance with her son. Never talked in depth and at length about it. She'd meant to, had always intended to. But the years rolled by and Maddox got a little older and... there it was. That old cliché: it was just never a right time. It had been better to smooth occasional troubled waters and change the subject than face the storm of emotions she'd buried herself and tried to protect her son from.

When he was about ten, he'd asked about his dad.

'What did he look like? Can I see some pictures of him?'

She'd told him she'd downloaded most of the family pictures from her old phone onto a hard drive which had since corrupted. The majority of photographs had been lost, she'd said. It was a lie, of course, but readily believed by her boy. She showed him a few snapshots and had given the police and press two or three photos when Rich had first gone missing and she'd made sure although they showed his face, they were just a little bit vague, taken at slightly off-centre angles. But the police and the press didn't know that. They'd even printed one of the old images when Rich had been declared as presumed dead.

Misleading Maddox might sound cruel to an outsider, but in Liv's opinion, it was far more heartless to show her son what he'd lost. She found it difficult enough to look at Rich's face herself, and to think back to the life they'd had together... before it had all gone so horribly wrong.

Liv stands up slowly and, her skull vibrating with each step, she climbs the stairs. Outside Maddox's bedroom, she listens in alarm. For the first time in possibly years there is silence. No TV on, no explosions or yelling from his gaming. Liv steels herself and then taps lightly on the door. There is no answer, so she taps again.

'Go away,' her son growls at last.

'Maddox, I just—'

'I don't want to talk to you.'

She pushes down on the handle and the door opens. He's lying on his bed, staring at something he's holding – a small, white piece of card – above his head. When she gets closer, she sees his face is streaked with tears.

'What's wrong, love? Can't you tell me?' She sits on the side of his bed, but he ignores her. Does not even glance her way. 'What have you got there?'

Slowly, he shifts himself up to a seated position and then turns the piece of card around so she can see it.

For a second or two Liv can't breathe.

When she speaks, her voice is hoarse, her throat instantly dry and sore. 'Where did you get that?'

She remembers the day she took the photograph. In the garden, at their chocolate-box cottage in Thunder Bridge. From the kitchen window, she'd watched as two-year-old Maddox and his dad kicked a ball about on the grass. It had been May or June, the two of them perfectly framed by the colourful wildflowers all around them. She had loved that house and garden so much, but they were another casualty. She'd had to leave.

Liv had gone outside with the camera. 'Say cheese, you two!'

Rich had scooped a beaming Maddox up in his arms and Liv had snapped the moment as they'd grinned at each other, her heart filled to the brim with love for the two of them. Rich looked so young in it. Taken from the side, his profile was slightly distorted by his wide grin and baseball cap. Liv frowns. She can't remember seeing this snap with the other photographs she'd scanned and then destroyed after Rich left.

She considers the possibility that Rich himself took it. But then how has it ended up in Maddox's hands? Unless...

Cold fingers close around her heart as she reaches for the grainy photograph, but Maddox snatches it further away.

'Don't you dare touch this. It's mine.' He presses it to his chest, his eyes welling up again. 'It's me and my dad.'

'Maddox, I need to know where you got the photograph,' she says again, more insistently. 'It's more important than you know.'

He narrows his eyes and glares at her. 'You told me they'd all gone. You said every single photograph of him had been burned.'

'That's true,' she says, swallowing down a barbed ball of guilt. 'This picture must have somehow escaped but... everything else was destroyed. So, whoever gave you this, they shouldn't have had it. I need you to tell me where you got it.'

'I needed *you* to tell me the truth about my dad, but you didn't.'

'Maddox!' She doesn't mean to snap but that's how it comes out. She needs to get it out of him. Whoever gave him that photo must know their history as a family. What if someone is trying to make trouble?

Nausea hits her and she has to battle not to throw up. 'Maddox, it's really important you tell me where you got it.'

'Someone gave it to me in the street,' he says petulantly. 'Just pushed it in my hand and walked off again.'

'What? Who was it?'

'I didn't recognise them,' he says, his voice deadpan.

'OK, so describe them to me.'

'I dunno. Some woman.' His expression darkens. 'I'm glad she did give it to me. At least I have something now.'

A woman?

Liv tries to breathe out the tension in her shoulders, but it holds fast. A year after Rich disappeared, she changed their names by deed poll and relocated to a completely different area of the country. All as she and Rich had agreed before he went.

So who is this woman who has a deeply personal photograph of Rich and Maddox? Someone who knows exactly who her son is and had the gall to approach him in the street all these years after Rich went missing?

Why would someone do that? The question has only one answer: whoever it is wants to cause trouble between Liv and her son.

She realises Maddox is staring at her. Expecting a reply.

'Whoever it was had no right to do that,' she manages to croak. 'I want you to think really carefully about what this woman looked like.'

'Why would I want her to get in trouble?' His face is pinched, his mouth set into a snarl. 'I respect her more than you, Mum. You've lied to me for years.'

'Maddox! Stop saying that. I have not lied to—'

'I saw stuff, Mum.' His voice drops quieter. 'On your laptop. So many locked files, but you must've forgotten to put a password on a few of them. I saw photographs of you and Dad. I know you've had pictures of him all this time and you've never let me see them. You've never talked about him; it's like you wanted to erase him from my life. As if he never existed. All I've ever had is the stuff printed in the newspapers... you kept it all from me. The truth.'

'Maddox, that's not true!'

Liv covers her face with her hands, silently berating herself. She might have known when she scanned the photos before destroying them, it would come back to haunt her. She'd been so careful. She'd hidden the folder and put a security passcode on each individual item in there but she must have missed some. Thought she'd got away with it after all this time.

The fact that Maddox has been given an actual surviving photograph fills her with terror.

She has no money and no way of contacting Rich. Now she knows there is someone out there who is clearly trying to cause trouble between her and her son. Liv feels like she's fading away. She has no leads whatsoever that can help her trace her supposedly deceased ex-husband.

And, as it stands, unless she wants to confess all to the two detectives and find herself in court and ultimately handed a prison sentence, there doesn't appear to be a single thing she can do about it.

THIRTY-ONE

RICH

THREE MONTHS BEFORE HIS DISAPPEARANCE

It was the failed Spanish property deal that floored him. His hundred-grand stake in a twelve-villa building project near Alicante had dissolved within hours when the developer unexpectedly declared bankruptcy.

Caleb had ignored Rich's calls apart from a short text message sent late which read simply:

Speak tomorrow, mate. Stuff to sort.

Rich howled in frustration, paced up and down the cottage's quaint beamed living room, only sitting down when Livvy appeared in her dressing gown in the doorway.

'Come to bed.' She yawned. 'I can see something's bothering you. I'll make some tea and we can talk about it.'

'I'm fine,' he said, snappier than he'd meant to be. 'Tea won't sort this out. Go back to bed, Livvy.'

He saw the hurt flutter over her concerned expression before she turned and closed the door quietly behind her. He'd stopped speaking to Livvy about anything to do with his business months ago, particularly as she'd expressed doubt and caution when he'd excitedly outlined the Spanish opportunity.

'So you're considering paying over a massive sum of money before the villas are even built yet?'

'It's called investing off-plan,' he'd explained. 'A bit riskier, but the rewards are often far higher. Besides, Caleb has green-lit this deal. He's sunk money in himself and that's good enough for me.'

'But Caleb's a multi-millionaire, Rich. You're just starting out and... well, it just sounds too good to be true, to me.'

He'd smarted, as if she'd slapped him across the face. He'd heard: *Caleb is a pro; you're just a clueless beginner.*

'I won't ask your advice in any business issues again,' he'd said icily. 'Now I know what you think about me.'

'What? It's the high-risk deal I haven't got faith in, not you!'

But he knew what she meant alright. He'd heard it constantly from his father, growing up: *You're not cut out to be a businessman, you're incapable of making sound decisions. You're a bad bet.*

He'd wasted a lot of time trying to prove Richard Arthur Askew Snr wrong, even though his father had been dead for ten years. But this deal was different. It had the power to give him all the validation he needed.

Livvy looked at him, her beautiful brown eyes full of hurt and worry. When he could stand it no longer, Rich grabbed his phone and car keys and left the house.

A sleepy, tousle-haired Caleb shrugged when he opened the door to Rich just before midnight. 'Mate, what can I say? You win some, you lose some in this game.'

'That's alright for you to say. That money's a drop in the ocean to you, but not to me.'

Caleb's bleary eyes sharpened. 'Hey, acting like a schoolboy won't make things any better. If you want to play with the big boys then you need to show some balls.'

'You said it was a sure-fire return.'

Caleb laughed and yawned. 'As far as any high-risk investment is a sure-fire return. Looks like I mis-judged you. I thought you'd mastered at least the basics.'

Rich's blood boiled in his veins. Someone else who'd written him off. 'I have! My problem was in trusting you.'

He bit back but it was too late. Caleb's expression darkened, his fists clenched. 'Be careful. Be very careful who you insult, my friend.'

'Sorry. I didn't mean to—'

Caleb raised a hand and Rich fell quiet.

'Tomorrow's another day, right? Get some rest. Something else will come along.'

Now the fury had left, Rich felt like a spent balloon. He could feel his eyes prickling. He'd considered Caleb a very good friend, but he was under no illusion now that Caleb's favourable attitude was conditional. Rich had seen how he could ridicule and ruthlessly put down people he didn't like or had gone off.

Rich had had enough ridicule growing up to last him a lifetime. He needed to get out of here before he became one of Caleb's casualties.

'Sorry for just turning up, but—'

'Hey, no worries, buddy.' Caleb reached forward and slapped his hand down just a tad too hard on Rich's shoulder. 'Take your mistakes and learn from them. That's how I do it and I reckon I know what I'm talking about, yeah?'

Rich nodded and turned away quickly before tears of frustration and panic spilled down his cheeks. The one mistake he'd learn from was trusting Caleb Mosley's investment tips.

He got back into his car and drove down the tree-lined avenue with its big, detached houses and sprawling front gardens. He turned left on to the deserted main road and pulled into a bus layby where he rested his forehead against the steering wheel and closed his eyes.

What the hell was he going to do now? The debt he'd incurred on the strength of this deal didn't bear thinking about. How the hell had his wonderful life suddenly turned to shit, literally overnight?

When he thought of Caleb Mosley's laughing, unconcerned face, a burning fury filled him again, rising through his stomach and chest and igniting a fire behind his eyes. Maybe it was time for someone to teach Caleb a lesson. Show him what happened when you played with other people's lives and feelings.

Rich opened his eyes, sat up and smashed his clenched fists down on to the steering wheel again and again and again.

'There's no way around it. My advice is to tell Olivia, and quickly, because I'm afraid you're almost certainly going to lose your house.'

Will Heaton, Rich's business lawyer for the last ten years, was notoriously laid-back. Over the time they'd known each other, Will – Rich's constant companion on the ups and downs of owning a small business – had constantly told him not to worry, that things were rarely as bad as they seemed.

There was no sign of that side of Will now. When Rich explained the situation briefly over the phone, Will cleared his diary and came over to the house while Livvy was at work. Now, he sat bolt upright, leaning forward across the desk, his face drawn and serious.

Rich felt prickles of sweat beading his upper lip. 'Surely there's something you can do legally to stave off the bank for a while. Caleb made it sound like a once-in-a-lifetime opportunity. I'd never have sunk everything I had in a risky deal.'

Will stared at him. 'You sank more than you had into this deal. You took out a huge bank loan secured on your house and—'

Rich's expression darkened. 'Thanks for the reminder.'

But Will was undeterred. 'That's why ninety-nine per cent of people check with their lawyers first and never, ever sign anything impulsively.'

'Yes, yes. Not helpful.' If Will couldn't help him then Rich just wanted him to go. Leave him to think. 'I've got another appointment soon, so we'll have to catch up later in the week.'

Will looked at him, incredulous. 'No appointment is more important than this one, Rich. Surely you realise that? We need to go through everything, see what the true impact of this disastrous decision is going to cost you.'

'I already know the answer to that,' Rich said vaguely, staring at the wall. 'It's going to cost me everything.'

THIRTY-TWO

KAIT

MONDAY

After another day of research, I'm consumed by the need to see Olivia Leigh and also to have sight of Maddox. With Daniel working away, that's what I pour my efforts into, driving to the school address on Maddox's student details form.

I'm taking a risk because there's no guarantee he'll be leaving after the bell. I know lots of schools have clubs that their students attend.

So I can't believe my luck when I see a woman with a dog standing at the gates and I realise it's Olivia. She must have decided to meet her son at the end of school.

The woman looks different in the flesh to her staff picture on the primary school's website. She is taller and older than me. Maybe five foot eight and in her mid-forties and her smooth-skinned face in the picture looks paler and slightly bloated. Dressed in casual loose clothes in dark colours, her mid-brown hair is pulled into a casual top knot with thick wisps escaping. She keeps sneezing and holding a tissue up to her face. Maybe that's why she looks so pale and worn out.

But it's definitely her.

I watch, barely breathing, as she scrolls through her phone, a frown playing between her eyebrows like something is bothering her. Every few seconds she looks across at the school gates and then back down at her screen again.

I stare at the sign on the boundary wall. *Fairlawns Forest.* Not a training place as Daniel had claimed. But a school. Possibly where his son attends.

Students begin to spill messily through the gates. All of them boys of around fourteen or fifteen carrying sports bags. Liv's face lights up as a tall boy with black curly hair and pale skin strides towards her. It's Maddox.

I sit in my car, rigid and staring, clasping my hands together and squeezing hard as I watch. The boy is tall for his age, but that's not what has shocked me. No, the thing that makes my blood run cold is that he is the spitting image of Daniel, even more so than in the pupil record photograph.

He once showed me a photograph of himself as a teenager and, from memory, Daniel and this boy could be twins at a similar age.

Maddox is scowling, clearly not happy to see his mum here. He ignores Liv and walks past her, looking around furtively as if he's checking who's noticed his mum has turned up to collect him.

Liv says something, slips her phone into her pocket and follows him. They are walking in the opposite direction to where I'm parked. Maddox strides ahead, swinging his sports bag back and forth as his long legs move quickly. His mum lags, occasionally calling out to him in what looks to me like a plea to slow down.

They get to the end of the street and it seems obvious by the way they're moving purposefully they're going to walk to their destination. It makes my pursuit a little more difficult in terms of not being spotted, but thanks to my previous digging, I know where they're headed if they're going home.

I get out of the car, grab my handbag, and slip it on cross-body style.

I'm wearing my trainers and trackie bottoms and I too am dressed in dark grey and black. I've got to try and take it easy but it's difficult when my heart is pounding and I feel hot and uncomfortable in the muggy weather. I lock the car and cross the road, staying well back until they turn the corner. Liv picks up the pace and, at the corner, casually slows to a stop as if she's unsure which direction to take, allowing me to catch up a little at my slower pace.

They are a third of the way up the street to the left and are now walking at a more leisurely pace. I turn into the street, slowing my pace, never taking my eyes off them. Another couple of turns into a modern housing estate and the woman opens a gate. Her son follows her up a tiny front path and they walk around the side of the house to use the back door.

'58 Pinewood Gardens,' I murmur to myself. The address on Maddox's student details form.

Since they went round the back, there is no sign of life from the front of the house. I imagine them entering via the back door and perhaps settling in the kitchen to have a snack and a drink. I open Google Maps and wait for my current position to load, scanning the roads around where I'm standing. I quickly spot that Pinewood Gardens runs adjacent to Raleigh Rise, a street of the exact same length just behind these houses.

I double-back on myself and take a shortcut, a small pedestrian track, that leads back into the estate. I don't walk the full length of the track but turn left on to the first road it traverses through. That road is Raleigh Rise and from here, I can see the back of the house Liv and Maddox disappeared into.

There are houses lining this road too, so I have to be careful not to draw attention to myself. I spot a small parking area with views over some of the back gardens. One of those houses is the one I'm interested in.

As if on cue, the back door opens at number 58 and Liv Leigh emerges, clutching a black bin bag which she dumps inside a wheely bin. Just then, she looks up and locks eyes with me. She hesitates just a second and goes back inside but I can see her shadow hovering by the kitchen window, still looking my way.

At that moment, one thought obliterates any other. Am I looking at my husband's lover and the mother of his teenage son?

THIRTY-THREE

LIV

When the woman who's staring into Liv's back garden realises she's been spotted, she quickly walks away from her vantage point – the small communal area at the back of the house.

It's clear this isn't a woman who's just standing around killing time, perhaps waiting for someone. She's not glancing around in that sort of harmless, nosy way people sometimes do. She'd been staring in purposefully and it had unnerved Liv, seeing a stranger just standing by the perimeter fence like that.

Her mind drifts to the photograph Maddox claims was given to him by a woman in the street.

'What's wrong?' Maddox says when he looks up from his iPad to see his mum distracted.

'Nothing... I thought I saw someone looking into the garden, but they've gone now.'

'Was it a man?' he says.

Liv looks at him. 'Not a man,' she says. 'A woman. But why would you think that?'

Maddox shrugs his shoulders. 'Just a fifty-fifty guess.'

There it is again: this new off-handed attitude he had on full display when the detectives were here on Saturday. It was all she could do to get two words out of him after she'd turned up at the end of school but – as she'd made clear to him as he'd stridden furiously ahead of her when she'd asked if he was still working at the café – she'll be doing exactly that until she is satisfied he isn't in contact with local drug dealers.

She's stopped sneezing as much, but her head is pounding thinking about if and when the money will arrive. Her energy levels are still rock bottom, sapped by the heavy cold.

'You seem very on-edge lately, Maddox.' Liv puts down the loaf of bread. 'If you were in trouble... you would tell me?'

'Not in trouble at all,' he murmurs, tapping his screen again.

Liv stands watching him for a few moments. He's always needed coaxing to talk if anything is bothering him. Way back in primary school – he must've been about seven or eight – he went quiet almost overnight, didn't want to go out, shut himself away in his bedroom. It took a bit of persuading him to talk but she managed it eventually. Turned out a boy in his class was bullying him to the extent he had taken his friends away. Allowing them to join in with the footie at lunchtimes if they ditched Maddox. That sort of heartless thing.

It didn't take long to resolve it all once Liv made his teacher aware, but sadly things aren't quite as easy to discover and fix now Maddox is older. He withdraws and refuses to let her in, and his ability to resist her efforts to talk about problems is much stronger now.

Maddox suddenly stands up. 'I'm going up to my room.'

'But your sandwich... it's nearly ready.'

'I'm not hungry.' He walks to the doorway and looks back at her, a glimmer of regret in his eyes. 'If you put it in the fridge, I might have it later.'

Liv knows when she's beaten. She's done all the pushing she can do for now unless she wants him to stay in his bedroom all night. She cuts the sandwich in half, wraps it in waxed paper and puts it in the fridge. Then she moves into the hallway and shrugs on the old Barbour jacket that Rich bought her brand new all those years ago. The Christmas before he went missing.

'Navy blue to match your eyes,' he'd said, holding it for her to try on.

Thanks to the quality, the jacket has lasted. Like so many other things have lasted when they could have done with being replaced before now.

Just three more years... two more years... next year...

It's what she's constantly told herself to get through. Living frugally, making stuff last. She has traded more than a decade of her life for a bright shiny future. That's the decision she made. And she's been good at it, living as ordinary and under-the-radar life as possible. But now she's questioning... what has it all been for?

Liv puts on a scarf and gloves and clips on Betsy's collar and lead.

'I'm taking the dog out,' she calls upstairs. 'Won't be long.'

She hears Maddox's vague response and sighs. Just a few months ago, he'd have come out with her and the dog. Made her laugh as they walked around the park with his embellished stories about what his football mates at school had got up to.

Somehow, she senses his whole routine has changed outside of the house. If he won't tell her whether he's still working at the café, she'll have to go there and ask.

Betsy strains on her leash, pulling her impatiently towards the door.

'Steady on, girl,' Liv chides. 'We'll be out in a second.' She shoves a couple of poop bags in her pocket and a handful of kibble and a minute later, they're walking down the street. Liv immediately feels better for getting out of the house and into the fresh air.

A short rain shower has cleared the air a little and now the sun has broken through and it feels fresher. Still feeling a bit shivery from her cold, Liv pulls on her fleece but leaves it unzipped. The light breeze feels refreshing on her face as she turns the corner and heads across the road to their go-to small park that provides Betsy with a quick loo break walk.

While Betsy sniffs around the bushes at the perimeter of the park, Liv finds herself thinking about Rich. What is he doing, right now, at this very moment? Has he broken all the rules they agreed on back then and found someone new? Has he decided he doesn't want to come back after all and turned his back on Maddox, too?

All those lost years that Rich has missed out on with their son. Years that can never be recovered at any cost.

She is deep into her thoughts, staring blindly at the back end of Betsy, who is still tirelessly poking around in the under-growth. She doesn't look up or register there is someone walking purposefully towards her on the narrow path that skirts the park until it's too late. The figure is right in front of her when Liv jerks up her head. Startled, she lets out a little yelp of alarm as they almost collide.

It takes Liv another moment or two to realise that this woman, with her straggly dark-blonde hair and upturned nose, wearing a dark-grey cotton top and currently apologising profusely, is the same woman who stared intrusively into her garden only about twenty minutes ago.

Liv turns to face her and Betsy stops sniffing for a moment as they both regard the woman.

'Sorry!' the woman says again and holds up her hands, and Liv notices she is wearing a white gold wedding band and soli-taire diamond engagement ring. 'I didn't mean to startle you. I wasn't watching where I was going.'

'I think I saw you earlier,' Liv say carefully. 'You were standing in the parking area at the back of my house.'

The woman's cheeks colour slightly. 'Yes. That was me.' She looks up again. 'My name's Kaitlyn Hatton. Kait. Can I walk with you a little while?'

Liv hesitates, discomfort gnawing at her throat as she thinks again of the photograph Maddox claimed he'd been given by a stranger. And this woman, *Kait*, her manner is furtive to say the least. Liv glances around the park, sees another dog walker behind the children's play area. Other than that, they're alone. She says, 'I'm literally just here for a few minutes... for the dog. I've got to get back.'

'It'll only take a few minutes. No more than that, I promise.' The woman locks eyes with Liv, willing her to agree. 'There's something really important I need to talk to you about.'

THIRTY-FOUR

MADDOX

From his bedroom window, he watches his mum and Betsy walking off down the street towards the park. When they turn the corner, Maddox goes downstairs and pours a glass of orange juice before taking his sandwich out of the fridge and wolfing it down in a few large bites.

He's starving but didn't want to come down before because he can't face his mum right now. The questions. The curious glances. The hurt and confusion in her eyes when he turns away. He's always been able to talk to her. Had a much better relationship with his mum than a lot of his mates at school have with their parents, judging by their constant complaints about being grounded or other punishments like reducing their allowances for bad grades.

But all that has pretty much changed now because what his mum has done to him is far, far worse than any of that.

When he'd taken the photograph Sammy gave him out of the envelope and studied it at the park, his stomach tightened into a cold, hard ball. For a crazy few seconds, Maddox thought the man in the photograph was Sammy. The expression on his face, the way his hair fell over his eyes. But he recognised himself as the small boy... so how could it be Sammy? And then it had clicked and he'd wanted to throw up.

He'd left the park and started walking quickly home. He had every intention of having it out with his mum, demanding to know the truth. But Sammy's words had come back to him. 'Say nothing to anyone about what you find in the envelope.'

Still, on his way back home, the knowledge of it had boiled up inside him, threatening to spill over. When he opened the front door, he was confronted with that detective and that took the heat out of him in an instant.

After that he'd got himself back under control, but he'd nearly died when he saw her waiting outside school for him. He was so nervous that Brandon would turn up unexpectedly as he has a habit of doing.

All the stress and bad feelings he has are bubbling just under the surface of his skin like a toxic swamp. Maddox's head is full of the pictures he'd found on her laptop and of the stuff Sammy has been talking to him about.

It was a relief when she went out because on the spur of the moment when he'd seen the worry and hurt in her eyes as he left to go upstairs, he almost cracked and told her everything that has been happening. Thank God he'd stopped himself because Sammy would have been furious and it would have been disastrous on every level after the coppers showing up at the house.

His mum would have exploded. Called the two interfering detectives right away. Contacted his school. Mr Patel and that grass, Mr Pinfold.

She will do all the things she thinks will protect him without realising it will increase the danger level massively.

Not just the danger to Maddox, but the danger to her, too. His mum hasn't got a clue just how lethal these people are. He pushes his plate away and absent-mindedly traces the knife welts and scratches on the old worktop. He has nobody to confide in, nobody he can talk to.

Somehow, Maddox must try and get out of this mess on his own and, at this moment in time, the only way he can see how to do that is by following Sammy's instructions and doing what he's told. If what Sammy has told him is true then he has every right to find out what's in those locked computer files.

He takes the pen drive he's been given and sits in front of his mum's laptop. He hesitates before sliding it into the USB port. Even though it feels wrong, it's something he must do.

He loves his mum dearly, but Sammy is right when he says Maddox's mum has no right to lie to him as she has done for all these years. He begins the process of saving all the files on to the pen drive just like Sammy instructed.

Maddox is taking his time and making sure he does the job properly because he very much wants to know the truth about what happened to his dad and find out why his mum has lied to him for so long.

Sammy wants to help him get to the truth. He really seems to get Maddox in a way that nobody else does.

He squeezes his eyes closed. None of this makes any sense because his dad is dead.

THIRTY-FIVE

LIV

They've been walking slowly, side by side, for about thirty seconds. The woman, Kait, has asked her a couple of questions about Betsy. How old is she? What sort of breed? It feels odd, being in the company of this woman who Liv has never set eyes on before. Pretending nothing is wrong when she clearly has a problem. She's pretty in a girl-next-door kind of way. Liv has noticed she's slightly out of breath even though they're not walking fast at all and she keeps touching her stomach. It just all feels quite odd and, frankly, she has enough on her plate and could do with some thinking time alone.

Liv stops walking. 'You said you needed to speak to me about something important?'

'Yes.' Kait shuffles from one foot to the other. 'It's... difficult to know how to start.'

'Well, you could just say it.' Liv shrugs. 'I need to be back home soon. I've got stuff I need to sort out.'

She has no idea what this is going to be about, but the woman is seriously starting to creep her out. That way she keeps looking at her, kind of curious but also as if she doesn't quite trust her.

'It's about your son.'

Liv stops walking. 'My son?' Icy prickles travel down her spine. Is this to do with the drugs thing... the new iPhone? He could be in some sort of trouble at school, maybe not just the stuff the police were talking about, but with this woman's son?

'Your son is Maddox Leigh, yes?'

Liv nods. 'What's the problem?'

Kait blinks. 'I don't know.'

'Is it to do with school?'

'No, it's not about school. It's... about my husband.'

The photograph Maddox had flashes before her eyes as Liv's fingers tighten on Betsy's lead. 'I'm listening.'

'This is going to sound crazy, but please, hear me out. I – I think my husband might be the father of your son.'

Liv laughs. A strange, high-pitched sound she doesn't recognise as her own. Her head is swimming as the possibilities begin to connect. She has to close this down.

'Maddox's father is dead.' Liv tries to look outraged, but she can already feel sweat beginning to pool at the bottom of her back.

Both women fall silent and Liv pulls Betsy closer as the dog walker who was across the park a few minutes ago shuffles past them with his feisty black-and-tan Jack Russell.

'Could we sit down for a few minutes?' Kait indicates a wooden bench a few feet away.

'I have to get ba—' The words die on Liv's tongue. What if it's *him*? What if Rich has broken their promise and got himself a new life? This could be the link she's been waiting for, an explanation of why he's reneged on their iron-clad agreement. If Rich has slipped up and his new wife has somehow found out about his son, this could be the link to the money she is entitled to. There again, it could be nothing at all. A mistake, a misunderstanding but she needs to know which it is. So she says, 'I can give you five minutes.'

Liv sits at one end of the bench, adjusting the lead length so Betsy can still meander around behind them.

When both women are sitting, Kait takes a deep breath before speaking.

'My husband's name is Daniel Hatton. We met three years ago and got married eighteen months ago.' Kait places a flat hand across her middle again. 'I'm almost five months pregnant and... well, something has been bothering me for a while.' She hesitates. 'Something has niggled at me about Daniel for the past few weeks. The feeling he's not quite telling me everything about himself.'

'What's this got to do with—'

'I know this might sound crazy to you but hear me out. Please.' Kait takes a breath before continuing. 'I'm talking about signs that probably wouldn't mean anything to someone else. A feeling, a strange look. It's hard to be specific.' Liv can see the worry etched into the other woman's eyes, pulling down her pretty features. 'In the last couple of months, I've sensed he's changed in some way and there have been other signs to back that up.'

Liv shivers and says nothing, nestling her chin down into the folds of her scarf. Three days ago, a sum not that far under a million pounds should have landed in her designated bank account as per the agreement she made with Rich nearly twelve years ago. That money has not arrived and she has yet to hear anything from her ex-husband. He's out there somewhere and Kait may have the key to exactly where.

Liv keeps her expression blank. She hardly dares to hope.

'At first, I wondered if he was having an affair,' Kait says, lacing together her fingers. 'The usual signs were there. He'd stopped coming home straight after work. Said he was going to the gym when I asked him about it.'

'What does your husband do?' Liv asks.

'He's a personal trainer to wealthy clients,' she says. 'He put his recent distractions down to losing a couple of customers and failing to fill their slots. But there was something he wasn't saying. I could feel it.'

Liv feels a slight release in her taut shoulders. Rich had always hated the gym with a passion. 'If fresh air isn't involved, I'm not interested,' he was fond of saying, much preferring to watch and sometimes take part in team sports like football and cricket.

'That doesn't sound like my late husband at all,' Liv says shortly, disappointment tamping down her sense of hope.

'Maybe not, but now there's something else. Something I can't ignore. I took this shot of a handwritten note that fell out of Daniel's pocket two days ago.' Kait taps at her phone and turns it so Liv can see the screen. 'He was very cagey about what the note meant but with the help of someone who works in education, I was eventually able to decipher it. It's the short-ened name of your son's school, Fairlawns Forest and this—' she points at the long number '—is the UPN, the Unique Pupil Number of Maddox Leigh.'

Liv squints at the screen, unsure whether it's relevant to Maddox. It's not as if any parent memorises the thirteen-char-acter UPN of their kid, although she can't deny the school's name is correct.

'So you looked at this note and thought: my husband must be this kid's dad?' Liv purses her lips. 'That's quite a leap to make.'

'No,' Kait says, her face falling. 'That realisation came when I saw a picture of Maddox. He's similar in looks to my husband. So similar, I can't ignore it.'

THIRTY-SIX

RICH

THREE MONTHS BEFORE HIS DISAPPEARANCE

The two-day property conference in Manchester had been booked for weeks and Rich was only away for one night. Before he went down to the bar for a few drinks to try and clear his mind of worries, he called Livvy to chat, see how she and Maddox were, but it was getting harder and harder to put on an act. Soon, the bank would hear about his big deal falling through and then... well, it didn't bear thinking about. Rich didn't have a clue what would happen, only that he would have to face it when the time came.

Caleb was still not returning his calls or texts. Rich had come up with a plan to ask him to lend him the cash to pay off the bank. When the next property investment came in – which Caleb had insisted would be very soon – Rich would start over again and pay Caleb back from the profits. He'd seen on Companies House that the most recently filed company accounts of his business, Mosley Property Developments, showed a balance of close to ten million pounds. A hundred grand, for Caleb, was like a drop in the ocean.

But with Caleb refusing to make contact, it was impossible to move towards this possible solution. Despite Rich's marriage being strained recently, he loved Livvy and his son. He'd do anything he could to wriggle out of this mess, so she would never need to know her husband was a lying scumbag.

Rich's eye was drawn to the back view of a woman at the bar. She was in some kind of altercation with a portly guy Rich had noticed around the conference's public areas, always gripping a drink in his fleshy hand.

Rich quickly moved towards the woman who had just raised a hand by way of indicating the man should back off out of her space.

Her ash blonde hair swept up into an elegant chignon, the silver grey gaberdine suit that clung to her hourglass curves... he knew this woman, recognised the shapely calves framed by a mid-length skirt and ankle-strap heels. She turned, as if she had sensed Rich's stare and he saw it was indeed her. Alicia! Caleb's wife.

He rushed over to the bar, glancing at the flushed, shiny face of her unwelcome company. Rich noted his name badge: Dougie Reeves, Centric Systems. Rich had seen him at property meetings in Nottingham, knew him just to say hello to. 'Everything OK here?'

'I was just trying to buy the lady a drink,' Reeves said, his words slurring into each other. 'But I think she's playing hard to get.'

'Come on, Dougie. Be nice,' Rich said mildly. 'I think you've had enough to drink.'

'I've told you three times, now,' Alicia said coldly, 'I don't want a drink. Please leave me alone.'

'Charming!' Reeves knocked back the rest of his whisky and grinned at Rich. 'Not very polite, this one, mate. If I were you, I'd—'

'Bugger off,' Alicia snapped, pinching her first finger and

thumb close together in front of his face. 'I'm this close to putting in a complaint about you to the conference organisers. And you know what that means... you'll be out on your ear.'

He staggered back as if she'd slapped him and shook his head at Rich. 'What's the world coming to, eh? Can't even offer to buy a lady a drink now.'

Rich and Alicia stared at him in silence until he turned and stumbled off sheepishly.

'Rich! What a nice surprise,' Alicia said, giving him a weary smile. Her usual infectious energy seemed to be missing. 'Thanks for helping me get rid of that pest.'

'To be fair, you didn't need any help from me.' He grinned.

'I didn't see you in any meetings today.' Alicia was MD of Caleb's property empire, her husband being the CEO. Rich had never had occasion to deal with her in a business capacity; all his interests were with Caleb.

'I decided to pop in, see who's around as I've had meetings nearby.' Her expression was vague, as if her mind was busy thinking about something else. She picked up her glass of white wine and drained the last of it. 'How are things with you? Haven't seen you around much lately.'

She was avoiding looking at him and he realised her make-up didn't look quite as perfect as usual. Her eyes were bloodshot and her mascara slightly smudged.

'Let's put it this way, it's not my finest hour.' He laughed, masking his devastation. 'I've had a big deal fall through, taking my sizeable investment with it. I'm not sure what to do with myself, if I'm honest.'

'Oh, you're talking about the Spanish villa development.' She pulled a face. 'I think Caleb might've mentioned it.'

As Rich had suspected: a major blow for him, but no more than a slight irritation for the Mosleys.

'Can I get you another drink?' Rich moved beside her,

leaning an elbow casually on the bar. 'Be nice to have a catch-up.'

She smiled a little then hesitated, stayed quiet for a few seconds before saying, 'You know what? To hell with it. Yes, I'll have another drink.'

Rich took a breath. He had to play this right... it was the best chance he'd get to earn favour with Alicia. She was the only person that could possibly help him resolve his issues with her husband. And at the very least he might be able to find out why Caleb was basically ghosting him.

They moved to a comfortable booth away from the main bar area where Alicia ordered them a bottle of quality Malbec.

While the wine warmed his throat, helping to relax his taut neck and shoulders, they talked for a while about things neither of them were really very interested in: holidays, and Alicia was keen to hear how Maddox was doing at school.

A few seconds into an awkward silence, Rich said, 'I'm glad things are going OK for you, Alicia. If I'm honest, I'm struggling with this failed investment. It's hard to keep trying to be upbeat.' He took a slug of his wine. Her face looked drawn and pale. He was boring her. 'Sorry. Sorry, I don't want to bring the mood down, it's just—'

Alicia took a sharp breath in. 'My marriage is in trouble, Rich. Caleb and I... we're splitting up.'

'What?' Rich felt jolted. They had seemed solid as a couple. He reached for something apt to say. 'I – I had no idea, Alicia. I'm so sorry. Livvy will be gutted.'

In all the time he'd known Caleb, Rich had never seen him with another woman unless it was strictly business. He wasn't a terrible flirt like some of the wealthy businessmen in the circles they moved in. Caleb was personable with everyone... unless he didn't like you anymore. Rich swallowed.

'I knew we'd started to drift apart, but we talked about it and things improved for a short time. Deep down I still felt as if there was a sheet of glass between us, you know? Like he was forcing how he felt on some level. But when I found out he'd been lying to me about money, that was it.' She drank some wine and stared into the glass.

'You guys have known each other most of your lives, right?'

Alicia nodded. 'Caleb and I met when we were young and we built the company together even though I admit MPD was his vision. He drove our rapid expansion but in the early years we scrimped and scraped, put the business first. I sank my grandma's inheritance into it. Wasn't a fortune, but still substantial and much-needed back then. I did it without a second thought and that's why this feels such a betrayal.'

He thought about Caleb, about his generosity and willingness to mentor Rich's own business even though things had now gone badly wrong. He wanted to think better of him. 'Could it be it looks like betrayal but isn't? I mean, have you spoken to him about it?'

Alicia gave him a sad smile. 'You think you know Caleb, Rich, but believe me, you don't. Not really. Nobody knows him past the very polished and genuine veneer he likes to peddle. Anyone who offends him or makes him angry is instantly excommunicated. And when you see that steel interior, it's already too late.'

Rich ran a finger inside the tight collar of his shirt. Alicia's words felt too close to home. He and Caleb had been good friends, rapidly moving towards becoming great friends. Maybe even lifelong friends. If they weren't together, they were chatting on the phone; Rich hadn't felt this close to a mate since his schooldays. He'd done nothing to anger Caleb and yet overnight he'd been completely ghosted. It didn't make sense. Nevertheless, Rich still felt the need to defend him, to speak up for Caleb in the face of his marriage dissolving.

'As a friend, I urge you to speak to him, Alicia. I'm not

trying to pry into what it is you've found that's made you feel so betrayed but... is it possible it could be a misunderstanding?'

'There's no misunderstanding.' Her voice turned steely. 'Whatever Caleb's up to, he knows exactly what he's doing. He always has.'

Rich topped up their glasses with the last of the red wine. 'You know him better than me, so I'm not going to argue about that. I really hope you two can find a way to stay together, though. Livvy will be as devastated as I am because we care about you both.'

Alicia looked away. 'Thing is, Rich, I didn't bump into you by accident today. Liv mentioned in conversation you were here, at the conference.'

'Oh?' He put down his glass. 'Is that because you wanted me to know about you and Caleb?'

'Not exactly.' She hesitates a moment before saying, 'I came here because there's something very important I need to tell you.'

THIRTY-SEVEN

Rich watched as Alicia poured herself a large glass of their second bottle of Malbec. She took a big gulp but still she didn't say anything.

'Alicia, you can't keep me hanging like this,' Rich pleaded. Caleb had obviously done something serious that had really wounded her. What he couldn't work out was why she wanted to discuss it with him so badly when, as far as he knew, she had lots of girlfriends to offload to, including his wife. 'What have you got to tell me that's so important you made the trek to Manchester when you've no need to be here?'

Alicia closed her eyes briefly before saying, 'I'm so sorry, Rich. I don't mean to make this harder than it is, it's just... I don't know how to begin.'

'That's easy. You just have to say it. We're friends, right? Just tell me whatever it is you need to get off your chest and we can talk about it. I'll help in any way I can, you know that.'

She nodded and put down her glass. 'Thing is, Rich, Caleb hasn't just lied and double-crossed me. He's also shafted you good and proper.'

Rich frowned and a nervous laugh escaped his mouth. 'Shafted me? How?'

'That Spanish property deal that's given you so many sleepless nights? It hasn't fallen through at all.'

'What?' He sat up straight, hope instantly flickering in his chest. 'That would be amazing news! But... are you certain about this?'

Could it be true he might not lose the cottage after all? Might not have to face the wrath of the bank... and Livvy?

'I'm absolutely certain. The investment opportunity is still on track and is still expected to bring excellent returns. It's just that Caleb has used his considerable contacts to cut you out of it. He wants to ruin you, Rich.'

Ringing started in his ears. 'You're mistaken! Caleb's lost his investment, too.'

She shook her head. 'Caleb's taken your investment as his own. They've redone the paperwork and you've been airbrushed out completely.'

He struggled to compute what she said. 'The developer told me himself. He's declared bankruptcy and—'

'It's all a lie, Rich,' Alicia said quietly, stopping him in his tracks. 'Have you had any official paperwork?'

He felt the colour drain from his face as he stared at her mutely.

'Caleb's known that guy – the developer – for over twenty years. They've done a ton of business together. The man controls multiple dormant companies and names dozens of other people as the various directors. On paper, he is not connected. It's nothing for him to declare bankruptcy on one of them and to say your investment sum has been a casualty of it.'

'It can't be true,' he murmured to himself. His hand shook as he picked up his glass and drained half of it in one gulp.

'I'm so sorry I've had to be the one to tell you, Rich. But the fact is, it is true and it's all Caleb's doing,' Alicia said, her face pained.

'But... *why*? We were friends, I loved him like a brother. Why would he want to ruin me and my family?'

'Livvy and Maddox are unfortunate casualties. But that's just it... once Caleb has set his mind on something, he won't let anyone or anything be an obstacle to getting what he wants.' Alicia topped up his glass. 'I've learned it the hard way.'

Rich knocked back great gulps of wine until his cheeks felt like they were burning up. 'I still don't understand. Caleb has been my biggest support and now he won't answer my calls. But why? There must be a good reason to want to ruin someone, to cut them out of your life completely.'

'He said he found out you'd lied, made a fool of him,' Alicia told him. 'He said he could never forgive you for that.'

Rich frowned. 'I've never lied to Caleb, much less made a fool of him. I'm sorry, but that didn't happen.'

Alicia bit her lip. 'He said it was when you first met. You told him your dad died of prostate cancer and... well, he did a bit of digging and found out your father actually died of cirrhosis of the liver.'

Rich felt the weight of the forgotten lie descend on him. His mind flicked back to that fateful moment he entered the conference foyer and his hand reached down and plucked a metal pin from the charity box. The subsequent hours of listening to Caleb's outpouring of grief and nodding with understanding, recounting the painful last moments spent with his own father...

'Rich?'

'It's true.' He hung his head. 'I lied because I wanted to build rapport with Caleb quickly. I didn't even give it a thought or consider that he'd be so angry.'

'Like I said, nobody knows the real Caleb,' Alicia murmured, twisting the stem of her glass before looking up again. 'But moving on from all that, let's look to the future. I have a proposal for you.'

THIRTY-EIGHT

KAIT

Liv Leigh is silent while she takes in what I've just told her about Maddox being the spitting image of Daniel. For a couple of seconds, she looks like she's been knocked sideways before recovering.

'There's a simple answer to this,' Liv says when she's collected herself. 'Show me a photograph of your husband.'

She folds her arms and watches me as I start to swipe through the phone's photo album. Shot after shot until I find a couple with Daniel on them.

'Here's the thing. He's always hated having his photograph taken,' I say. I feel like a fraud, but it's true. He shies away the moment a camera comes out. Insists he'd rather take pictures of me framed by a beautiful view on holiday. 'It's one of the things I found strange about him but pushed away. Now I'm wondering if there's a reason.'

I hold up the phone. 'Here's one. It's not great shot because he's turning his face in it.'

Liv studies the photo, pinches the images of Daniel out and

back in again. I wait for her verdict, but she remains poker faced. 'Do you have any more?'

I suddenly remember I've got some from our wedding day on here. 'Hang on.'

I scroll through the photo albums looking for the right one when my phone flickers and the screen goes black. 'Oh no,' I say faintly. 'I was on low charge, but... let me try and restart it.' But the phone is dead as a dodo.

'Well, from the one photo you've shown me there are similarities, but I don't think it's Rich.'

'Are you saying you don't know Daniel?'

'My husband died eleven years ago.'

'Yes, you said. So you've never met Daniel? You're not—'

'Having an affair with your husband? No.' Her face is expressionless, and I can tell she's getting fed up with my line of questioning. But when all's said and done, I don't know her well enough to take her word for it.

'Right, OK,' I say. 'I had to ask.'

Liv's expression softens a little. 'I'd ask you back to the house for a cup of tea, but my son is home, and I wouldn't want him overhearing our conversation for obvious reasons. He still struggles with losing his dad.'

I nod. 'I understand.'

Then she says, 'But there's a little café around the corner from here. They're dog-friendly, so we could go there for a quick drink if you want? I can see you're worried and, believe me, I know what that feels like. Maybe we can piece things together after a chat? It's your call.'

She seems to be holding her breath, wanting me to agree.

'OK.' I nod, surprised at her new openness. 'Let's go there.'

At the café, I get the coffees in. I'm suspicious of her, but I won't get very far if I show it, so I make an effort to be amicable.

'It must've been unnerving for you, me, a complete stranger turning up and making wild accusations,' I say, opening a sachet of sugar and emptying it into my decaf latte. 'It's just... there's no way of softening something like that, is there? I couldn't think of doing anything else until I'd spoken to you.'

'It was a big shock, but I can see you had to follow up on it.' Liv gives a small smile. 'And of course the mystery still stands of why your husband – Daniel – had Maddox's confidential student details at all.'

I shake my head. Like her, I'm still confused. 'It doesn't make any sense. And the coincidence of Maddox looking so much like Daniel... it's really unnerved me.'

Liv reaches down and scratches Betsy's ears. 'Out of interest, where do you live?'

I hesitate. Daniel has always been obsessed with maintaining our privacy to what I thought was a paranoid extent. 'Working for wealthy clients has opened my eyes to the dangers out there,' he'd explained one day when I kicked back about his obsession with locking the door as soon as we stepped inside the house after a trip out. 'Most of them have sophisticated alarm systems, CCTV cameras and electric gates. It's made me realise how vulnerable we are at home.'

'But your clients have plenty of high-end stuff to rob.' I'd laughed. 'We have nothing, in comparison.'

'We have the most precious thing in the world to protect now,' he'd said, gently touching my stomach. 'It doesn't cost us anything to stay private and tell people nothing. Trust no one, Kait. It's the best way.'

I look at Liv, who is still waiting for an answer. This woman I don't know at all who's staring at me over her coffee cup asking me for personal details. I realise I must seem a bit odd, turning up out of the blue questioning... *accusing* her of stuff like that. If anyone is acting weird, it's me, not her.

'We live in Hucknall, moved there about a year ago.'

'Oh, not far away then. That's what... about a twenty-minute drive from here?'

I nod and sip my coffee.

Liv grins and her manner is gently teasing. 'Close enough for me to be having an affair with Daniel. Is that what you thought?'

I press my fingertips to my forehead. 'I did wonder if he was having an affair but when I saw the picture of Maddox, I realised the link with your son. You two have a shared history together.'

She glances at my stomach. 'It's natural you'll be feeling more anxious with the baby and all.'

Is she trying to say I'm imagining Daniel's link with her and the boy? I fold my hands in front of me.

'I remember I was just the same when I was pregnant with Maddox,' she continues. 'Worrying about everything in the world that could go wrong.'

I've missed having someone to talk my worries through with... another woman. I neglected and finally lost my friends when I climbed in a bubble just with me and Daniel. I love my sister dearly, but she has no experience and no real interest in my pregnancy beyond a new fascination with the fact she'll be an auntie for the first time. Kirsten has never been a worrier.

'Pregnancy is the most wonderful thing in the world and the most terrifying all at the same time. Is Daniel supportive?'

It feels weird to talk about him with her. Especially about the baby.

'He's very supportive,' I concede. 'In fact, I couldn't wish for a better husband, if only I could stop worrying that he's hiding something.'

'I can understand that. You're feeling a bit vulnerable at the moment and that's perfectly normal.' She smiles. 'He's an attractive guy. How old is he... early forties? He looks very fit for his age, if so.'

'Forty-three next month. He's seven years older than me but you wouldn't think it to look at him. I suppose that's what spending all day in a gym does for you!'

'Is it a local gym? I could do with firming up a bit!' Liv pokes her belly, and we laugh.

'No, he's freelance. He trains business people mostly. Wealthy clients who have their own training facilities.'

'Sounds impressive.' Liv raises an eyebrow. 'Sounds like I wouldn't be able to afford his services anyway.'

I smile. 'He's determined to build a great life for us. He's adamant the business will be ready to sell out for a sizeable sum in the near future, but I think that's probably a bit of wishful thinking.'

'That's interesting,' Liv murmurs, sipping her tea. 'Sounds like Daniel is expecting a big windfall quite soon. Lucky you.'

THIRTY-NINE

LIV

When they finish their coffees, Kait begins to gather her belongings.

'I don't know why Daniel has those details about your son. But if what you say is true, my previous theories obviously don't stand up to scrutiny. I guess I'll just have to ask him again.'

They'd got on OK in the café, but Liv bristles at Kait's remark that seems to cast doubt on what she'd told her. She decides to ignore it and go on the defensive.

'When you've had a chance to speak to Daniel, it would be great if you could put my mind at rest about why he had the note containing Maddox's personal details. That information should be confidential, but I'm sure there's a reasonable explanation.' Liv smiles to show there are no hard feelings. 'Let's exchange numbers.'

When they've swapped contact details and Kait has left the coffee shop, Liv sits and stares into her empty latte glass.

How she held it together during their exchange, she'll never know. The second she set eyes on the photograph on Kait's phone – even though it was a bit blurred and only showed his profile – her insides had involuntarily clenched.

That told her it could be Rich. It probably was Rich.

A considerable amount of time has passed and he doesn't look exactly the same. There again, Liv herself had changed a lot, too. 'Daniel' looks older, as you'd expect, although in a good way. He's shaped up, changed his hair style, possibly had his nose refined – he'd always hated the bump in his nose from his amateur boxing days – but he can't disguise everything. His eyes. That unusual shade of piercing navy blue. The way he holds himself and the curve of his smile mostly on the left-hand side of his mouth.

It's more than possible that Daniel Hatton is the man who used to be Rich Askew. If it is true, that means he has an awful lot of money that is rightfully hers. It means he turned out to be a lying, cheating scumbag who she now knows has taken her for a ride. Betrayed not just her, but their son, too. In the worst way possible. He's set himself up in another nice, cosy relationship while failing on his promises to deliver the money to her and their son.

But why would he have Maddox's details if it's not his intention to contact him?

Somehow, Liv had battled wanting to throw up and managed to keep her face as immovable as a waxwork until Kait finally put away her phone and stood up. 'Just need to pop to the bathroom before I go,' she said. 'Back in a mo.'

The second she was out of view, Liv dipped her hand into Kait's straw tote and pulled out her purse. Quick as a flash, she opened it and plucked out the other woman's driving licence. She took a couple of snaps with her phone and then slipped the ID into her own bag. She fastened and replaced the purse, all within a few seconds.

Kait's phone sat tantalisingly close to her on the tabletop, but it was locked. Liv knew she wouldn't have a hope in hell of guessing the passcode so had to resist the temptation to try.

She stares now at the remnants of congealing milk around

the rim of her cup. The fury she'd instantly felt upon realising she'd been betrayed is dissolving now, melting into stone-cold fear when she thinks about the note Kait showed her on her phone.

A note that contains precise personal details about Maddox.

What is Rich up to? What's he planning to do with that information? Maybe Liv is already too late and Rich is back in touch with their son. Is it him who'd given her son the photograph? Maddox said a woman had given it to him but was he lying? Maddox has certainly developed an attitude problem – with her in particular – over the last couple of weeks.

Has Rich already contacted Maddox?

It was a shock when Kait approached her in the park, but now she's calmed down a little, Liv decides she will treat the encounter as the gift it is. She can't afford to waste any more time dithering about what ifs and maybes. There are too many irrefutable signs this man is likely to be Rich. The photographs, the connection to Maddox, the stuff he's told Kait about their future and his past. How he very conveniently worked on the rigs and so does not need to account for the lost years with no audit trail.

The most important thing now, Liv thinks, is that she must not scare Kait off. Instead, she must work to build and strengthen their connection. Win Kait's confidence in talking and confiding in her about Daniel.

Liv opens the recent photographs on her phone and studies Kait's driving licence. Her full address is there. For the last year, she and Daniel have lived in Hucknall, a market town seven miles north of Nottingham. Just a twenty-minute car ride from Liv's house. Oh, the irony.

Liv must get this right. With Kait's emotions running high, who knows when she might come clean with Daniel, tell him she's approached the mother of Maddox, the boy she'd thought was his son.

If he discovers Liv is aware, who knows what he might do?

Her priority, without doubt, is to find Rich. To see 'Daniel' face to face with her own eyes. She cannot be fooled seeing him in the flesh.

And she needs to do it now, without delay.

FORTY

NOTTINGHAMSHIRE POLICE

Brewster sits in his car outside the house, a curdling sensation starting in his stomach. He shouldn't have come here, he knows that but... the opportunity is just too good to miss.

The downstairs light is on, and he sees a shadow cross the room and disappear, as if someone just walked in and sat down. A constant faint flickering crosses the closed curtains, a tell-tale sign that the television is on.

When Brewster first joined the force, DI Jarrod Hutch was his supervising officer. The men got along like a house on fire from the off, Jarrod a seasoned detective with a bold north-east accent and no-nonsense approach to the job. Brewster was young and keen and eager to listen to Hutch's humorous but informative anecdotes when others quickly grew tired of his manner. The two men had genuinely liked each other and Brewster had missed him when he went to work in West Yorkshire.

He gets out of the car and walks across the road. Hutch had retired on a full pension at the age of sixty after thirty-two years in the force and he had returned to live in Nottingham. That was ten years ago now and Brewster has only bumped into him two or three times at various leaving events in that period. It has been a couple of years at least since the men have seen each other despite them living only a couple of miles away.

Brewster had thought about calling ahead but in the end, he decided just to drive by on the off-chance he'd catch his old colleague in. When he'd seen the light on in the front room, he'd impulsively pulled over. There is no time like the present, he reasoned.

He walks up the short path, stepping over the cracks where clusters of unchecked weeds have burst through and sprawled across the concrete slabs. The front garden is small, the tiny lawn patchy and thin with no flower borders to speak of.

There is no doorbell, so Brewster raps smartly on the blistered blue paintwork of the wooden door. This close to the house, he can hear the loud volume of the television. He catches movement as the curtain shifts slightly before immediately falling back into place and then the TV noise stops abruptly. A few moments later, the door opens.

Brewster manages to catch himself before his face falls. The grey-skinned, slightly stooped man who stands in the doorway is a mere shadow of Hutch, the dynamic detective with a reputation for cracking the toughest of cases. For a moment, Brewster recalls the once lean and wiry guy with piercing eyes who took him under his wing and mentored him so effectively all those years ago.

'Yes?' Hutch croaks, squinting his eyes as if he's been in darkness too long.

'Alright, boss?'

He peers forward before recognition flashes across his unshaven face. 'Is that you, Brewster? Come in, man, come in! Good man.' He stands aside and pats Brewster's back as he squeezes by him and into the dark, narrow hallway. 'Long time no see, eh? Go straight through, door on your left. Ignore the mess, mind; I wasn't expecting any company.'

He looks genuinely delighted to have a visitor and Brewster feels a squeeze of pity.

In the living room, the TV is still turned on but the volume has been muted. The room is in disarray. The coffee table covered with used glasses and a couple of crumbed plates. A takeaway pizza box sits on the floor next to the armchair and several items of clothing are strewn over the furniture. More of a concern for Brewster are the empty gin and whisky bottles lined up like soldiers next to the tiled hearth.

Although there's a comfortable three-piece suite, a carpet and a fireplace in here, the room seems stark. There are no comforts like scatter cushions or blankets, no personal items that add comfort and interest to a room such as framed photographs or ornaments.

The room is at the front of the house and although the curtains are pulled loosely closed, it's too warm in here. The air is muggy and feels a touch fetid. Brewster watches a dozy fly buzzing around at a low level.

He feels a twinge of regret he hasn't made the effort to pop in to see his old friend now and again, but it's easier said than done. Life gets in the way, people have a way of fading from your circle of interest, of good intentions. Before you know it, they are way down your long list of priorities, of stuff that shouts louder. It's just the way things go. Still, it is sad to see the great man diminished like this.

'Warm in here, mate. You should crack a window open,' Brewster says, pulling at his shirt collar. 'You looking after yourself?'

Hutch shrugs. 'Stella went and left me, didn't she? Ran off with some bloke she met on a night out.' He waves a hand around the room. 'More of a lad's pad now, this place. Suits me, never did like fuss.'

Brewster's eyes fix on the empty bottles. 'You doing OK, Jarrod?'

'Aye, I can't complain. Just got to get on with it, haven't you?' He grins as Brewster juts out his bottom lip and blows air up on his face. 'Truthfully, I don't really notice the temperature once I crack open a bottle. Want a cuppa?'

'Nah, I can't stay that long. Just thought I'd pop by – long time no see and all that.'

Hutch's eyes twinkle. 'Let me guess... need a bit of help? You wouldn't be the first one turning up at my door, asking to pick my brains about a case.'

To be fair, Brewster thinks, with the amount of hard liquor Hutch seems to be putting away, his brains are probably too pickled to pick.

'Ah, don't let that fool you.' Hutch nods to the empty bottles. 'I'm still sharp, and your luck's in, 'cos I haven't cracked open a bottle yet. I've got standards, you know. Rule is never to pour a drink before six. That's six in a morning, mind.' He nudges Brewster and grins, revealing nicotine-stained teeth. 'So, what's vexing you?'

Brewster smiles, recalling Hutch's jokey attitude when they worked together. It had helped them get through some tough times at work and maybe it does the same for Hutch now.

'Now you mention it, there is a closed case I've been looking at.'

Hutch taps his head. 'Closed, eh? Might not be worth me dusting off the old archives then.'

'I'm not so sure. You were the senior investigating officer on this particular case about eleven years ago in your West Yorkshire days. Richard Askew, a guy in his mid-thirties, went missing.'

Hutch frowns, takes a moment or two to think before nodding. 'I know it. Took his son out to fly a kite just as a storm was brewing. We found the kid but not his father, as I recall.'

Brewster nods. 'They never found him, and four years ago Richard Askew was declared presumed dead by the courts.'

'Gobsmacked they never found him. I felt sure they would, even if it was some time after he disappeared.'

Brewster regards his former colleague thoughtfully. 'What made you so sure, Hutch? All this time there have been no clues, no sightings, nothing.'

'You've been in the job long enough now to know you just get a nose for these things. Take people lying. Lies leave a trace in the air as soon as they're spoken, right? Bit like the rusty scent of fresh blood.'

Brewster doesn't comment, but he knows exactly what Hutch is getting at. Sometimes you can almost sense something in the ether, like Helena had at Liv Leigh's house when she'd felt something was off in there – not quite right.

'That's how it was for me when we questioned Rich Askew's wife. Can't recall her name.'

'Olivia Askew,' Brewster provides. 'Now Olivia Leigh, calls herself Liv. She changed her name a year after her husband went missing and her and the lad moved to Nottingham.'

'That figures,' Hutch mutters.

'Why do you say that?'

'It's just... oh I don't know. It's a long time ago now. Just me and my super-sensitive nose again. Ignore me.'

Hutch stares at the window in such a way that Brewster can tell he's back there for a moment. Back in the case.

'I'm interested in what you thought at the time,' Brewster says. 'I saw confidential notes on the file. Stuff officers were thinking that they couldn't quite prove.'

'Can you tell me why you're interested in the case?' Hutch says after a few moments.

Brewster hesitates. Giving details of a current case is problematic. Helena doesn't know he's poking around for information and so he's on dodgy ground. Especially when he's pretty certain the recipient of the information is an alcoholic. 'I sort of stumbled on the old case by accident,' Brewster says truthfully. 'Liv Leigh spooked my boss with her initial reaction when we came to the door. That "sniffing out" of the truth you were talking about? DI Helena Price got a whiff of something she couldn't quite put her finger on.'

Hutch grinned. 'I bet she freaked out, didn't she, that Olivia? Thought you'd finally worked it out, I expect.'

Brewster frowns. 'Worked what out?'

'That she had something to do with Richard Askew's disappearance.' He sighs in frustration. 'I could never work out exactly what she did to him, and God knows I tried. To this day I'm certain she lied to us during the interviewing process. In fact, I'd bet my current booze stash on it, and I can assure you I wouldn't do that lightly.' Hutch looks at him. 'Sure you don't want a cuppa?'

'Go on then,' Brewster says, hope rising in his chest that there might be more to uncover here. 'I'll have a quick one with you.'

Five minutes later, the two men sit with mugs of strong tea. Brewster wants to dig deep, but instinctively feels it's best to stay quiet and hope that his old colleague volunteers more information.

'Thing is,' Hutch says after a few moments of companionable silence, 'I had a bit more than a hunch that Olivia Askew was dodgy. But I couldn't use my source or find a way to otherwise reveal it.'

'Who was your source?'

Hutch laughs and takes another gulp of tea. 'Doesn't really matter now after all this time, I suppose. My Stella had a good friend who lived across the road from the Askews. She gave Stella some information and swore her to secrecy, but of course Stella told me and then made *me* swear I wouldn't reveal it.'

'Not that the senior investigating officer's wife could testify anyway, I suppose,' Brewster murmurs.

'Correct. I mean, I made a point of speaking to all the neighbours personally, just so I could get to this woman, but she was poker-faced. Swore she didn't know a thing.'

'Frustrating.'

'Aye, but she did me a favour because then I knew I was on to the right track. The other officers couldn't understand why I was like a dog with a bone when they all took Olivia at her word.' Hutch makes a derogatory noise and puts down his mug. 'The grieving wife and mother. I don't think so.'

Brewster hesitates before saying, 'Could you... I mean, can you tell me what Stella's friend told her?'

Hutch looks at the bottle of whisky on the mantlepiece and licks his lips, his hands skittish.

'Obviously I'm here off the record. I'm not going to divulge anything you tell me.' Brewster checks his watch. 9 p.m. 'I'll be getting straight off after.'

Hutch sighs, shuffles to the edge of his seat cushion. 'Out of what must be tens of hundreds of cases, there's just a handful of 'em that have never left me. The Askew disappearance is one of them. That small lad, just three years old... I can still see his little face to this day, you know?'

Brewster nods, thinking about the tall, brooding teenager with attitude he and Helena had encountered. 'This could be the only chance we have of pinning something on Liv Leigh,' he says, fully aware there will be no guarantees the super will approve of him raking up an old, closed case anyway. And it has to be said that Rich Askew is no longer missing. He has now been legally declared presumed dead. Still, you never know where these things could lead. 'What did Stella's friend tell her about Liv Leigh that convinced you of her guilt?'

Hutch stares at his hands and then looks longingly at the bottle of whisky. Then he stares straight at Brewster and he tells him what Stella said.

'You should read through those interview transcripts with fresh eyes,' Hutch says, wiping the palms of his hands on the front of his grubby trousers as his eyes fix on the bottle of whisky in front of him. 'Now, if you don't mind, I have something that desperately needs my attention.'

FORTY-ONE

RICH

Rich placed a hand over his glass when Alicia tried to pour him more wine. She'd said she had a proposal, but she hadn't said what that was yet.

'With what I've heard so far, I need to keep a clear head,' he said. Although, it had to be said that after drinking the best part of a bottle of wine to himself, he felt remarkably sober. And no wonder. What Alicia had just told him about Caleb felt like being repeatedly dunked into freezing cold water and barely allowed to come up for air.

She put down the bottle without topping up her own glass. 'You're right, of course, and I'll do the same. It's important we both keep our heads clear if we're to be partners.'

'Partners?' Rich frowned. 'In what?'

Every time he thought about Caleb ripping him off, willing to destroy his life because of one lie when they'd first met, he felt sick. The last thing he wanted was a new business involvement with Caleb's wife that would almost certainly make things worse.

Alicia's eyes burned into his. 'Think about it. We're both victims of Caleb. He's cut you off completely and thinks he's succeeded in ruining your life. But he doesn't know I'm on to him yet. That gives me some power, but I don't know for how long.'

Rich didn't quite follow, but he waited.

'I have an idea, a proposal of sorts. You might think I'm crazy, but I've already spent a lot of time thinking this through since I found out his seedy little secret. Are you willing to hear me out?'

Rich nodded. 'I haven't got any other options jumping out at me.'

'A few weeks ago, I felt a bit under the weather, so I didn't drink. Caleb on the other hand got happily blotto and, as has happened a few times before when he hits the bottle, it made him lax. He didn't lock his office door, his desk drawers were also unlocked and even the small safe he uses for various important legal papers.'

'So you went in there? Did you already suspect he was up to something?'

'Yes and no. His drinking has got steadily heavier. A couple of months ago, I found a woman's diamond stud earring in his suit pocket, which he swore he'd found on the floor in a restaurant and had intended to hand in before he got distracted by a phone call. On top of that, he's slowly stopped discussing current business matters with me. If I ask for an update, he's purposely vague.'

'So it was your chance to have a little look around, put your mind at rest?'

'You got it. At least that's what I hoped to do.' Alicia gave him a wry smile. 'To cut a long story short, his laptop was open at an online banking page... a financial institution I'd never heard of. The page had expired and required passwords to log back in, but I knew it must've been the last thing he looked at earlier in the evening. Caleb has always been shocking at remembering his passwords, so I hunted around in the drawers and the safe and it didn't take me long to find a security letter from the bank giving log-in details.'

Alicia looked longingly at her empty glass but pushed it away.

'That's when I discovered he had a secret bank account with just over three million pounds in it.'

Rich pulled a face. 'That's a lot of money not to tell your wife about,' he said.

'It gets worse. The account was in joint names.'

'He'd opened it in your name too?'

Alicia shook her head, her expression darkening. 'The account names were Mr Caleb Mosley and a Miss Jenna Beck. I hired a private detective and turns out Miss Beck is a twenty-five-year-old dancer who just happens to be six months pregnant. With Caleb's child.' Alicia kept her expression blank, but Rich understood how painful it must have been for her.

'I'm so sorry,' he said softly.

'Not as sorry as he'll be, trust me,' she said darkly. 'Luckily for me, Jenna Beck has turned out to be quite a loudmouth. My PI did a week's worth of digging and found out she'd been telling anyone who'd listen that she and her fiancé were preparing to start a new life together in Spain just after the baby's birth.'

'Jeez. Caleb is her *fiancé*?'

'Yep. News to me, but it's perfectly legal to get engaged while you're still married, apparently. But forewarned is fore-armed. So now you understand why I have to do something soon unless I want to be left with nothing to show for a fifteen-year marriage and a business built on blood, sweat and tears. My own, as well as Caleb's.' Alicia's usually soft brown eyes looked harder now, a flush creeping into her cheeks. 'He wants to ruin both our lives, Rich. He's arguably already managed it with you but I for one am not about to roll over and let that happen. I'm hoping you feel the same way because if it's got any chance of success, my plan needs your input.'

Rich nodded. 'I'm listening. What do you have in mind?'

Alicia looked around. The booths either side of them were now taken and the waitress had already been over twice to see if they needed more drinks. 'It's not really the place to be talking about revenge tactics, but I booked a suite here for tonight. Only because there were only expensive rooms left, but... I have a comfortable sitting room up there with a mini bar. Why don't we move upstairs and then we can talk in privacy?'

'Sounds like a plan,' Rich said, his head spinning. It crossed his mind Livvy might not be too happy if she knew he was going up to another woman's fancy suite – even if it was with her good friend Alicia – but Livvy didn't know their lives were about to fall apart and that was as much thought as he gave it. The important thing here was to see what Alicia had in mind. Caleb had shut him out completely and Rich knew he hadn't a chance of getting close to Caleb without Alicia.

His mind continued to reel from Alicia's revelations about Caleb's duplicity. Sure, Rich had lied about his dad's cause of death the day they met, but did that really warrant having his life so ruthlessly destroyed like Caleb had almost succeeded doing? Caleb had been the one keeping the lie alive in wanting to talk endlessly about his own father while asking Rich questions about his dad. Since the men had become close, Rich hadn't lied about a thing apart from making up the odd anecdote about his dear old dad when in reality he'd despised him. Was that really so bad? As far as Rich was concerned, it didn't matter in the scheme of things.

The one good thing about not being in touch with Caleb now was that Rich didn't have to talk about his own dad anymore. Didn't have to think about the old bastard. About what he'd done to him... and how he'd treated Rich's mum over the years.

He much preferred to forget his old man ever existed.

FORTY-TWO

KAIT

I open the text message from Daniel.

> *Training course went well. Met a couple of useful contacts. I'll*
> *go straight to the office from the train tomorrow morning and*
> *I'll see you tomorrow evening. Missing you. xx*

I close the message without replying, my heart squeezing hard as I read those two words again, loaded with meaning. *Missing you* with a couple of poisoned kisses. The phrase I love sounds twisted now. Spoiled. His emotive sign-offs always used to make me feel cherished. Now, it's just another reminder of his duplicity.

How do I know he's not the only one lying? Liv seemed adamant she and Daniel aren't having an affair and that her son's resemblance to him is pure coincidence.

At the time I believed her to be genuine. Now, I'm not so sure. Liv said she doesn't know Daniel and insists that her husband, and Maddox's dad, sadly died.

But that still leaves me with questions. The very large sum in a bank account I never knew existed when he'd tried to tell me he was worried about money. Why did Daniel feel he had to lie rather than explain the contents of the note that fell out of his pocket? Why has he written down personal details of a teenage boy who looks just like him?

I can't let him carry on like this. I've battled the past, tried to make a fresh start but now... I know it's time for me to take control.

Daniel isn't due back until the morning, so I decide to get my thoughts in order ready to face him on his return. I open my laptop and start to make a list of all the things that are worrying me. I'm just adding my concerns about the note when my mobile rings. Liv Leigh's name flashes up on screen. I answer right away.

'Kait? Hi, it's Liv. So sorry to ring late, but I wanted to let you know I found your driving licence on the floor of the café after you left. Thought you might be panicking if you've noticed it's missing.'

'I hadn't even realised I'd lost it,' I say, racking my brains as to how this could have happened. It must have somehow slipped out of my purse when I paid for our coffees. I've got too much on my mind, getting careless. It's been my downfall before.

'Thing is, I had to pop out, and I'm passing the Hucknall turn-off on my way home anyway. I could drop it off, if you're in?'

'Oh! That's really kind of you.' My mind works furiously for an excuse. 'It's just that I'll be heading to bed soon and—'

'I'm literally five minutes away. I can even drop it through the letterbox if you'd prefer. What's your address?'

'No, no.' I don't know why I'm being so tetchy, probably because Daniel's always been so paranoid about home security. Liv is doing me a big favour, after all.

I give her the address. It's only when we end the call, I realise that if she has my licence, she already has it.

. . .

'Have you got time for a cup of tea?' I ask Liv when she arrives. I've been thinking about how I can capitalise on her being here. She checks her watch as I usher her inside.

'That'd be nice, thanks. It's been a long day. Here.' She hands me the driving licence and I clasp it to my chest.

'Thanks for this. It would've been another thing on my plate to register it lost and go through all the rigmarole of applying for a new one. I can't believe I've been so careless.'

'No harm done. I know you've got a lot on your mind,' Liv says kindly. 'OK if I use your loo?'

I direct her to the upstairs bathroom as, despite me asking him to move them every other day, the small downstairs cloak-room is cluttered with Daniel's golf clubs propped up between the tiny sink and the loo.

I potter around making the drinks and take them over to the comfy sofa in the kitchen that overlooks the garden. A few more minutes pass and I glance towards the hallway. I thought Liv would be down by now; she seems to be spending a long time in the bathroom and it crosses my mind she might not be feeling so good. I take a sip of my drink and stare outside while I wait.

Daniel and I keep the garden tidy together. It's my job to keep the borders tidy and Daniel mows the lawn. He never seems to have time to cut it lately though, so the grass is longer than it ought to be. 'I'm too busy with work to worry about the garden,' he'd said when I mentioned it. That had happened in my last relationship, too. He'd lost interest in our life together before announcing he didn't feel ready to get married.

'You have a lovely home.' I look around as Liv walks into the kitchen and joins me on the sofa. 'It's really stylish.'

'Thanks, we've still got lots to do. Daniel wants to extend above the garage, giving us another two bedrooms, but I can't stand to think of living in all that mess with a new baby.'

'Sounds like you're planning more kids after this one.' Liv takes a sip of her tea.

'Not really; I'll be happy with just the one, I think. I'd like to go back to work and well, kids are expensive, aren't they?' I grin. 'Daniel's keen to have another though. Says we'll have plenty of money soon enough.' I fall quiet. I shouldn't have said that; it could sound as if I'm bragging.

'Oh, really? Is he expecting a windfall?' Liv grins. Her face looks slightly manic, as if she's desperate to appear upbeat.

I shake my head. 'He's hopeful of growing his business to the extent it becomes lucrative enough to sell on.' I think about the scanned bank statement and my heart sinks. He already has so much more money than he is letting on.

'If his plan works, you'll be very happy, I'm sure.' Liv puts down her cup. 'Did you say he's back tomorrow?'

'That's right; he should be home around teatime.'

'Hope you don't think it forward of me to ask, but are you going to speak to him about the note you found... about Maddox, I mean?'

'I am, yes. I'm hoping it's something simple, like he got confused with another note that was about the training platform he told me it was. But...'

Liv waits. 'But... you don't believe that.'

'No. Because it just seems a coincidence too far that Maddox looks so much like Daniel.'

Liv stares at me. 'I swear I'm not having an affair with your husband. I can't say any more than that.'

She seems completely genuine. She doesn't look away, doesn't fidget or scratch her nose. The more I get to know her, the more I believe she's telling me the truth.

'I'm not accusing you of having an affair with him and I'm sorry for your loss. Sorry you've lost your husband and Maddox's father. Do you mind me asking what happened to him, to Rich?'

Liv hesitates, as if she's reluctant to revisit the trauma of the past. I get that, I feel the same way. She's never wavered in her certainty that she and Maddox have nothing to do with Daniel. Rightly or wrongly, I'm starting to believe her.

'Sorry,' I say. 'I don't want to make you feel uncomfortable.'

'It's fine,' she says, looking down at her hands. 'It's still so hard to grasp after all these years. He took his own life when Maddox was three years old.'

My hand flies to my mouth before I can stop it. 'Oh no. I'm so sorry, Liv. I had no idea.'

'You weren't to know,' she says quietly. 'Rich was unhappy for a long time. For as long as I knew him, he had demons inside him that he could never rid himself of. Demons that whispered in his ear night and day telling him he was useless. One day after talking about the release death would bring, he just disappeared and...' She squeezes her eyes closed, obviously in a great deal of pain just thinking about what happened back then.

The demons inside... I know plenty about them.

'Please, no need to go into details. I see now why it must have been such a shock when I turned up suggesting Daniel might be Maddox's father.' And yet I'd had no choice. I had to do it.

She gives me a weak smile and looks around the kitchen, her eyes settling on the cluster of decorative copper-bottomed pans hanging from a rack above the island. 'It's a nice bright room in here. Who's the cook?'

'Both of us really. I kind of take care of the weekday meals and Daniel usually cooks on a weekend. He's got a thing about copper pans – bought that set when we had the kitchen done. In fact he designed our new kitchen pretty much himself.'

She's still staring at the pans. 'They're nice,' she says, her eyes shifting to the exposed beams and the cream Aga. 'All of it is very nice.'

We finish our tea and she reaches for her handbag and shuffles to the end of the seat cushion. 'I'd better get off now. You'll let me know if you find out how Daniel got Maddox's details?'

'Course.' I walk down the hallway and she follows me. 'Thanks for bringing the driving licence. It's saved me a job and...' My voice trails off as I sense she is no longer behind me.

When I turn around, I catch the edge of her back disappearing into the living room. 'Liv?' I turn around and walk back to the doorway. It's as if she hasn't heard me. She's standing in the middle of the room, distracted by something.

I follow her line of sight, wondering what it is that's captured her attention so completely.

Even though she's told me there's no way Daniel is her ex-husband, she's staring at the framed photographs of Daniel and me on the windowsill.

It almost looks like she might have changed her mind.

FORTY-THREE

LIV

She can't wait to get out of the house. What the hell was she thinking?

She thinks, *thinks*, she's covered herself. The kitchen was bad enough – almost an exact replica of the one she had when she and Rich were together. But when she walked down the short hallway behind Kait, she looked through the open doorway of the living room and saw the photos. A step or two into the room and she'd just stopped, her body rigid.

Seeing what appeared to be Rich, large as life with another woman. Could it really be him? Living his life, forgetting his promises and their pact because he's got so much money in the bank. *Her* money. Maddox's money.

She'd had a little snoop in his office when Kait was making drinks and she excused herself for the bathroom. Put her head around the door enough to see them there, hanging on the wall behind his desk. The same two signed prints of Muhammad Ali he'd had in his office at home. Before his disappearance.

Initially, he'd wanted to hang them in the living room, which Liv had laughingly outlawed. He'd been so proud of those prints back then, had bragged about them on Facebook, taken friends to show them.

He'd got it all planned out: sink his efforts into his new life. His new wife and his soon-to-be-born baby. The past firmly ditched and conveniently forgotten.

Fury and heartbreak flooded through her like a thousand volts of electricity. She'd forgotten where she was until she heard, 'Liv? What's wrong?'

Kait stood in front of her, looking concerned. She'd looked at Liv and then looked at the photos.

'Is it something to do with Daniel?'

'No,' Liv answered quickly. 'Just... a vivid memory of when I was married. These photos are so lovely; I can see you and Daniel are close.'

Kait smiled then. 'I do love him. If I can only get this blip cleared up, get some answers from him, I'll be happy.' She'd laid a hand over her stomach. 'I can properly look forward to our future together as a family.'

When she gets out to the car, Liv can't stop shaking. Kait had shown her a single picture on her phone in the park but it wasn't clear or at quite the right angle for her to be completely sure about what seemed an impossibility. Sometimes, after so many years, she finds it hard to summon up Rich's detailed image at all. But the photos she's seen here are extremely troubling. So close to who Rich was and what he looked like. So close and yet... she just can't quite hit that one-hundred-percent sure mark. Years have passed, people change. Rich will have changed. Is she in denial it's him? That her passport to a better future is dissolving into thin air in front of her very eyes?

The expensive copper pans Rich had been obsessed with at home. Hung them over the island in their chocolate-box cottage exactly as he has done here. The cream Aga and leaving the original beams exposed... they were his idea, too. Kait's throwaway comment about how he is expecting a substantial sum of money soon, supposedly from the sale of his business.

And then the photographs on the windowsill. Clearer shots, taken while he was relaxed and off-guard.

If it's true, if Daniel Hatton is really Rich, then there's something far more pressing Liv must address.

She must figure out how to get her hands on the money she and her son are entitled to. The money she's given up over a decade of her life for.

FORTY-FOUR

RICH

THREE MONTHS BEFORE HIS DISAPPEARANCE

The suite was spacious and cool. As they came through the door, Rich saw a collection of elegant cream sofas as he kicked off his shoes. A full-size dining table and chairs stood in front of floor-to-ceiling windows without blinds, which, on this high floor, gave a bird's eye view over Manchester's city lights.

'Make yourself comfy and I'll get us a drink,' Alicia said, closing the door softly behind him. He sat down on a large, squashy sofa, and she padded in barefoot with two large glasses of red wine a few minutes later.

'So let's hear your plan,' Rich said, taking a sip. He knew Alicia was an intelligent woman who excelled at thinking outside the box. He felt optimistic that her plan would be a good one, particularly as she'd mentioned she'd given it some thought. Hopefully, it would be good enough to get them both out of a fix.

'I mean, it's more of an outline at this stage,' Alicia said, her brow furrowing. 'But the main points are there. Essentially, using the online security details I've discovered, I plan to move ninety per cent of the money in the secret account out into a new, separate account.'

Rich frowned. 'Why not all of it?'

'Completely emptying an account as big as that can be difficult. Plus closure would probably mean an email and possibly letter confirming to Caleb this action had been taken.'

Blackcurrant and aniseed flavours exploded on Rich's tongue. 'Good point.'

She really had thought about this.

'Once the transfer of funds is complete, you and I will split the cash sixty-forty in my favour and then I disappear. I plan to move abroad.'

'A sixty-forty split?' He frowned, confused. It sounded like too good a deal. After all, he was only a hundred grand down – even though that was more than enough debt to bankrupt him – but he'd be happy with just the money he'd lost refunded. Alicia was offering him well over a million of Caleb's money. *A million!* He wasn't stupid enough to argue... soon, it would be Alicia's money and it was up to her how she carved it up. Rich decided to play it cool.

'Sounds like I might need to disappear, too,' he murmured.

Alicia pressed her lips together. 'That will be your decision. I'll explain fully later, but you only need to play a very small though essential role.'

Rich stared at her. 'Couldn't you get half of this money through legal means?'

Alicia gave a bitter laugh. 'Trust me, Caleb would find a way to cheat me out of most of it. I had no idea about this account and I've no doubt he has more cash stashed away where nobody will ever find it. If he realises I know what he's up to behind my back with his exotic dancer, he'll lock me out of his life overnight. He's only keeping me around for convenience while he puts his plan into action.'

Rich nodded slowly, considering what she'd said. He knew how that felt.

'It sounds fairly straightforward, but you might need to move fast if he's got plans to move in with this woman.' Rich hesitated. 'I don't want to talk myself out of an enormous sum of money, but as a friend, it seems to me you could do this on your own without my input at all.'

Alicia sighed. 'Thing is... it's not nearly as simple as it sounds. I can't just move the money into one of my existing bank accounts, or even a new account in my own name. When he realises the money has gone, I'm the first place he'll look. His lawyers will comb every inch of my personal finances to prove I took it.' She hesitated. 'This is where you come in, Rich. Initially, I would need to transfer the money into an account that you set up. He'll never suspect your involvement and his forensic lawyers would never think to look at your personal finances.'

'*My* account?' He felt his face blanch. Maybe she'd not offered such a generous split after all. When Caleb realised his money was gone and that Rich's name was the withdrawer, he'd come after him with a vengeance. If Alicia was to be believed, he would stop at nothing in order to find him.

Alicia glanced at his expression and held up a reassuring hand. 'It's not what you think. We'll be using the dark web.'

He frowned. *The dark web.* He'd heard the phrase many times. Had read an article once that said it was some kind of hidden internet portal for looking at dodgy stuff like extreme porn, or a place you might hire a hitman and fake passports. It had seemed to him to be a bit of an urban myth.

Alicia glanced at his concerned expression. 'The dark web is just a name for a search engine that guarantees anonymity online. The biggest search engines like Google don't index it, so we need to use special software to access it.'

'So your actions can't be traced.'

She nodded. 'Let's just say I'm paying an expert a lot of money to help me execute my plan. That person only communicates via the dark web, but it's not all dark stuff. Some people just want to feel they can speak freely, discuss things openly without being monitored.'

'You said yourself Caleb will come after the name the bank give him when he realises he's been duped.'

Alicia nodded. 'He'll try. But the account won't be in your real name either; it will be a false name. I just need another person to enable our man to set up the forged photographic ID to open the account. As you know, bank accounts don't carry a photograph, just a name and address. When Caleb's people try to find out who's taken the money, they'll find themselves running around in circles. I need to be squeaky clean in that there's no link whatsoever to myself no matter how deep they dig.' She stared into space for a moment. 'And believe me, they'll dig very deep.'

'And that's the extent of my involvement?' Rich said.

'That's right. Safe to say, once the money is out of Caleb's account and safely in yours, I'll transfer my share to various offshore holding accounts. The UK banking system is watertight, but once the money is out of circulation here, it's far easier to distribute without leaving an audit trail.'

'And I'll be left with my share?'

Alicia nodded. 'Correct. And it's entirely up to you what you do with your percentage, Rich. I realise I'm asking for a tremendous amount of your trust here, but we must have faith in each other, or this will never work.' Worry shadowed her face. 'I'm not going to mince words, here. Caleb will do whatever he needs, in order to protect his assets. Make no mistake, he has the power and the dodgy contacts to make us both disappear where no one would ever find us.'

'What are you saying?' Rich's eyes widened.

'Exactly what it sounds like. Caleb will never recover from

this. His reputation will be ruined, and if that happened and he found out what we'd done, he'd want to wipe both of us out. You haven't seen that side of him but believe me when I say it would be entirely possible for him to arrange. What I'm proposing is a big ask, I know, but the rewards are high. It's your decision in the end, I won't put pressure on you, but I need to know if you want in by tomorrow at the latest. I can't afford to leave it any longer.'

Rich thought about his scant options. He could just accept what had happened: that he had been shafted by Caleb Mosley and had lost all his money thanks to the businessman discovering a white lie involving a charity pin, of all things. Talk about being over-sensitive! It was still an option for Rich to try and put it all behind him, get a job, get himself back on his feet and never set eyes on Caleb again.

He thought about his own bank and how they could foreclose on his loan as early as next week. If that happened, it was a certainty they'd lose the house.

He couldn't bear to think of how he would begin to explain it all to Livvy.

Then his thoughts returned to the cool million-pound balance that could be sitting in his bank account within a matter of days. The answer to all problems. *All of them.*

Rich turned to Alicia and fixed her with a determined look. 'OK then, I'm in,' he said.

When Rich returned to his own hotel room, his heart felt heavy. He'd been given the chance to dissolve all his problems in record time, but it wasn't without risk. Alicia was insistent Caleb would never find out about his involvement, but she couldn't be one hundred per cent certain of that outcome. If something went wrong, the true cost Rich might have to pay was sobering. Was his safety and the safety of his family *really* worth a million pounds?

A million pounds! The answer to all his problems in life for a *little* risk. A very small risk, that was all. The money had the power to save his marriage, prevent his house from being repossessed and it would keep the bank onside. They'd have time to sell up and start a new life, maybe abroad, like Alicia also planned to do. Somewhere warm and safe where Maddox would flourish and he and Liv could become closer again. On top of that, Caleb Mosley, the smug liar, would pay for double-crossing him with the aborted Spanish deal.

He and Alicia had talked in and around the subject for hours before he left her hotel room, but in the end it came down to this: all Rich had to do was to allow Alicia to transfer the funds from Caleb's secret bank account into his own false account for one day only. That was it. His entire contribution for the reward of saving himself and his family from certain ruin. Only a mad man would turn a chance like this down.

Alicia would be the one doing the hard work and Caleb would never know about Rich's involvement. More importantly, neither would Livvy... until he was ready to tell her. Rich believed and trusted Alicia. She had been a good friend to both him and to Livvy, and on top of that, she thought the world of Maddox.

Before he'd left her suite tonight, the two of them had shaken hands to cement the deal and Alicia had said, 'One thing I need to make crystal clear: you can't tell a soul about this, Rich, not even Livvy. If Caleb becomes the least bit suspicious, Livvy will be forced to lie or get dragged into this mess.'

Rich nodded. That was true enough and it was the last thing he wanted. But with every step down the carpeted corridor as he neared his own small room, he became more and more compelled to do it. He couldn't turn down such an offer and he had no choice but to keep it all a secret for now because Livvy was a born worrier. If he involved her in any way, there was no way she'd be able to cope with the knowledge of what was about to happen. Plus, there was another powerful reason for keeping his wife in the dark.

It wasn't just the million pounds – it was the fact Rich himself had all but bankrupted them and she knew nothing about it.

'Neither of us can trust anyone in this situation, Rich,' Alicia had said. 'I hope you realise that.'

Before he'd left, they'd pencilled in some initial fake meeting dates under the tag of 'Investor A' in their diaries.

He swiped his key card against the door and entered the bedroom with relief. He loosened his tie and opened the top two buttons of his shirt. He felt hot and his heart was pounding.

After splashing some cold water on his face in the bathroom, he undressed, pulled on a robe and lay on the bed staring at the ceiling. It was all decided.

He'd paid his fare and climbed on to a rollercoaster ride that would either save him or destroy him. Now, it was just a waiting game.

FORTY-FIVE

MADDOX

After he's dealt with something that's been on his mind, Maddox walks to the place he's agreed to meet Sammy, feeling like a zombie. The sports bag he carries feels so heavy with him being so tired and his stomach is churning. He'd barely slept last night after opening that envelope. So much stuff going round in his mind... trying to make sense of something that defies belief.

In the early hours of this morning, unable to stand it any longer, he'd texted Sammy on his 'work' phone.

Is that me and you in the photo? Are you my dad??

There has been no reply and now Maddox is scared Sammy is annoyed he'd texted him instead of waiting for their meet-up as Sammy had arranged with him.

At the agreed meet place, he gets into Sammy's car and they high-five in their usual greeting.

'I'm sorry about sending that text but... the photo?' Maddox tries to bite his tongue but he can't. He has to say the words. 'Are you... I mean, is it—'

Sammy presses a finger to his lips. 'Fasten your seatbelt, lad. We'll talk about it later.'

'Where are we going?' Maddox asks when Sammy pulls away. He watches Sammy, takes in the slicked back hair that he knows is curly like his own. His profile the same as the man in the photograph.

'Tonight, we're going somewhere very special,' Sammy says mysteriously, giving him a strange smile. 'Now you've seen the photograph, it's the perfect moment.'

His mum's face appears in his mind's eye, and he pushes it away.

Maddox feels his guts beginning to swirl. Why is he worrying about his mum? If Sammy is really his dad then she's been lying through her teeth to him.

Sammy lets Maddox choose a playlist and he's so busy scrolling through Spotify, it's a shock when he looks up. 'Why have we come here?' he says faintly.

Sammy pulls on to the car park, the gravel kicking up under the big tyres of the SUV. 'Told you it was a special place,' he says, turning off the engine. 'Not Frog Hill, but somewhere very similar. Special for you and me, anyhow.'

Silence settles around them and both stare out of the windscreen, gazing up at the big hill in front of them. 'This is just like the last place we saw each other.'

Maddox looks at Sammy, opens his mouth and closes it again. When he was about ten, his mum drove him to the place in West Yorkshire where it happened when he was three years old. For the first time, she'd explained exactly what had happened that day. The kite flying, the storm. All of it. He'd been old enough to understand and imagine how it must have been.

While his mum walked Betsy around the bottom, he'd climbed Frog Hill and willed his dad to come back. Maddox could almost imagine him just walking in front of him, his mum crying and them hugging like a proper family again.

Shortly after that his dad was officially declared as presumed dead and he's never been back there since.

Sammy clears his throat and breaks the spell. Maddox looks at him but can't speak.

'That's right, Maddox. I'm your dad,' Sammy says softly. 'I had no choice but to disappear that day. I'll explain everything, but for now—'

Maddox wrenches open the car door and stumbles out, vomiting into a tangle of weeds at the side of the car. He wipes his mouth with the back of his hand, drawing in big gulps of cold air before straightening up.

Sammy appears at the side of him and slides his arm around his shoulders. 'It's a shock, I know. But try and look on the bright side. We're together again now.'

'But... why didn't you tell me before now?'

'I wanted to, believe me. But see, it was your mum, Maddox. She's kept secrets from you all your life and she threatened me with the police if ever I made contact. But now you're old enough to make your own decisions and she has my money – cash that's meant for you and me to start a new life away from here.'

'But... why would Mum lie to me all this time?' Maddox believes Sammy. He's called his mum a liar to her face now, but in his quiet moments, he still finds it hard to believe she really has betrayed him.

Sammy sighs and takes off his baseball cap, running his hand through the wild, dark curls that are so like Maddox's own. 'This is hard to hear, I know. But there's a lot you don't know about your mum, Maddox. Now's not the time to explain every detail, but she's done you wrong, for sure. That's why I needed you to get the information. I needed you to do it for us. Do you see that?'

Maddox nods and glances at Sammy's tense expression. He's usually so cool and laid back, but now he just looks kind of desperate. Maddox hasn't seen him this stressed before. Apart from the first time he met him, when Sammy was in the car and talking to him in the rear-view mirror, he's been chatty and relaxed.

'Hey!' Sammy snaps his fingers. 'Did you get it?'

Maddox nods and pulls out the pen drive from the front pocket of his denim jacket.

Sammy takes it, his eyes glinting. 'And everything is on there, right?'

'Yep. Just like you said. I downloaded every folder and document on my mum's laptop.'

'Good lad.' He nods to the big weekend bag Maddox carries. 'See you brought some clothes for our travels.'

'Yeah, I can't wait!' He knows Sammy wants him to be happy about their trip, but he keeps thinking about his mum. What she'll feel like when she realises he's gone. Even after all her lies he still feels something in his heart. He's an idiot and he needs to toughen up.

Maddox looks up sharply as another vehicle – a brand-new Range Rover, black with tinted windows – pulls into the parking area, the pebbles scattering beneath the extra wide, low-profile tyres.

Sammy watches the vehicle's approach and Maddox can tell by his expression he was expecting it.

Sammy puts a hand on his shoulder. 'Wait here. I just have a bit of business to attend to.'

Maddox nods and turns to look back up at the hill. His throat tightens as he realises this looks like the exact spot his dad... Sammy... had left him all those years ago. If only he could remember.

He turns when he hears voices. Sammy has climbed into the passenger side of the Range Rover but his door isn't fully closed.

In the quiet surroundings, Maddox can hear snatches of what sounds like an uptight conversation.

'Is this all there is?' the driver of the Range Rover says.

'Everything on her laptop is on there,' Sammy says. He sounds curiously polite, Maddox thinks. Like he's speaking to his boss. 'You'll have to go through it properly and let me know if—'

'I don't need to go through it.' The man sounds irritated. 'I can see at a glance that what I'm looking for isn't there.'

'So what do we do now?' Sammy asks.

There's a pause. The voices drop lower still and Maddox can no longer hear what's being said. Then Sammy says in surprise, 'Is that really necessary?'

The man replies in a low, menacing tone. 'Absolutely it's necessary. We're running out of time and it's the only way we'll get the truth out of her.'

'It's just that—'

'Jeez, stop dithering, Sammy. You always knew there might be a Plan B and there's no time like the present,' the man growls. 'So let's just get it over with.'

Sammy opens the door, his boots scraping on the gravel as he walks over to Maddox, a forced smile on his face.

'Before we go, there's someone who wants to meet you, OK?'

Maddox's heartrate picks up. Sammy looks pale and he won't meet his eyes.

'Who is it?' Maddox swallows. 'I heard him getting annoyed with you.'

Sammy looks taken aback for a moment before saying, 'He just wants a quick word. Jump in, yeah?' Sammy nods to the passenger side door.

'But... who's in the car?' Maddox doesn't move. He feels sick and he's staring at Sammy, willing him to say what's happening. 'I don't like this. I heard you talking and—'

Maddox turns at the sound of the driver's side car door opening. A tall, broad figure dressed in black looms and instinctively, Maddox steps back. But the man steps into the light and smiles at him.

'Remember me, Maddox?'

Maddox takes a good look at him and frowns. He's handsome with a square jaw and short dark hair. When he smiles, his eyes crinkle at the corners like he means it.

Maddox's shoulders relax a little but he shakes his head. He doesn't know who this guy is.

'That's a shame because you and me, we used to be mates, you know? When you were little more than a toddler. My wife loved you, used to say she wished you were our own boy.' The man takes another step forward and, this time, Maddox doesn't feel threatened.

'Sorry,' he says. 'I don't remember you.'

The man holds out a hand and Maddox shakes it. 'I'm Caleb,' he says. 'And I was good friends with your dad. Before he double-crossed me, that is.'

Before Maddox can speak, or cry out, a muscular arm gets him in a headlock and presses something wet and cold over his face.

It sticks to his skin and smells like chemicals. Maddox tries not to breathe. But the cloth is held fast over his nose and mouth and in another few seconds, he is forced to gasp in air.

He feels himself slumping, feels darkness close in around him as Caleb's face looms above him.

His legs give way, and he drops down. All his thoughts, his hopes and his fears are gone.

FORTY-SIX

LIV

When she gets home, it's 10 p.m. but Maddox isn't in yet.

Liv heads for the kitchen, annoyance burning in her chest, and pours herself a large glass of wine. Just the one. She's expressly told him if he goes anywhere at all, she wants a note or text message saying where and who he's with. Otherwise, he's not to go out.

Her instruction went down like a lead balloon as she expected, but that's irrelevant. Liv is taking the detectives' concerns about this county lines business at school very seriously, and more than that, she's got to somehow find out if Rich has made contact with their son... without expressly saying that to Maddox when he thinks his father is dead. Now that she's over her weekend sickness, and can think straight, she's got to sit down and properly grill Maddox tomorrow, about exactly what had happened outside the school gates when a teacher stopped to see if he was OK.

There's now a far more worrying danger on the horizon. It's not just some spotty kid trying to get Maddox involved in drugs – she still prays and believes that her son is too smart to get involved in dealing – but his *father*. What boy wouldn't want to get to know his dad, particularly after believing he was dead? This would be a new way she could lose him. That comment he'd made when the detectives called, about Liv lying to him. It seemed to prove that Rich had already revealed his identity to their son and blamed Liv for everything.

She shivers at the thought of it.

Before she goes to get her phone out of her bag, she gulps down half her wine and walks back to the fridge for a top-up. That's when she sees it: a folded piece of notepaper propped up against the kitchen canisters.

Sorry, Mum.

That's it. That's all it says in Maddox's distinctive scrawl.

But... sorry for what? Liv looks around the kitchen, her heart thumping against her chest wall. Her laptop is where she left it and nothing else appears to be missing. It's the same story in the living room. Nothing out of place, nothing damaged or ruined... *so what?*

At the bottom of the stairs and stooping to pull her phone out of her handbag, Liv stops and frowns. Stares at the hardwood floor between the front door and the first step. It's clear of Maddox's several pairs of trainers. She's grumbled periodically about him leaving them there and his defence has been, 'I don't know which pair I'll wear until I'm heading out of the door.'

But they're all gone.

An instant wave of panic rises inside her. Liv pushes the phone into her back pocket and bounds upstairs into Maddox's bedroom. The room looks in disarray as per usual, but something has changed. No clothes strewn over his gaming chair, no dirty underwear and socks left in a trail on the floor.

Liv rushes over to his double wardrobe and flings open the doors.

'No... oh no!' she wails, staring into the wardrobe as if this all might be a bad dream.

A good chunk of his clothes are gone including the track-suits and hoodies he wears constantly after school and at weekends.

With shaking hands, she pulls out her phone and calls him. The call connects and she's disorientated for a moment when a ring tone starts up around his bed. She stumbles towards it and spots the lit screen amongst the folds of his tangled bedding.

Tears sting her eyes as she stands staring down at the phone – his old Samsung. She makes a quick search of the bedding and in his bedside table and desk.

The new iPhone she'd seen a couple of nights ago is not here.

'Where are you, Maddox?' she whispers. 'Where has he taken you?'

She reels back against the wall as a familiar face flashes into her mind. She squeezes her eyes closed hard but the image does not leave her. Her fine features, her beautiful eyes... a woman she used to call a friend and who didn't deserve to die. *Alicia Mosley.*

Why now? Why, after all this time when she's coped so well?

The image twists and turns and now those beautiful eyes are staring blankly at Liv. Her face covered in blood.

It's hard to breathe. She's gasping for air.

FORTY-SEVEN

KAIT

I'm just about to get into the shower after a long day when my phone rings. It's Kirsten.

'Kait? It's me. Thought you'd have called me by now. Are you OK?'

I gather myself, already pre-empting her reaction. 'I'm fine. Unless you want the truth which is that I'm exhausted. A lot has happened since we last spoke.'

'Really? In what way?'

'I'll explain everything when you get back from your trip and—'

'Can we do it now? I'm relaxing in my hotel room with a drink from the minibar and I'm interested where this is going. This is the perfect time to tell me everything. From the beginning.' She seems hellbent on getting every detail from me.

I start by explaining how I managed to trace Olivia Leigh from the contact form.

'So now you know exactly who she is?'

'More than that, I've been to see her,' I say, filling her in about finding the photograph on her workplace website.

She makes a noise of disbelief. 'You're a fast worker, I'll give you that. So what happened?'

'When you sent me the form and I saw the picture of the student, Maddox, it felt as if my world was falling apart. I couldn't just sit here dithering, I felt like I had to do something.'

She falls quiet for a moment. Then, a little more subdued, she says, 'He's the image of Daniel, isn't he? What happened when you confronted her?'

'Confronted is the wrong word really, although it might have felt that way to her. I stayed calm and tried to be reasonable. I went to the school to see the boy with my own eyes and his mum was waiting outside. I hung around the house until she came out to walk the dog.'

'And that's when you spoke to her?'

'Yes. We spoke in the park and then went for a coffee. She was friendly enough. Probably more than I would have been, if I'm honest.'

'And what did she say about her son?'

'She was adamant Daniel isn't Maddox's father, that his biological dad died years ago. She seemed genuine, but I'm not about to just take her word for it.'

'Maybe you should,' Kirsten said. 'Maybe you shouldn't go digging, Kait.'

'What?' I let out a little laugh. 'You're the one who initially commented on their likeness! Plus, the fact remains that Daniel had the boy's personal details for a reason and I need to find out why.'

I hear Kirsten's wine glass chink on a hard surface as she puts it down.

'What else did she say?'

'She told me Maddox's father died when he was three years old.'

'Anything else?'

'I asked her if she was having an affair with Daniel.'

'You asked her straight?'

'Yes. And she completely denied it.'

'As you might expect, I suppose.'

'Exactly and at the moment, I have no other evidence apart from her word... which means nothing to me because I barely know her.'

I hear the giveaway tinkle of liquid being poured. She's topping up her glass. Kirsten can quickly become combative when she's had a few drinks.

'If I were you, I'd back off a bit,' Kirsten says. 'I'm worried about you.'

'I'm not going to back off. It's a bloody big coincidence that the kid has such a striking resemblance to Daniel.'

'Thing is, you're stressed and that's when you... that's when it becomes difficult for you to cope. Promise me you're not doing anything silly, like last time.'

'I'm not even going to answer that,' I snap.

'Sorry. I shouldn't have said that. It's just—'

'Daniel is due back tomorrow evening, so I'll be tackling him then. I'll let you know how this all pans out. I have to go, Kirsten. Speak soon.'

'Wait, I want to—'

I end the call as if I haven't heard her and think for a moment. She's never usually so interested in my life.

With Daniel, I'm going to make a big effort to start things off in a pleasant and relaxed manner. Even though it's exhausting me. It's not just Maddox Leigh I need to tackle Daniel about, it's also the loaded bank account I now know about that he has in his own name. Plus finding out what was behind the doorbell camera footage I discovered and why he's deleted it.

FORTY-EIGHT

RICH

TWO DAYS BEFORE HIS DISAPPEARANCE

He'd met up with Alicia regularly.

'I've never known you to have as many meetings,' Liv had remarked one day when he'd kissed her on the cheek and said he wouldn't be long.

'You know how it is,' Rich had said mildly. 'Nothing one minute then a few good properties come on to the market all at once.'

He'd felt sick as he'd said it, noticed her sideways glance. As it stood, he hadn't a penny to put towards buying a garden shed then, never mind investing in a multi-million-pound residential development. But it wasn't as if he could share that with Livvy.

'I'm researching exactly what I need to do,' Alicia had told him at the café they'd met at on the edge of town. She'd opened her laptop. 'It won't take more than a few days. We haven't got that luxury, but I want you to open an account in a false name today. Watch carefully.'

Alicia had looked up when Rich hadn't answered. 'Don't look so worried. It'll all be over soon.'

. . .

Over the next few days, Livvy had become increasingly restless. Rich had been pretty sure she'd sensed something was wrong, she just hadn't figured out what yet. But she was sharp-eyed enough and he'd known he had to watch everything he did which only increased the tremendous pressure he'd felt like a real thing bearing down on him. Waiting, waiting, waiting for news from Alicia that she was able to proceed.

He'd stopped trying to contact Caleb since speaking to Alicia that night and finding out the truth of what his so-called friend had done to him. Rich was still a member of a couple of popular online property business forums, and it had rankled to see Caleb's name mentioned regularly. Several people were clearly in awe of Mosley Property Services.

by TowerBlockBuilder: I see MPS won the big leisure park contract in the South-West.

by VeganGirl1989: MPS is awesome. Caleb Mosley is the new big beast in property development.

by Minky.MooX: I've met him several times. Lovely guy.

He'd felt the same himself when he'd first met Caleb and had been in awe of his reputation. Now the mere mention of his name sickened Rich.

He'd begun wearing a belt with his loosening trousers. He pretended to watch TV or pushed food around his plate at dinner when he felt Livvy's eyes on him. She'd had always had what seemed like a sixth sense that kicked in when he was anxious about something. It was as if she could effortlessly zero in on the troubled vibes that were rolling off him in messy waves he felt unable to control.

Friday night, he poured them both a pre-dinner drink while Livvy stirred a rich ragu sauce at the hob. Maddox had turned three earlier in the week, and the three of them had planned a day out the following day to celebrate together. Maddox was tucked up in bed – it had been a busy week.

His phone screen lit up briefly with a notification from *Investor A*. His hand jolted and red wine splashed clumsily off the lip of the glass just as Livvy turned around from the hob.

'Everything OK?' she said lightly as he put down the bottle and snatched up his phone.

'Yes, fine! I'll just pop to the bathroom before we have drinks.'

Faintly aware of Livvy's eyes tracking him across the room, he got out of there as quickly as possible and closed the cloakroom door behind him before opening Alicia's message.

We have a problem. Need to speak to you urgently.

He pushed the phone back into his pocket and wiped prickles of perspiration from his top lip. His body sagged with the leaden weight of his dilemma.

Dinner was almost on the table. He couldn't possibly get away for another hour at the very earliest. *Shit!*

'Could you put the heat mat on the table?' Livvy called, her voice light and relaxed. 'I'll be serving up in two minutes.'

He walked down the hallway and stood outside the kitchen – gathered himself.

'Did you hear me?' Suddenly her face was there in front of him, in the doorway. 'I'm nearly ready to—'

'I'm sorry, I can't,' he said, his voice cracking.

Livvy frowned. 'What?'

'I can't stay for dinner. I have to pop out. I just got a call and there's an emergency. In one of the properties.'

'What kind of emergency?' Livvy's cheeks inflamed. 'What's got into you?'

Rich shook his head and stared at the floor. He couldn't sustain this for much longer. 'I will tell you, I promise. But... I have no choice but to go. I'll be back as soon as I can.'

Livvy's mouth settled into a hard line. 'Rich, what the hell is going on? You can't just walk away from this, I need answers.'

'I'm sorry.' He turned to leave. He needed some breathing space. 'Soon, you'll know everything. I swear.'

Outside in the car, Rich called Alicia.

'Jeez, I didn't think you were going to call me. What took you so long?' Her voice sounded strained. Panicked. 'I need to meet with you. Right now.'

Rich swallowed. It sounded serious, as if something might have gone badly wrong. 'What is it? What's the problem?'

'I can't talk here,' she said tightly. 'Meet me in the small bar at the Randall Hotel as soon as you can. I'm on my way there now.'

He started the car and said, 'I'll be there in about thirty minutes.'

He found her at the back of the bar area, sitting in a dimly lit booth, a closed laptop and a half-empty bottle of red wine on the table with two glasses, only one of them unused.

Alicia started when she saw him, her hand pressing her chest in what looked like relief that he'd arrived.

'What is it?' Rich said urgently, looking around the bar. 'It was difficult to get away and I can't stay long. I think Livvy suspects—'

'Caleb's planning to leave me next week. We must move immediately, or it'll be too late.'

'What? You said it would be another few weeks before—'

She cut in, her voice slightly breathless. 'The private detective called me two hours ago. Caleb's fancy piece has been spouting to her friends again. Apparently, they've brought their plans forward because they want to be settled together for when she has the baby.'

Rich studied her face. She looked pale and drawn, her fingers twisting and working against each other.

'If I don't get the funds out in the next day or so, he'll take everything, and I'll be left with nothing.' She looked up, meeting his eyes. 'As will you.'

Rich poured himself a small glass of wine but he didn't top her up. 'OK, what do I need to do?'

She reached down to a bag on the seat cushion next to her and pulled out an envelope. 'Here are your documents back. My contact has opened an account and you'll find full details in there. It's untraceable to you.'

'I thought we'd have more time,' he said weakly. 'But if it has to be done now then that's all there is to it.'

Alicia nodded slowly. 'It's going to be OK. The money will stay in your account for just one day before it's moved again. Destroy the details about the new account when you've absorbed them. Don't make any electronic notes or refer to it on email or by phone and nobody will ever know you had a part in this.'

Optimism surged inside him, helping to disperse the fear. When it came down to it, he had no choice but to comply unless he wanted to continue this brutal, short path to bankruptcy. Abiding by Alicia's instructions, he hadn't told a soul. His involvement would be over in just one more day from now and then, when they had the money, he would tell Livvy everything and beg for her forgiveness so they could start a new life.

It was going to be alright. He was going to make something

of his life. He was doing this for himself but, most of all, he was doing it for his family.

FORTY-NINE

LIV

She stares at her phone, the shrill ring hurting her ears. It's the school she works at, no doubt enquiring as to when she's going to be back. She turns the phone face down; she forgot to let them know she still felt ill yesterday, but she can't possibly go in today, not with Maddox missing. Besides, she has to get herself to River Gate Care Home.

She'd been out of her mind with worry until she simply couldn't think straight worrying where Maddox was and who he was with. Her son's note saying he was sorry showed he'd willingly gone somewhere. Which, bearing in mind the police concerns about county lines activity, was worrying to say the least. But deep down, Liv didn't think Maddox was involved in drug dealing. Her gut told her that Rich, aka Daniel Hatton, was back in town and if that was true, then what man wouldn't want to see his son?

She barely slept a wink last night, worrying. And when exhaustion finally knocked her out, she woke herself up sobbing and wailing... at the scene of the accident again. Alicia waving and beautiful one minute, dead and bleeding the next.

And it was all her fault.

She'd gone downstairs to make a hot drink, to take her mind off the dream. She'd been afraid of the breathless panic making a return and it had worked to some extent. She'd sat up drinking coffee as the sun rose and had eventually nodded off on the kitchen sofa for an hour.

Before she went up to bed, she'd made the decision not to involve the police. Just in case Maddox came home very late or even in the early hours. She had to give herself the chance to discover if Rich was involved in her son's sudden disappearance. If Rich *was* involved, she didn't want the detectives anywhere near. Couldn't risk everything that happened being exposed and dragging them all down with it.

It was then, like an epiphany, she thought about her mother-in-law, Shannon, and her supposed night terrors. It is clutching at straws, but maybe, just maybe, it means something. He'd always thought the world of his mother to the point he couldn't see any wrong in her whatsoever. Could it be possible he'd made contact with her, too?

It is a dull day, but already too warm. Her head thumps from the wine she knocked back last night – nearly two bottles in the end. Trying to cancel out the thoughts that were torturing her. She needs help with her drinking but that is the least of her worries.

Liv parks up at River Gate and buzzes for entry. The routine is just the same: signing the visitor book, asking for a brief update of Shannon's care.

'Nothing new to report save for a small tweak in Mrs Askew's night-time medication,' the desk clerk says.

'What medication is that?'

'One sec.' The clerk scrolls down her computer screen. 'Ah, here we go. A mild sedative has been prescribed by the doctor.'

Liv frowns. 'Does it mention the night terrors she's been having?'

Again, the clerk scrolls through. Liv thinks she sees a shadow flit across her face but she looks up and smiles. 'Can't see anything here, but if you take a seat, I'll ask one of the lead carers to come and have a quick word with you. They'll know more than me.'

Liv nods and takes a seat in reception. Several visitors come in, sign the book and are buzzed straight through to the main building. She checks her watch; she's been waiting ten minutes now. What's going on?

At the very moment she's about to speak to the desk clerk again, a courier arrives with a sack barrow loaded with cardboard boxes. The security door is wedged open and he begins ferrying the packages through to an inner storeroom. The phone rings and while the clerk is busy on the call, Liv slips quietly through and makes her way down the corridor to Shannon's room.

She doesn't knock on the bedroom door but pushes it open softly.

Shannon is sitting by the window and staring out at the small garden and car park beyond.

Before she speaks or walks inside, Liv looks around the room. Everything looks ordered and neat, just the same as usual. Shannon's bed is made, there's a jug of water and a glass on the small coffee table and a vase full of her favourite flowers. Freesias.

Liv narrows her eyes and looks at the vase. There are far more freesias there than she brought with her last week and they look fresh. Then she sees the box of new, cellophane-wrapped Milk Tray chocolates on her dresser. A bigger size than the one Liv brought her.

'Hello, Shannon.' Liv walks inside the bedroom and closes

the door. Shannon wheels around in her chair and narrows her eyes. 'How are you? It's me, Livvy.'

'You!' Shannon narrows her eyes. 'I told them I don't want to see you anymore. He's told me everything and you're a wicked person.'

Liv feels a weight descend on her chest. *He's told me everything.* Has Rich been here?

'Who said that about me, Shannon?' Her throat tightens. 'Who was it?'

'He told me about what you did.' Her voice rises in volume and pitch. 'You're a liar and a bad person! You've done such bad things and now you're after his money.'

Liv reaches for the edge of the table to steady herself. Her head is spinning.

'Shannon... be quiet!' Glancing at the door, she walks towards the older woman. 'Stop shouting.'

'Stay away from me... help!' Shannon wails. 'Help me! She's going to hurt me!'

The door opens and two carers appear. 'What's happening here?' one says while the other attends to Shannon, trying to calm her down. 'It's probably best if you step outside, Ms Leigh. The desk clerk said she'd asked you to wait in reception until someone spoke to you.'

'Who brought Shannon the flowers?' Liv says, following her out. 'It sounds to me like someone has been here without permission, upsetting her.'

'I'm sorry?'

'She says someone has been frightening her and there's a vase full of fresh flowers in there and a new box of chocolates. I didn't bring those in, so she must have had another visitor.' Shannon's wails still emanate from the bedroom into the corridor. 'I'm not going anywhere until you check your visitor log.'

The carer consults her handheld tablet.

'It looks like she had a visitor yesterday evening at seven o'clock.'

Liv's throat burns with fury. 'That's unacceptable. I've made it perfectly clear that nobody else is permitted to visit my mother-in-law without my permission. Someone has really messed up here and I'm going to take it further. What is the name of her visitor?'

The carer looks at her then turns the tablet around to show Liv a screenshot of a completed visitor log. 'It was a Maddox Leigh. Says here he's Mrs Askew's grandson.'

FIFTY

NOTTINGHAMSHIRE POLICE

Case Number: 0045789
Date: 13 October 2012
Location: Huddersfield Police Station: Inter-
view Room 2
Time: 17:21

Present:

- Detective Inspector Jarrod Hutch
- Detective Sergeant Emma Dunsforth
- Mrs Olivia Askew (Interviewee)
- Constable Sara McGuinness (Witness
  Care Officer)

Interview Begins: 17:21

DI Hutch: This interview is being audio and
video recorded. I am Detective Inspector Jarrod
Hutch, and this is Detective Sergeant Emma

Dunsforth. We are conducting this interview at Huddersfield Police Station. The date is Sunday thirteenth of October, twenty twelve, and the time is five twenty-one p.m. Can you please confirm your full name and date of birth?

Mrs Askew: Yes, my name is Olivia Jayne Askew. I was born on December ninth, nineteen eighty-one.

DI Hutch: Thank you, Mrs Askew. We understand that this is a difficult time for you, but we need to ask you some questions about your missing husband. Can you tell us the last time you saw him?

Mrs Askew: Yes. He was heading out with our son around ten a.m. this morning. We'd had dinner and drinks at home the night before to celebrate Maddox turning three earlier that week, and I'd felt worse for wear on waking up and Rich had offered to take our son up to Frog Hill.

DS Dunsforth: This is Frog Hill near Thunder Bridge?

Mrs Askew: That's right, yes. Rich often takes Maddox up there to look at the kites, and Maddox had got one for his birthday.

DS Dunsforth: And while they were gone what did you do?

Mrs Askew: I jumped at the chance to take a long, hot bath and take a bit more rest.

DS Dunsforth: So you didn't leave the house?

Mrs Askew: Not at all.

DI Hutch: So when did you start to get worried about the whereabouts of your husband and son?

Mrs Askew: The time went so quickly. I fell asleep on the sofa for a while, and woke at eleven a.m. I tried to call Rich but it went to voicemail. Then I took a bath, thinking they'd be back when I'd finished, as I'd expected them to be gone for maybe an hour and a half. When they weren't back by one o'clock, and with no word from Rich, I called his phone again. It still didn't ring, instead continuing to go straight to voicemail.

DS Dunsforth: What happened next?

Mrs Askew: I'd opened the Find My Friends app again but the location wouldn't settle, just kept whirring around. Frog Hill is notoriously bad for signal; there are parts higher up where it disappears completely. I tried not to over-react, but given I was unable to contact Rich by phone and text — even emailing and using Messenger came to nothing — I pulled on some warm clothing and jumped in the car.

DS Dunsforth: You drove out to where they were flying the kite?

Mrs Askew: That's right. It's a twenty-minute drive to Frog Hill from the house. As I approached the rough ground the locals use as a free car park, I saw Rich's car. It was the only vehicle parked up. I got out of the car and looked up at the hill. I couldn't see anyone up there, no kite swirling above the ground.

DI Hutch: How long did you spend looking around?

Mrs Askew: A while, but by this time in the day it was getting cold. The wind was picking up and the temperature seemed to be dropping. When I couldn't spot them up on the hill, I walked over to Rich's car.

DS Dunsforth: This is the black Mercedes GLE registration ending UTW?

Mrs Askew: Yes. Rich wanted plenty of room for his fishing gear. The car was locked and although we keep a spare key for it in the kitchen drawer, I didn't think to take it with me. But I could see there was nobody in the car. Nothing in there that rang alarm bells.

DS Dunsforth: Was this the extent of your search at this point in time?

Mrs Askew: Not quite. Next, I walked around the base of the hill, all the time looking up towards the top, calling out. I could see the big frog-shaped rock that gives it its name. My son loves that rock, has named it Freddy Frog.

Pause

DI Hutch: Do you want to take a short break, Mrs Askew?

Mrs Askew: No, no. I want to carry on if it helps you find Rich.

DI Hutch: You were telling us about walking around the circumference of the hill.

Mrs Askew: Oh yes. I could see the rock. When I've been up there with them, Maddox always makes a beeline for it. Climbing up, jumping off, even lying on top of it and counting the clouds. But I… I could see my boy wasn't up there.

DS Dunsforth: So what did you do at this point?

Mrs Askew: It took me a good five minutes to walk around the circumference of the hill, staring up until I'd seen all sides. The hill is too high to completely see over the top of it, but I would have expected to see moving figures at some point. But I couldn't spot

them. There was nobody up there. If it wasn't
for the fact that Rich's car is still parked
there, I'd have assumed they were on their way
back and that our journeys had crossed. Now I
know that can't be the case.

DI Hutch: Did you think about calling the
police?

Mrs Askew: I felt sick and confused. So I
called my mother-in-law. She tried to calm me
down, saying if Rich's car was there then they
must still be around. She didn't seem overly
worried and it calmed me down a bit. Shannon
suggested that if I couldn't see them on the
hill, I should search nearby. See if they'd
gone for a walk.

DS Dunsforth: So you then began to search the
vicinity?

Mrs Askew: I wouldn't say search, exactly. I
looked all around me, at the flat stretches of
fields and rough land with its bracken and
long grass. There were clusters of trees and
bushes dotted here and there but it was clear
there was no one else out walking. I called
Rich's phone again and got his voicemail. I
yelled his name at the top of my voice. I
tried again and again, turning full circle.
The wind was getting up, taking the power out
of my voice.

DI Hutch: You must have felt quite desperate
at this point.

Mrs Askew: I was. I'd done everything I could
think of and I just stood there. It felt like
my insides were turning to liquid. Then I
looked at the Mercedes again and it suddenly
occurred to me that there might be something
wrong with the car! I thought maybe it
wouldn't start and so Rich had left it there
and called a cab to pick them up, not wanting
to drag me out. But then I remembered his
phone was off. And wouldn't he have called me
as soon as he got into the cab?

DS Dunsforth: But you still didn't call the
police?

Mrs Askew: No. I got back into my car and sat
for a couple of minutes staring up at the hill
as if they might suddenly appear. When that
didn't happen, I started the engine and drove
home.

FIFTY-ONE

KAIT

Ellie's wellbeing studio is a large unit in the regenerated Market Avenues of Sneinton, a suburb to the west of Nottingham city centre.

I park on a nearby road and walk a few minutes, across Sneinton Marketplace and into the warren of mainly independent niche businesses. Ellie has owned Calm-a-rama for a couple of years now after giving up her stressful role for a medical company as UK sales manager where she was expected to travel up and down the country most days.

I walk into the small foyer and inhale the floral, sandalwood scent of Nag Champa incense. I immediately feel calmer and smile at the young woman who sits behind a curved reception desk.

'Hi,' she says, glancing at the large wall clock. 'Are you here for the yoga and Pilates session? Only I'm afraid it's already started and—'

'No, no. I came to see Ellie, the owner. Is she teaching?' My heart sinks. I wanted to surprise Ellie but should've known she'd be taking classes today. Although she employs a couple of staff, Calm-a-rama is a small operation and I know Ellie enjoys being a hands-on owner.

The young woman looks guarded. 'Can I ask who you are?'

'Sorry! I'm Kait Hatton. I'm the sister of Kirsten, Ellie's partner.'

'Oh, I've met Kirsten.' She pulls a regretful face. 'I'm afraid Ellie is off work at the moment and I'm not sure when she'll be back.'

'Really?' I frown. Ellie had only called me the other day and hadn't mentioned she was off work. 'What's wrong with her?'

Stupid question, I realise as soon as the words are out of my mouth; she's never going to divulge that. But I do wonder why Kirsten hasn't mentioned she's not well.

'I'm not sure exactly, but she's at home. I've already had to call her this morning about a messed-up class booking.'

I thank the receptionist and walk back across the market-place. There are a few teenagers and families with young children lounging in the sun around the edges but no market stalls today.

Kirsten and Ellie live in a small block of plush new apartments in Mapperley which is only a short drive from here. So I decide to surprise drop in on Ellie and have a cuppa. We're long overdue for a catch-up and she'll probably be glad of the company if she's feeling under the weather.

I park in the visitor section and walk around to the front of the apartment block, ringing the bell of number 16.

'Hello?' Ellie's guarded voice says. She's obviously not expecting a visitor.

'It's me, Kait! I called at Calm-a-rama and they said you were at home today.' Silence. 'I thought... I dropped by for a chat, if you feel up to it?'

After another beat of silence when I wonder if the intercom has cut off, Ellie says, 'Sorry, Kait. Come on up.'

The door buzzes and clicks and I pull it open ensuring it closes behind me. The foyer is clean and pleasant with a dark green wiry carpet. I press the lift button and it arrives quickly, the doors closing smoothly when I press the button for the fourth floor. There are only six floors in this modest block comprising two and three bed apartments with far-reaching views. When Kirsten told me they'd bought one, I checked Rightmove and saw the cheapest one available was three-hundred-and-fifty thousand pounds.

When the lift doors open and I step out into the pleasant corridor with troughs filled with artificial plants and framed prints on the walls, Ellie is waiting at the open door to their apartment.

Inside we hug and I feel like she holds on just a tad longer than usual.

'So lovely to see you, Kait,' she says, both her hands on my shoulders. 'How are you doing?'

'I'm good, Ellie. How are you feeling?' Her short, feathery blonde hair and smooth, blemish-free skin tell me she's not unwell in the same way I expected.

'I'm OK,' she says quickly. 'Come through, I've just put a pot of coffee on.'

She doesn't look ill exactly, but she looks... upset. Pale. I slip off my flat pumps and follow her through the elegant entrance hall furnished in neutral shades with tasteful wooden furniture and an eye-catching cream runner on the polished wooden floor. No pets and no kids here.

She shows me into the living room. 'Make yourself comfy in here and I'll get our drinks.'

I choose the end seat on the oversized squashy cream boucle sofa which must be new because I've been here a handful of times and they used to have a leather suite. An enormous flat screen television sits on the wall above a modern, oblong electric fire suite that's also set into the wall. Scattered around the various tables and shelves are photographs mainly of Ellie and Kirsten at various events and on holiday in Scotland. They have a good life together and have made it clear they don't feel the need to start a family yet.

'I'll wait until you give me a niece or nephew to spoil instead,' Ellie has joked to me a few times in the past.

Ellie comes in carrying a tray bearing coffee mugs and a small plate of dainty shortbread biscuits.

'You look well, Kait,' she says. 'If not a little frazzled.'

And that is all it takes. The floodgates open and tears begin streaming down my face. 'I'm sorry, I'm sorry!' I hear myself keep wailing on repeat. 'I came here to have a nice chat and now look.'

She comforts me, offers tissues, strokes my arm. I tell her everything that has been happening. Talk about my fears about Daniel, his lies and my fears about the baby.

When I've calmed down, she says softly and gently: 'Kirsten told me, Kait. She told me what happened... in your previous relationships.'

Instinctively, I cover my face, but she gently peels my hands away. I feel rigid with shame. Kirsten promised, swore, she'd never share what happened with anyone. Ellie strokes my arm and I shrink away. I feel nauseous and for a moment I think I'm going to throw up.

'I'm sorry,' I croak. 'It's just... she promised me she'd never tell a soul about all that. I trusted her completely and it's a shock to know she's broken her vow. I would have never believed she'd do that.'

Ellie looks down, sadly. 'I'm afraid Kirsten is... different to how she used to be.'

She looks so down, it breaks me out of my own misery. 'Are

you OK, Ellie? It's just they told me you were off work and yet you look... well in yourself.'

'Not in here.' She taps her head and gives me a weak smile. 'I don't mind admitting I'm struggling at the moment, Kait.'

'Have you... spoke to Kirsten about it?'

Ellie shakes her head and crosses her hands in front of her, rubbing her upper arms to give herself comfort. 'Kirsten gets bad-tempered these days if I say the wrong thing. I tend to keep my feelings to myself.'

I shake my head, not understanding. Kirsten has seemed a bit off lately, but she's been helpful in finding out about Daniel's interest in Maddox and it was through her assistant digging I got Liv Leigh's home address.

Ellie reaches for her mug on the coffee table and her sleeve rides up, exposing some nasty bruising on her forearm. I gasp involuntarily. 'What have you done?'

She immediately pulls down her sleeve and folds her arms, leaning forward and looking at her knees. 'It's nothing,' she whispers.

'It's far from nothing! What happened?'

She looks up then, her eyes shining with tears. 'Maybe you should ask your sister,' she says.

Helena puts down the phone and sighs. What started off as a county lines investigation seems to be spiralling into something else altogether and Maddox Leigh at the centre of it.

She stands up, about to call out to her colleague when she sees he is deeply distracted with whatever he is reading. She watches as Brewster stares at the wall, frowning before picking up the documentation again.

Helena walks across the office. 'You look perplexed, Brewster. Anything I can help with?'

He looks up, surprised to see her there. 'I'm reading through the last part of the police interview with Olivia Askew again, boss. Bit inconsistent.' He pinches the top of his nose.

'Really? In what way?' Helena says tightly. Brewster seems obsessed with the disappearance of Richard Askew and this is not the focus of their investigations. He's even confessed to visiting an old colleague, Jarrod Hutch, the retired detective who'd been the senior investigating officer on the Askew case.

'I checked back in the records and checked on the timing of Olivia Askew's call to police. It proved that her claim, in her initial statement, to have returned home without ringing the police was inaccurate.'

Helena waits. So far as she is concerned, this is not crucial information or anything that might assist them in the county lines investigation.

But Brewster isn't finished yet. 'There was also a brief interview with Richard Askew's mother, Shannon. The session had been terminated early due to Mrs Askew Snr becoming upset.'

'Fascinating, Brewster, but if the super hears you're digressing, she'll have your guts for garters. A closed case doesn't really have any bearing on—'

'In the middle of questioning, Askew's mother went off on a bit of a tangent, accusing Olivia Askew of keeping dark secrets but had then seemed to gather herself and refused to elaborate.' Brewster runs a hand through his hair. 'And as far as I can see from the records, officers never followed it up. I think we should—'

'Stop, please,' Helena says, interrupting him. 'We've just had a call from Olivia Leigh. Maddox Leigh is missing. Let's get over there now, I'll give you the details of the call on the way.'

FIFTY-THREE

KAIT

Liv's phone rings once before she answers. 'Hello?'

'Liv? Hi, it's me, Kait. I was calling to make sure you were OK; you seemed a little unsettled leaving tonight. And to say thanks again for bringing back my driving licence.' Daniel's back home tonight, so at least I don't have to tell him about a missing licence; he's paranoid about our personal information at the best of times.

Liv doesn't reply, but instead lets out a heart-wrenching sob.

'Liv?' She sounds devastated. 'What's happened?!'

'Maddox has run away. He went yesterday, took some clothes and... Daniel's not around either, is he? They must be together! Daniel might have pressured him to—'

'What do you mean? If Maddox has taken his clothes, then he must have willingly gone! And what are you saying about Daniel? What do you think he has to do with anything?'

Liv falls silent and then groans. 'Oh God, what am I going to do? I've not slept at all, and no matter how many times I run through it in my mind, none of it makes any sense.' She groans again. 'It's all such a mess. I don't know what to do and I keep seeing her face... her poor, broken face...'

'Keep seeing whose face?' I say, puzzled.

'No one!' Liv snaps. 'Not your concern.'

She sounds deranged. It must be the lack of sleep.

'I think Daniel might be Rich. I think he's taken Maddox,' Liv says, her voice monotone and vacant.

'It sounds like you've not been telling me the truth after all,' I say bitterly. 'Daniel can't be Rich if Rich is dead. So what do you mean?'

A few moments of silence, then she says, 'Listen... can I come over?'

'But... won't you need to stay home in case Maddox comes home? Have you rung the police?'

'Only just. You come over here then and I'll explain,' Liv says. She sounds exhausted. 'I really need to talk to you, Kait. I should have been honest with you before now about... just come, quick as you can.'

I try Daniel's phone again and leave yet another voicemail before I get into the car. 'Daniel? I'm worried sick. Call me, please. I need to know where you are.'

In the car, I fasten my seatbelt, battling the sickness feeling that's getting worse. I look down at my stomach and squeeze my eyes closed. I've made such a mess of everything. I have so many thoughts whirling in my head. Thoughts that don't fit together and don't make sense. I love Daniel but at the same time, I hate him for lying to me. I can't figure out a way he can have a secret bank account and seek out personal details of a boy that looks just like him and not have been betraying me.

Twenty minutes later, I pull up outside Liv's house. I've no need to park down the road now or skulk around the rear of the house, trying to spot her in the kitchen. She opens the front door before I reach the small front gate.

'Kait, thank goodness you're here.' She looks cagily up and

down the road before stepping back into her hallway and beck-oning me inside. 'Thanks for coming right away. I'm waiting for the police to call back after reporting Maddox as missing,' she says and I follow her into the kitchen room.

Without asking me, she pours two glasses of cool, still water from the fridge and brings them over to the small sofa.

I take one and watch her as she fidgets and twists her fingers together. She looks really pale and her scraggy short ponytail has bits of hair sticking out at strange angles. Liv leans back and then sits bolt upright, but now I'm here, she doesn't seem able to look at me, never mind talk to me. I'm anxious and worried myself, but Liv looks off the scale.

'Where do you think Maddox is?' I say. 'More importantly, who do you think he's with?' The time for dithering is over. She's asked me over here and I've obliged because I need to find out what is so important she wants to unburden herself.

A few more moments of silence and then Liv finally looks me in the eye. 'I'm sorry,' she says in little more than a whisper. 'I'm sorry it's taken me this long.'

'To tell me the truth, you mean?'

'Yes. I'm sorry I didn't tell you before now, Kait. We only just met but... I trust you. You see, I must trust you to be able to tell you the truth.'

'The truth about what?' My chest feels tight and my fingers flutter there.

She falls quiet again. I think we could go on like this forever unless I say something.

'Liv, please, tell me! You're worried about Maddox and you mentioned Daniel... do you think he's with my husband?'

'I don't think, I *know* there's a connection.'

I shake my head. She's not making any sense at all, but the air around us is charged and it feels bad. Whatever she's about to tell me is bad.

I raise my voice. 'This needs to stop! You must tell me the truth or—'

'Ssh!' she says sharply, holding up her index finger and inclining her head.

Knocking. On the front door.

Liv jumps up and runs into the hallway. I put down my cup and follow her.

'Oh God, I thought they'd just ring,' she cries softly to herself before turning to me. 'Kait... it's the police.'

Brewster rings the doorbell a second time before Liv Leigh comes to the door.

'Hello, yes?' Helena thinks how she looks flustered and in disarray similar how she'd looked last time they were here. Then, she'd been ill, and Helena had detected her words slurring at times. Now, her cheeks are flushed as her fearful eyes dart between the two detectives.

'Could we step inside please, Liv?' Brewster says. 'It's about Maddox.'

'Gosh... yes! Do you know where he is?'

'I'm afraid not. We were just informed you'd reported him missing and we were alerted because of our county lines investigation.'

She slumps slightly. 'I see. I can't sleep. I keep thinking where he can be and... she won't leave me alone.'

'Who won't leave you alone?' Brewster frowns.

Liv freezes, as if she's just realised she spoke out of turn. 'I can't sleep,' she says faintly.

Brewster turns to Helena and shrugs as they step inside the hallway and Helena immediately notices a woman hovering at the kitchen door. 'Hello,' she says.

'This is Kait, my... friend. My friend.'

Helena notes the hesitation and the jittery demeanour of the other woman, who keeps nervously touching her stomach.

'Hello, Kait,' Helena says, eyeing the woman's agitated expression. 'Everything OK?'

'I don't know. I—'

'Everything's fine,' Liv says quickly. 'But we've got some stuff to sort out so...'

'Mind if I take your name, Kait?' Brewster says lightly, waving his notebook.

'There's no need!' Liv snaps. 'She's only come over on a quick visit. Right, Kait?'

'I... yes. Right.'

Brewster ignores Liv and beams at the other woman. 'Name and address if you don't mind, madam. Just for the record, you understand.'

'Kait Hatton,' she says quickly, adding her address. 'I'm not really a friend... just a sort of acquaintance I suppose...' Her voice fades away to nothing under Liv's accusatory glare.

'I see,' Brewster says mildly.

Liv's face flushes. 'So what was it you wanted? I don't want to talk about the past, just Maddox. I need to find my boy.'

Brewster raises an eyebrow at this new, rather brisk manner Helena is picking up. 'So, can we confirm how long Maddox has been missing?'

'From last night. Maybe he went to stay at a friend's, but he's supposed to tell me where he's going and...'

'And?' Brewster takes out his notebook and takes down details of when she last saw him and his movements twenty-four hours before he went missing.

Liv's eyes glisten with tears. 'He's supposed to leave me a note which he did, but not telling me where he is.'

Brewster is staring at Kait Hatton's hands. When Helena follows suit, she sees the woman's hands are trembling.

Helena and Brewster share a look as he says, 'Excuse me a moment while I step outside to make a call.'

'Have you got the note?' Helena asks when her colleague has left the room.

Liv takes it out of her pocket and hands it to her.

'"Sorry, Mum",' Helena reads out loud. 'Sorry for what?'

'I don't know,' Liv mumbles. 'He's never gone missing like this before. Not for this long although he's been staying out later and I found out he's finished his job at the café without telling me.'

'Is there anything else you can add?' Helena says. 'Anything at all that might help us?'

Liv looks distraught. 'Not really. I mean, his favourite clothes are gone. So he knew he was going somewhere and had time to plan... oh!' She covers her face with her hands and Kait steps forward to offer her some comfort.

'You came over because Liv was distressed, I take it?' Helena says to her.

She watches as the two women look at each other. That strange undercurrent is there again, as if there are a lot of things going unsaid. Brewster comes back into the room and gives her an almost imperceptible nod.

'It's very important you tell us everything,' Helena says firmly, looking at both women. 'We can't help until we have all the facts. As you know, we're concerned Maddox might be in touch with some dangerous people, so it's imperative we find him as soon as possible.'

Liv makes a low moaning sound. 'This is all my fault.'

Brewster sits down and takes out his notebook again. 'How so?'

After a few moments of silence, Liv says, 'We've grown

apart over the last few weeks. I just thought it would pass but, in fact, it's got worse and now... now this has happened.'

'When we were here on Saturday, Maddox seemed quite stressed. He mentioned something about his dad,' Helena says gently. 'About you lying to him.'

Liv chews the inside of her cheek and nods. 'He sometimes gets angry because he hasn't got a dad. The older he gets, the more it seems to bother him.' She looks up at the detectives. 'Maddox had just turned three when Rich... died.'

'Yes.' Brewster taps the notebook with his pen. 'Just to confirm, your husband, Rich, disappeared eleven years ago – twelve in October – but was only declared as presumed deceased four years ago, is that correct?'

Helena watches as the other woman's mouth falls open. 'What's that?' Kait says faintly.

Liv looks unnerved. 'It was a paper exercise, that's all. We had to wait because they never found his body, but as far as Maddox and I are concerned, Rich died that day.' She looks at her hands before regarding the detectives again. 'Rich was... very troubled. Look, I'm worried about my son. I really don't want all this raking up again when it's not relevant.'

The woman, Kait, stands rigid as if she is in shock. 'You didn't tell me they didn't find a body. You just told me Maddox's father was dead.'

Helena catches the fleeting glance Liv shoots at Kait, as if she is silently trying to convey a thought of: *Keep quiet and say nothing.*

Brewster immediately latches on to the tension between the two women.

'You seem surprised at this revelation, Ms Hatton,' he says to Kait. 'Did you know Mr Askew?'

'It's nothing to do with her,' Liv snaps. 'And none of this is anything to do with Maddox going missing.'

Kait's cheeks inflame and she looks, to Helena, like she might be about to explode.

'In fact,' Liv continues, clearly in her stride, 'forget I ever reported Maddox as missing, OK? He'll have stayed with a mate, probably. Best you leave now and if I hear anything, I'll let you know.'

Brewster speaks with a quiet formality. 'Doesn't quite work like that, Ms Leigh. We have concerns about the sort of people Maddox has been speaking to, and we know he skipped school last Friday. It's our duty of care to follow up on his disappearance.'

Liv is looking increasingly stressed as she repeatedly tucks wisps of hair behind her ears. In the light of Brewster unearthing the old case file of Richard Askew, which contains suspicions from the investigating team and inconsistencies in her statement after his disappearance, Helena thinks Liv is certainly acting in an anxious, possibly guilty, manner.

It is Kait Hatton who speaks next, ignoring Liv and addressing the detectives. 'So, in the decade since Maddox's father went missing, his body has never been found?'

'Correct, sadly,' Brewster says. 'The investigation stayed open until the declaration of his presumed death.'

Liv clenches her fists tightly. 'Maybe if you lot had done a better job, me and my son wouldn't have suffered all those years hoping he'd return home,' she says viciously.

'The investigation remained open for seven years,' Brewster repeats, looking at Kait. 'There was intensive questioning for weeks and months after Mr Askew's disappearance.'

'Yes, and most of it focused on me when you should have been finding out the truth.'

'Why did their questioning focus on you, Liv?' Kait's brow furrows as she visibly begins to join the dots.

'Easy to pick on me, wasn't it?' Liv says bitterly, giving Brewster a look.

Helena watches her colleague. She knows Brewster enough to see he is getting close to telling Liv Leigh a few home truths. It is time to intervene.

'We haven't come here for an argument,' Helena says. 'Suffice to say, it looks like the investigation was conducted in a thorough manner.'

The corner of Liv's mouth curls up. 'Well, I suppose you would say that, wouldn't you!'

Brewster, calmer now, asks, 'Is it possible Maddox could be troubled about his father? I recall when we were here last time, he made a comment that he felt you'd lied to him.'

'He didn't mean anything by it.' Liv is dismissive.

Helena says carefully, 'Could it just be hitting home now that his father is presumed dead? That must have been very difficult for you both, giving up all hope like that, and trauma can be delayed in kids.'

'Unless he isn't dead at all.' Kait's voice, clear and strong, cuts through the air like a sharp knife. 'If Maddox's father is alive and well then everything that's bothering me starts to make sense.'

FIFTY-FIVE

RICH

TWO DAYS BEFORE HIS DISAPPEARANCE

Two hours later, Rich and Alicia walked out into the car park. The air still felt warm against his cheek but it was refreshing to be outside. Cleansing.

It was quiet out here; most people had left the hotel bar after end-of-week work drinks and meetings and the people who were staying over were safely installed in their bedrooms.

Alicia laid her hand on his arm, and they stopped walking. 'How's it feel to be a millionaire?' She smiled. 'Soon, my cut of the money will be moved out of your dud account and into my own offshore arrangements where it can't be traced.'

'I hope to God it works,' Rich muttered, his heart pounding.

'My regular bank accounts are the first place Caleb will look when he realises his money is missing. Your involvement ensures the money goes nowhere near my UK accounts. It won't occur to him to scrutinise your finances,' she said. 'You can keep your cut in the dud account until you decide what it is you want to do. If you need help setting up off-shore arrangements, my contact – whose details I've included in your information pack – can help with that. Remember: memorise and destroy.'

Rich nodded. 'Got it. So, you'll let me know how things are progressing tomorrow?'

'Best we don't make contact tomorrow, but I'll contact you the day after, just to confirm everything has gone through OK. Then we're both free.'

'I guess this is it then,' Rich said as they looked at each other.

Alicia gave him a weary smile, clutched his hand and laid her head on his shoulder affectionately. 'You and Livvy have been good friends to me. Maybe one day our paths will cross again,' she said. 'Until then, we owe it to ourselves to make the best of our lives. Will you move abroad?' She hesitated. 'Remember the second you transfer that money into a UK bank account in your own name, you risk being found out. And Caleb will not be merciful, trust me.'

He nodded. 'I need to speak to Livvy, explain everything to her and hope she forgives me.' He pushed the thought away. It was too much to wrestle with right now. 'Are you going to be OK, Alicia? It must hurt like hell, what Caleb has done to you.'

She lifted her head. 'I'm going to be fine. Yes, it hurts, but Caleb... well, he's grown into someone very different now. I don't think we could find happiness together again. Not after all this.'

Rich slid his arm around her shoulders. 'Thanks for giving me the chance to save my skin, too,' he said. 'You didn't have to do that.'

Alicia laughed softly. 'Hey, you've done me a favour too, you know. Maybe we couldn't have done it without each other.'

They shared a hug of gratitude and, for Rich, a sense of pure relief it was nearly over. Both looked up at the sound of gravel scuffling close by.

'Oh no,' Alicia whispered, her eyes widening.

'Had to take a leak.' Dougie Reeves, the drunken guy who'd bothered Alicia in Manchester, weaved out of the bushes, towards them.

'Is this a private love-in, or can anyone join in?' he leered, lurching forward while trying to do up his zip.

'Get lost, Dougie,' Rich snapped. 'You're out of order.'

They watched as Dougie staggered towards his car, fumbling for his keys.

'We should stop him getting in his car,' Alicia said. 'He can't drive like—'

'Don't get involved,' Rich said. 'Let's just get out of here.'

His hand slid into his pocket and cradled his phone but he didn't take it out. He'd seen missed calls and text messages from Livvy when he'd glanced at it halfway through his meeting with Alicia. He didn't need the aggravation. Livvy would know what he'd been up to soon enough, and hopefully she would come to understand he'd done it for her and for their son.

Rich walked back to his own car. He'd parked in a quiet spot under an overhanging tree but he could see it from the door. As he walked, he savoured the space that had been created both inside his head and physically in the cold, fresh air. It was done.

He pointed the remote key at the car and the side lights flashed. He squinted as he drew closer. It looked like... there was someone sitting in the driving seat!

'Hey!' He ran to the car and as he wrenched open the driver's door, he stopped dead. Froze. 'Livvy?' he said faintly. 'What... what are you doing here?' He glanced in the back. 'Where's Maddox?'

'Where else? Your mum has him.'

She got out of the car and they stared at each other across the bonnet. 'I was just...'

'I knew you were up to something when you took off like

that. I came to the bar. I saw you with her.' She walked around the front of the car to stand in front of him.

The way she said that. *I saw you with her.* A crawling dread started up in his stomach when he realised the assumption she'd made.

'I wasn't *with* her, as such. We were talking. About a business deal.'

Livvy threw back her head and laughed. A hard, bitter sound. 'You must think I was born yesterday.'

'It's true, I swear! I'm going to tell you all about it soon, it's just that—'

'It's just that... what?'

'I can't say anything yet. Another day or so and I'll be able to tell you everything.'

A tear popped from the corner of Livvy's eye as her outrage gave way to sadness. 'You know, I would have thought... hoped, you'd have had enough respect to tell me the truth,' she said. 'I saw you, cuddling up to each other in there. Touching hands. Don't treat me like an idiot, Rich. Don't be that person.'

'Hi, Livvy!' Alicia's voice carried across the car park. Rich looked up to see Alicia waving and starting to walk towards them as a car engine started up nearby. This was all he needed!

'Livvy, you don't understand. You've got this all wrong!' He reached for her hand and she pulled it roughly out of his grasp, her eyes fixed on Alicia. 'Let's just calm down a moment. Please.'

'Don't patronise me,' she said behind bared teeth. 'It's too late for calming down. And now it's not just me who knows, either.'

The thread of steel in her tone made Rich feel dizzy. He walked a few steps in front of her to try and block her view of Alicia. 'What are you talking about?'

A flash of something passed over her face. Regret or fear, he couldn't tell.

'I snapped a couple of pictures of you both in the bar and I—'

'You what?' He grabbed her arm and she cried out. 'What did you do?'

'You're hurting me!' she yelped, tears spilling down her face. He let go and she snatched her arm away, started the car. 'I sent them to Caleb, OK? He has a right to know what you two are up to, like me!'

He felt bile rising in his throat.

'Oh no, tell me you didn't. Oh Jeez. There's nothing going on between me and Alicia. How many times do I have to—'

'Speak of the devil!' She spat out the words as he looked up and saw Alicia rushing towards them. No longer calling out with a smile, her face was a mask of terror and panic as she waved her phone in the air.

In a flash, Rich understood. She'd really done it. Livvy had sent the photos to Caleb and he'd already been in touch with Alicia. Now, Caleb would know they'd been together just before his money disappeared. Their plans... in ruins. 'You stupid, stupid bitch,' he hissed, reaching for the door handle. 'What have you done to us?'

'*Us*? You and Alicia?'

'No! I mean—'

The words died on his lips as Livvy looked at him, the strangest expression on her face he'd never seen before. His head began to pound, and he opened his mouth again to speak but suddenly a car shot forward out of a parking spot before hitting the brakes. Dougie Reeves' manic face grinned at him from behind the wheel.

The engine revved, the wheels spinning before it lurched forward again. Livvy let out an anguished roar as she bolted and pushed Alicia hard into the path of the careering vehicle. Rich heard himself scream as there was a hard muted thumping sound and Alicia suddenly flew up into the air and landed, bloodied face against the windscreen. Her eyes wide open and staring right at him.

FIFTY-SIX

He and Livvy froze, both staring at Alicia's limp body, draped over the bonnet of the car, her pale cheek pressed against the windscreen, the same lively brown eyes he'd looked into less than ten minutes ago, now glassy and sightless. Livvy's whimpering echoed in his ears and he tried to break away from the invisible thread tethering him to Alicia's face, but he couldn't. He couldn't do it.

Behind the wheel, Dougie Reeves' head was lolling this way and that. He clutched his chest, his mouth open as he groaned in pain. Rich's stare averted and he looked at the hotel. All was quiet and still nobody around. Yet. If they stood here much longer, someone was bound to come outside for a smoke or to leave the bar after a nightcap.

Rich slid his arm around Livvy's shoulder and she quietened. Began to sob into his chest. He began to walk towards his car, guiding her alongside him. 'Livvy, listen to me,' he said, his voice stern and low. 'Listen. To. Me.'

She sniffed, her sobbing subsiding as he walked a little faster. 'We're going to get into the car and drive away. Do you understand?'

She looked up at him, puzzled. 'But—'

'Everything will be fine. They'll think the drunk guy did it,' he said as his stomach roiled, not sure if he believed it.

'But I can't! I mean... I did it. It was my fault and...'

Her words were lost as he opened the passenger door and pressed Livvy inside before walking around to the driver's side. He got in and started the car, pulling away, driving past the sign that said, *Vehicles are parked at their own risk. These premises are not monitored by CCTV.*

Back at the house, Livvy paced up and down the living room. 'We shouldn't have just left her. We should have called an ambulance.' Both hands were on her head, fingers pulling viciously at her hair. 'Oh God forgive me. What did I do? Oh, sweet Jesus.'

Rich reached gently for her wrists. 'Livvy, Alicia was plainly dead. You'd have gone to prison and that can't happen. Do you hear me? You're a mother, Maddox needs you and there's other stuff happening that you don't know about.'

'What stuff?' She was trembling, but she allowed him to untangle her fingers. She needed something from him. Not all of it, but the outline. To prove he was trustworthy.

'Caleb will come for me, and soon. If I don't get away, he'll kill me.'

'Because I sent him the photos?' She gave a shrill, hysterical laugh. 'I'll tell him it was just a joke. That we set it up... as a prank!'

Rich shook his head. 'I wasn't having an affair with Alicia, Livvy, and that's the truth,' he said sadly. 'There's no other woman for me but you. But you were right in that I was up to something behind your back.'

'But I saw you... you and her. Holding each other.'

'We were in the process of stealing Caleb's money. Nearly

three million pounds.' He ran a hand through his hair. 'What you saw was just two scared people offering support and reassurance to each other. Alicia thanked us – me and you – for the friendship we'd given her.'

Livvy looked at him. 'I don't understand—'

'Alicia had found a secret bank account Caleb was offloading funds into. He had a secret relationship, got a young woman pregnant. He was about to leave Alicia and take everything they'd built together.' Rich paused for breath. This felt rushed, surreal, but he owed Livvy an explanation and he had to get her onside. 'He'd shafted me on an investment I'd made and not told you about. I lost over a hundred grand. We were going to lose the house and—'

'I can't take all this in.' Livvy pressed her fingers to the sides of her head. 'This is crazy. All the lies...'

'I know,' Rich said, his voice catching in his throat. 'I know and I'm so, so sorry. But I was trying to put it right, do you see? I had every intention of confessing I'd lost everything when Alicia came to me with a plan. I agreed to shield the money, just for a short time and then... then it would have all been OK and I was going to sit you down and explain it all. We would've had money to start a new life abroad: you, me and Maddox.'

'Why couldn't you have just confided in me?' Livvy squeezed her eyes closed. 'You could've trusted me.'

His mum had Maddox overnight at her house, so at least that was one less thing to worry about right now. Rich had texted his mum and asked if she could drop him back in the morning.

Shannon had replied: *No problem!*

Rich helped Livvy into the shower and then wrapped her in a fluffy bath towel and sat her in front of the gas fire in the living room. After a small brandy, she seemed less shaky although she still stared silently ahead, not responding to anything he said.

'Everything is going to be fine, Livvy,' he said again but he didn't feel nearly as confident as he sounded. 'Provided we stick to our story, it's all going to be fine.'

That was the deciding factor in whether they could pull this off or not. *Sticking to the story*. That's what he had to impress on her.

Livvy's eyelids grew heavier, closing then flicking open a couple of times, her eyes dull and startled. Eventually, she closed her eyes and mercifully drifted into sleep.

Rich stood up and went upstairs. He had a quick shower, washed his hair and changed into a T-shirt and a pair of jersey bottoms. That felt better, as if he'd washed some of the drama and anxiety away. He added his cast-off clothes to the small pile of Livvy's clothes then scooped the whole lot up and took them out into the garden.

Rich shivered and poured a small amount of petrol over the clothing before flicking in a lit match and stepping back. He stood and watched as the garments they'd worn that evening burned quickly in the dry, cold air of the evening. He kept the waste incinerator at the bottom of the garden behind the shed on a bed of loose paving slabs so there was no fear of the neighbours seeing he was burning clothing and not twigs and dry leaves.

It was another step towards making the story real.

As the flames began to die down a little, Rich poked at the pieces of fabric still intact. He'd give it another five minutes and then that would be it. Job done.

He stared into the embers, Alicia's dead, wide eyes still burning into his. It was monstrous, terrible. Would Caleb know yet what had happened? That his scheming wife was dead? He thought she and Rich were having an affair.

Little did he know it was far worse for him than that. Soon he'd discover his money was gone. Money that was now in a fraudulent account and accessible to Rich. When Caleb checked out Alicia's accounts, the next place he'd come was to him, thanks to Livvy's photographs taken the day his money disappeared.

Rich was a multi-millionaire and yet now, he had nothing at all.

FIFTY-SEVEN

RICH

ONE DAY BEFORE HIS DISAPPEARANCE

On Saturday morning, Rich's phone chimed and he checked the screen. It was a message notification from Caleb Mosley. Rich's fingers trembled slightly as he opened it.

Where's she stashed my money? You have 24 hours.

He didn't mention the message from Caleb to Livvy. Not at first.

After their lengthy discussions half the night, his wife went to the trouble of preparing a meal on their last evening together, after a little birthday celebration for Maddox. Although Livvy looked a bit put out, Rich was pleased when his mum made an impromptu visit in the afternoon, even though they'd already seen her in the morning when she had dropped Maddox back. It gave him a chance to see her again. One last time.

When she'd drunk her glass of champagne and Livvy was busy at the hob, he hugged Shannon and when she'd broken free, she tilted her head to the side slightly and looked at him.

'Everything OK?' she said lightly, her voice low enough to be disguised from Livvy by the noise of the oven. 'You can tell me if something's wrong, Richard.'

He looked at her. 'Everything's fine, Mum,' he said softly.

She nodded, keeping her eyes pinned to his. 'That's good. That's what I'd hoped you'd say.'

Livvy turned around, watched them break apart. 'Are you staying for something to eat, Shannon?' she said in a tone that made it clear it shouldn't be taken as an invite.

'No, I have to get off,' Shannon said and she kissed Rich on the cheek. 'See you soon.'

'Yeah, see you soon. And Mum?'

Shannon turned back to him and raised an eyebrow. 'Yes, love?'

For a moment, he had to gather himself before he could speak.

Then he said, 'Thanks for everything you do. For us and for Maddox.'

'That's alright, love. I'm always here for you all, you know that.'

When Shannon had gone, he explained to Livvy about the money.

'It's in your account now... all of it?' Her eyes were wide when he nodded.

And that's when he told her he had no choice but to disappear.

FIFTY-EIGHT

KAIT

Three pairs of eyes – two detectives and Liv's – turn on me like laser beams.

Liv takes a step forward and growls through gritted teeth, 'What did you just say?'

I swallow, brace myself. 'I made the point that, as his body has never been found, there might be a chance that Maddox's father isn't dead at all. That maybe those drug dealers, or whoever it is you keep mentioning, have nothing to do with it and Maddox is with his dad right now.

DS Brewster's phone begins to ring and he stands up to answer, walking out of the room and closing the door.

'You're speaking out of turn. Saying things you've no right to say.' Liv's eyes are sparking as she tries to warn me off saying anything else in front of the detectives. But she's misled me, been selective with the information she's told me. When she said Maddox's father had died when he was three, she'd hoped I'd instantly abandon my suspicion that Daniel could be his dad. But why would Daniel have had information about

Maddox? 'Kait, please. We can talk later.' Her eyes have softened, the sparks have faded and now she looks at me pleadingly.

'Talk about what, exactly,' DI Price says. 'What's the connection between you two?'

'We're just friends,' Liv says quickly as Brewster returns to the room. He walks over to Price, says something quietly in her ear that causes her to raise her eyebrows before sitting back down again. I see a look pass between the two detectives, and I know it's time to start protecting myself instead of worrying about Liv's reaction.

Liv Leigh has cost me a lot of time. All those hours I've spent ruminating about what Daniel could be up to, racking my brains to try and make it all fit and make sense. All because she knowingly gave me just half a story about her ex-husband when I asked for her help. She's seen photographs of Daniel and still insisted I was imagining the likeness between him and her son.

'Liv asked me here today because she said she has something to tell me,' I say, my hand hovering over my stomach. 'But now, I have something to tell you.'

'Really?' DS Brewster raises an eyebrow. 'What's that then?'

I have no reason to continue to play Liv's game. I remind myself I barely know the woman and she's misled me all along.

'My husband's name is Daniel Hatton,' I say. 'He's away at the moment – at the exact same time as Maddox Leigh, it seems – and there has been a previous link between them... Now I'm thinking that...'

'What are you thinking?' Price prompts me.

'Kait, don't!' Liv cries out. 'Don't say something you'll regret.'

I avoid looking at her and keep my eyes firmly on the detectives.

'It might sound crazy to you without the background to this, but I'm thinking there's a possibility that my husband used to be

Richard Askew. I don't think he died at all, and I think Liv knows that. I think Maddox has left here to be with him.'

'Shut up!' she shrieks. 'You're not thinking straight.'

'And have you got proof to back up your accusation?' Brewster asks coolly.

I can't believe what I'm hearing. He's ignoring Liv and focusing on me. As if *I'm* the liar here!

'Not yet,' I say, keeping my voice level and reasonable. 'Isn't that supposed to be your job... to follow up on leads and dig for information?'

'Oh yes, that is our remit exactly,' he says pleasantly. 'Which is why I took the liberty earlier of requesting one of our team to take a look at your own history.'

'What?' For a second, the whole room fades out and then rushes back at me again. My fingers dig into the arm of the sofa. 'I'm not the one lying here.'

'That's debateable,' he murmurs and directs a loaded glance at his colleague before continuing. 'The call I just took was the result of a quick sweep of your details, Ms Hatton. Seems you've not been entirely transparent in your own previous relationships.'

Liv shifts to the edge of her seat cushion and leans forward. 'What's this?'

Kirsten told me, Kait. She told me what happened... in your previous relationships.

A damp panic rises in my chest and I push away Ellie's recent words. Instead, I press my hand to my stomach to calm myself and focus on the life growing there.

My daughter. She's all that matters now.

'My previous relationships aren't relevant to where my husband and Maddox Leigh are,' I say steadily. 'My past isn't your concern.'

'I'm afraid your past is very much our concern in this case, Ms Hatton,' Brewster remarks, referring to his notebook. 'A caution for stalking and a twelve-month court order preventing you from contacting your last partner could be deemed highly relevant to your accusations against your husband.'

'I don't believe it!' Liv gasps but I don't look at her. I'm not going to let them intimidate me. They don't know what I went through. They don't know anything.

'The past has nothing to do with my current marriage.' My face feels hot and my throat is like sandpaper. 'I don't wish to continue with this conversation. I have my unborn child to consider and I'm starting to feel unwell. So unless you want me to put in a complaint, I suggest you stop this right now.'

I fold my hands neatly across my stomach and challenge him with a look.

'Certainly,' Brewster says. 'We can continue this conversation down at the station if you prefer.'

'To talk about what? There's nothing left to say about me, so I suggest you put your efforts into whether my husband is, in fact, Rich Askew.' I'm feeling stronger, spurred on by his mild manner. He's got nothing on me. I've done nothing wrong then, or now. 'You should listen to me. Liv knows her husband isn't dead.'

She glares at me. If looks could kill...

'She's a liar,' she tells the detectives. 'I know nothing of the sort. Rich died and left me and my son alone.'

'It's important we understand your motivations, Ms Hatton,' Brewster says carefully. 'And to that end, there's an issue we need to discuss with you at the station.'

Bright sparks of fury shoot before my eyes. 'Anything you have to say, you can say it here. Now.'

He looks at his colleague before continuing.

'The information my colleague found also details you have a history of pseudocyesis.'

'Pseudo-what?' Liv frowns.

Kirsten told me, Kait. She told me what happened... in your previous relationships.

I look down at my hands. I swear I can feel my baby's heartbeat spurring me on.

'Pseudocyesis,' the detective says again.

That word. Like a knife plunging into my chest. *How do they know?*

'Also known as false pregnancy,' Helena says gently. 'Are you really pregnant, Ms Hatton?'

Rage channels through me. I jump up and pull up my T-shirt high enough to see my skin. 'Look! Look at my bump!'

Silence shimmers in the air like a cool breeze. I follow their stares and look down. Tears spring into my eyes when I see what they see.

A perfectly flat stomach. Not the slightest hint of a bump with plenty of room to spare in the waistband of my jeans.

FIFTY-NINE

MADDOX

He opens his eyes with difficulty. The lids are stuck with gunk in places but he rubs them and blinks and then squints against the light that comes from a lamp in the corner.

He's lying on a single bed, on top of a quilt and pillow. It's a proper bedroom with a wardrobe and some drawers. There's a plain, biscuit-coloured carpet and one wall decorated in floral wallpaper. The blind is down and he can see it's dark outside.

What happened before comes back to him in a flash. The strange-smelling cloth held to his face, someone behind grabbing him and now he's here, in a room he's never seen before.

Maddox can hear a TV on through the open door. Out there is another room with much brighter light. He sits up on the bed and stays still until his head stops spinning. Swinging his legs over the side, he waits again. Then gets to his feet. His head is pounding but he doesn't feel dizzy. He pats down his jeans, but his phone isn't in any of the pockets.

He takes a step, then another, giving himself time in between to breathe. Finally he gets to the door and peers into the other room. A man sits with his back to Maddox, his long legs propped up on a coffee table in front of him, a can of beer in his hand. *South Park* is playing on the TV and the man laughs and takes a swig of beer.

This is not Sammy, who he now knows is his dad. Despite his situation, he feels that new warmth in his chest that comes from knowing he has a dad. His blood runs cold again when he remembers his mum has lied to him all these years and kept them apart.

Although Maddox didn't get a clear view of him, he looks more like the guy who knocked him out with chloroform or whatever it was. He stands there, holding his breath for a few moments until he spots the door over in the far corner, behind the TV.

It would only take seconds for him to sprint across the room, taking the man by surprise as he passes him in a blur and disappears out of the door to make his escape. Maddox is young and fit. The school football coaches are always impressed by his 'dexterity', as they call it. But Maddox is also feeling pretty crap right now. His head hurts and his thoughts seem slow, his movements clumsy. He must make it count when he does decide to make a run for it, so maybe he needs a little more time to recuperate from whatever they knocked him out with.

'Hey, sleepyhead! Back in the land of the living at last?'

Maddox stays quiet, leaning on the doorframe to keep himself steady. He'd like to see this guy after he's been drugged for hours, see how dozy he is.

'Want some water?'

'Yes,' he replies in a grudging tone. 'Where's Sammy?'

He grins, takes another gulp of beer. 'Your dad, you mean?'

Maddox feels a draught of heat rise inside him. 'Why are you saying it like that?'

The man gets up, opens a fridge and takes out a small bottle

of water, handing it over. 'Let's get one thing straight. Rule one.
I ask the questions around here.'

Maddox takes the water, opens it and takes a long drink. He
has so many questions. Where is Sammy? Why have they
brought him here? How long has he been out of it, and when
can he go home?

For now, he stays quiet.

'Pull a chair up if you like, kid,' the man says. 'You're gonna
find yourself feeling pretty whacked for a while.'

'I want to go home,' Maddox says shortly.

The man laughs. 'Hey, I want to watch tonight's game in a
sports bar staffed by girls in low-cut tops instead of babysitting
you, but we don't always get what we want, right?'

'My iPhone isn't in my pocket.'

'Yeah, I know.'

Maddox turns and goes back to his small bed. He isn't going
to get any answers from this idiot and he's not in the mood to
watch TV with him, pretending everything is OK.

He watches the man with disdain as he laughs at the TV,
drinks another beer and burps loudly.

The best thing, Maddox thinks, is to get some rest and build
up his strength until he feels stable enough to get to that door.

When he gets his chance, he's going to take it.

SIXTY

NOTTINGHAMSHIRE POLICE

TUESDAY AFTERNOON

In the brightly lit, smart office, Dr Edith Simms sits across from the detectives, her expression calm but serious.

'OK if I record your comments, Dr Simms?' Brewster waves the Dictaphone in the air. He places it on the desk when the psychiatrist nods.

'I read through the notes you sent through and so have a good handle on what you're dealing with here.'

'Phantom pregnancies,' Brewster says.

'The condition you're referring to is pseudocyesis, commonly known as false or phantom pregnancy.' Dr Simms glances at her notes before hitching her spectacles on top of her short red hair to regard them both with astute green eyes. 'It's a rare condition, but very real for those who experience it. The woman in question may genuinely believe she's pregnant, despite the absence of any physical evidence. This isn't simply lying or faking for attention – it's a psychological condition where the body is capable of mimicking pregnancy symptoms.

She may exhibit morning sickness, weight gain, or even report feeling foetal movements, all without an actual pregnancy.'

Brewster leans in, clearly fascinated and listening intently as the psychiatrist continues.

'In genuine cases, the mind has convinced the body so deeply that she might even test positive on pregnancy tests due to hormonal fluctuations.'

'That's astonishing,' Helena murmurs.

'Indeed. It's important to understand that from her perspective, she is not being deceitful. She believes she's pregnant, and her emotional responses are real. That's why it's critical to approach this with care – she's dealing with a psychological condition, not a deliberate act of deception.'

Helena blinks, recalling their rather abrupt conversation with Kait Hatton earlier.

'Ms Hatton has received therapeutic support in the past,' Brewster adds. 'But we haven't yet established whether her current pregnancy is genuine. It's not really a police matter but gives us some insight into her state of mind and the accusations she's making.'

'It's good news she's been open to therapy in the past but of course she may have had some kind of relapse,' Dr Simms says. 'If that's the case then my advice is to tread carefully in the interview and don't put her under too much pressure. It's the best way to avoid her closing down and saying very little.'

Helena watches Kait Hatton with interest as Brewster goes through the interview preliminaries.

Kait maintains a surly expression but looks nervous and every so often, despite Brewster's revelations at Liv Leigh's house, she cradles her stomach protectively with a hand. Kait agreed to take part in the interview and has not hesitated to agree to the session being recorded. She also refused a solicitor on arrival, stating, 'I've nothing to hide.'

They need to get to the bottom of the relationship between Kait and Liv Leigh and untangle her rather cryptic comments about her husband, Daniel Hatton, specifically that she believes him to be Richard Askew, who was declared as presumed dead four years ago. And now, according to Kait, Daniel is also missing at the same time as Maddox Leigh.

It had all sounded a bit fantastical until Brewster had checked the Police National Computer regarding Daniel Hatton, too.

'His documentation checks out OK, no previous convictions but something's off.' Brewster had frowned. 'The PNC records are incomplete in that there are no previous addresses and workplaces listed earlier than the last three years.'

It is unusual, but not unheard of. Incomplete records can occur due to human error or some kind of technical failure. Sometimes it can be due to data protection and privacy issues.

Still, under the circumstances and paired with the discovery regarding Kait Hatton's past, it makes both detectives suspicious. Particularly when incomplete records have thrown up more questions of a missing person.

Now, Brewster begins. 'Putting your own past to one side for the time being to avoid any confusion or ambiguity, could you tell us how you know Olivia Leigh? Feel free to start at what you consider to be the beginning of your suspicions even if that's a while ago.'

Kait's face remains surly, but she obliges. Runs through how she found a note which gave personal information about Maddox Leigh, including a photo in which the teenager resembled her husband. 'I was convinced Daniel was Maddox's father and that he was probably in a relationship with Liv Leigh. So I found her and asked her.'

Brewster raises an eyebrow. 'That was very bold of you. What did she say?'

'Liv told me Maddox's dad died eleven years ago so Daniel couldn't possibly be Rich. She also denied knowing Daniel, having seen photos of him, never mind having an affair with him.'

'But you decided to keep in touch with her?'

'Yes, because she was concerned, as I was, that Daniel had Maddox's personal details in his possession. We both wanted to know why that might be and why he'd lied to me about the note.'

'But you were shocked when you realised Richard, her husband, was only declared presumed dead, and that no body had been found,' Helena says.

'Yes. She'd led me to believe it was uncomplicated and straightforward. Then when Maddox went missing, and Daniel's away, I got suspicious. I think Liv is hiding something but I'm not sure what. You probably think I'm paranoid.'

'No,' Brewster says evenly. 'We don't think that at all. We're keeping a completely open mind.'

'You mentioned you were pregnant at Olivia Leigh's house,' Helena says lightly, mindful of Dr Simms's advice. 'When is your baby due?'

'November,' Kait says defensively. 'But I've had some health problems including pre-eclampsia which can have very serious consequences. So I'd rather not tempt fate by talking about the baby in this interview.'

There's a pause before Brewster says, 'Mrs Hatton, as part of our enquiries, I did run your details through the Police National Computer and the results were interesting to say the least. A little more detailed than our earlier enquiry.' He picks up a printed sheet. 'According to our records, during the past six years, you've been charged twice under the Protection from Harassment Act 1997.'

For a moment, Helena fears Kait Hatton is going to keel over. Her face turns deathly pale and she looks wobbly on her chair. She does not respond.

'The first time, six years ago, you were charged with Harassment, Section 2,' Brewster continues. 'But four years ago, you were charged with the more serious offence of Harassment Putting People in Fear of Violence, Section 4.'

'I told you, it was all a misunderstanding,' Kait blurts out, twisting her hands.

'Furthermore, four years ago, you were issued with a restraining order.' Brewster looks up. 'You were in relationships with both men?'

Helena watches as Kait's previously pale cheeks now flush with heat. She clears her throat. 'Yes. And they both betrayed me. Had affairs, one cheated me out of savings. But the police chose to believe their lies and charged me.'

'Both lied about you stalking them and faking pregnancy?' Brewster presses on.

'I thought I was pregnant and it turned out I wasn't. End of. That's not a crime, is it?' Kait presses her lips together. 'I've had therapy since. But both times I believed I was pregnant.'

'And you believe you're pregnant again now, a third time?'

Kait narrows her eyes. 'I *am* pregnant. Not as it's any of your business.'

Helena shoots Brewster a look and opens up a new angle. 'Your husband, Daniel, hasn't returned home from his work trip as expected, is that right?'

'Correct.'

'You approached Olivia Leigh because you suspected Daniel might be having an affair with her. You also suspected your husband may be Maddox Leigh's father and Mrs Leigh's missing husband, Richard Askew, now declared presumed dead. Is that correct, too?'

'You're making it sound like I'm crazy!' Kait's voice has risen to a shrill cry. Beads of perspiration line her top lip.

'That's not my intention, but it's entirely relevant to our enquiries,' Helena replies. 'I need to formally ask, do you have any knowledge on the whereabouts of Daniel Hatton or Maddox Leigh?'

'What? No, of course I don't!' Kait touches her stomach. 'This is not good for me and it's not good for my baby. You should be looking into who Daniel really is instead of hassling me.'

'You were also warned on both occasions that the City Hospital would take matters further if you continued to harass their staff with false claims of illnesses including pre-eclampsia,' Helena says.

'The same condition you currently claim to be suffering from,' Brewster adds. 'Does your husband know about your false pregnancies and your harassment charges?'

Kait looks momentarily stunned but recovers well. She grabs her handbag and stands up. 'I'm not staying to listen to this crap. It's victimisation, that's what it is!'

'Before you go, Mrs Hatton, it would be useful to have the name of your GP, hospital consultant or named midwife please,' Brewster says easily.

'That's personal information and it's nothing to do with you,' Kait says scathingly, pushing her chair away. 'It's nothing to do with where my husband or Maddox Leigh is, either.'

Helena almost has some admiration for the complete trans-formation in Kait Hatton's personality. It must have taken a lot of effort to keep it hidden.

'We can't stop you leaving, Kait,' Helena says calmly. 'But we may need to speak to you again quite soon.'

'I'll see how I feel,' she snaps. 'As it stands, I'm not feeling too good right now.'

SIXTY-ONE

MADDOX

TUESDAY MORNING

He thinks that maybe five or six hours have passed. In that time he's had another lengthy sleep and when he'd woken up, the man in the other room brought through a cheese sandwich, some fruit and more water.

He ate, waited for what he thought was another hour and then he did some stretches and a few squats in his room and he felt nearly normal.

When the guy is fully lounging back in his chair, leafing through a sports magazine with the TV on, Maddox bursts out of his room and takes long, powerful strides towards the door.

'Hey! Get back here, you—' As far as Maddox can tell, the man has been drinking all through the night and he struggles to get upright, spilling beer down himself as he curses and calls out threats to him.

Maddox yanks open the door and finds himself in a corridor. He runs down it and through the door at the end and stops dead. There, playing cards, are three men – and one of them is Sammy. His father.

'Dad?'

Sammy jumps up and rushes over to him, raising an arm. Maddox gasps and shrinks back, but Sammy slides the arm around his shoulder and guides him back down the corridor to another room. Just as they step inside, the guy who'd been watching him in the small bedroom thunders past, stopping to glare at Maddox.

Sammy closes the door and sits down on one of two chairs either side of a desk.

'Sit down, Maddox,' Sammy says. 'I think I owe you an explanation.'

For a few seconds, the room is deathly quiet. Maddox can hear a television on further down the corridor and there's a clock on the wall that's ticking loudly but shows the wrong time.

Maddox sits on the edge of the hard, wooden chair, fidgeting with the cuffs of his denim jacket. He doesn't know what to expect. This could be really good or very bad and he can't tell by Sammy's expression which one it is. But he's sick of waiting now.

'Why did you let that man – Caleb – take me? They drugged me and you...' Maddox can feel his eyes burning with fury. 'You just stood back and—'

'I'm sorry about what happened, Maddox. But it's not what you think... please, just hear me out, OK?'

Maddox folds his arms and clenches his teeth to remain silent. He's trying to show he doesn't care but inside, he's filling up with tears like a little kid. And he hates himself for it.

'There's something I have to tell you,' Sammy begins, his eyes avoiding Maddox's brooding stare. 'It's time you know the truth and there's no easy way to say this. I'm not your dad.'

Maddox stares. His stomach gives a sharp twist as his arms fall limply down by his sides. He tries to blink but he can feel the warning sting of tears surging forwards, so he stops.

The fury he'd been trying to stoke up against Sammy has gone and now he just feels empty inside.

'Why did you lie to me?' he says, his voice emerging as little more than a whisper. 'Why would you do that?'

'I'm sorry, Maddox. I feel like shit telling you this, I really do but I had no choice.' Sammy sighs. He takes off his back-to-front baseball cap and runs a hand through the dark hair that looks so much like Maddox's own. 'See, Caleb Mosley, he's my boss and, as you've found out, he's not a very nice guy. I can't give you all the details, but he paid me a lot of money to—'

'To say you're my dad? But why?' The tears finally win the battle, and Maddox roughly wipes his damp cheeks with the back of his hand.

'It's not that simple. I can't say much about it all. I just wanted you to know the truth about me because I can't carry on pretending.'

Maddox stands up, balling his hands into fists. The photo Sammy had given him, their imagined future together... now it is all falling to pieces in front of his eyes.

He swallows hard, his voice raspy. 'OK, you want me to know you're a dirty liar? I get it. But what I really want to know is this. What happened to my real dad?'

Sammy opens his mouth to answer when the door flies open. Caleb Mosley stands there filling the gap, his face red, eyes blazing.

'Leave me with him,' he snaps at Sammy. 'I'll beat him and then his bitch mother.'

'You better not hurt my mum!' Maddox shrieks. He jumps up, his teeth clenched.

Caleb throws back his head and howls laughing. 'Going to take me on, are you, little man?'

Sammy stands up and presses on Maddox's shoulder,

urging him to sit down. He affects a friendly tone. 'Caleb, why don't you leave this to me? It's not the kid's fault and—'

'No. You get out and leave this little loser to me,' Caleb snaps. He pulls a long kitchen knife out of the long pocket of his combat trousers and Maddox gasps and shrinks back in his chair. 'In fact, you can just hold him while I—'

'Wh–what? What are you gonna do?' Maddox cries, looking wildly between Caleb and Sammy.

Caleb grins and walks forward. 'Don't panic, kid. I'm just going to cut off some of those girly curls of yours, send 'em with a note to your mother, see if that loosens her tongue about where my money is. Something along the lines of "Next time it'll be his fingers."'

'No! Get away from me!' Maddox springs up and backs away.

'Hold him down, you idiot!' Caleb bellows at Sammy. He lunges for Maddox, who easily sidesteps the larger, slower man. Caleb's face is puce. 'Tell you what, let's ignore the haircut and go straight for the fingers. Grab him, Sammy.'

But Sammy doesn't grab Maddox. Instead, he moves towards Caleb. 'Leave him be. I'll not tell you again. You're obviously on something.'

Momentarily, Caleb looks confounded then his face changes, his mouth stretching wide in the semblance of a smile. 'You dare to tell me what to do? Maybe you need your fingers cutting off too.'

'I'd like to see you try. Just leave the lad alone,' Sammy says again, turning away as if he's trying to defuse the situation.

Maddox feels like he's going to throw up at any moment. How did everything go so badly wrong? One minute he's found his dad again, the next there's a psycho trying to cut his fingers off. His head jerks around as he spots Caleb start to move quickly towards him again. Maddox cries out and launches himself to the side just as Sammy throws himself in between the two of them. Caleb throws a powerful punch into Sammy's chest. Sammy reels back and lets fly with a counter punch that crunches into Caleb's jaw.

The force of that blow sends Caleb staggering back... and closer to Maddox. In a split second, Caleb seizes his chance and whips round, grinning manically. He raises the knife in his left hand and roars, flying forward to attack him.

Maddox presses back against the wall and closes his eyes. He's going to die right now. Away from home, away from his mum.

His eyes snap open at the sound of Caleb's roar as he's caught by Sammy in a headlock. He jumps out of the way as the men grapple with each other, falling to the floor. A bloodcurdling cry and then a moment's silence where both men are still.

Maddox presses his hands to his temples, his head pounding with the worst headache he's ever had in his life. His breath catches in his throat when he spots the blood. A rapidly expanding pool of syrupy crimson emerging from the tangle of their limbs.

Then Sammy moves. Pushes himself up and away from Caleb. A small noise escapes Maddox's throat when he spots the knife in Caleb's chest.

'He fell on his own sword like Brutus,' Sammy says quietly. 'How apt.'

Maddox stares at him. They've read *Julius Caesar* at school. 'Caleb would've killed me if you hadn't stopped him.'

'I would never have let that happen,' Sammy says, standing up and brushing himself down. He crouches and feels for Caleb's pulse. 'He's gone... and the world's a better place,' he says without emotion.

Maddox's expression darkens. 'Why did you stop him, though? It's not like you're my dad.'

'That's true. I'm not your dad,' Sammy says, looking directly at him. 'But I'm the next best thing.'

Helena glares at her ringing mobile phone and makes a noise of frustration. 'Get that for me, would you, Brewster? If I don't save these database changes, I'll lose the best part of an hour's work.'

Brewster snatches up the phone. 'DI Price's phone, DS Brew— oh, hi... *what?*' Helena looks up at his new, urgent tone. 'We're on our way. Hang tight. Don't go anywhere.'

'What is it?'

'That was Liv Leigh, boss. She's just had a guy at the house threatening her and she remembered your card and rang in a panic,' he says, grabbing his jacket from a nearby chair. 'She said he told her Caleb Mosley has Maddox. She sounds in a bad way.'

Helen's eyes widen as he hands her back her phone. 'Let's go. You drive, I'll speak to dispatch and get officers out to Mosley's address if they can find it.'

When they arrive at Liv Leigh's house, the front door is wide open. Both detectives jump out of the car and rush up the path.

Helena is first inside and is stopped in her tracks by the scene in the living room. Liv and Maddox Leigh embracing, both sobbing and holding on to each other for dear life.

'Maddox is back!' Helena exclaims, walking over to them. 'Are you unhurt?'

'He's fine.' Liv wipes her eyes with a shaking hand. 'He walked in here just a few minutes ago! I was just about to call you; I thought I was dreaming. I can't believe he's back and he's OK. You're OK, aren't you, love? You're OK?'

Liv sounds a little crazy and hyper, but Helena can understand that.

Maddox nods but he doesn't look at the detectives. Helena thinks how pale and shaken he looks. 'Let's sit down a moment, shall we?'

Everyone takes a seat. Liv sits close to her son, a protective arm around his shoulders which he doesn't shrug off.

'Where did you go, Maddox?' Brewster says carefully. 'Who were you with?'

'I've asked him that and he won't tell me,' Liv says. She stands up, wrings her hands and sits down again. 'He's barely said two words since he got back, have you?' Maddox doesn't reply but fixes his attention on the wall opposite.

'I think he might be in shock,' Helena says quietly. 'Could you possibly make him a drink, Liv? Hot, sweet tea, perhaps?'

Oh!' Liv looks crestfallen. 'I thought he was just a bit tired. I feel terrible now. Are you OK, Maddox? Are you OK?' She looks at Brewster, taking uneven gasps. 'Will he be OK?'

Brewster takes stock of her. The beads of sweat at her temples. 'I know it's difficult, Mrs Leigh, but you must try and calm down. Maddox needs you to be calm for him.'

'We can organise a medical check-up to ensure everything is

as it should be,' Helena says. 'And the tea should help get his glucose levels up.'

Liv stands bolt upright. 'Yes. The tea. I'll go and make it now.' At the door she turns back and says tearfully, 'Will you be alright, Maddox, while I'm in the kitchen?'

There is no response from Maddox.

'Did you leave home willingly, Maddox?' Brewster asks him when Liv has left the room. 'Or did someone force you to go?'

Maddox shakes his head. 'Nobody forced me, but...' He glances at the door. 'I was lied to, so I didn't realise what I was getting myself into.'

'Where did you go?'

He looks at Brewster. 'I don't know. A farmhouse in the countryside not that far from here, I think.'

Helena glances at Brewster. 'Is this something to do with a county lines drugs ring, perhaps what Brandon McFadden tried to get you involved with? Were you recruited?'

'No! It was never county lines and Brandon never mentioned that. The stupid school just assumed that's what it was.'

It is a curious answer, Helena thinks. If it wasn't county lines... then what? Then it hits her. 'Maddox, was this something to do with your missing dad?'

He doesn't respond.

'Are you hurt, Maddox?' she asks.

'No,' he says. Then, 'I nearly was hurt, but... I'm OK.' Again, Helena notices, that furtive glance at the door. He may be in shock, he certainly looks as if he's been scared out of his wits, but he's clearly also very cautious of speaking in front of his mother.

'Your mum is making some tea, Maddox. Don't worry.'

'She's acting really weird,' he says. 'Like she's going to have a breakdown or something.'

'How did you get home from this farmhouse?' Brewster

says. 'Your mum rang for our help and it sounds like minutes later you were back.'

Maddox opens his mouth and closes it again.

'We need you to be honest, Maddox,' Brewster says. 'We have no choice but to get to the bottom of this whether you want us to or not. The sooner you can tell us everything, the quicker you can get on with your life again and we can give your mum some support.'

Then another voice speaks. 'Don't be afraid, Maddox.'

The three of them look at Liv, who is standing at the door holding a mug. 'The time has come for us all to tell the truth about your dad. About what happened all those years ago. I'm not going to get upset. I need... I need help... I—'

Helena rushes forward and takes the tea before helping Liv into a chair.

Maddox seems to visibly relax, as though he's been holding his breath. 'Sammy brought me home,' he says. 'He stopped Caleb Mosley stabbing me. He broke my heart because I really thought he was my dad. He's a liar, but I owe him my life.'

SIXTY-THREE

KAIT

I get a cab home from the police station. When I get back, I collapse in the hallway, sobbing.

It felt like nothing I said to the detectives made any difference in their opinion of me. I'd lost those babies. I'd grieved for them.

I yell and slap the floor with flat hands. The sting feels almost cathartic. It feels good to let it out but once I let my guard down, I lose track of how long I lie there, my cheek on the cold, hard floor tiles.

Finally, I force myself to get up. I'm filling the kettle when I hear the front door open. When I rush from the kitchen into the hallway, there he is. Daniel.

'Hello, Kait,' he says, stepping inside the hall and closing the door behind him.

'Why are you wearing those clothes?' I say faintly, placing a steadying hand on the wall, looking him up and down. 'Where have you really been?'

He looks different, dressed in dark clothing, a baseball cap worn back to front. His manner seems rougher at the edges. 'Let's sit down,' he says.

There's a stabbing pain in my chest that's carving me up inside, but I feel so weak that I follow him through to the sofa.

There are a few moments of silence before I say, 'What's going on, Daniel?'

'I'm not who you think I am, Kait,' my husband says. 'I'm not Daniel Hatton.'

I feel so dizzy, hearing him say those words even though deep down, I've known for a while.

'We got married. Legally,' I say. 'Our wedding certificate states your name is Daniel Hatton. You need documents and solid proof, to get that certificate.'

My chest is cramping and I feel sick. I press back into the soft cushions, but I can't bear to look at him. At the same time, I feel like pouncing on him, scratching and hitting. Beating out all the lies.

The old inadequacies and terror brush against me and I feel the hairs on my arms prickling.

Daniel moves closer to me. I want to shrink away, but I can't move. 'I lied to you, Kait. I betrayed you in the worst possible way. But the plan... it went wrong.'

'The plan?' I swallow down the lump of bile in my throat.

He touches my face gently but his fingers feel rough and he doesn't smell right. He doesn't smell like Daniel.

'Let's just say I was given an opportunity. A one-off opportunity that would set me up financially.'

'I was part of a *job*?' The words nearly choke me and I fall silent.

'Not really a job. It meant more to me than that. But rightly or wrongly, I took it. I was tasked with finding a partner, settling down to blend in, to look as normal as possible and there was someone to help me. Someone close to you who drew you in like a spider.'

And suddenly, her face floats in front of my eyes, the way she tried to convince me to let go of my association with Liv

Leigh. The bruises on Ellie's arm and the way she called me from her hotel and wanted to know every last detail about Liv and Maddox.

'Kirsten,' I whisper. She knows everything; I've confided in her and she's betrayed me.'

'Not Kirsten. Ellie.' He looks down at his hands. 'That's who I was on the phone to when you caught me on the doorbell footage. I had to ring her with regular updates of how things were going.'

I gasp. 'Ellie?'

'She helped set things up between us. Arranged for you to be in the bar when I went in. Reported back to Caleb on our relationship. That's why I hated your closeness with Kirsten... because of Ellie.'

'Who is Caleb?' I manage to say. I have to swallow my emotion and find out exactly what's happening here.

'He's the guy behind all this who offered me an amazing opportunity to make a lot of money. But this *opportunity* turned out very differently because I fell in love with you, Kait. I broke the rules. When you told me you were pregnant, I felt torn between the best feeling in the world and dread of what I was doing to both you and our baby.'

'So when you were so happy at the prospect of having your first child, that was one of the rare times you were actually telling me the truth.'

Daniel nods and looks down at the floor. 'She's my first baby and despite everything I've done, I love you both, Kait.'

'You're not Maddox's father after all?'

He shakes his head. 'But I had to tell the lad I was his biological dad, and the worst part was, he believed me without question.'

I can't look at him. I feel the baby move and my hand gravitates to my bump.

'You look just like Maddox. Strikingly so.'

He nods and a strange expression comes over his face. 'I'm not his dad but... I am related to him.'

I frown, my pulse roaring in my ears. 'What are you talking about?'

'My name is Samuel Askew, Sammy. Richard Askew Snr was Rich's father, and he was also mine. He had an affair with my mother just after Shannon gave birth to Rich.'

'You're Maddox Leigh's... *uncle*?'

Daniel nods. 'I'm Rich Askew's half-brother. My mother told me the truth on her death bed. Before that, I just knew she brought me up alone because my dad dumped her when his wife – that's my brother's mum, Shannon – found out.'

'You knew Rich?'

'Yes. After Mum died, I looked him up. I was an only child and I got this stupid romantic idea in my head that we'd become close. I had to find him.' Daniel's expression turns morose. 'Big mistake. He wasn't interested. Nor was his mother. She called me a mongrel, an unwanted runt. I appealed to Rich as his brother but he told me he had no brother. He was his father's only son.' He falls quiet for a moment and I can see the hurt etched into his face. 'We looked really similar, like full brothers.'

'Did you keep trying to change his mind, or—'

'No. I grew bitter and it only got worse over the years. But that's another story. The most important thing to talk about is us. Our family. You and our baby are my world. Kait, you've got to believe me.'

'You've just told me that our whole life together is nothing but a lie. How can you expect me to believe what you just said?'

'I know that's how it seems but... what we have together, that bit is very real. It's so pure.' Daniel watches me, tenderness sweeping across his face. 'We can get through this, Kait. I beg you, don't take her away from me. I need you both.'

I shrink away from his touch. Being near him feels toxic. Despite everything he's saying and the emotion he's showing, the unavoidable truth is that Daniel is a liar and a cheat. He's lied to me, and he's lied to a teenage boy in the most despicable way. I haven't the slightest clue why he's done all this, I only know I can never trust him again and now, I only want him to hurt. But the time isn't right. Not yet.

'Tell me what I can do to make things better, Kait. I swear I'll never lie to you again. I'm begging you... I'll do anything.'

I want him to leave, but I know this is probably the best chance I'll get of finding out the truth of how all this came about.

'Tell me what happened,' I say. 'The full truth of how you became involved in this mess. Don't leave anything out.'

Daniel sighs, pinches the top of his nose. 'It all started three-and-a-half years ago when I was approached by a woman in a bar.'

SIXTY-FOUR

NOTTINGHAMSHIRE POLICE

Dr Simms's secretary shows them through to the psychiatrist's office for the second time.

'I didn't expect to see you both again so soon.' She smiles, indicating for them to take a seat.

'Thank you for seeing us at such short notice, Dr Simms. We requested guidance on interviewing a person who possibly suffers from dissociative amnesia.'

'According to your notes, I understand the female in question is displaying signs and behaviour that suggest her past recollections are surfacing.'

Helena nods. 'She's now under the care of a doctor, but it will greatly help our case if she were to open up during an interview and tell us what happened eleven years ago. We have no time to waste and your thoughts would be invaluable.'

Dr Simms leans forward. 'The first thing to remember is that dissociative amnesia isn't really about someone choosing to forget. It's a way the brain instinctively protects itself from something too painful to process... a kind of defence mechanism. In your suspect's case, the memory of a traumatic event was likely repressed because her mind couldn't reconcile the guilt or fear she felt at that moment.'

'You're saying it can be an automatic reaction, without effort on her part?' Brewster asks.

'Certainly over time, this repression can become automatic – part of her mental landscape that she doesn't have to think about doing consciously.'

Helena purses her lips. 'Until there's unexpected and disruptive change in her life, perhaps.'

'From what I can gather in your notes, something like her husband's reappearance may have triggered that memory to surface and disrupted her ability to repress the incident. Then she finds herself unanchored and struggling to cope. It can be a time of dangerous possibilities if she feels cornered or pressured.'

The detectives exchange a glance as Dr Simms continues.

'So yet again, you're suggesting we'll need to tread carefully,' Brewster remarks.

'Indeed.' Dr Simms steeples her fingers together on the table. 'And if trauma memories surface during the interview, remember they might well be fragmented and disjointed. They may come back in flashes and your job is to help her retrieve those pieces without overwhelming her or pushing her into a defensive state. If she feels too pressured, she could either shut down or revert to her original dissociation which will in effect be a brick wall.'

Helena nods. 'That makes sense. So how do we get her to tell us what really happened? If she's blocked it for this long, how can we encourage her to talk about it when she knows there'll be consequences?'

Dr Simms smiles. 'It's not about making her talk, it's more about creating the right conditions for the memory to emerge naturally. First, my advice is to be patient with her; try and gain her trust. Not the easiest thing to do in a formal interview, I know, but she needs to feel safe enough to confront the emotions she's buried for over a decade. If she feels accused or cornered, her mind will protect itself again and revert to the dissociation.'

She pauses. 'I suggest you approach the interview gently. Use open-ended questions. For example, instead of asking her directly if she remembers pushing the woman, ask her what she remembers about that day. Let her talk through it at her own pace. Pay attention to her emotional responses, even if the details seem mundane. A sensory detail – a smell, a sound – could be the key that unlocks the memory.'

Helena says, 'If she starts to recall it, how do we guide her?'

'Carefully,' Dr Simms warns. 'Once she begins to remember, avoid leading questions. Don't feed her details or push her toward a conclusion. Trauma survivors can be highly suggestible when memories start to resurface. If you try to fill in the blanks for her, she might latch on to something false. Let her do the work. Encourage her to describe what she sees, what she feels, but always leave room for ambiguity. The memory will either come back in full, or it won't. But if she trusts you, she'll be more likely to reveal the truth.'

She leans back, meeting their eyes with a steady gaze. 'You're not just looking for facts here. You're dealing with a mind that's been protecting itself for over a decade. My advice is: treat her gently, with patience, and you'll stand a much better chance of getting to the truth.'

'Thank you, you've been extremely helpful, Dr Simms,' Brewster says, picking up the two case files the psychiatrist slides across her desk. 'All of that is invaluable information for our interview.'

Liv Leigh sits stiffly at the table, her fingers twisting the edge of her sleeve, eyes locked on a spot on the interview room floor. She hasn't made eye contact with the detectives since they walked in here and Helena thinks how pale her face looks, her skin almost translucent under the harsh fluorescent lights.

She is coldly silent compared to her hyper mood when Maddox returned home. Helena can imagine it's probably not going to be an easy task to try and get her to speak about the past.

After Brewster runs through the preliminaries, Helena clears her throat 'We're aware of your impending medical assessment and we're going to take it slowly today, Liv. Our priority is Maddox and the truth of what happened.'

Liv's fingers tighten around her sleeve, her knuckles white. She indicates she's heard with a jerky nod but doesn't lift her head. Helena notices the tremor in her hands and the way her shoulders hunch slightly inward, like she's trying to somehow make herself smaller.

'We're not here to accuse you of anything,' Brewster adds, keeping his voice calm and measured in line with Dr Simms's advice. 'We just want to talk. See if we can fill in some blanks about what happened back in 2012. We realise it's been a long time.'

Liv says nothing.

'We know how hard it can be to think back on something so obviously traumatic,' Helena says quietly. 'Your mind might have blocked out parts of it, maybe even the whole thing, but sometimes, talking through the day, just remembering small details, can help bring things into focus.'

Liv's eyes flick up and meet hers for a split second, just long enough for Helena to catch the flash of fear in them. 'I've spent so many years trying not to think about that day,' she says finally in a small voice.

Helena nods. 'I get that, Liv, I do. We just want to start with the basics, OK? What do you remember about that day eleven years ago, in the Randall Hotel car park? Take your time.'

After long moments of silence, the tension in the room is palpable. Liv seems to track the dust motes circulating in the light filtering through the Venetian blind and Helena spots panic building in her eyes. She looks like she wants to run, but her body is rooted to the chair.

'I–I remember...' She closes her eyes, her hands gripping the arms of the chair now. 'It was dark, I think. I was waiting for Rich in his car. I felt angry. That's all.'

Brewster gives her a nod of encouragement, careful not to let his eagerness show as they'd agreed. 'That's good,' he murmurs. 'You were waiting for your husband in his car. What happened next?'

Liv stares at the table, her breathing growing more rapid. 'I honestly don't remember,' she said quickly, her voice shaking.

Brewster leans in slightly, his voice soft. 'You can remember, Liv. You remember more than you think, you just have to want to unlock the memories. Let's just walk through it together, shall we? You're sitting in Rich's car and you're feeling angry about something. What is it that's made you angry?'

Liv looks up, her eyes flashing. 'I'd seen them in the bar. Drinking together. She turned to him and leaned her head on his shoulder. They looked... like a couple in love. I took out my phone and snapped a couple of pics and then I waited back in Rich's car.'

Helena can almost imagine the flickering memory, clawing its way up through the cracks. 'That's good,' Brewster says. 'And how long did you wait in the car?'

'Until they came outside.' Helena winces as Liv bites down on her lip so hard it draws a spot of blood. Her hands clench into fists on the table. 'I don't want to remember. I just don't!'

Brewster leans forward, his voice firm but gentle. 'I know it's hard. But it's already there, isn't it? You just need to let it out, set yourself free. Do it for Maddox... so you can both move on from this.'

Liv takes a deep breath and looks up at the ceiling. 'Rich came out first and Alicia followed him. He walked towards the car and saw me. His face... he was shocked. He asked what I was doing there and wanted to know where Maddox was.' She blows out air and looks down again.

'OK, then what?'

'I let rip and told him I'd seen what they were up to and that I'd sent a couple of pics of them together to Alicia's husband, Caleb. At that moment, Caleb must've texted Alicia to say he knew what she was up to because she cried out and waved her phone into the air. That's when she started walking towards us.'

Helena feels her pulse quicken. They're getting closer. Nearly there. 'You're doing great, Liv. Alicia started moving towards you and...?'

'I ran forward and I just went for her, screaming and shouting like a banshee. When she denied they were having an affair, it made me angrier still. I pushed her hard, really hard... and that's when it happened.' Liv covers her face with her hands, moaning softly.

'What happened, Liv?' Helena prompts gently.

'A car... I heard the engine and then it just shot towards us out of nowhere. Alicia was still staggering back and she fell right into its path. People say stuff like that happens in slow motion, but that night it didn't. It happened in a heartbeat. One moment I pushed her in a jealous fury and the next...' Her voice breaks. 'The next, she was dead on the bonnet of the car.'

A sob breaks through her voice as she wraps her arms around herself, rocking slightly in the chair. 'She was just there... her eyes wide and staring. I couldn't look...'

'You say the car came out of nowhere after you pushed her?' Brewster clarifies. 'Is it possible you pushed her into the path of the vehicle?'

'I pushed her, yes,' she whispers, the words barely audible through her tears. 'I pushed her, but I didn't mean for the car to... I'd already pushed her when it zoomed forward. In that moment I hated her, but I didn't mean for her to *die*.' Liv sobs harder then, her body curling in on itself. 'Rich took charge of the situation... he took the blame. He told me not to say anything, that it would ruin us... He said he'd fix it, but I didn't... I didn't want...'

Brewster leans forward, his voice soft but firm. 'Rich took the blame to protect you, did he? He didn't want you to carry this alone.'

She nods. 'He said he had to go away anyway because Caleb would kill him to get the money back. He took the blame because he said the entire thing was his fault and it made sense to let Caleb think Alicia was killed by a drunk driver. The man behind the wheel... I saw his face, the horror of what he'd done.' Tears stream down her face. 'I didn't mean to kill her,' she cries out, her voice raw. 'I swear on my son's life, I didn't mean for any of this to happen!'

Helena sits back, her heart pounding in her chest. After eleven years, the truth has finally surfaced. Although Dougie Reeves had got behind the wheel of his car drunk, he had little chance of avoiding a careering Alicia Mosley, suddenly staggering in front of him. The shock had been too much, and Reeves had suffered a massive heart attack at the wheel, dead before paramedics arrived.

He should never have got into his car drunk, but he wasn't to know Alicia Mosley would lurch out in front of him. Helena feels sure the truth will provide some closure and relief for Mr Reeves' family.

SIXTY-FIVE

KAIT

TUESDAY AFTERNOON

I wait while Daniel goes into one of his weird, staring silences.

After a minute of this, I prompt him. 'So, you're in a bar...'

He jolts slightly and nods. 'I'd never seen the woman before but she was smart and professional. Attractive, too. Now I've had time to reflect, I think if it'd been a man who'd approached me, I would have instantly been more suspicious.'

I say nothing and listen. As it stands, I honestly don't know whether to believe a word that comes out of his mouth.

'This woman, who tells me her name is Elena, she buys me a drink and we start to talk. I tell her my line of work and she tells me she's a recruiter with a difference; she finds unique people to fill positions for very high-profile people. It sounds really interesting; I quite like hearing myself described as unique. I'm happy to stay a while to hear what she has to say.

'So we chat and it's all very friendly and low-key but then she mentions she's got a really important position to fill. So confidential and niche, it's making it difficult to fill the vacancy but that I would be the perfect candidate and did I fancy making more money than I could dream of?' He looks at me sheepishly. 'Of course, I feel compelled to ask her about the job.'

'A job that's absolutely nothing to do with a legal business, I assume?'

He shrugs. 'I didn't know that at this point. She started talking in riddles, things like: "there's so much money in it for the right person", "there are certain qualities we're looking for", "it's highly confidential"... that sort of thing.'

I stare at him. 'Did it cross your mind that this random woman had just approached you in a bar and pulled you straight into a supposedly confidential chat?'

'It wasn't like that,' he says a little irritably. 'She seemed very genuine, and she didn't say that much the first time I met her apart from she was invested personally in this particular job.'

I feel a frisson of shock. Foolishly, it didn't occur to me that he met this woman more than once. Now, something else occurs to me. All those suspicions I had about him...

'Did you have an affair with her, Daniel?'

He looks back at me. 'No. I swear I didn't, Kait.'

I nod, vowing to keep quiet to get to the crux of how he got drawn into a nightmare. What does it matter now, anyway? Betrayal is betrayal, no matter how it takes shape.

'We met a few times, and in the meantime I met you – one of the best days of my life – and we started dating. Sometimes during those times you asked me why I was late home, sometimes on the occasions I'd pop out on one of my "deliveries". I'm sorry I lied to you.'

'Sounds like it was just the beginning of your lies to me. Carry on.'

'We became more comfortable in each other's company, and one day she told me that she'd agreed to find someone to do this particular job because of her dad. Someone framed her father in a potential hit and run but he died at the wheel.'

I frown. It isn't making any sense to me.

'She told me it had taken them the best part of a year to find me.'

'What? You mean she knew who you were?'

Daniel nods. 'They'd used a private investigator.'

'But why you?'

'I'm coming to that, Kait. They offered me five hundred grand to go through with it, but there was a catch. I had to agree to some minor cosmetic surgery. Just a couple of tweaks to my nose and my mouth.'

Then it dawns on me. 'So you look like Rich Askew?'

'Yes. To look even more like him. Close enough I'd resemble him on a banking app.'

I narrow my eyes. 'Fraud.'

He nods, looking away from me. 'These people knew for sure that Richard Askew didn't take his own life all those years ago. Don't ask me how. They knew it was an elaborate, and possibly not that smart, hoax, to shield the money he'd cheated Caleb Mosley out of. What they didn't know is whether his wife, Liv, was involved and if she had access to the money.'

I shake my head. 'But why did Caleb wait so long to take action?'

'The money. Over five million was at stake. Alicia, his then wife, was killed by a drunk driver just as she put a plan in place to scam her husband. In a jealous rage, Liv had texted photographs of Alicia and Rich the night his wife died. So he knew they were together the day his account was emptied. After her death, Caleb found notes in her personal effects to say she'd met with Rich Askew, told him the amount in her husband's secret account was three million when in fact she'd lied. It was five million.'

'Then Rich went missing, Alicia was dead and they didn't know where the money was?'

Daniel nods. 'Caleb waited until Rich was declared

presumed dead and then came up with a plan to infiltrate Liv's life to find out if she was involved and knew where the money was held. Caleb was always certain Rich would come back from the dead once he thought the coast was clear and with that amount of cash at stake, Caleb set out his stall to wait for him.'

'And the woman who got you into all this, Elena... you're saying that's Ellie. Married to my sister?'

Daniel looks into my eyes.

'Yes. Ellie Reeves. She's avenging the death of her father, a man called Dougie Reeves.'

Banging on the door makes us both jump. I rush to the window, see the marked cars scattered all down the road with a cluster of officers at the door. 'It's the police... lots of them!'

Daniel is calm. 'Now I've spoken to you, I'm ready for the police. I'll tell them everything: where they'll find Caleb Mosley's body and who I really am. But I had to tell you first.'

The banging comes again, louder still. I rush to the door and open it and the officers storm past me and into the living room.

I hear, 'Samuel Askew, you are under arrest for...' Then they're marching who I thought was my husband by me, out into the street as neighbours tip out of their front doors to watch the show.

Daniel starts to shout from the moment he leaves the house. He shouts the same thing down the path, to the police car and he's still shouting when they press the top of his head down as he climbs into the back seat.

He shouts, 'I love you, Kait! I love you and our baby!'

He shouts it again and again and again.

SIXTY-SIX

RICH

ONE YEAR AFTER HIS DISAPPEARANCE

For a while, the remote Scottish island with its rugged mountains and wild crags offered Rich a feeling of safety, a reassuring barrier to the outside world. At daybreak, he woke to the wild cries of the gulls and numerous other seabirds: a constant, screeching backdrop to his self-imposed isolation. But as the days and weeks turned into months, Rich found himself getting more distraught.

It wasn't that he felt afraid. He was unrecognisable with his beard and much longer hair. On his diet of mainly fresh fish and vegetables, he'd lost weight and dressed in baggy, dark clothing with a wool beanie he even slept in sometimes in the coldest weather. Anyone, even his own wife, would have difficulty spotting him, and no paper trail clues existed. None.

Rich sometimes felt he'd taken a time machine back to the distant past. He lived frugally in a small, rented cottage with the barest of amenities. Crucially, there was no Wi-Fi or phone signal here. He had to travel by boat to the mainland for that.

Yet, in some ways, this bare, harsh life suited him. It felt like a punishment of sorts to live alone without his family. Without his wife and son. It was thoughts of Maddox that filled his days and haunted his restless nights. The pain of realising he could never get this time back. He'd never see his boy growing into the fine young man Rich knew he would be. All the lost nights stretching ahead he would never lie with his wife, holding her gently in his arms, his face buried in her soft, clean hair.

The five million glittering pounds full of promise he had squirreled away in an off-shore account felt like Monopoly money for all the use it was. He wouldn't be able to spend a single penny of it for a long, long time. As the days rolled on, the excitement of a future he'd planned now felt empty and utterly pointless.

The money could only ever buy *things*. It could never bring back this precious lost time with his family. There was no two ways about it; Rich had willingly made a pact with the devil.

In the last couple of months, a new thought had burrowed into his daydreams and nightmares. Although he could not speak to his son, or make himself known to him, there was another tantalising possibility. If only he could simply *see* Maddox, it would be like a balm to his troubled soul, helping to get him through each unbearable year until he was free again.

His boy had turned four six weeks earlier, and Rich tortured himself for hours on end, imagining Maddox and a small group of his school chums, perhaps at a bouncy castle or inflatables party. He loved those.

The drive to see his son grew in him like an aggressive tumour, getting bigger and stronger with each passing day. It took Rich by surprise, this need so strong, he felt more unable to fight it as time went on.

One day, he decided he wouldn't fight it. He planned a trip, back in the time machine, to revisit his old life for a few precious hours where he would observe Maddox at his Thursday evening football practice from a safe distance.

As with everything he did, Rich took his time thinking things through and planning meticulously until the day arrived.

On the mainland, he hired a car with the new identity credentials that had cost a small fortune to procure on the dark web before he left a year ago. It took the best part of a day to drive with frequent stops along the way, eating and drinking at roadside pop-up cafés.

He felt like his insides began to thaw as he broke through the isolated scenery of his life and entered this parallel universe of traffic, shops and people. He'd already forgotten the sheer number of people there had been in his old existence.

He parked up close to the school playing field but on a quiet side road well away from the gates. Here, he knew there to be a small stretch of open ground that bordered the school grounds but had a decent vantage point of the field the kids ran around on during P.E. lessons.

He pulled down his beanie and stood, hands in pockets, to wait. Twenty minutes later, his heart swelled as the small children ran out in their P.E. kits followed by a couple of teachers. Rich's eyes searched frantically for the dark curls of his son and, just as he became fearful that Maddox was off school ill, he saw him, one of three boys running out last, their faces vibrant and alive.

He watched his son's agile moves, marvelled how he had grown, how his legs and shoulders had thickened out. Then he looked over to the parents that had gathered to watch the mini-races. Dads he recognised, standing together laughing and chatting, watching their kids. And then he saw her. Livvy. Dressed in dark clothes, hair pulled back, her features etched with an indefinable sadness making her look older than her years.

He lowered the binoculars. He had done this to her: he'd set them all on a terrible trail of awful events because of his stupid, stupid mistakes. He did it to save his skin, cover up his terrible error of judgement, but back then he'd claimed his only thought had been for his family's future.

He had deprived his son of a father, his wife of a husband. And for what? Tears filled his eyes, the need to embrace them both rapidly growing so frighteningly powerful. He knew instinctively he had to get out of here.

So Rich left. Scurried back to the car like a rat running to save its skin. He was a coward and a fake.

Had his pain made him more careless? Had his planning been less than perfect? He would never know. Swaddled in his own misery and regrets, Rich had reached the southern uplands of Scotland before he noticed the black Audi. His stomach tightened at the realisation that every time he'd glanced in his rear-view mirror, the same car had been there. A bolt of panic hit him when he had a flashback to stopping at a roadside café just past Carlisle. A black Audi had pulled in there too, although the driver had not got out to use the facilities, as Rich had.

A sinking sense of doom enveloped him. He'd been expecting them. One day, he just knew they'd come for him. He dropped his speed and the Audi did likewise. He sped up and away and the Audi stuck to him like glue.

When two other vehicles joined the road and forced him off the A74(M) on to a remote stretch of Duneaton Water, Rich thought about his wife and son. When they pulled him out of the car and Caleb Mosley stood over him with a shotgun screaming, 'Where is my money?' he saw Maddox running out on to the school field, his face alive and animated.

When the end came, Rich turned away from Caleb's expression of hatred, closed his ears to his demands for Rich to reveal the whereabouts of the money. Instead, as the cold, hard barrel of the shotgun struck his skull, he placed himself in Livvy's warm embrace, her soft skin next to his, her hair silky on his face.

SIXTY-SEVEN

NOTTINGHAMSHIRE POLICE

ONE MONTH LATER

Just before the two detectives enter the superintendent's office, Brewster takes out his notebook in readiness. Their remit is to brief the super on the conclusion of the case and this one might be described as one of their most complicated cases.

'There are so many twists and turns in this one, I don't trust myself to get it right,' Helena said before they left the incident room. 'And if there's one thing the super can't stand, it's people who don't get it right.'

'Don't worry, boss, I've got it all in here.' He touched his shabby notebook. 'More reliable than the PNC, this thing.'

Upstairs, Helena taps on Superintendent Grey's door and listens for the order to enter.

'Ahh, Helena. Hello, Brewster.' She checks her bright orange Apple Watch. 'Nice and prompt, that's good. Take a seat, I'm looking forward to hearing how the Askew case wrapped up.' She taps her computer screen before turning to the detectives, smiling first at Helena and then at Brewster. 'Fire away. I'm all ears.'

'As you know, ma'am, West Yorkshire Police began investigating the missing persons case of Richard Askew back in 2012. But they were never aware of a crucial hidden part of the story that would come to provide all the answers.'

'You're referring to the fact that Askew and Alicia Mosley made a pact to steal her husband, Caleb Mosley's money and that she was pushed in front of a car by Liv Askew – as she was still called back then,' Grey says, patting down her short silver hair.

'That's right. But those details had been kept secret by Caleb Mosley all these years because he never believed Rich Askew had gone missing. But he was utterly convinced Askew had stolen his money and was determined to recover it using his own ways and means. Not something he'd want the police involved in.'

'He was under the impression that Rich and his wife were having an affair courtesy of the photographs Liv Askew had texted him when she discovered them together in the Randall Hotel on that fateful night,' Brewster adds. 'Mosley allowed West Yorkshire Police to assume his wife was a victim of a drunk driver. He never let it be known that Rich and Liv Askew had also been there as the police would have only become involved in the theft and wanted answers as to where his money came from. Mosley had bigger plans on the wrong side of the law.'

'So this actual case has always been far bigger and more complicated than anyone realised back then,' Grey remarks.

'Correct,' Brewster agrees. 'Mosley murdered Askew about a year after he disappeared because he swore he hadn't got his missing money. He waited and waited until Rich Askew was declared presumed dead and then waited some more before he put his master plan into action.'

Helena nods. 'Waiting and watching Liv Leigh. He didn't think Liv knew where the funds were – which was correct – but

Mosley was convinced that Askew might well have put some-thing in place that meant Liv and his son, Maddox, would get the funds even if it took him many years.'

'Meanwhile, Liv Leigh was completely unaware her "miss-ing" husband had been murdered and she waited, believing – as was always their plan – that he'd eventually come back years later and give Liv and Maddox their cut of the money when the coast was clear,' Brewster explains. 'It was only when Kait Hatton contacted Liv questioning if he was Maddox's dad that set the cat among the pigeons for want of a better phrase.'

'OK, well the good news is that I'm following you so far,' Grey says, leaning back in her padded office chair. 'Do carry on.'

Brewster clears his throat. 'Just to stick with Mosley's moti-vations for a moment, after his money disappeared, Mosley was forced to diversify his business interests. From general property development – although some of his interests seem dubious – he took a turn towards illegal gains after his wife, Alicia, died.' Brewster glances at his notebook. 'He'd lost an enormous sum of money and consequently found himself unable to pay back his powerful financial backers and honour his investments. His younger, pregnant girlfriend left him, and he began himself using drugs to cope with the pressure.'

Grey raises an eyebrow. 'A textbook case of crashing off the rails.'

'Whether it was the drugs use or not, perhaps we'll never know. But Mosley became more and more obsessed that Liv had the answer, but he grew tired of waiting and decided to play a cleverer game. He discovered through a private investigator that Rich Askew had an estranged half-sibling. His name was Samuel – known as Sammy. And he also enlisted Dougie Reeves' daughter—'

'Dougie Reeves?' Grey frowns.

'Reeves was the drunk driver who mowed down Alicia

Mosley when Liv Leigh pushed her into the path of his out-of-control vehicle, ma'am.'

'Ah yes. This man Reeves had a heart attack and died at the wheel on the same night as Alicia Mosley died, is that right?'

'That's right. His daughter, Ellie, was given the opportunity to avenge his death by Mosley. She took it.'

'And just when we thought we'd uncovered the main threads of this never-ending tale,' Helena says, 'we discovered Reeves' daughter is no other than the wife of Kirsten Reeves. Kait Hatton's sister.'

'Which brings us around to Ms Hatton again.' Grey taps her pen on the desk. 'She's proved to be a major player in revealing the whole sorry tale, by all accounts.'

'Yes, ma'am, she was the catalyst in setting off quite a chain reaction,' Brewster says. 'Kait Hatton was married to Daniel Hatton – aka Sammy Askew, Rich's half-brother. She became increasingly suspicious about his behaviour and then she found a note bearing details of Maddox Leigh and knew she had to act.'

Helena adds, 'Her sister, Kirsten, used a contact to find out Maddox's details including a photograph of the boy. Kait was so alarmed by his similarity to her husband, she contacted Liv Leigh to ask her if she and Maddox were connected to him. Actually he turned out to be Maddox's uncle.'

Grey purses her lips. 'And the rest is now history, as they say. A big explosion and everything hidden is blown out of the water. What are the expected outcomes for our wicked cast?'

Brewster flips a couple of pages on in his notebook. 'As you know, Caleb Mosley died by his own hand attacking Sammy Askew. Sammy has been charged with Assisting an Offence, Abuse of Trust and Child Endangerment. Serious as they include manipulating a minor to steal information from his mother and Askew was also the kingpin of Mosley's plan, successfully deluding a lot of people. Sammy Askew is currently on remand awaiting sentencing.'

'Particularly wicked considering he was related to Maddox Leigh.' Grey frowns. 'What about the others... Liv Leigh and Ellie Reeves?'

'Mrs Leigh is facing multiple charges including Perverting the Course of Justice in lying about her husband's disappearance in 2012 and Manslaughter in relation to Alicia Mosley's death,' Helena says. 'It's expected her legal team may go for a diminished responsibility defence on account of her diagnosis. For now, taking into consideration she has Maddox, now fifteen, she has been released on unconditional bail. Ellie Reeves has disappeared and is currently listed as a wanted person in terms of the continuing investigation. Her wife, Kirsten Reeves – Kait Hatton's sister – was unaware she had set Kait up. Ellie became abusive in the last few months so the relationship was already in the process of breaking down.'

'Yes, I can imagine Ellie Reeves was not impressed when Kirsten provided information to Kait about Maddox and Liv Leigh. Without that Kait may never have pursued the fact her husband might be his father.'

'I think that's highly likely. Kait Hatton herself has not been charged of course. She's currently undergoing therapy in relation to her previous problems including her phantom pregnancies but was found to be telling the truth about this current pregnancy. She's due to give birth in November.'

'And of course her child's father is Samuel Askew – aka Daniel Hatton. So the baby will be related to Maddox... his cousin?'

'Yes, ma'am,' Helena says. 'Which is one reason why Liv Leigh and Kait Hatton have come to a decision to get on for the sake of the children.'

'Finally, sense prevails,' Grey remarks. 'Anyone else to consider in the aftermath of this chaos?'

Brewster consults his notebook. 'Shannon Askew, Rich's mother, is still in River Gate nursing home. She has advanced dementia so remains mercifully unaware of events. She is visited regularly by Liv and Maddox, her grandson.'

'And all the criminals on the periphery... Caleb's Mosley's thugs, for instance?'

Brewster smiles. 'In a turn-up for the books, a wayward lad called Brandon McFadden has actually been very useful. Mosley paid him to recruit Maddox for a job and then introduce him to Sammy Askew.'

'So that was nothing to do with a county lines drugs ring?' Grey asks.

'No. But when he found out what happened, Brandon gave us some names of Mosley's thugs who'd kept Maddox at the farmhouse and when we took a closer look, some of those men provided us with very interesting leads in county lines activity elsewhere in Nottinghamshire.'

'Excellent!' Grey beams. 'Well, all that remains to be said is very well done indeed, you two. It's a satisfactory result, everything considered. Very nicely tied up.'

'Thank you, ma'am,' the detectives murmur in unison.

She sighs. 'Of course, the missing money still remains a complete mystery. After Rich Askew's death, I suspect it's probably lost forever in an endless web of off-shore accounts.'

'Agreed. And with Caleb Mosley and Rich Askew dead, there's nobody left who knows enough to pursue it.' Brewster shrugs. 'I doubt we'll ever know, ma'am.'

SIXTY-EIGHT

KAIT

TWO MONTHS LATER

The wind stirs softly around us as I sit side by side with Liv on the same worn park bench over the road from her house. Betsy sniffs around our feet and then wanders a few yards away on her extended lead. We chatted here when I first approached her with questions about Maddox's father. That conversation had been awkward too, but the silence between us now no longer feels like a brick wall. Liberated by the awful truth we both have to bear, it's morphed into something else – something heavier, perhaps, but not hostile. More like a truce.

I stare out at the small pond, watching the ripples spread across its surface. My fingers fidget with the edge of my jacket sleeve. 'How's Maddox doing?'

'He's doing really well,' Liv says, the ghost of a smile playing on her lips. 'He's back into his football training and school have been brilliant. They've arranged for him to see the school counsellor and I feel like he's getting back to his old self a little more every day.'

'I'm really pleased. I feel so sorry for Maddox and what he's been through.'

'Strangely enough, he finds a lot of comfort in visiting his gran these days in her nursing home. When they told me a man whispered to her at night sometimes, it was Maddox, calling by on his way home in the summer when her window was cracked open for some air. He even visited her just before he went missing.' Liv looks down at her hands. 'It's been tough on him and I hate myself for my part in it. I'm guilty of lying to him all these years. So many lies...'

'I know the news about Rich must have been a big shock to you, too,' I say. I'm treading carefully but some things just needed saying in order for us to move on from it. 'All these years you thought he was alive and coming back.'

Liv sighs as if she has the weight of the world on her shoulders. 'Yes. I'm not sure I'll ever come to terms with it but... it's weird to say this, but I'm glad I can think better of Rich, you know?'

'Now he's gone, you mean?'

She nods. 'I thought he'd let me down and worse still, I thought he'd let Maddox down. Run off with the money and left us without a backward glance. I'm glad that wasn't the case. It's just so ironic he squirreled the money away so well no one will never, ever find it.'

'I understand. I feel the same about my sister, Kirsten. I thought it was her who'd betrayed me. I'd believed her wife, Ellie, above her when she said Kirsten was abusing her. I'm so glad that wasn't the case.'

'You and your sister are close?'

I nod. 'We're close but she's gone to work in Germany for a year. Her marriage is over, and Kirsten has always dealt with stress and emotional pain by working. But we're in touch regularly.'

'Daniel, or Sammy, is the one who's really losing out on

happiness,' Liv remarks. 'He must think about that every day in prison.'

'I don't know whether Daniel – I just can't call him Sammy – meant it when he said he loved me and our unborn daughter, but I want to believe it. Nobody wants to think someone they love doesn't care at all.'

'Do you...' Liv hesitates before continuing. 'Tell me to mind my own business, but do you think there's the possibility of a future for you and Daniel?'

I squeeze my eyes closed briefly. 'Honestly? I don't think so. That's all I can say at the moment.' I cradle my bump. 'She's due in another month. That's my focus... my little girl.'

Liv smiles. 'Nothing phantom about her, Kait. She's very real.'

I nod. 'They didn't believe me, you know. The police, the doctors... you should have seen their faces when they did an ultrasound scan.'

We share a chuckle, and it cracks the awkwardness like ice.

'I lied through my teeth to you and I'm sorry,' Liv says quietly, her voice barely rising above a whisper. 'When you first contacted me. I thought if I ignored you, you might just go away. I didn't want to have to deal with my own mess. Anything was better than reliving what happened back then.'

I don't respond right away; I can't pull my gaze away from the water. I know Liv has been suffering from some kind of serious memory disorder. I know how powerful the mind can be because of my own problems in the past. The therapy is helping me with that.

'I thought if I held on to all that anger, I could... I don't know. Just keep pretending I'm better than I am. But I'm not.' Liv's voice cracks, the weight of her own words sinking in.

'I've made mistakes, too. Worse than mistakes.' I exhale slowly, my shoulders loosening just a fraction. When I glance sideways at Liv, she's already looking at me, her eyes softer than I've seen them.

'I know that feeling,' she says, her tone low but raw with emotion. 'I've been running from who I am for years. Pretending like I'm this person who has it all together, when really, I'm just—' Her voice catches, and she shakes her head, frustrated with herself.

'You're just what?' I ask gently.

'I'm just tired, Kait. Tired of pretending. Tired of hiding from my son what I've done and who I've been. All these years I've been waiting for someone to expose me, to punish me... and now that time has come. I don't know whether I'll get a prison sentence but if that's the case, then so be it. It's time for me to stop running.'

I nod, my throat tight. I can feel the truth of those words deep in my bones.

Slowly, I reach over and place my hand over Liv's. 'We've both done things we're not proud of but maybe soon we can stop punishing ourselves. At least with each other. We can find the strength to do it because of our children and their family link.'

Liv gives me a small, almost sad smile. 'We have to try, don't we? We can't change the past, but... we can stop letting it control us. Maybe even face it.'

I nod. 'I think we've already made a start on that.'

She squeezes my hand. 'Yeah,' she says. 'You know, I think you might be right.'

And for the first time, it feels like finally, we actually agree on something.

SIXTY-NINE

In a small modern office near Huddersfield, about an hour and a half's drive from Nottingham city centre, family and property lawyer Will Heaton stares at the national newspaper's online post.

He reads through the article once again before closing the window and turning to stare out of the window at the wet pavement and grey clouds circling ahead.

His heart feels heavy now he knows the reason the years have rolled by with no word from his old friend Rich Askew. He died ten years earlier.

In the walk-in cupboard, Will taps a numerical code into the safe and removes a letter. Back at his desk, he stares at the envelope and the words written by Rich's own hand.

FAO: William Heaton Esq

Instructions: This sealed, private and confidential letter to be handed to my son, Maddox Askew, on the day of his twenty-first birthday.

Signed: Richard Askew Jnr, 5th July 2013

Now he is sure of Rich's death, Will makes a vow to himself it will become his utmost priority to carry out his dear late friend's wishes.

He opens a new Word document and begins to draft a letter to Rich's widow, Liv, to say how sorry he is to learn of recent events and to offer help and support to both her and Maddox should they need it at any time.

He will not divulge to her his possession of Rich's private and confidential letter. That time will come soon enough when he carries out his friend's instructions.

SEVENTY

RICH

My dear son,

As I sit down to write this letter, my heart is heavy with the thought that I may never get to see you again. It breaks me more than words can say, knowing that I won't be there to watch you grow into the man I know you're destined to become. I've always been so proud of you, Maddox. Prouder than you'll ever know. You're smart, kind, and stronger than you realise. Knowing you, even for such a brief time, has been one of the greatest joys of my life, and I only wish I had more time to stand by your side as you make your mark in the world as I know you will.

I regret so deeply that I won't be able to see you finish school, or drive your first car, or celebrate your successes with you. But I need you to know that I believe in you with all my heart. Whatever life throws your way, I know you'll handle it with courage and conviction. You're going to be a fine young man – one the world will be lucky to know. See, son, they're coming for me. The bad people. I've made a terrible, terrible mistake and although I'm never sure when or how, I know I will pay for it. It's the way the world works.

Before I go, there's one more thing I want you to know. I've left something behind for you. The man that has personally handed you this letter is called Will Heaton. He is a good man who I've trusted all my life. You can trust him, too. He will answer all your questions, and he'll make all necessary arrangements for you to receive my last gift.

Don't think of it as just money, son. It's an amazing chance. A chance for you to chase your dreams and find the happiness you deserve. I hope that you use it well, not just for buying things, but for moments that will make you smile when you think back on them.

Don't ever feel like you must carry the weight of my absence alone for I am always by your side. Your mum adores you too and you should forgive her weaknesses because ultimately, everything that has happened is my fault alone.

Take my final gift and build the life I always wanted for you, son.

I love you, always.

Dad xx

A LETTER FROM K.L. SLATER

Thank you so much for reading *The Married Man*, I really hope you enjoyed the book. If you did and would like to keep up to date with all my latest releases, just sign up at the following link. Your email address will never be shared and you can unsubscribe at any time.

www.bookouture.com/kl-slater

The seed of this idea began as a kind of love triangle, but one not everyone in the book knew existed. In this story I knew there would be two women possibly married to the same man, and I wanted the reader to know from the outset that one woman is not as innocent as she initially appears to be. I was interested in writing a twisting, turning tale where things weren't quite as they seemed to be. No surprise there then! But I never get tired of trying to misdirect you, my dear reader... and I suspect you enjoy it when I succeed!

This book is set in Nottinghamshire, the place I was born and have lived in all my life. It also refers, in parts, to areas in West Yorkshire. Local readers should be aware I sometimes take the liberty of changing street names or geographical details to suit the story.

I do hope you enjoyed reading *The Married Man* and getting to know the characters. If so, I would be very grateful if you could take a few minutes to write a review. I'd love to hear what you think, and it makes such a difference helping new readers to discover one of my books for the first time.

I love hearing from my readers – you can get in touch on my social media or through my website.

Thank you to all my wonderful readers... until next time,

Kim x

https://klslaterauthor.com

facebook.com/KimLSlaterAuthor

instagram.com/klslaterauthor

x.com/KLSlaterAuthor

ACKNOWLEDGEMENTS

Every day I get to write stories that excite me for a living, a fabulous career I'm lucky enough to do full-time. Best of all, I'm lucky enough to be surrounded by a whole team of talented and supportive people.

Huge thanks to my editor at Bookouture, Lydia Vassar-Smith, for her expert insight, editorial support and valuable brainstorming of ideas.

Thanks to ALL the Bookouture team for everything they do – which is so much more than I can document here and who ensure the completed books are ready for the keen eyes of my wonderful readers!

Thanks, as always, to my wonderful literary agent, Camilla Bolton, who is always there with expert advice and unwavering support at the end of a text, an email, a phone call. Thanks must also go to the wonderful Jade Kavanagh, who works so hard on my behalf. Thanks to the rest of the team at Darley Anderson Agency and Associates.

Thanks as always to copyeditor Donna Hillyer and proof-reader Becca Allen, who have worked hard to make *The Married Man* as smooth a read as possible.

Thanks as always to my writing buddy, Angela Marsons, who has been a brilliant support and inspiration to me in my writing career. Like all good friends, she's my go-to person for a moan, a laugh and to share our latest news.

Massive thanks as always go to my family, especially to my husband, Mac, and my daughter, Francesca, who works as my social media manager. Both are always so understanding and willing to put outings on hold and to rearrange to suit writing deadlines.

Special thanks to Henry Steadman, who has worked so hard to pull another amazing cover out of the bag.

Thank you to the bloggers and reviewers who do so much to support authors and thank you to everyone who has taken the time to post a positive review online or has taken part in my blog tour. It is always noticed and much appreciated.

Last but not least, thank you SO much to my wonderful readers. I love receiving all your wonderful comments and messages and I am truly grateful for each and every one of your support.

PUBLISHING TEAM

Turning a manuscript into a book requires the efforts of many people. The publishing team at Bookouture would like to acknowledge everyone who contributed to this publication.

Commercial
Lauren Morrissette
Hannah Richmond
Imogen Allport

Contracts
Peta Nightingale

Cover design
Henry Steadman

Data and analysis
Mark Alder
Mohamed Bussuri

Editorial
Lydia Vassar-Smith
Lizzie Brien

Copyeditor
Donna Hillyer

Proofreader
Becca Allen

Marketing
Alex Crow
Melanie Price
Occy Carr
Cíara Rosney
Martyna Młynarska

Operations and distribution
Marina Valles
Stephanie Straub
Joe Morris

Production
Hannah Snetsinger
Mandy Kullar
Jen Shannon
Ria Clare

Publicity
Kim Nash
Noelle Holten
Jess Readett
Sarah Hardy

Made in the USA
Middletown, DE
02 November 2024

63728530R00215